THE CAPTAIN AND THE KING

Jack Champlin

Cover design by Jesse Champlin

With gratitude for the following resources:
Early Nineteenth-Century Sealing on the Falkland Islands: Attempts to Develop a Regulated Industry, 1820-1834 by Anthony B. Dickinson (for the quote on page 63)
Hawaiian Dictionary: Revised and Enlarged Edition by Mary Kawena Pukui and Samuel H. Elbert
Men, Ships and the Sea by Capt. Alan Villiers

EMPRESS
PUBLICATIONS
WWW.EMPRESSPUBLICATIONS.COM

JOURNEY OF
KAMEHAMEHA
STATUE

AUTHOR'S NOTE

I have travelled to Hawaii from the mainland many times. Nearly three decades ago, I explored the Kohala district of Hawaii's 'Big Island' for the first time. On the dead-end road at the far north of the island, which passes through the small village of Kapa'au and ends at the Polulu Valley overlook, my wife and I stumbled on—and that's the best way to describe it—a statue of King Kamehameha the Great. It looked the same as the famous one in Honolulu that millions of people have visited and, indeed, is said to be the most photographed statue in the world. However, this statue in Kohala was much less ornate, its surroundings were severely modest and we'd never before heard anyone make mention of it.

When we got out of our car, we were the only ones there to look at the stately bronze of Hawaii's most famous historic figure. The small, wood-frame courthouse standing behind it was locked and deserted. On the porch wall was a wood-frame display case with several faded pages pinned inside, giving an abbreviated version of the statue's history. Even though it was difficult to decipher through the hazy glass, I read enough to be struck by the extraordinary journey the statue had taken to arrive at that spot: In 1880, the wooden-hulled cargo ship *G.F. Haendel,* under the command of Captain Gerhard Schrock, filled its sails and set out from Germany bound for the Sandwich Islands (as the Kingdom of Hawaii was still largely referred to then) carrying coal, gunpowder, and a large bronze statue of King Kamehameha I. The ship burned and sank near the Falkland Islands. But the statue was later salvaged, and two years later sold as scrap to another sailing captain who brought it to Honolulu. Eventually, it was placed on Hawaii's Big Island close to Kamehameha's birthplace. Because this original had been given up as lost, within a year of the ship's sinking, a replica was cast that is the one that now stands in Honolulu.

Every year in June, celebrations are held at the sites of these statues and other places in Hawaii to pay homage to Hawaii's pre-eminent warrior, diplomat, leader and *all'i* god figure who united the

Hawaiian Islands into a single kingdom in 1795, after centuries of conflict.

I couldn't forget the account of the statue, and years later, research led me off the regularly taken paths of visitors to Hawaii, as well as through the doors of its libraries to find out more about this story. Although this writing gives broad allegiance to an intriguing slice of Hawaii's past, in the end it is a novel.

Jack Champlin

CONTENTS

PART I

AUGUST 1880
COAL AND BRONZE

CHAPTER 1

Bremerhaven, Germany
August 1880

The warm Pacific waters and the Sandwich Islands tugged at his core like unseen tow lines. Gerhard Shrock hadn't seen clear sky for two weeks and wondered if it was because he wanted to be warm again or it was that something else he couldn't describe—an elusive pull that spirited like a lone firefly in the back of his head.

The moored and anchored ships pushed up a forest of masts in one of Europe's busiest cargo ports as Schrock leaned against the forward rail of the ship he now commanded. He stared down at water lapping at the pilings below, wearied from the monotonous chug and rattle of the steam-driven conveyer belt lugging coal up to the main hold, trailing black dust on either side. He pulled his attention back to the shouting dockhands working beneath the derrick, hoisting multiple pallets of netted cargo aboard his three-mast merchant freighter. The *G.F. Haendel* was being readied for another voyage to the Pacific, this time to Honolulu. Captain Schrock wasn't pleased to be carrying coal, the bulk of the cargo for this voyage, coal that was running the engines of commerce even in such faraway places as the Sandwich Islands. In his mind this was his ship but he couldn't help be vexed by the thought of the real proprietor. All the same, if the owner didn't get the coal to Honolulu then any number of competitors would.

Several rain drops pelted Schrock's head. He waited, but the conveyor belt kept running. He grabbed a billed seaman's cap out of his cabin and headed for the gangplank to search out the cargo supervisor on the dock. He turned around and rapped on the cabin door of First Mate Deetjen.

"Mister Deetjen," he said when the door opened, "we have some rain coming on. I'm going down on the dock to make sure the coal loading is suspended until it's clear there's no rain. You know the problem."

"Yes sir. Wet coal—." Deetjen didn't have to finish his sentence. They both knew.

"You'll see to it the hatches are covered as soon as the conveyer is stopped then."

"Yes sir."

By the time the conveyor belt ground to a halt, it was a steady rain. Schrock started his way back up to the helm where he'd last seen First Mate Deetjen. Now he was wet and irate that he'd had to tell the dock supervisor to shut down the coal loading. On deck he was relieved to see that the bosun's mate and a seaman were nearly done covering the holds. He stopped at the top step to the officer's quarterdeck. At first glance, Captain Schrock knew that something was bothering his first mate. Deetjen was clearly agitated and talking to himself, going through the motions of securing the cover over the ship's sextant, oblivious to the rain dripping over his cap brim onto his face.

Schrock stood and waited for the first mate to address him. He couldn't help but again be perplexed by the contrast of this behavior with the mate's sober bearing. Ludwig Deetjen's earnest nature and diligence to duty was reflected in his ramrod-straight posture, exaggerated by his ever-present waistcoat of a somewhat military cut he wore tightly over his torso. At that instant Schrock wondered if the mate ever unbuttoned the coat. Never on deck, as far as Schrock could recall.

"What is it, Mister Deetjen? We've known each other long enough that I can tell when you're out of sorts."

Deetjen cleared his throat and faced Schrock. "I don't like it, sir."

"And what's that, Mister Deetjen?" Schrock asked, addressing the mate formally. Deetjen had always expressed discomfort if it was less proper.

"If I may, Captain, it's something very grave I heard from a God-fearing man on the dock this morning."

"Really?" Schrock wondered just how Deetjen knew the man was God-fearing. Did people have a special sign they gave to each other when they talked?

"Yes—that," he said, pointing down the quay, "the big crate waiting to be loaded onto this ship. Well, sir, it has an image of a heathen god inside it." The mate's square face with a trimmed beard was rendered even more intense by dark eyes just visible below his mate's cap. "Were you aware of that, Captain?"

"Umm," replied Schrock, noncommittal. That was it, he thought—the other man on the dock also had a deep-rooted fear of heathen images.

"It should not be in our cargo, sir," the mate continued in a tone of religious authority. "Mark my words, if you allow that foreign devil-god to be on board, it will be a curse on the whole voyage." His voice grew more urgent. "And it'll be a curse on them blinded dockhands if they take part in loading it!"

Schrock gritted his teeth. He had always considered Deetjen to be in a category by himself. The man was very competent and dependable at what he did, taking his position seriously as the ship's chief mate. But another side to Deetjen was an evangelical fervor that in fact had gripped him as tightly as the call of the sea. And to Schrock's occasional uneasiness, Deetjen's zeal always seemed to be searching for opportunity. The difficulty for Schrock was that his religious ardor always manifested with a God of judgment and punishment rather than a God of mercy, the fires of abomination always close at hand. It left the first mate little room for humor.

Deetjen became more insistent as he stared at Schrock. "It is evil in the eyes of our Lord and need be in yours—and the owners of this ship, Captain. That graven image will be this ship's Jonah."

Schrock didn't look directly at Deetjen or reveal any concern. "It will be all right, Officer Deetjen," he said as calmly as he could manage. "It's only metal—not something unearthly."

"But it's clear, Captain, the Good Book warns us in Leviticus: 'Turn ye not unto idols, nor make to yourselves molten gods.'"

Schrock was aware that this piece of cargo was indeed a statue of the first king of the Hawaiian Kingdom's island chain. Apparently called the "Savage King" by even the Europeans who knew about him, he also heard this king had been highly revered, if not something of a god to the native people there. Though he might have predicted Deetjen's reaction, he was still surprised at the fervor of his diatribe.

Schrock turned away from his first mate, looking out at the dark water. "As long as we're not bowing down to it, I'm sure it won't be a problem for us. Remember, Mister Deetjen, whatever we carry pays your wages and then accounts for your well-being."

"But sir—."

"And for that matter," said Schrock, looking back at Deetjen, "this statue can't be any viler to us poor sinners than the gunpowder or the cases of spirits we'll carry—or even all that coal down in the hold. I would imagine that the statue is a fairly innocent thing measured up against those three cargoes. Why, each one of those by itself can muster up untold misery and destruction."

He looked directly into Deetjen's troubled face. "So now, why don't you make yourself useful and do what you can to make sure this rain doesn't get into the holds?"

Deetjen started to say something else, but with his head lowered, instead started back toward the main cargo hatch. Schrock hadn't thought too much about the enormous crate on the dock when he first saw it. He'd go talk with the shipping agent and ask him if there was another ship that could take this piece of cargo. There was a slim chance of that happening, but it was worth a try.

Back down on the quay he found the agent, a short man whose hair stuck out at odd angles from under a battered bowler hat. When he looked up from his small wood dais, Schrock saw a man crumpled by years of schedules and tedious ledgers.

"No," he responded to Schrock's inquiry, "and I must remind you that you'll need to keep the crate upright, otherwise the arms on the statue can be damaged."

"Impossible!" Schrock shot back. "With all that coal and my other cargo in the holds, there isn't space enough to position it upright."

"Then you'll have to secure it on the deck, won't you?" the agent answered, entirely too insolent for Schrock's liking, and from a man who clearly had never worked a day at sea himself. Because Schrock didn't own the ship, like the coal, he didn't have much of a choice about what else was on the cargo manifest. But it didn't keep him from wanting to yell at him more and then push the smug little man down into the dirty water sloshing below the pier. Schrock decided to leave before saying anything he might regret. As he walked back to the *Haendel's* gangplank, he took one more sniping look over his shoulder at the agent. This piece of cargo was becoming much more of a problem to Schrock than he could have expected when he'd woken up this morning. For a moment he reflected back to how his mentor, Captain Sanders, would have handled the situation; what Sanders might have done with this unwieldy and apparently superstitious piece of cargo.

Sanders—Schrock's recollections of him were indelible. It had been two years since the former shipmaster of the *Haendel* had come to such an untimely and bad ending. But right now the circumstances surrounding his death weren't what Schrock needed to remember about Captain Sanders.

By mid-afternoon the rain had come and gone and coal loading had resumed. Schrock walked down to the main deck and made his way to the cargo hold. He peered down into the dark of the hold as heaps of black coal poured past his head from the conveyor. Men down below spread it with shovels, grunting and cussing as they did the dirty work. It made him uneasy, even though his ship had carried coal before without a problem. He'd heard enough stories to know coal fires were thorny to extinguish. And the sizable cargo of gunpowder stowed forward in the between-deck compounded the threat.

He'd always had a choice to refuse a deck officer appointment. But with Germany's lingering financial depression, the consequences were serious. Competition for officer berths on merchant ships was high. A shipmaster's post was even more difficult to secure. Schrock couldn't take any risk of not getting another berth.

Two hours later, Schrock heard the sound of the dockhand's whistle from his cabin. He came out to see the loading chute being pulled away from the ship. The coal loading had been completed, the two main holds filled with seven hundred tons of the dark rock. In addition, the remaining hold was jammed with a hundred tons of steel bars, a hundred-fifty casks of gunpowder, fifty barrels of tar, thirty cases of gin, fifty cases of wine, and hundreds of miscellaneous-sized boxes and crates filled with items ordered by businesses in Honolulu. The crate of the nine-ton Savage King stood waiting on the dock, at eleven feet high and seven-by-seven feet wide. Schrock scrutinized the operation while the dock workers fixed it with lines to a massive boom. They began slowly winching the enormous statue up the side of the ship. At the point where it was suspended high over the deck, swinging lightly back and forth, without being able to see into it, the crate seemed ominous to Schrock. His imagination was beginning to fashion something borne out of Deetjen's rant.

When the statue crate was swiveled to the deck, he thought to have his first mate oversee some crew to get it shimmed, lashed down, and covered. But he realized it probably wasn't the best plan to have Deetjen on that task. He called over second mate Ronitz and ordered him to take charge of securing the statue. "Make sure it's roped firm,

Maus. We can't be losing it in weather." Captain Schrock called his second mate 'Maus' when he was distracted or hurried. Second Mate Ronitz had been called that by others for years, since despite his stocky torso, his face somewhat resembled a mouse.

Maus ordered Seaman Kullrich to help secure the statue behind the foremast. They spent the next hour securing it tightly with thick hemp ropes. Periodically, Schrock checked their work. He thought his mind was playing tricks when he was overcome with a peculiar sensation that somehow the statue had brought its presence to the ship. He actually felt something, like a wind, but not the same, because there wasn't a breeze at the moment. His organized mind dismissed the notion as absurd.

He went back to his cabin to go through his checklist of final preparations for a morning departure.

Schrock sat at his cabin desk, leafing through the pages in front of him. Distracted, he lifted his gaze and stared out the port window, wondering what Honolulu would have in store for him. He'd taken little leisure time in Bremerhaven. With no wife or family, he figured there was little point to it. Besides, he always preferred foreign ports: the allure of the sights, the food, novelty wherever he looked.

His thoughts were broken up by a gull that landed on the window sill, lost its balance and then flew off. He was blocking his thoughts about Australia—about Susan McGinnis—the subject his idle mind liked revisiting to trample that dismal ground. Even though the memory of her had at times been a respite during months at sea, it was more of a curse, one that he'd brought on himself. And now that he would never see her again he didn't know if he could ever get his mind right to be that close to a woman.

CHAPTER 2

Molokai Island, Hawaiian Kingdom
August 1880

The palm thatch roof of the bamboo structure, set back in the forest, kept the occupants dry in the afternoon rain. Unwashed gray hair hung down around the man's head, obscuring the dark skin of his face as he leaned over. He lifted a gourd container and filled three hollowed-out coconut cups sitting on the floor in front of his crossed legs. As he poured the *awa*, the tremor in the aging Hawaiian's hands made him dribble some of the shrub-root euphoriant over the edges of the cups. The two young apprentices watched stone-faced as Naholehua's stained fingers embraced his cup. He drank it slowly and gestured for them to do the same. The man then began a chant, which lasted several minutes. When he finished, he opened his eyes and appraised his two apprentices. Makia, the larger of the two young men, shivered, unable to avoid seeing the scaly skin on his face as the man's black eyes tunneled into his. He had his reasons to be afraid of Naholehua. This teacher, once a *kahuna kilokilo uhane*, a spirit diviner, having found he acquired more business as a *kahuna 'ana'ana* sorcerer, was also Makia's stepfather. And his sometimes successes at praying people to death had turned out to be lucrative. Makia didn't find it surprising how often people wanted someone dead for one reason or another. Besides his stepfather's disconcerting conversion and now reputation as a death sorcerer, his years of drinking too much *awa* had caused the old man's tremors and scaly skin. But worse for Makia, the *awa* had made him unpredictably bad-tempered, especially around Makia's mother, who preferred to know little of the extent of Naholehua's *'ana'ana* practice.

"It has been a hundred years," Naholehua pronounced, "and our family has yet to take revenge on the first Kamehameha for killing our forefather, *Moi* Kalanikapule, the rightful ruler of these islands. They burned his corpse and took away his *mana*. And now I will tell you what I have seen in my sleep vision that disturbs me but also shows us divine intervention has finally come to us. A ship that carries *mana* of Kamehameha sails from far away. Listen as I say this. I will not let his *mana* reach *Hawaii nei* in this way. I will make sure that it dies!" His bony finger pointed toward Makia. "If required, the two of you will assist me in this calling."

CHAPTER 3

Shaken from sleep, First Mate Gerhard Schrock's first thought was that it was someone else—that the forward watch had it wrong. "He's died. It's the captain—out on deck—he's died," the sailor kept telling Schrock, his voice sounding as if he'd rather cry than speak.

Captain Sanders was a relatively young and healthy man. It was surely another man who had fallen dead on the deck. "It can't be," were the only words Schrock could muster, bolting out of his cabin.

In the next days and weeks, First Mate Schrock kept thinking how he was going to run the ship and not let on that the crew would maybe see him a fraud, a ship's officer pretender. Sanders was a decisive captain, leaving very little to others' judgment about the ship's day-to-day matters. For the most part, Schrock's job as first mate had been without much stress, with major decisions always made by Sanders. By maritime law, now he was in charge. He was *at the helm,* and they were at least a two-month sail away from their destination: Bremerhaven.

Schrock's first night was nearly sleepless. In the morning he steeled himself to go into Sanders' cabin to retrieve the ship's log and look through the captain's personal effects for anything of importance. He couldn't remember ever feeling so ill at ease with a task. His respect for Captain Sanders was such that this was a personal violation.

Schrock rubbed his hands briskly through his hair in the hope of stirring himself out of this bad dream. He wondered how the captain could up and die and leave him with these responsibilities. He tugged at his trousers and started looking through the items in the neatly arranged desk area. After a while he saw it, in the metal strongbox along with his shipmaster's certificate, ship's orders and other essential documents. The envelope had instructions clearly written on the outside: *Last Will and Testament ⅃ For Examination Upon My Death*. As Schrock read through it, he couldn't have been more mystified about the part that mattered most. Sanders' wish was to honor his family's tradition: to be buried in the churchyard of the small German town where he was born.

Schrock made his way back to his cabin, sat on his bed and stared at the envelope containing the will. He remembered there was probably good reason for the sailors' saying: 'What the sea wants, the sea will have'. It voiced the mariners' necessity of burials at sea. Worse, he hadn't considered what was to come.

"I've done a thorough accounting," the bosun announced to Schrock late the next morning, "and we don't have extra salt or spirits on board to preserve the body." He and the bosun looked at each other vacantly. They knew the implications—keeping the un-preserved body for the long voyage to home port was an absurd notion. Schrock knew he would be blamed by the family if he did other than Sanders' wishes, and that blame would inevitably go down as a black mark on his sailing record or his reputation.

On his first berth as a seaman it was Heinrich, the ship's sailmaker, who advised him that all sailors knew a ship carrying a dead body will always sail slower. Heinrich said putting the deceased to rest in the sea was the only practical way to attend to this predicament. This was advice from the man whose job it was to ensure there were firm sails for swift ship movement and that there be nothing to impede this task.

"Son," he'd told Schrock, "don't keep the sea from having what she wants. Just sew the unfortunate bastard in his hammock with some ballast stones and slide him into the drink—and do it quick before something else bad happens on the ship."

During Schrock's apprentice years he'd been witness to three sea burials: one for a sailor after he'd died of illness, and two for men in falls from high in the rigging. He'd been near one of those men as his body smacked onto the deck. It was a sound unlike any other. By the time he'd become a first mate, Schrock had come to assume that when far out at sea, slipping the wrapped and weighted body of a deceased mariner into the waiting arms of the deep was an inviolable tenet. But that was all long before he'd read Sanders' confounding will.

They were on a long sail through the Indian Ocean, around the African Horn and into the Southern Atlantic. Knowing that this ship's voyages were usually three and four months in duration, he wondered what Sanders had been thinking—this intelligent and venerable seaman that he'd respected so much—when the captain had fixed that declaration to paper. He must have assumed or somehow trusted that if he died at sea, he'd die in or near a port and then be embalmed and preserved before being shipped home.

Schrock huddled in his cabin with the second mate, Beckmann, hoping to get some other thoughts about the problem they were faced with.

"I don't know if you can go against the man's wishes and not have his family be irate if you don't deliver him," the second mate said.

"Even if the sailing goes well, what of him will we be delivering a couple months from now?" said Schrock. "He'll be far gone by the time we could make it to any port where he could be embalmed. I don't want to even think about it."

Beckman hesitated a bit before saying anything. "I hate to say this, sir, but we could put him in a net and drag'im in the sea for a while to get him good and salty. Then we could wrap him in sail cloth and put him in the rope store at the lowest deck—where it should be coolest."

Drag him in the sea? Jesus, what an irreverent thing to do, thought Schrock. Then again it made some sense, given what few options they had.

"Or what if he was in the net and it accidently broke, you know," said Beckmann, "and—no, sorry, I don't know what I was thinking."

"Yes, we could say we were trying to wash his body in the sea when we lost him…"

After a long pause and a glancing search into the corners of the cabin for better ideas, Schrock finally said, "Okay, we have to do it. Pick another couple of crew who won't blab about this and put the body out in a net tonight for a good soak—a half hour or so. Then dry him off, wrap him up good and put him below in a rope store—one you can lock up that'll hopefully keep out the rats."

"Yes sir," Beckmann said without conviction.

"Oh, and Beckmann—thank you for the—the suggestion," said Schrock.

In the next three weeks, the ship rounded the Horn of Africa and worked its way north up the west coast past Namibia and Angola.

Schrock assumed the routine duties of being master of the *G.F.Haendel*, though his days felt long and joyless. The men rarely talked, and weren't heard to joke or sing. Because Sanders had been a captain respected throughout the crew, his loss was especially palpable. The shroud of his death inescapably hung over the ship despite their movement through the water.

As they began nearing the equator and the ship entered the often windless and humid seas, Schrock noticed the smell becoming more noticeable each day, working its way up through the cargo from below.

"Beckmann, bring her about thirty degrees starboard to see if we can catch more of that westerly." The second mate, his back propped against the mast nearest the helm, wiped the sweat as it dripped off his nose.

"Aye, Captain." He grabbed the wheel gingerly at first. "You know, this wheel's heating up to the touch. Ain't no pleasure here, me being the big man runnin' the rudder."

Schrock nodded at Beckmann's sarcasm, feeling too lackluster to reply. The temperature rose daily with no relief at night, and the wood and massive cargo of the ship began to absorb the heat. He knew only too well that down in the rope locker, the heat would be quickening the body's decay. And as a result, the men complained to the ship's bosun about the smell, who had passed it on to second mate Beckmann, who told Schrock something he already knew.

After that, the stench grew even worse when the ship came to a dead still in flat water without the slightest breeze. Schrock scanned the sea the first evening of what was to become more than a week of being totally becalmed. Futilely, he hoped to sight any movement, any ripples across the water. Three days later, the unabated heat drove Schrock out of his cabin in the middle of the night. He stood at the railing, where even there, there was nothing to carry the smell away from the cadaver below, from the smells of the other men, or from the ship's sewage that he couldn't see in the dark but knew was floating in the water below. Each day dragged interminably, and he watched the patience of the crew wear thin. Two fights broke out between men squabbling over water rations. Schrock kept them separated for the duration, enforced by the second mate.

Sitting a hundred miles off the Ivory Coast, Schrock wondered how long they'd be able to survive in this heat, not moving. At the same time, he mused about how much longer the crew would respect his command of the ship… not that a mutiny would do much for them.

It was only by chance that Sanders' demise had made Schrock the captain—or was it half of one? Being the provisional captain stirred up a circular dialogue he continued to have with himself: Was he suited to be a ship's captain? But wasn't this what he'd always wanted to do? Well, for damn certain not in conditions like this.

He had put in the customary four years' time as an officer to be eligible for his shipmaster certificate; however, he had yet to take the examination, or in truth, to embrace the responsibility of commanding a ship. His rank as first mate on the *Haendel* should have bolstered his confidence to be captain. But Sanders' abrupt death was prodding his cautious timeline for ship's officer advancement. He had imagined several more years as a chief mate. It was hard to admit that it had been comfortable being mentored and, to some extent, protected by Captain Sanders. Schrock had heard of captains dying in the middle of voyages. He just hadn't thought it would ever be on a ship he sailed with.

The shirtless men were scattered about around the deck under makeshift tents to protect them from the sun, unable to sleep in stifling cabins or the forecastle. Schrock kept their deck duties to a minimum to prevent dehydration. It helped save on water usage, and in truth, there was little for them to do.

It was late afternoon of the eighth day of their becalming; the slightest breeze came up out of the southeast. There was movement and murmuring all around the deck. It was a tease that stopped as quickly as it had started. Then, a half hour later, it picked up with enough force to fill sails. Cheers erupted throughout the deck.

"Praise the Sea Gods, sir!" Beckmann blurted out to Schrock. "Maybe we won't be fish food after all."

"You have that right, Mister Beckmann. Quick, see to manning the stations! Tight those sails!"

The southern blow had reached them and they were on their way again. In the hours that followed, Schrock was invigorated by their change in fortune. The crew chatted and moved about with a sense of purpose, feeling relieved from the smells of each other and the cadaver below.

Five and a half weeks later the ship mercifully reached port in Bremerhaven. The fat and blustery ship's owner, Carl Pflueger, met Schrock in his office within an hour after berthing.

"Damn shame about Captain Sanders. One of the most capable I've ever had. But these things happen. Of course I'll let his family know to make arrangements. This sailing is a tough business. I can't believe you brought his body back. Never heard of that before— without a mortician's preparations."

"What was I supposed to do—the will and—no ports of call—."

"Yes, I suppose—but still—," Pflueger said, shuffling papers on his desk. "Anyway, your skillful return of the ship showed that you are ready to command. You know, Mister Schrock, I have two ships that need to go out of here within the month, including the *Haendel*. You should have taken your master exam a year ago," he said, his jowls flapping. "It's clear you're ready, my man! I want you at the helm of this very ship."

Schrock was first taken aback by Pflueger's token recognition and almost summary dismissal of Sanders' death. And he wasn't ready for the abrupt endorsement to be a shipmaster. He suddenly felt besieged by the months of stress and then having to be with this repugnant man. He knew he could hardly tolerate another minute in the same room.

"I have some things I need to take care of," Schrock said, rising from his chair. "I'll let you know."

Astonishment that Schrock wasn't grateful for his praise or his offer played out in Pfleuger's raised eyebrows. As Schrock started to leave, Pfleuger said, "I need to know what your plan is in the next couple days or—," he hesitated as he held up a fist full of papers and stared at Schrock. "I'll have to recruit a master elsewhere."

"I'll let you know."

Hours later, as the ship's berthing papers were cleared and he walked down the docks, Schrock knew moving up to being a shipmaster had nothing to do with Pfleuger. It was about his father. He'd never overcome the sense that the man hadn't been the strong character he needed in his youth. His father lacked... what was it— confidence. And his father often seemed reluctant to take sides when things mattered. Once when Schrock was wrongly accused by a neighbor's father of stealing a bicycle, his own father wouldn't side with him. It was those things that ran deep, that he never forgot. He remembered how silently grateful he'd been when, by chance, he'd acquired an officer's berth under Sanders' command—a man who carried himself the opposite of his father—with relaxed authority as a captain, navigator and man of integrity.

Schrock knew where he'd go to sort through his quandary. In the evening he walked to his favorite hofbräuhaus on Bremerhaven's Posener Strasse. The timeworn and ivy-covered beer garden had been an unofficial maritime officers' club for more than a century. As expected, when he entered, he saw a few men he'd known over the years. He sat down at a long wood-plank table next to Hans Brunner, a man he liked who had once served on the same ship as he. He knew several others at the table of ten or so men, including a man named Schmidt who sat across the table. Schmidt had been in some of his same maritime academy classes and held a reputation for being a mouthy antagonist.

Over more than a few steins of beer, Schrock slowly began to confide his dilemma to Brunner and those sitting closest. "I think I'd rather spend another year or so as a mate—make sure I'm ready. I'd hate to lose a ship to something brainless I did."

Brunner, although half drunk, pretended to be serious. "You certainly wouldn't be any worse than most of the captains I've sailed under." Laughing at the obvious irony of his joke, Brunner nearly fell off his chair. Schrock, not enjoying the humor, made to laugh with them. This clearly wasn't the helpful endorsement he was looking for. Taking the cue, others at the table continued telling stories of the mistakes and poor seamanship they had witnessed from shipmasters they'd sailed under. It only made Schrock more uncomfortable.

Then out of nowhere, a drunk Schmidt said, "Here you have a chance to jump up the ladder, Schrock, and you're just like the pussycat we always knew you were."

The table quieted noticeably as the men glanced around uncomfortably.

"Maybe it's time for you to shut your pie-hole, Schmidt," said Schrock.

"And I suppose you're the one to make that happen. That will be the day."

Talk around the table ceased as all eyes shifted back and forth between Schrock and Schmidt.

"Now there, we're all friends here," Brunner said, attempting to broker a peace.

Schrock ignored him. "I am that man, Schmidt, and this is that day for you," he said, rising from his stool. "I'll meet you outside."

Schmidt, unused to seeing Schrock as someone who would get into a fight, seemed to be surprised by the confrontation. He hesitated, glanced around the table, and then with a smirk stood up across from Schrock.

Standing, Schmidt looked up to a much taller man who was every part a seasoned sailor. At two inches over six feet tall, Schrock was nearly as fit as he was when a decade earlier he had played for one of Bremen's first rugby teams. And at this moment, the veins on his full neck bulged out while his eyes revealed the fury of a brewing storm. Schrock's stare found the pliability of Schmidt's core. Sweat dripped down the side of the agitator's forehead.

In vain, Schmidt's eyes searched the table for support. "Ahh—like Hans said, we're all friends here—I, uh—I didn't really mean all that. I guess we don't need to take this any further."

Walking back to his hotel that night, Schrock realized that as difficult as the stories from the men at that table were to hear, the accounts were fitting. They clarified questions he'd been trying to pose to himself: Could he do everything required to run a ship and not meet disaster? Would he always be able to act with the confidence he'd need in front of his crew? Could he show a captain's self-assurance in all the business transactions required of him when the ship called at foreign ports? But the exchange with that weasel Schmidt was actually the timeliest thing that could have happened. It broke a dam. It left him feeling almost euphoric, revealing he had confidence—and that maybe he'd be a decent shipmaster. Someday he'd have to thank Schmidt for his reckless outburst, or knock him around if his attitude hadn't changed.

He examined the embossed certificate in his hand. A few more days of pondering his options and Schrock had accepted Pflueger's offer. And in the next two weeks he had applied for and passed his shipmaster's examination with little difficulty.

Even though he was pleased to be finally licensed to command a ship, a residue of uncertainty grated the corner of his mind. He knew it wasn't his seafaring competence that had been holding him back. It was self-assurance. Putting Schmidt in his place was nothing compared to what awaited him. He wondered whether this new captain's title would merely be disguising his confidence demon in new clothes. If the message of courage against peril in all the sea stories he'd read had any worth, the sea would tell. The plaque that hung in the hall of the maritime academy said it: *You Can't Cross the Deep Until You Have Your Stern to the Harbor.* It seemed cliché, almost inane when he was a cadet. Not now.

CHAPTER 4

North Atlantic Ocean
September 1880

Every time Captain Schrock peered off toward the bow, it irritated him that the outsized crate seemed out of balance with the appearance of his vessel. The *Haendel* had sailed out of Bremerhaven loaded full with coal, gunpowder, and the statue fixed awkwardly on the deck. Although it was a three-mast tramp freighter built sturdy for heavy cargo, he considered her lines to be clean and rakish. He thought of ships constructed and rigged like this as the true workhorses of Germany's remaining sailing fleet. Their bark-rigged sail-spread gave them the ability to attain passage times that often matched those of the full-rigged ships, even some of the Clippers. He had grown to feel at home on the *Haendel*. He didn't own her, but by now it was his ship.

Captain Schrock lowered the spyglass from his eye just as Gepken, the sailmaker, came up the stairs to the quarterdeck. "We have a small tear in the topgallant foremast sheet, sir," said Gepken. "Need to pull it before it gets worse. We have the spare, but I can sew it proper in about an hour. I'll reef it in, loose the ropes and clewlines, get her down on deck and back up—about three hours. Shouldn't lose but a couple knots of speed."

"Very good. Get after it, Mister Gepken."

"Aye, sir."

Schrock found a benefit in the *Haendel's* lighter sail rigging. Because this type of cargo-hauler could operate with a smaller crew, he'd reasoned that being able to get by with fewer men gave him better odds against a having a disagreeable crewmember signed on. Through experience he knew that in a three-to-six month voyage—and that could be just one leg of the passage—it only took one conniving sailor to make for miserable sea time. He felt lucky with the likes of Gepken. This was a good crew, all in all.

Important for Captain Schrock and his two officers, so far the six passengers, all businessmen, hadn't voiced any serious complaints about the voyage. One at a time, Schrock had invited each of them for dinner to get to know them. He'd even found one of them, Johann Kessler, someone with whom he got on well. The man listened and could speak with nuance—and humor, and liked to drink, too. The dark-haired forty-year-old said he and his family had lived in Honolulu for ten years. Schrock had been there twice before on short turnarounds, knew little about the most isolated landmass on the earth and liked hearing the fellow German's engaging stories about the Hawaiian Kingdom.

Schrock was normally reserved about his personal life. But about the fourth time he dined with Johann Kessler and they had consumed wine and several brandies, he found himself sharing with Johann some about his family.

"I'm the first of two sons of professional parents. They were both teachers. I say were, because they are both dead of the cholera."

"I'm sorry to hear that," said Johann.

"It's been more than a decade, so I don't think of it that often. They were along in years—didn't marry until they were in their thirties." Schrock stared at the brandy in the glass he held before setting it down. "I think it's a sound idea—marrying late—if at all."

"What's your age, if I might ask?" asked Johann.

"I'll be thirty-six in a few months," replied Schrock.

"It won't be long before you'll be unable to chase children around if you were ever to be lucky enough to have any."

Schrock's brow lifted as he glanced up at Johann. "You go for the jugular, don't you?"

Johann held up both palms, gesturing his innocence.

Schrock shook his head and added, "But hear me out, will you, dirt lover. This life at sea is dangerous business—and," he shook his head to loosen his alcohol cobwebs, "I've thought a great deal about it. I'm not sure I want to give a wife the considerable chance to become a widow."

"You're not convincing, Captain Schrock."

"Wait," said Schrock, "besides that, most captains are wedded to their ship. Hard to admit, but I love this ship. You've got to appreciate the irony of my acquiring an officer's berth on the *G.F. Haendel*. Here we have a ship named not after a monarch, noble or place, like most ships, but after one of Germany's more beloved composers."

"I—well—I had never considered that. Curious."

"Yes, and God help me, I will always go out of my way to hear a Haendel performance, especially his Water Music Suite."

"I believe you, Captain. And I see the significance of it all," said Johann, with a twisted grin, "and therefore propose a toast to our long-departed national composer, George Frideric Haendel, who was, I will point out, spirited away from Germany by the damnable British!" They laughed as they touched glasses.

"Then I'll make a toast to Frideric's namesake ship," said Schrock, "which has brought me both profit and pain. May the former be prolonged and the latter exiled into the depths." They raised their glasses again as the *Haendel* rolled south through a vast stretch of ocean that passed off the coasts of Spain and then Portugal.

The sailing went well for three weeks, with good wind and fair skies. Schrock was puzzled he'd heard nothing directly from First Mate Deetjen about the demon nature of the statue. He sensed, however, that his mate hadn't let go his bleak convictions.

It was twenty-three days out and several hundred miles off the coast of West Africa, near Cape Verde, when First Mate Deetjen sent for Captain Schrock to come out on deck. The quarterdeck was slick with rain mist. "See there, Captain, sir," the chief mate said, pointing out the storm clouds coming toward them from the south. "This could be a troublesome squall by the looks of it."

Schrock scanned the horizon. "You're probably right, Mister Deetjen. We can most likely get through. but let's keep a close eye to it."

"I'm not so sure. I'll keep watch."

Fifteen minutes later, Schrock scanned the skies from the foredeck and grunted to himself. He had been charting the course to Honolulu in his mind—continuing across the Atlantic toward the east coast of South America, then around Cape Horn to the Pacific. He turned and headed to the quarterdeck.

"Mister Deetjen, if we have to turn away from that damn storm it will divert us from our Atlantic course crossing," his voice edged in irritation. "I should really like us to get past it. We both know it will cost us dearly if we can't—maybe a week or more bonus money as happened last time." He didn't have to voice any of this to Deetjen. He needed to vent. Schrock and Deetjen stood side by side at the forward rail of the quarterdeck and for the next half hour saw three-foot waves transform into twenty-foot swells. Spray whipped from the wave caps, stinging their faces.

Schrock raised his voice over the wind. "I've seen enough of this ruin. It's too big to sail through, isn't it? Let's bring her about and run with the wind until it blows itself out." He took another look at the black, bulbous cloud formations just at the same moment a blast of wind nearly tore both of them off their feet. "It might be too late to turn us around!" he yelled over the howl in the spars and lines overhead. "I'll get the watch to take in all canvas but jib and staysails!" His tone was urgent. "You take the helm from Kullrich—send him forward to man the winches. Push that rudder tight to starboard and get us away from this fiend!" He appreciated Deetjen's experience; the mate knew what to do well ahead of being given those orders. It was the protocol that his first mate expected. He thought the man was overly rigid in that way. Maybe it was just a wedge of insecurity in his makeup. In some measure, he himself had also been a little like that as first mate under Captain Sanders: always waiting for orders. He and Deetjen cut of the same cloth? A disturbing thought.

For the next several hours, the ship fought the wind in retreat. Then with little warning, the strong gusts from the south veered, shifting the tempest into a malicious northeast blow that descended on them at frightening speed. Within minutes the ship was pounded by huge waves of what could only be described as two intersecting storms.

"What in hell's name—," Schrock muttered through clenched teeth. The mongrel northern Atlantic weather was always unpredictable, but given the time of year, this was most likely the far edge of an Atlantic hurricane meeting a southern blow. He anxiously eyed his sailors high in the rigging above, attempting to furl main and foremast topgallant sails. Thrashed by gale winds, they leaned over the yardarms with their feet spread back on footropes, pulling in the canvas to secure it with cleats. The tall masts tipped closer toward the sea as the ship rolled with ever-larger swells, the men struggling to hold fast while they worked.

Most of the crew was a band of young men—boys really, and if any one of them lost his grip he would fall to the deck or into the sea. The horror of just such an event was inscribed in Schrock's memory. And when a man is killed or lost at sea, no one comes to take his place. Others must do his work. A pall sets over the ship and for the rest of the voyage, nothing is the same. Fault is assigned, superstition grows and morale deteriorates. The captain is not seen to grieve. When he does, he does so privately.

With the sailors aloft, Second Mate Ronitz rigged safety lines along the cabin rails to the fore and aft masts. It took an hour for the men to finish with the sails and make their way down the webbed ratlines to the deck. The deep furrows relaxed on Schrock's forehead. At the same time, a fear he wouldn't have been able to name creased his insides.

Schrock saw the waves turn into small mountains. "Tether up to the lines!" he shouted. "Ronitz, make sure the passengers stay inside and tell them—tell them just hold on."

First Mate Deetjen stood rigid at the helm, white-knuckling the ship's wood-spoke wheel. He shivered as he looked through frigid wind at the large crate, still lashed firmly to the foredeck. "This is all because of that devil statue," he said loud enough for Schrock to overhear.

But the first mate had no time to contemplate his epiphany as two ferocious waves smashed into the *Haendel's* port side in quick unison. Deetjen, Schrock and several other crewmen were thrown to the deck as the ship swiftly heeled over forty-five degrees. Schrock lay splayed out, stunned by his fall, his chin dripping blood that ran small streaks into the water on the sodden deck. He lifted his head in time to see the port rail disappear in a surge of frothing water that rolled up the partially sunken portside. The water swept up over him to the center of the deck, spilling through the hatch vents into the holds below. Soaked through, Schrock struggled to a sitting position and gripped the safety line. The *Haendel* held there, inert, listing sharply, the lower sail yardarms dipped oddly into the sea.

Suppressing his panic, Schrock guessed they hadn't yet heeled over all the way because of the heavy cargo and ballast. He got to his feet even as more swells broke over the high side of the hull, dropping waterfalls over all the crew on deck. As the waves continued breaching over the high side, they all held tight to weather rails and lines to keep from being slammed onto the deck or bulwarks. Seaman Fafsing, a small, wiry man on his first voyage with the *Haendel*, couldn't keep his grip. A deluge ripped him down the deck, his eyes wide with terror, while the tether around his waist jerked him to a wrenching stop two feet before he smashed into the gunwale. Sopping and shaken, Fafsing grabbed his tether and, hand-over-hand, pulled himself up the slanted deck through the foot deep foamy water to the safety line on the cabin wall.

Schrock counted silently to confirm the others were still holding on. Dread heaved in his gut. Without tethering, any of them could have been swept overboard. And if he were to drown, the ship would fall to Deetjen's command, just as happened to him when Captain Sanders died—a disconcerting notion. Interrupting this thought, another massive wave washed over the high side and plunged down on his head. The tons of crashing water shook him and his crew like rag dolls. Just like Fafsing, most of them were slammed to the end of their tethers and onto the deck. After the wave of water had cleared his head, Schrock looked up to see through a sprung cabin door that some of his passengers had fallen into unforgiving walls and storage lockers, leaving them sprawled in awkward positions.

Schrock and the crew each did their best to cling to their tilted ship. A brief lull slowed the waves breaching the portside. The upper part of the deck drained of seawater. In those seconds, Schrock felt a tremor through the deck. He looked back to the helm and shouted to Deetjen. "Did you feel that?

Deetjen nodded vigorously.

Tethered near Schrock, Maus shouted. "Them black rocks slipped down!

Schrock and the older crew members knew it meant a portion of the coal had shifted all the way over to the submerged side—with a dreaded keel-over next. They were all gripping their handholds in terror. Schrock heard screaming and saw Seaman Kullrich at the rail, submerged chest deep in violent, frothing water struggling with both arms on a line. "Christ in a tarhole! Oh shit save me Blessed Virgin!" his shouting a mix of prayers and curses welling up from some maelstrom of heaven and hell. At the same time, out of the passenger cabin, a man kept calling out "Lena!" His wife? His mother? Yelling loud enough that Schrock could hear him over the storm's din and Kullrich's outbursts. Instantly, Schrock thought of his own mother and then Susan McGinnis, a momentary flash to wonder if he'd see them both in an afterlife.

It didn't happen. Even as more waves hit the ship, it refused to heel all the way over. Responding to a gravity pull of the ballast and the remaining heavy cargo load, Schrock felt the ship begin to gradually heave itself upright, rising like a phoenix. First the yardarms came up out of the water, then the ship's masts pushed to vertical, slowly pointing up toward the roiling sky, water gushing off the mizzen sails. Hesitant to believe they'd been fetched from disaster, one of the crew finally let out a scream of relief. Schrock realized he had been holding his breath. His mouth dropped open as he exhaled heavily. Blood continued to drip from the inch-long scrape on his chin, quickly washed away by wind-driven seawater that flew from all directions.

Captain Schrock knew the ship's salvation was only a respite. The accumulation of the shifted coal was still piled up against the starboard wall of the hold. It would leave the ship awkwardly tilted and impossible to sail. And he could see enough through the saltwater in his eyes to know the sea still wasn't through with them. From all sides, brutal waves continued to pound the nearly immobile ship, lifting it up over mountains and down into valleys of churning seas. Schrock looked high into the ship's rigging.

"Mother of God, we need to move," he mumbled to no one, sure that if the battering kept up, even the hull would be splintered. "Mister Deetjen!" he screamed as he turned his head toward the helm where his first mate laid splayed on the deck, "pin the rudder over to starboard!" The first mate pulled himself off the deck and grabbed the wheel, putting his back into it. They waited as more waves pounded. Jerking leeward with one wave smash at a time, the *Haendel* turned its stern to the wind. But just as it had come three quarters around, this time a crushing wave slammed into the starboard side. The ship shuddered heavily and then rolled nearly thirty degrees back over to port. Shouts of panic erupted from crew scattered throughout the deck. Schrock felt another tremor under his feet as the displaced coal likely slid back to somewhere near level in the hold. The effect brought the ship wholly upright. Although still being assaulted by waves, the *Haendel* managed to complete its turnaround. Immediately, she began picking up momentum as the gale-force wind from the south found purchase with intact jib and staysails.

Schrock checked on all the crew he could see, then scanned the rigging to assess damage. He was stupefied. No spars were broken and the sails not furled weren't completely in tatters after the devastating winds they had endured. Some miracle had allowed the ship to skirt disaster. But respite from the battering of the waves was momentary, as furious rain came on the ship in blinding sheets, forcing Schrock to protect his eyes with his arm. Already soaked and cold, he had the feeling this near catastrophe might be a herald of worse to come. His body shivered—but from something other than cold. He hadn't thought it would ever happen to him. He'd finally run face-first into the hard bulkhead of a mariner's livelihood—the conditions where fear begins to outweigh any pretense of adventure.

Schrock's confidence wasn't bolstered when he turned and moved back toward First Mate Deetjen, at the helm during the whole episode except the times he'd been thrown to the deck. The mate gripped the wheel, staring transfixed at the wood-crated statue that stood firmly where it had been lashed in front of the forward cabin. Deetjen didn't see Schrock approaching as he shouted at his unseen God, "Why didn't You use Your storm to rip away that heathen idol? You could have thrown it to the depths—where it belongs!"

Schrock checked his watch. The helm change for Deetjen would come in ten minutes. It would be none too soon. In the remaining hours of daylight, even as the ship continued to wallow in massive seas, every time Schrock peered forward, the statue crate of the Savage King stood there, massive, disparate, seemingly immovable.

CHAPTER 5

The two apprentices followed *Kahuna* Naholehua into the low palm-thatch *hale* where the sorcerer conducted his rituals. He'd said that today he would instruct them in his most recent dream-spirit journey and continue them on their path of learning the intricacies of dreaming. As Makia stooped down to enter the hut through the opening, he had his usual mixed feelings, fearing it wasn't beyond possibility that his *kahuna* stepfather might just kill him for any misstep he made in the instruction. And it would be the impulsive act of a man with strange ideas of honor. Since the man had married his mother, Makia had never had anything that could be described as a good relationship with Naholehua. To Makia's thinking, Naholehua had taken on the father role with the skills of a wild dog. He had been impatient, demanding, quick to anger and too ready to use a stick on him. He always flew into a jealous rage when there was a mention of Makia's real father, an unselfish fisherman who had died in a storm at sea. As time wore on, Naholehua resented that Makia's mother now showed more affection toward Makia. Sometimes when the *kahuna* thought that she was too dismissive of him, in his fury he would allude to making her sick or even killing her. In response, she would wag her finger at him and then bare her voluptuous breasts, reducing him to a whimpering puppy. It amazed Makia how such a powerful sorcerer could easily become subject to a common man's weakness.

The other side of the stone was that there was much to learn from his stepfather before the effects of *awa* rendered this talented *kahuna* useless. If Makia wanted respect and a vaunted place in his community, being a *kahuna* sorcerer was the easiest path he saw to achieve it. And it would take Naholehua's knowledge, public designation and blessing to have that happen—all before the man lost his memory or died.

The three had all sat and drank *awa,* and repeated a ritual incantation. As Naholehua spoke, Makia thought his stepfather looked more awake than he could remember having seen him in recent memory. "I have had a sleep vision that took me to a ship somewhere far out at the sea, and I saw an image of the first Kamehameha on that ship. There was a storm, and I was helped by that storm as I tried to push the figure off that ship and into the sea—."

CHAPTER 6

South Atlantic

In the hours that followed, the storm subsided enough that Schrock was able to raise the sails and edge southwesterly around it. The second mate had reported no hull ruptures, and the sailmaker was in the process of repairing the ripped sails as the cook saw to the passengers. None had been seriously injured. But Schrock wondered what more this voyage had in store for him before they made port in Honolulu. He wasn't as superstitious as many sailors and unlike his first mate, didn't have any convictions about heathen images. Nevertheless, this was his closest near-sinking since he'd gone to sea. It had scared him to the core. There was a breach in whatever equilibrium he'd enjoyed before hoisting sail in Bremerhaven.

When he saw the statue standing tall in its casing, it still annoyed him how out of place it was on his ship's usually well-ordered deck. And to his first mate, this statue was a sailor's Jonah. He'd heard Deetjen fix the ship's destiny directly to the statue, and it wasn't any good fortune that he was foreseeing. Was it possible there was some kind of bad luck coming from the statue? He needed to dismiss the thought. Deetjen could never know he'd even considered it.

Other than giving him orders, Schrock had said little to the first mate since they'd left port. Other than matters related to ship duties, Deetjen never seemed to talk with other crew or passengers. He'd kept a sullen face since the storm and near-knockdown of the ship, but as far as Schrock could tell, he was doing his job. Although Schrock knew the reasons he'd again taken on Deetjen as first mate, he now had to question that decision. Deetjen had been a very competent first mate in the past, not so detached from others. Before, apparently he had been able to keep his demons in check.

The *Haendel* endured two more weeks of gales during which the vessel labored and rolled, continually pounded by the heavy seas. The duration of the bad weather took its toll on the crew and passengers. Even Johann Kessler had turned to sarcasm. After a short exchange about the weather and the ship's position, he told Schrock with a bit of a smirk, "If I didn't think I was going someplace, this voyage would be all but intolerable."

To Schrock, everyone else looked and acted beleaguered. There was none of the usual humor or camaraderie among the crew. And with uninterrupted sleep such a precious commodity, the gray faces of the other passengers gave him the impression the dead were now loose.

The seas became calm after another week of unsavory weather, and with the exception of Deetjen, the dispositions of everyone on board the *Haendel* improved. Schrock entertained the other passengers to dinner in his quarters on occasion, not wanting to appear partial to Johann Kessler. But it was Johann with whom he still looked forward to dining and conversing.

Johann eased back into a chair in the captain's spare quarters. "So, you were telling me before about the unfortunate circumstances that made you captain of this ship—before your account was cut short by the call of your duties."

"And you had determined that I had been denied common sense by virtue of being a mariner."

"Ah, yes. But your memory has little to do with common sense—so continue."

"If I must, as much as I want to remember about all that. Some of it is hard to think about." Schrock took a long drink of his wine, his mood shifting to that of child whose dog had just died. The image was there; the crew unloading the sailcloth bundle of what remained of Captain Sanders' body.

He still hadn't said anything when Johann said, "You're not obliged to tell me."

"What the hell; you might as well hear it. The ship, this ship, had been twenty two days sail out of India on our return to Bremerhaven when he died. It shouldn't have happened—Captain Sanders was only nine years older than me—too young to die. Because I was pilot and first mate I had to take command of the vessel. If I hadn't discovered Captain Sanders' will, I would have gone ahead and given him a customary burial at sea.

"His will? Did you have the right to read it?"

"As master of a ship, I have complete authority while at sea. And while we're on the subject, don't you forget that part!" Schrock said, feigning importance. "Where was I? Then we discovered there was precious little salt or spirits remaining on board to preserve Sanders' body. So I had him wrapped in sailcloth and put in the rope-store at the lowest deck. When we entered the hot equatorial seas, it quickened the body's decay. We noticed the smell as it worked its way up through the cargo decks below.

"My god, what a dilemma for you."

"It was bad—the crew all complained. At that point I decided that was not the kind of officer life I'd signed on for. It got even worse when we were becalmed for more than a week in the 'Horse Latitudes'—you've heard the phrase?"

"No, I can't say I have," said Johann.

"It's the thirty degrees of latitude on either side of the equator that has a belt of calms mixed sometimes with these baffling winds. You've been in it, so you know. And that name, Horse Latitudes—it came about when the Spanish Armadas carried horses across the Atlantic to invade the Americas. When the Spaniards' ships became stranded for weeks in these motionless seas, they would run out of water for the horses. Their solution was to shove all their parched and dying animals overboard—while the creatures were still able to stand. Dead horses floating all around the ship—an ugly picture, wouldn't you say?" "I can't imagine myself in those soldiers' place, even though I've never been sympathetic with Spain about much."

"After a week and a half of the boredom and stink, the nagging crew and I would have been thankful to see my captain's quick dispatch into the ocean. Every day I had to reason why, if the Spanish could push live horses overboard, we couldn't slip just one deceased and weighted down mariner over the side. And I would have it done with a good deal more ceremony—because I cared deeply for that man."

Off the coast of Argentina and on the morning of the twelfth of November, nearly three months after leaving Bremerhaven, Schrock noticed a gas-like smell from somewhere on the ship. He called for Second Mate Ronitz, sending him down the forward hatch to see if he could discover anything below. When Maus returned above deck, the mate's face was crumpled in worry.

"What'd you find below, Mister Ronitz?"

"I couldn't see anything, but the smell was stronger in the between-deck." Schrock stared intently at the deck as if he could see through the wood into the cargo hold. He tried to focus his mind on the probable cause of the odor. He knew the way this ship was constructed there was no means of through-ventilation. The main source of air that reached the holds came through the wooden crisscross ventilators over each of the hatches. There were two other small ventilator-shafts that passed from the fore and aft of the ship's main deck into the lower hold. Except in extreme weather it was always his policy to have the fore and after-hatch vents and the ventilator-shafts left open for airing. He shook his head as he thought about it. Regrettably, they hadn't covered the vents before the ship was beset by that first storm, and as they heeled over, seawater had likely flowed down into the coal cargo. He knew the problem was what every coal-carrying ship's captain knows, that the oxygen in water makes wet coal more dangerous than dry.

Schrock went down through the forward hatch to see for himself. Like Ronitz, he didn't carry a lantern, fearing an explosion from possible coal gasses. Barely able to find his way in the gloom, he crept along the between-deck's narrow passageway to the after-hatch ventilator, reaching down through small openings, feeling the coal with his hands as he went. He didn't sense any heat, but the smell was strongest in the fore of the holds. His shoulders slumped as he began to reach an unwanted conclusion. Somewhere in that mass of black rock it was smoldering. He continued crawling, feeling, hoping he was wrong. He stopped and put his head down on his forearms to rest and think. His mind raced now. Seven hundred tons of coal loaded into the holds twenty-two feet deep. The coal had to be under terrific pressure down deep. It was wet and it had been jostled about because of the storms. The circumstances were a perfect combination for spontaneous combustion. If that was the case, just where the hell in all that coal was he going to find it if he couldn't detect it down here?

Still down on his knees in the suffocating passageway, he thought of one way to maybe trace it to the source, maybe get to it. He had to. They were far out at sea, a miserably long way from any help. He slowly worked his way back to the ladder, his body aching, and climbed as fast as his legs would move. Stress constricted his throat. The sudden exertion made it difficult to breathe. When he reached the upper deck, in between gasps for air, he told Maus to order the sails luffed and to lower the anchor in drag. He needed to bring the ship to a near-stop so they could concentrate their efforts on clearing some of the coal from the hold. That would give them space to search for the heart of the fire. He went to Deetjen's cabin to wake him. He was awake, sitting on his bunk and staring at the wall.

"Mister Deetjen—there's fire somewhere in the coal. Wake up the other watch and get the main hatch open. We need to dig."

Positioned close to Cape Horn off Tierra del Fuego, Schrock knew it was a small piece of luck they were in the lee of Los Estados Island. Their location out of strong winds would help keep the ship from being pushed off course and into dangerous channel currents. When the remaining sails were luffed and the anchor put out in drag, Schrock ordered the crew to begin shoveling coal, hauling it up to the deck and throwing it overboard.

The crewmen took turns shoveling dirty coal into barrels as Captain Schrock paced and watched the work. He didn't want to show his own sense of foreboding as he glimpsed the dread in the faces of his crew. Shovel in hand and sweating profusely, Deetjen climbed out of the hold following a barrel of coal hoisted through the hatch by winch and boom. He thrust the shovel into Kullrich's hands and turned to face Schrock, frustration carved in his face. "The deeper we get, the hotter it is," he mumbled.

Before Deetjen could say anything else, Schrock turned to the ship's carpenter and shouted, "Mister Brandt. Let's find the source of this. Drive the iron pike ten feet into the coal and let it stay there."

The time passed with nervous anticipation after Brandt did as ordered while the crew continued to shovel the piled coal overboard. When the iron pole was finally withdrawn after fifteen minutes, Schrock felt along the length of it. "It's warm, about four to five feet down from the surface," he said to Brandt. "This end pushed deepest is cool. That tells me we need to dig more to the fore."

Schrock went to check the navigation charts while the men resumed digging, hauling more coal topside. After another hour of work, smoke began sifting up through the coal at their feet. The farther down they dug, the denser the smoke became.

For a second time, Schrock halted the work and told Brandt to drive the bar into the coal. "How far, Captain?" Brandt asked.

"About twelve feet, but this time, angle it toward the bow. The center must be somewhere down in that direction."

Two sailors helped Brandt drive the bar in with a sledge. The minutes passed and the smoke thickened, wafting up from the hold and around the deck. The men pulled out the bar an agonizing half hour later, teary and coughing. Schrock reached out to feel it, quickly jerking his hand back, his fingers singed. Looking down at his hand and then around at no one in particular, he mumbled, "There, it's happened, an ass-wiping coal fire—and down where we'll pay hell trying to get to it."

CHAPTER 7

South Atlantic Ocean, Near Cape Horn

A ship fire could be any sailor's worst fear, but for Schrock it was gnawing away his insides. Fire had been a personal demon since his family's home on the outskirts of Bremen went up in flames during a cold winter night. He was five when his mother yanked him from sleep and dragged him outside through thick smoke. His little brother's screams were so loud when his father carried him out that Schrock thought he had been burned—even though it was only his cries of terror. The four of them stood in the snow and watched the house become an inferno. For the first time he saw both of his parents crying, and for the first time in his short life, fear and despair were inscribed in his core.

He tried suppressing the disturbing memory. The smell of smoke only sharpened his sense of dread. The *Haendel* was his home now. He couldn't lose another home to fire. Jesus and Mary, it would tie his brain into a knot he would never be able to undo.

Schrock looked up and saw the men all staring at him, waiting for his orders. *What the hell do they want of me?* "Well, what are you waiting for?" he asked, ripping himself back to the present and pointing toward the hatch.

With his gesture, the crew began their rotations of climbing back down the ladder to shovel coal or man the deck-winch to haul up the barrels. All sailors know the consequence of a fire on board, and the *Haendel* deck-watch worked without complaining, shoveling and filling barrel after barrel with the dirty black rock. Within an hour the pace took on more desperation as they dug deeper, working more feverishly but still unable to locate the fire in the many tons of coal. One, then two of the men passed out from the smoke and had to be hauled up to the deck with ropes. With few men not completely exhausted, Schrock knew he'd need to pitch in. But first he had to steel himself to go down into the hold—closer to wherever the fire was.

He watched Seaman Kullrich stumble up the ladder and collapse, rubbing his blackened eyes. Without saying anything, Schrock climbed down into the dimness and grabbed a shovel. For an instant the drum-tightened muscles in his arms wouldn't move as he imagined the fire somewhere down below him. A terror overcame him, of burning to death, which gave him the momentum to finally plunge his shovel into the coal. He put his back into it despite smoke thick as early morning fog, but he'd only filled half a barrel before it tormented his eyes and he found it difficult to breathe. Tunnel vision followed ragged coughing and then the feeling of collapse, within and without, as he neared blacking out. He shuffled blindly to the ladder, grabbing onto it until some of his vision returned. He climbed to the top and crawled from the smoke-bellowing hatch. He staggered toward the rail, coughing and gasping, his body frantic to reach cleaner air.

Large hands grabbed onto him as he lurched out of control, catching him before he plowed into the rail and pitched into the water. The second mate still had hold of him when he retched over the side. After a minute Schrock's mind cleared enough to croak out new orders to Maus.

"Stop the digging. Get all the gunpowder kegs hauled topside from the forward hold." As Maus turned to pass the order to the crew, Schrock said, "Maus."

Maus looked back at the captain.

"Thank you."

The second mate gave Schrock a slight nod of his head.

Confronted with oppressive smoke in the forward hold as well, crewmen still able to function traded quick trips down to retrieve the gunpowder kegs. As Schrock watched them fasten the kegs to the winch rope and hoist them up, the men he knew seemed strangely transformed, their faces and arms blackened by coal dust and smoke. Deetjen approached nearby, just beginning his new watch. As he came upon the men, apparently he saw something that was more sinister than what Schrock had seen. The first mate's face screwed up in confusion, then in fear.

"Those are the Devil's henchmen, come from that cursed idol," Deetjen yelled. Several crewmen stopped what they were doing to stare at him. "Holy Mother of Jesus," he pleaded as he backed away and headed toward the aft deck. Deetjen's hands trembled as he held on to the rail to keep his balance. He shook his head back and forth, seemingly to clear away the disturbing vision. Schrock followed him for a few steps but stopped, not sure what he could do for the man. He'd have to hope Deetjen wasn't too far gone to be of help again. They'd need him.

The crew hauled all the kegs of gunpowder up on the deck and away from the hatches when Schrock embarked on his next step. He would try and starve the fire of air. Sealing off the holds might buy them some time. There was little chance of smothering the fire this way since a ship's wood swells and shrinks constantly—it can never be air-tight. But he had to try.

"Maus, tell Brandt to seal all hatches and vents right away."

"Aye, Captain." The second mate was moving as soon as his mouth closed.

"One more thing, Maus," Schrock yelled after him. "Keep with this watch until I see that Deetjen's good to take over." Maus raised his hand in affirmation without looking back.

His eyes still watering, Schrock went aft to his cabin and tried to wash the soot from his face and mouth. When he'd recovered some, he looked at his charts to approximate the ship's position. He poked his head out the door and called Deetjen in from the quarterdeck. When the first mate entered, Schrock said, "You don't look well. What's wrong with you?"

"The smoke's made me a little sick."

"A little sick—do you know what nonsense you were spouting up at the forward hold?"

"I was just—a bit dizzy. I'm good now."

"You'd best be or your men won't listen to anything else you tell them. Nor will I." Schrock felt a mix of both impatience and sympathy for his mate. "We're in serious trouble. I need your mind in the right place and this is not the time to get peculiar. All right?"

"Yes sir. I won't, sir."

"That's good, because you're the best navigator I know." Schrock was silent for a moment as he looked at Deetjen's face, reaching deep inside himself to find compassion for this broken man. He put a hand on Deetjen's shoulder. "Now look here," he said, pointing at the chart on his desk. "You need to see this. There's a small chance to save the ship. You know we're still here, in the lee of Los Estados Island, well north of the Horn. With strong southerlies and full canvas we can make a run back to Port Stanley in the Falklands—maybe three or four days. If we do, we just might get a water-pumper to the ship in time."

"We just might, Captain," Deetjen said, his words flat.

Schrock rubbed his eyes. "You check the course to see if I've set it right. I had a devil of a time seeing the charts." He left his cabin door ajar, hurrying to get back to the helmsman. When he got close to the man holding the wheel, he saw a face of weariness and fear.

"Seaman Gepken! Come about for a course east-northeast," he rasped. "We're turning back to the Falklands. I'll have better coordinates soon. And chin up! At least we're not thirty days somewhere back out in the middle. We'll get ourselves to Port Stanley."

Schrock peered out through his still-watering eyes toward the horizon. He figured they were lucky not to be that far out from the Falklands. Otherwise there would be little hope of putting out a fire, let alone surviving if flames took hold. He pulled his pea coat collar tight around his neck and his cap down to his ears, heading to the fore to find his second mate.

"Mister Ronitz," he shouted over the rising wind, his voice still hoarse. "Set a full press of sail. We're to Port Stanley! Then you're off your watch."

CHAPTER 8

South Atlantic Ocean
53₀ Course NNE to Port Stanley

Schrock settled back onto his bed and pulled a blanket over him without taking off his coat or shoes. He was too agitated to sleep. He'd have to hope it would come in time. There were too many nautical miles and hard seas if they could even reach The Falklands. He would need rest for what lay ahead.

The memory of holding Susan McGinnis welled up inside him again. Sydney more than a year ago was fading in bits. But it was something he could cling to. There were so few sweet memories in his life; as long as he was in this hell it felt wasteful to ever let go of her.

For the next two days, the *Haendel* ran with heavy winds northeast toward the Falkland Islands. With freezing weather, the passengers had been spending most of their time in the cabins. But by the end of the first day the smoke was so thick it forced both the passengers and crew to leave their quarters. Schrock explained to the passengers that the fire was smoldering and still flameless, somewhere deep in the tons of coal, not yet presenting an imminent threat.

"Mister Kessler," Schrock said as he approached Johann. "I'm telling all the passengers that if there is any sign the fire reaches the wood bulkheads, you will be notified straight away to go to the lifeboats. I'm still hoping that won't happen and we will make it to Stanley. Mister Kessler, you're the first I'm telling this to, but I'll have to share this much with you in confidence. It's just that—if I'm to guess—we are in a race against the movement of this fire below. So if you're a praying man, well—I don't know, do what you can."

Johann Kessler stared at Schrock with vacant eyes. "When was it you said that you secured your first berth on this ship?"

In the next days the six passengers settled out on the deck where the smoke was dispelled by the wind, huddled in makeshift tents. At one point, Schrock was able to overhear a conversation between Johann Kessler and another man situated close to the quarterdeck.

"God, I can't die," the man said to Johann, the pitch of his voice rising in anguish. "I'm the only breadwinner for my wife and five children. If I don't make it back to Bremen, I don't know how my family will get by. None of our damned kin would be of any help to them." The man's head sagged and it sounded to Schrock as if he were crying. "For Jesus' sake," he sobbed, "I should have waited 'til spring to make this trip."

"There now," Johann said as he reached out and put his hand on the man's shoulder. "I'm confident we'll get through this in one piece. We've a good captain and crew."

Johann seemed composed. Schrock considered that perhaps this man feared dying less than he did. He made his way up to check on two other passengers sitting under a canvas lean-to fixed against the forward cabin, both wearing gloomy expressions. "I'm sorry we're in this state," he told them. "There's not much more we can do right now. But we're at a pace that should get us to Stanley in good order." Schrock was taking his lead from Johann and he wanted to believe what he was telling them. But he didn't have much reason to be optimistic.

Another full day passed as the *Haendel* plowed through the unseasonable weather toward the Falklands, spray whipping wildly across the deck while the ship trailed a stream of smoke as if it were a coal-fired vessel lacking a smokestack. The air temperature was frigid as the crew and passengers dozed for short periods on hard surfaces of the raised quarterdeck and cabin roofs. When night fell, Schrock finally lay down and curled up with a blanket in front of the helm, dropping into sleep almost immediately. No more than ten minutes passed when the whole ship lurched violently with a tremendous explosion. Schrock bolted upright, his thoughts frozen in half-sleep and confusion. He heard yelling over his shoulder and saw Gepken at the helm, gesturing for him to get up, frantically pointing with his free hand. "Sir, the three main hatch covers have blown out—lifted ten feet before they hit the deck—it's awful, sir!" He heard more crew and passengers shouting and cursing and looked to see black clouds of smoke billowing out of the holds and swirling over the deck and around the ship. He struggled to his feet just as Seaman Kullrich bounded up the stair to the quarterdeck, coming at him like he had seen the devil again. "Sir, Captain, sir! I think a keg of gunpowder's been touched off by fire—the main hatches all blew off."

Schrock stood at the rail and saw Deetjen on the forward deck below. "Any injured?" he shouted. His mind raced as he waited for a report. A gunpowder explosion would have blown a massive hole in the deck or even the hull. They had pulled all the kegs out of the hold and put them up on the forward deck, hadn't they? They didn't seem to be sinking—not yet. The heat buildup—the weakest spots—the hatches. He heard more frantic yelling forward deck. From the quarterdeck rail the smoke obscured what had happened beyond the sight of two of the hatch covers thrown up against the gunwales. He took a breath and closed his eyes to quell his panic.

Maus had run back from the foredeck. "I didn't see anyone hurt—but everyone's scared sick."

Schrock waved his hand. "Go see if there are any flames down the hatches and what damage we have."

Schrock tried to clear his mind to consider what options he had now. He was sure of one thing. Whatever he did, they'd probably not reach Port Stanley before the fire burned up through the deck.

Deetjen approached through the smoke. "No injured to report, sir, crew or passengers. All three main hatch covers blown off but still on the deck."

At least the man is functioning, thought Schrock. "Have the watch quickly shove all that bastard gunpowder overboard—and keep the kegs away from the hatches when they're being moved. I'll be damned if we'll be blown to bits before we can even put out in lifeboats."

Deetjen left him, mumbling about the curse, but quickly scrambled several crew toward the powder kegs. Schrock coughed from the smoke and then expelled a deep breath. *How dense of me—thinking I could somehow save that powder. The kegs should have been cast off days ago. I could have killed us all.*

Maus came back to the quarterdeck. "I didn't see any flames below—a lot of smoke and heat. The hatch frames are intact but the covers are pretty torn up."

"Shit-o-dear," said Schrock. "Get the lifeboats provisioned and ready to launch. When that's done, you and The First tell the crew and passengers that if things get worse we'll need to abandon ship."

The second mate looked more unnerved from Schrock's words than from the explosion. He slowly backed away from Schrock, staring at him, his mouth slightly agape. Then he closed his mouth and turned toward the closest lifeboat.

Schrock bit his cheek as a small fortune of gunpowder rolled into the sea, trailing a ragged line of barrels in the waves behind the ship. He felt only a small measure of relief.

He still hoped he could slow the burn below. Spotting Carpenter Brandt, he pointed forward and yelled to him. "I want all those hatch covers repaired and secured right away."

Brandt stepped away to make a quick survey, needing to walk nearly the entire length of the ship to examine the damaged covers and latches. He repeatedly shook his head and cursed. As he neared the quarterdeck on his way back to report, he told Maus who was following close behind him, "How the hell am I supposed to quick-up secure these busted pieces of junk?"

Maus turned red as he grabbed Brandt's arm with an iron grip and whirled him around, getting close up into his face. "However you damn well can, Brandt!" he hissed. "Our worthless lives could depend on it!"

Another half day and the ship was still underway with the hatch covers back in place and nailed tight. In the early light of dawn there was little talk on board. Schrock could see both fatigue and anxiety in the faces of crew and passengers. But within a short time their disquiet rose to near panic.

Nearby, Kullrich pointed down to the smoke that was curling up from the deck as the caulking pitch melted away in the seams of the decking. "Bitch of Davey's locker—have you ever seen anything like that, Mister Brandt?" Staring down at the thick wood under his feet, Brandt shook his head in disbelief. "I'd say we're in a race against being burnt-out or sinking, neither of which is good."

Schrock saw the same thing and felt his throat constrict. They were plainly in a run for their lives. From the quarterdeck, he could also see First Mate Deetjen in the foredeck, where the statue crate stood in the swirling haze. He watched Deetjen turn and walk directly toward him. Deetjen carried himself military straight, his squinted eyes exuding a sense of righteous affirmation. Schrock knew that look meant his first mate still wasn't right. He didn't need this. As Deetjen came nearer, Schrock was ready with an order to avert another of the first mate's likely expositions about the antichrist figure causing the fire.

"Mister Deetjen," he said, pointing toward the gunwale, "see that the scupper holes are plugged and then get your crew on the pumps to flood the whole deck."

Deetjen stopped in his tracks, looking like he'd run into a wall. After a stunned pause, he turned to do as ordered. But his stiff retreat said he wasn't ready to give up on enlightening his captain.

Throughout the morning, hand pumps flooded the main deck with seawater. The passengers and the crew did their best to stand clear of the water sloshing about. Because smoke was still finding its way through cracks in the vent covers and broken hatch knee walls, Schrock believed the flooded deck gave them some hope the fire wouldn't burn through the deck before the ship made land.

Facing the wind, Schrock pulled off his cap and rubbed his hands through his hair, feeling the pinpricks of the icy droplets of water work their way to his scalp. In all his years at sea he'd never faced such an array of problems at the same time. He wondered if this could get any worse.

Then, as if in answer to his question, heavy snow squalls came up from the east-southeast, true to South Atlantic weather. The crew had managed to retrieve all the smoky-smelling blankets and foul weather clothes from the uninhabitable cabins, but they offered scant protection from the snow and near-freezing temperature.

Hour after hour, the *Haendel* continued to push toward the Falklands for what seemed like an eternity to the miserable crew and passengers. Because of the crew's lack of sleep and the cold, Schrock put himself in the rotation of one hour shifts at the helm with Gepken, Deetjen, and Maus. They were each hit hard in their faces by an Antarctic sleet as they took their turn at the wheel.

Though there was little conversation, Schrock overheard the passenger who was worried about his family say to another man, "The steam coming up from the deck feels good, doesn't it?"

How ironic... even diabolical, thought Schrock. *The fire below that's causing that steam will in all likelihood kill us all if the ship doesn't make it to the Falklands.*

Schrock was having dizzy spells from sleep deprivation when just before dawn of the fourth day in their retreat north, the Cape Pembroke lighthouse on Falklands' William Island was sighted. The shout of "liiiigt-hooo, starboard!" came from a lookout high in the *Haendel's* mainmast. The sighting brought wild cheers from everyone but Deetjen, even though they were still ten miles out. Schrock allowed himself to think they might yet escape the fire or foundering in lifeboats, boats unfit for any duration in heavy sea. But the ship would still need a fireboat, and need it quick. He could feel the heat through the deck, the water sloshing about warm as a bath.

The dawn itself came with the gray Falklands land mass taking form like the back of a sleeping animal. As Schrock watched with a sense of hope, suddenly there was another deafening explosion, louder than the first. "Oh no," he managed to voice as he fell to the deck while the boat rocked thirty degrees opposite the wind lean. This time Schrock glimpsed one of the hatch covers falling back down to the deck.

"Jeez-us," Schrock sputtered, his ears ringing. "Deetjen, Maus!" he shouted, scrambling to his feet on the slanted deck. Smoke poured out of the holds with pent-up force with no place on deck to escape it. The crew and passengers coughed and swore, all pulling themselves up after being knocked down as well. Schrock looked to see that despite the explosion, the ship was still making headway with full sails. He yelled orders to get what was left of the hatch covers nailed and roped down. As the crew struggled to get the covers secured, the stifling smoke pressed at them through large cracks in the sides of the damaged hatch walls that extended two feet above the deck.

Schrock tolerated Seaman Kullrich's mixed prayers and curses throughout the remaining hours it took before they finally passed the Cape Pembroke lighthouse and rounded the cape. "Holy hell, we've made it," Schrock mumbled to Maus.

As they neared the bay a few miles from Stanley, a pilot boat came to intercept the *Haendel*. Schrock ordered the sails luffed, the ship slowed, and the harbor pilot boarded the ship to bring it into Port William. Reaching the top of the ladder and coming on deck, the pilot looked around at the makeshift shelters and water spilling about on the deck. "What's happening? Where's the fire?" he asked, gingerly stepping through the water on the deck, clearly annoyed.

Schrock gave the pilot a quick account of what they'd been through while the pilot made his way to the helm to guide the ship toward the port, seeming irritated at having to get his feet wet. All the sails but the mizzen and staysail were reefed to further slow the ship in the bay as they approached Stanley. Near land, Schrock ordered the anchor dropped in about thirty-five feet of water. The coughing, relieved pilot quickly got off the heavily smoking ship to his small tender. Schrock could see several other small craft coming toward the ship.

With all eyes looking toward the boats that could get them some help, Schrock noticed Deetjen moving quickly toward the fore of the ship. Only later did Schrock hear Kullrich's account that a crazed-looking Deetjen had ordered him and four other crew members up front of the mid-ship cabin to the statue. He had them undo the crate's lashings and covering, then directed them to lever it up to the portside main rail with cargo poles. They were only able to move the container inches at a time. "Push, push. Hurry!" Deetjen urged them with frantic whispers. When the crate came up against the rail, the sailors stopped to catch ragged breaths, the smoke encircling them, cloaking their doings. In an urgent but hushed tone, Deetjen gave his directives: "You three, put those poles under the bottom. You two, place the ends of yours up at the top. When I say push—," and as his order came, they gave a final heave with their poles. The crate partially tipped. For an instant the rail held it back. Then, with grinding, splintering noises, the massive, encased statue slid and scraped over the railing, breaking away the lower half of the crate as it toppled, the statue sliding halfway out, head first. The men stood back and watched it hit the water with a thunderous splash and push-out wave. The remaining wood-crating kept the statue afloat a few seconds. Then it disappeared down into the dark water of the bay.

Schrock had heard the splash and, through all the smoke, peered off the starboard trying to make sense of the sounds. Not seeing anything, he shouted out toward the foremast. "What's happened—is someone overboard?"

He felt strange, lightheaded, like he too was sinking beside the ship. It was almost like something was pulling him underwater. He shook his head to try and clear the sensation.

He looked up and saw Deetjen moving toward him through the smoke.

"Sir," Deetjen said, trying not to sound breathless. "I took the liberty of pushing the deck cargo overboard—where it can be salvaged instead of damaged by any fire."

Schrock's eyes narrowed as he took a long look at the first mate. He knew the demented reasoning behind Deetjen shoving the statue overboard, and turned over in his mind what he should do. What the hell did it matter? It might be useful to leave the statue salvageable. But Deetjen should still be flogged. Damn this man.

"Mister Deetjen, let me make this clear to you. I don't want any more essential actions taken by you without my consent. If it happens again, I'll have your papers suspended. Do you understand?"

"Yes sir, Captain," Deetjen responded, sounding contrite. Except Schrock could see what appeared to be months-long tension of this religious dilemma roll almost like waves from his enigmatic first mate.

"Get the passengers ready to off-board," Schrock said without expression.

As Deetjen moved away, Schrock looked down into the water. He couldn't see a crate or any sign of the Savage King statue. But he felt it—as if some part of him was down there as well. It was ludicrous and troubling at the same time. Damn Deetjen, and the statue, and this voyage.

A few minutes later the boats came alongside and Schrock sent the passengers with their effects to shore and on to the town of Stanley. Johann Kessler approached him before heading to the ladder.

"I'm sorry, Captain. I hope you're able to get this fire out. I'll do my best to see that you and your crew have rooms when you get into town."

The gesture surprised Schrock. He nodded as Johann turned and was gone through the smoke and over the side. Schrock had a momentary, distracted thought that he had wanted to talk more with Kessler about Hawaii. But there were things to do and do quickly. When Maus reported hearing there was a fireboat in Port Stanley, Schrock asked men in one of the boats heading in to alert the fireboat crew. He also asked them to have the port's marine surveyor sent out to advise him about what he might do to save the ship.

An hour later, the marine surveyor arrived to assess the situation. Schrock accompanied the man as he took furtive looks down in the hatches to estimate the advancement of the fire. It only took a few minutes until he turned to Schrock to provide his verdict. "I'm sorry, Captain," he announced with a clipped British accent, "you need to scuttle her if there's to be any salvage."

The truth hit Schrock like a broken spar in a gale, flailing wildly across the deck.

Jesus and Mary—this is it. The *Haendel* will go down.

CHAPTER 9

Falkland Islands
November 1880

Schrock stood motionless by the quarterdeck rail. Drifting snow settled on his cap and shoulders while he watched the marine surveyor's quick departure from the *Haendel*. Take your pronouncement to hell with you, he thought, looking down at the surveyor's sloop rocking in the swells below.

"Brandt." He signaled to his carpenter to come closer. "The surveyor says to scuttle her—maybe can be some salvage. Get a boat down, start on the starboard and bore holes just below the waterline."

By the time Brandt and two other crewmen had finished boring the five, three-inch holes, the waterline was creeping up the side of the hull. The fireboat schooner arrived minutes later, pulled up alongside the ship, and immediately began spraying the deck with water. There was a lot of shouting before Schrock convinced the fireboat crew to instead get a hose on board and direct their water down through the hatches. He was determined to drown the beast that seethed somewhere deep in the coal. Moreover, if there was any hope that would happen, by God he'd have Brandt plug those same scuttle holes and save the damned ship.

The fireboat pumped seawater for the rest of the daylight hours while Schrock and the crew clambered around, helping to shift the hose from hatch to hatch. The fireboat's steam engine chugged incessantly, stoked by its crew, pouring out acrid smoke mixed with the black fog that came from the *Haendel's* fire. The irony of a coal-fired pump being used to put out the *Haendel's* coal fire wasn't lost on Schrock. The hellish air on deck and around the ship gave him and everyone else relentless coughing fits.

Ragged with exhaustion, Schrock and his men had all been awake for most of three days. After the first seven hours of pumping from the fireboat, there was twelve feet of water in the holds; and in another two hours they had pumped nearly sixteen feet of water inside. The ship's hull was now low in the water, though far from sinking. Schrock still didn't want her to sink. He assumed that by now the fire had to be extinguished.

Then a daunting sight erased what little hope he had. Flames were breaking out on the foredeck, the blaze coming from ahead of the forward cabin in the exact place where the statue had been lashed on deck.

"Can you believe this?" he yelled, aiming his remark toward Maus and Brandt standing nearby. They both shook their heads with faces that showed equal exasperation.

A crew member from the fireboat waved up toward Schrock to get his attention. "It's too dangerous to lie close alongside!" he shouted. "We'll try and spray those flames down after we back off!"

Schrock could only shake his head as he watched them reel in their hose and then move the fireboat away through the pall of smoke.

No sooner was the fireboat away than the Stanley port magistrate again pulled up close in his boat. "You can't scuttle the ship here!" he yelled up to Schrock. "The masts will block other ships in the channel. If it sinks here, you're responsible for the removal of the wreck inside three days or you'll be fined for every day after."

Schrock waved at the magistrate and reluctantly nodded.

"For Christ's sake," he said to Maus after the magistrate's boat pulled away. "You'd have thought that cretin surveyor might have said something after he told me to scuttle her and then jumped ship like his ass was already on fire."

"You'd a thought, sir," growled Maus.

He turned to Deetjen who stood behind him on the quarterdeck, close enough to have heard the magistrate's warning.

"Cut the chain and slip the anchor free," he ordered his mate. "There's no time to weigh it in."

The fireboat hadn't abandoned them. Its crew managed to stay close enough to spray water at the flames in the fore of the ship. It gave Deetjen and three of the crew the additional minutes they needed to free the ship, held by the chain to the five-thousand pound anchor on the sea floor. For the next few pulse-pounding minutes, each of them took turns hack-sawing the chain links as the fireboat's water sprayed over their backs. Finally, the second two-inch thick link was cut through. The men leapt back as the massive chain tore through the hawse-pipe with an explosive, raking noise, then plunged down to the bottom, pushing a boiling wake of bubbles to the surface.

Schrock peered over the side as the sea closed around where it had swallowed the mass of iron. Almost certainly the chain had landed in a heap close to where the statue had sunk to the bottom.

"Maus!" he yelled. "Give all the canvas full set. We'll need all sail until she's grounded!"

Exhausted crew made a final climb aloft to set sails and then on deck to haul the sheets up with clewlines and halyards. Schrock, Deetjen and Maus all worked with the crew to hurry the set. Coughing, Schrock made a final walk through the smoke into his cabin and grabbed his money purse and the ship's log, stuffing them into his shirt.

Despite all the water in the holds, there was enough wind to push the ghostly *Haendel* on its last crossing, trailing smoke the remaining three hundred yards to the shore. With the flooded holds dragging the hull low in the water, the ship eventually ground to a stop, the keel bottoming-out in ten feet of shoal water, still thirty yards from land. Above deck, chaos reigned as the wood around all the hatches was overtaken by flames. Schrock's yell to abandon ship appeared pointless as crew were already piling into the first boat being lowered over the side.

When the boats filled with Schrock, Deetjen, Maus and the remaining crew at last made it to shore, they gratefully accepted wool blankets handed them by an older sailor from the Port Stanley seamen's union. The grizzled veteran went about his mission in such a matter-of-fact way that Schrock guessed such disasters happened with frequency in these waters.

Lung-seared and fatigued beyond anything most of them had ever endured before, Schrock could see there was nothing more to do to save the ship or remaining cargo. He and his crew stumbled a few yards up from the beach to sit on the rocks and watch the ship burn.

PART II

NOVEMBER 1880
CHOICE

CHAPTER 10

It was afternoon of his third day in the Falklands capitol of Stanley as Schrock sat on his bed in the Globe Hotel and stared out the narrow window facing the harbor. A heavy mist, blown sideways by the unfailing southern Atlantic wind, all but obscured the dozens of ships anchored offshore. He could just make out what appeared to be the tops of detached masts floating on a sea of gray. He wondered why it never rained hard here. The island seemed beset with continuous, dismal seepage.

In this distant outpost, it was unclear when he'd face a maritime enquiry into the loss of the *Haendel*, only that he would. His only respite from waiting for the bureaucratic wheels to turn was spending time in conversation with passenger, Johann Kessler. As he had promised, Johann had secured a room in Stanley for Schrock, two blocks from the waterfront. Schrock was a mariner and found it intolerable to stay inside for any length of time when he wasn't sleeping. Despite the cold, he and Johann, who had insisted he be called by his first name, met up to take a walk. Schrock donned the frayed coat he'd been given by the sailors' refuge organization and they set out in the direction of the harbor seawall. They walked easily, side by side, like old companions.

"So, were you able to secure a berth on a ship?" Schrock inquired, trying to conceal his envy about the possibility of leaving.

"Yes, I just did," Johann answered. It departs in three days for Honolulu. And if I have better luck than my last journey," he said, grinning as he spoke, "I'll see my wife and children in about three months."

"I feel terrible about this delay for you and the other passengers, keeping you from your families," Schrock said.

Johann stopped and looked at Schrock. "You've got to know you're not responsible for what happened. Storms occur all the time, and your ship wasn't the first to have a coal fire. If it wasn't for what you did to save the ship, I might not be here feeling the breeze on my skin. I have you to thank."

"I—I appreciate your saying that, Johann."

Schrock's eyes followed the pattern of the cobblestones as the two resumed walking. "There's something I've wanted to talk to you about," Schrock resumed, giving a side glance at Johann. "I've been thinking—I know this may sound irrational—as I told you before, First Mate Deetjen believed that statue we carried on board had cursed the ship. You know I attended the university, studied philosophy, science; I should know better. But in the last couple of days I've been having thoughts—that he was right." Schrock wagged his head, exasperated with himself. "I would never tell this to any of my crew, especially Deetjen. But I wanted to know what you think, Johann. What are your thoughts about these things sailors believe in?"

For a moment the only sound was the clicking of their heels on the cobblestones. They stopped at the seawall, facing the harbor.

"Well, sir, there are sailors and then there is your first mate," said Johann. "But tell me first, good Captain, don't you remember the common beliefs passed around when we were children—and we thought of them as true? Like, if you walk under a chicken roost and a hen poops on you, it will bring you bad luck? But if it's the rooster that unleashes his messy load on you, amazingly, you get good luck?"

"Sure, I remember," said Schrock.

"Well then, if you still believe that superstition today, you might as well believe you lost your ship because you once walked under a hen that shit on you."

Schrock made a half-attempt at smiling. He could tell Johann had more to say about it.

"Or how about the one that says if a man wears a shirt spun by a girl between five and seven years of age, it will protect him against bad magic?"

"I think I had an uncle who told me that one," Schrock replied, seeing this storytelling was livening up Johann.

"Well then, Captain, you see your problem was that you weren't wearing just such a shirt."

"You're joking with me," Schrock said, taking his cap off and running a hand through his unkempt hair. "And you don't need to call me captain. Either Gerhard or Schrock is fine. But what if—what if there are some superstitious beliefs that are reliable, that almost always bear out as true?"

"I don't accept any of it," Johann shot back. "Forgive me, but you should know that superstitions are usually made up by those who want to control the gullible. Take the story of the cloth spun by a child. It's easier for unscrupulous merchants to get away with having young children work in factories if they've spread around these phony stories."

"I get that, Johann—but I assure you it's rare that mariner superstitions are made up by ship owners. In their eyes, sailors' superstitions just slow things down—get in the way of their making money."

Johann chuckled. It was infectious, and the two men laughed more as Schrock described thoughts he'd once had about the *Haendel's* owner as he'd watched him talk. "I imagined the man's jowls puffed out like squirrel's cheeks because he had them stuffed with money."

The sun broke through the mist for a short time and Johann opened the top button on his coat collar. Continuing to walk the road out of Stanley, the two men gradually had a view of the bay unobstructed by the mist or any ship anchorages. Schrock pointed out a square-rigged freighter coming into the harbor, passing not far from the *Haendel* wreck site. He felt his shoulders go tense.

Johann shielded his eyes as he looked at the ship. "It occurs to me," he said, "in Mister Deetjen's already unstable mind, he has mixed religious and superstitious beliefs in a way that conveniently finds a way to place blame when things go wrong. But you, you're the sane and sober shipmaster. I would think of you as a man who makes decisions based on specifics and hard evidence. Or have I misunderstood what's required in your profession?" he asked, tilting his head.

"Well, yes, you've understood," Schrock nodded. "But sailors have many superstitions, and sometimes I've found myself needing to go along with them. When you're at sea and things go awry, those are times you may need to indulge all the possibilities—just to try and keep your crew and the ship safe. I don't have to tell you that sailing is like living on a knife's edge, and sailors don't like the idea of tempting fate."

Johann gestured out toward the water. "I don't remember you using any superstitious tricks during our ordeal at sea. All I saw was clear, decisive actions on your part."

"But Deetjen did," Schrock explained. "After you left the ship, he pushed the statue overboard, right out there, without my orders. He was trying to rid the ship of a curse, still hoping it would keep us from sinking."

"Since the ship burned and sank," Johann snorted, "I guess that speaks to how well that worked."

Schrock shook his head and turned his eyes on the rutted road as they started walking again. "Let me tell you a story and maybe you'll see what I mean. There was an instance when my crew's superstitions influenced my command and, in truth, I think saved the ship."

"Tell it, friend. I'm listening," said Johann.

"It wasn't that long ago, on my first voyage to Australia as master of the *Haendel*. We ran into intense northerlies bending off the Cape. The ship was blown off course, south toward Antarctica. Nothing I did to get us back worked, and we were pushed into waters with ice floes and massive icebergs. Eventually we hit submerged ice that tore a big gash in the hull. We took on water and for a while I was worried we could sink. However, I was fortunate my carpenter was able to make a temporary fix to the damage. Then for the next five days around the clock, we never stopped tacking, trying to move northeasterly toward Australia. In all that time, the bastard wind direction never changed and all we did was lose ground. We were all exhausted and winter was coming on fast. The crew on watch was always fighting frostbite, and I was sure the ship was about to be locked in by ice at any time— something we were wholly unprepared for. Even if the ship wasn't crushed in the ice, we didn't have food or clothes to keep us through a winter there. I had premonitions of freezing to death. Worse, I knew I'd be taking all those men along with me."

"That's unimaginable," Johann said, his brow furrowed in sympathy.

"I didn't want the men to see I was beginning to lose hope. But then—I don't know how to describe it—an extraordinary thing happened. An able-bodied seaman named Welshans came to me out of the blue—and he was apologetic—asked me for some wine. I was the only one who had any wine—kept a small store of it locked in my quarters. He said it was a cure for the mess we were in. Like some Portuguese ships he'd sailed on, he'd seen this rite bring good luck and intended to pour it on the deck. I was desperate, because I gave him a bottle of my best wine."

Johann nodded. "All in, I'd say."

"I suppose that was true for me. Anyway, the word was out what Welshans was going to do and all the crew came out on deck. I knew everyone was scared, and these kinds of rituals aren't trivial to sailors. He mumbled a few words and then started spilling the wine on the deck. The wind caught it as he was pouring and it sprayed around on some of the men. But no one said a word."

"Forgive me, but it all sounds rather pagan," said Johann. Signs of agitation crept up the corners of Schrock's mouth. "Sorry," Johann said. "So then what happened?"

The recollection of the event buoyed Schrock. "I have to tell you— what followed was astonishing. Within two hours of Welshans' ceremony—and by God I'm telling you the truth—the winds shifted and we were able to pull northeast. In two days we were clear of the ice, and in three more weeks we'd sailed to the coast of Australia."

Johann looked at Schrock and shook his head. "But Gerhard—now that you've had some distance from that, surely you recognize it was coincidence the wind picked up at that point. Isn't weather always unpredictable, especially at sea?"

Schrock's jaw dropped open. "Damn, you're impossible. Listen, Johann, I think there's more to this than we can see. I'm not ready to dismiss these practices because I can't tie the results to something logical. As odd as some of these rituals are, I'm open to the possibility they had something to do with saving my life more than one time."

"Think what you will," Johann quickly responded. "As far as we know, the universe will only bend so many ways."

"As far as we know," Schrock repeated pointedly. "That's the key, isn't it?"

Johann's demeanor was patient as he looked at Schrock. "And I'd say to you—that when some acts of nature aren't understood, it doesn't mean we have to consign them to some ethereal realm."

Schrock put his head down as cold raindrops began to peck at his face. He'd have to think about how to work this argument more with Johann. Contentious as this conversation had become, Schrock was glad to be able to talk it through with someone he could trust. "I'm not giving up on this, but there's another troublesome notion that I'd like you to tell me about."

"And what's that?" asked Johann.

"It's about the king for whom this statue was cast—the one out there," he said, pointing out though the mist into the bay. "Do the Europeans and Americans living in Hawaii still refer to that man as the Savage King?"

"They do," Johann answered, shaking his head, "especially a good many of the British and the Americans. They like to label anyone they deem as primitive or not Christian as a savage. If they're seen as not fully human, it makes it less complicated to cart off everything they have."

"I can't believe the Germans are much more enlightened," said Schrock.

"True enough, although I'm trying hard to break the mold. And a few of us know how the king should be referred to. It's King Kamehameha the Great. It was because he was a remarkable warrior and leader. With, guile, tenacity and brutal force, he was the one who brought all the warring islands of that archipelago under one kingdom."

"I know almost nothing about him. Not in our history lessons, was it?" said Schrock.

"If you come to Honolulu, you are always welcome at my home. You'd be able to learn as much as you'd want."

"Thank you for your offer. I'm not sure what the outcome of the enquiry will be. If for any reason the court determines I've been at fault in this disaster, I could lose my license to sail."

"Is there any chance that could happen?" asked Johann.

"It's hard to say. There are a lot of unknowns here in this strange outpost. It worries me."

"Whatever happens, if you should ever consider doing anything besides being a shipmaster, perhaps there's other employ that I could help you find in Hawaii. I'm fortunate to be well-established in commerce."

"Thank you, Johann. I may have to come begging."

"This must be hard for you. I hope the court gets this right."

Schrock held his hands together in mock prayer and blew on them. "The thought of not having the choice to sail makes me feel bitter. I think I'd probably be lost."

CHAPTER 11

Schrock walked in the direction of the Ross Tavern, one of the few in Port Stanley. He disliked the confinement of his room but being outside held little promise. Nearly two weeks had gone by since the fire and sinking of the ship and he felt like there was no end to his involuntary internment in the Falklands—these land fragments that maps, upon close examination, confirmed were no more than leftover pieces of South America's incomplete assembly. What's more, with Johann Kessler already on a ship to Honolulu, he no longer had a companion to spend time with. It came as a gradual revelation. He'd rarely had close friends since childhood. It was part of the formula for the loneliness that in some ways he'd deliberately cultivated in the last two decades. Closeness equaled complication. It was easier to stay unattached, where social expectations were few and life's simple pleasures were more accessible. He'd almost forgotten what close friendship was until Susan McGinnis, and more recently Johann. And Susan was no longer alive. It was times like this he continued to resurrect her.

Schrock had not yet been to the Ross. Some of his crew told him the English-style food was barely tolerable but that at least they stocked Bavarian ale. His men would know. Maus said he'd already logged generous time there, using their ale to wash down kidney pies and mackerel. Like Schrock, all the crew would be obliged to appear at the Court of Enquiry and then they'd need to wait until it was over to get a berth on a ship out of Stanley.

Schrock squinted through the mist, almost missing the tavern's sign. He stepped through the doorway across a worn wood threshold and into the dimly lit space. Through the smoky haze he surveyed the short bar and a dozen wood tables filled with men. Even though he could hear traces of other speech, he heard mostly English. He saw Maus, Brandt and Kullrich and picked his way over to sit at one of the few empty chairs at their table. Each of his three crew members spoke passable English and seemed comfortable in their new environs. Glad to see him, they offered to buy him beer. "I'm buying," he insisted. He caught the eye of the bartender and motioned in a circle around the table with his index finger. He didn't recognize some of the faces, but the usually rough-edged Maus was polite enough to introduce him around. When the last man at the table was introduced, Schrock thought he'd seen this sharp-featured man before.

"You remember me, right?" the man said. "I'm Captain Radcliffe, the pilot who ferried your passengers ashore—just as soon as your burnin' ship made it into the bay."

His memory revived, Schrock nodded. Besides the odd face and slicked-back hair, something about Radcliffe's nature made Schrock want to distance himself. But he could tell by Radcliffe's alcohol-fortified stare that the pilot was going to continue the conversation whether he was ignored or not.

"Yes, Captain, it's me that got your passengers ashore," Radcliffe repeated with a tone of self-importance.

"Thank you for the help," said Schrock. "I don't remember all the details of the day, what with all the smoke and commotion."

"It's bad luck about your ship, but I imagine she was insured."

"As for the loss, the cargo was insured." Having said more than he intended, Schrock turned his attention toward the other end of the table, hoping to end the conversation.

But Radcliffe went on, his voice a little louder. "Now and then, I myself does some salvage work."

"Do you now?" said Schrock, looking back at Radcliffe. He could tell the pilot wasn't the least sympathetic about the loss of the ship, and it dawned on him that Radcliffe counted on ship calamities to make what was probably most of his income. In a few days of salvage work, the man would make more money than in three months of piloting, particularly if the cargo happened to have items of high value he could sell off.

"Yes, I've got more'n ten years of salvagin'—." Schrock stopped listening to him. He knew salvagers served a useful function, all allowed under international law, but he couldn't shake the impression that he was being clutched at by more of a parasite than a salvager.

Carpenter Brandt sat next to Schrock. Over his shoulder, he tried to catch Brandt's eye in the chance of being freed from Radcliffe's attention. Brandt caught his look.

"Captain," Brandt said. "I've been meaning to talk to you."

"Mister Brandt. How are you doing?"

"Suitable, Captain, considering everything. I'm content not to be burnt or drowned," he answered with a smile. "So, what do you think we should do about getting work again after this is all over?"

The two men conversed for a while about what the future might hold for them. As they paused to drink their ale, Schrock overheard Seaman Kullrich excitedly talking to Radcliffe, hearing the word 'cargo'. He glanced across the table and saw Radcliffe listening intently. He jostled Brandt with his elbow and motioned with his head for Brandt to listen, for it was Brandt who had told him that Kullrich was one of the crew who'd helped Deetjen push the statue overboard. And it had been Brandt who'd queried Kullrich for the details.

It didn't take Kullrich long to mention the statue.

"All that cargo we didn't throw overboard or that got burned was mostly coal. Besides them steel beams, the bronze in that statue is the only other thing worth your trouble—and maybe some of the gin or wine if it survived." Schrock and Brandt watched the two men. Radcliffe's face lit up, just as Kullrich's rum-hazed eyes showed a conspiratorial squint, giving away his eagerness to share what he knew, especially about the fascinating statue of a savage king, cast in valued bronze.

"That statue is not where the ship was burned and sunk near shore," stated Kullrich. "No. It would be laying a good two hundred meters out—in about six fathoms of water. I know, because that is where we shoved it overboard before we slipped the anchor and grounded the ship."

Schrock assessed Radcliffe as the man took in the information with rapt attention, tucking it away in his crow-faced head, hoarding it, he supposed, until the parasitic salvager could find out what was out there in the cold waters of the bay. Why was it he disliked the notion of this salvager going after the statue? He shouldn't really care.

———————————

In the morning, Schrock left his small hotel room for the dining room, walking down the dark hallway lit by a single gas light. It was best to be at breakfast on time. Later arrivals at the six-person dining room always seemed to get smaller portions. Maus was sitting at-the-ready at a two-person table; fork in hand, his mouth and eyes fixed with a pained expression.

"Good times, eh, Maus?" Schrock said sarcastically, settling into the hard chair across from him.

Maus returned a wry smile to his captain. "We're marooned while they dally, Captain. Tell me what this quorum thing is all about, anyways."

Schrock looked toward the kitchen to see if someone was coming with food. Quietly he responded to Maus. "Remember, these Enquiries are conducted to see if the captain or crew were slack in their duty, maybe caused the ship's destruction."

"Ah course not!" Maus fumed.

"And I was told," Schrock responded, doling out his words, "by the clerk of the court—that they need a certain number of assessors who have master mariner standing to convene a legal enquiry. But one of the shipmasters called to serve supposedly had other commitments, keeping him from being available for another two days."

Maus looked mockingly at his fork as he held it in front of his face. "Couldn't 'His Honor' make an exception to how it's done here on this rock?"

"The man's flexing his tiny muscles," answered Schrock. "He's not going to make exceptions."

The cook, who was also the server, quickly laid two plates in front of the men. Maus dug into his sausage and potatoes, shaking his head. Schrock stared at his plate.

"Aren't you gonna eat nothing, Captain?" Maus asked while he chewed.

Schrock wanted to be anywhere but here today, eating this food, facing this enquiry. As he left the table and made his way back to his room, a thought held its grip on him: if not for the coal fire, he would never have chosen to come near this place, this place where ships come to die. And now some part of him was feeling like he could burn and sink here.

He lay back on the bed and wondered what he should do to pass the time. After a while, he picked up the book on Falklands Islands history he'd found in the anteroom of the hotel. He'd come to a chapter written by an officer whose ship was held in the Falklands for repairs a century earlier. As he read, it was evident Schrock wasn't the only one who'd labeled the Falklands a disagreeable place.

The officer had penned a description of stinking smoke he'd gone outside to investigate. He'd discovered it came from beneath one of the island's sea cliffs, where men from a schooner anchored nearby boiled down seal fat to use for lamp and cooking oil. He saw that feeding their fire with seal parts and peat moss created the noxious smoke and fumes that had reached the inn where he stayed.

The desolateness of the place, the subterranean cave, the whirling gusts of smoke and flame gushing from under the rocky canopy—all contributed to give the setting an extremely depressing look. The men, while writhing about with their grim faces and ash-powdered hair, stirred their cauldron amid curling smoke, like the scullions of Pluto stewing down a dish of the damned for the supper of their infernal master.

He'd gotten that just right. This place had the air of a barren hell. He tossed the book back onto the bedside table and leaned his head back. Staring at the ceiling darkened by more than a half century of lamp, pipe and cigar smoke, it occurred to him that during the days the *Haendel* was on fire, he and his crew had been pressed into stewing down a similar dish for the devil. Then they'd been forced to come here along with that fiend to share in the eating of it.

The next afternoon, out of boredom, Schrock returned to the Ross, looking forward to another one of their ales, hoping Radcliffe wouldn't be there. As expected, Maus and Kullrich were sidled up at a table along with several others of his crew. He didn't see Radcliffe in the room. He took the vacant seat next to Kullrich and ordered a round for the table. "Kullrich," he said, taking a long swig of ale, "have you seen Mister Deetjen here at all? I haven't seen the man but once since we arrived."

"No sir, Captain, I ain't seen him, and he sure never comes in here."

"Do you think he's okay, I mean—."

"Well, it's hard to say, sir. I guess he is. I'm not always sure." Kullrich put his head down, looking embarrassed.

"Is there something you want to tell me about him? You don't have to. But if you want to."

Kullrich took a drink and wiped his mouth, buying time. "Well sir, it's like this. I woulda thought you knew about this more than me. Maybe you do. But anyways, it happened like this, see. He and I served on the same freighter for a couple years. Then I got a berth on another ship, but him, he stayed with that one. Well, later that year, he was on that ship when it struck rocks off San Francisco Bay—at night. It foundered, broke up and sunk... real quick. Everybody died but three. And, well, he was one of them that made it."

"No, no. I—he never told me about that."

"Yessir, I think it messed him up some. You see, he told me about it when later I ran into him in Bremen. I'm surprised he told me, him being an officer and all. But he knew I'd been on that ship and was lettin' me know I was lucky to be alive."

"I would guess you are," said Schrock.

"What else he told me is that the ship had a port of call in Valparaiso, Chile to take on water and fruit that would make it to California. But then they set sail on a Friday. You know as well as I do, Captain," he stared at Schrock, his eyes wide open, "it's the day Christ was crucified, and cross myself, the day witches gather. That's exactly what he told his captain, and they shouldn't leave 'til the next day. But the captain didn't seem to pay no heed to Mister Deetjen or to any of the gospel truth of the sea. You've never set sail on a Friday, have you, Captain? I ain't ever known you to do so."

"No, Mister Kullrich, I don't believe I ever have."

"You see, Mister Deetjen believed... yes, he knew that ship went down because of what that captain did—setting sail on a Friday. It and that reckless captain killed all those men. And he wasn't able to talk the captain outta makin' that horrible mistake. Because of that I do believe Mister Deetjen's head ain't been quite right ever since, after seeing all that death and him havin' to live through it. I've always felt sorry for him, sir. He's a damn fine sailor and a good man."

CHAPTER 12

It had been two weeks to the day after the fire and sinking, and to Schrock another day of gray skies in Stanley. But this date was singular. The Court of Enquiry was convened, as the posted notice declared in front of the small courthouse: *Assess the Circumstances Attending the Loss of the Bark G.F. Haendel of Bremen.*

Stanley's Chief Magistrate rapped his gavel and announced he had impaneled the required number of maritime assessors. Schrock sat uncomfortably in a straight-backed chair facing the front of the small courtroom. He surveyed the five men who would decide his future. Thin, bespectacled and wigged in the British court fashion, the formal-looking magistrate introduced the case.

"This Enquiry is now called to order. On November Fifteenth of this same year of our Lord, the *G.F. Haendel*, a German bark under the command of Captain Gerhard Schrock, put into Port William on fire and later burnt out."

Schrock was jolted. That was it—that was all that happened? This officious bastard had reduced their terrible experience to these few words. It seemed like an immense disservice to everything that had taken place. There had been such uncertainty, such chaos and anguish, smoke and bitter cold suffered over so many days by every one of them on board that ship. Was this judge at all aware of the hardship they had endured? But he knew the hard truth. Those were not things on which the case would be decided.

While the magistrate continued to speak, Schrock made up his mind he wouldn't be able to trust in 'His Honor's' impartiality. The judge sat ceremonially behind his raised oaken desk, looking and sounding self-important as he conducted the deliberations in English. Schrock did allow that this man knew how to look the part of a potent jurist, even if he was consigned to carry out his judicial intrigue in a small courtroom, far away from England on this godforsaken island.

"The court will enquire into the circumstances attending the loss of the ship and its cargo. I will now swear in all of the assessors chosen by this court," he said.

Each of the assessors put on a face of seriousness as, one-by-one, they placed a hand on a Bible and took an oath. Schrock thought the magistrate's demeanor probably didn't help to put any of them at ease. The four included Port Stanley's Police Magistrate and Receiver of Wrecks, a British Master Mariner, a German Master Mariner, and the Consul of the Imperial German Empire. Having the two countrymen would hopefully provide some safeguard against any unreasonable attack on his actions during the disaster.

Schrock was the first one called to the witness box. After he took the oath, the magistrate looked at him over the top of his eyeglasses.

"Captain Schrock. I'd like you to provide us with a detailed account of the events that led up to the loss of the ship."

Referring to the ship's log he'd stuffed into his shirt when he had abandoned ship, he began reciting his account of what happened. The court interpreter for the German speakers sat at his left, translating his testimony to English. Schrock couldn't remember ever being so anxious. He tried his best to provide a composed recounting. He couldn't show his nervousness.

"I have been Master of the *G.F. Haendel* since July 1878. I have held a certificate as a Shipmaster since that time. My certificate was burnt with the ship. I sailed on my last voyage from Bremerhaven with destination Honolulu direct on this last Twenty First of August. The ship was laden with seven hundred tons of coal and a general cargo that included four tons of steel beams, twenty-seven kegs of gunpowder, forty barrels of tar, one hundred cases of spirits, about one hundred miscellaneous cargo crates, and a large bronze statue, cased and stored on deck."

He proceeded to describe the loading of the cargo on the docks, the fact that it had rained—getting it wet as it was loaded by the dockmen—and that his concerns had been ignored for some time by the cargo supervisor. He paused after each sentence so it could be translated. The interludes allowed him a brief moment to consider what came out of his mouth, before he'd say something he might regret. He began to explain how the weather had deteriorated as they were well into their voyage. That was all it took to trigger a flood of unpleasant memories of everything that went wrong, encroaching on his hoped-for dispassionate delivery. Though the courtroom was cold, sweat trickled down his forehead. He struggled through his account for at least an hour.

"I could see that the ship would burn out completely, and that is when I walked from the beach to Port Stanley. That is the sum of what happened, Your Honor," Schrock concluded, his voice trailing off with fatigue.

"Thank you for your testimony, Captain Schrock," the magistrate said. "Now, do any of you on the panel have questions for the captain?"

The British shipmaster, John Scott, leaning to the side of his chair with his elbow on one of the chair's arms, casually raised his bent index finger from the same arm while keeping his eyes focused on Schrock like a cat eyeing his prey. The magistrate didn't appear pleased at Scott's demeanor, but nonetheless acknowledged his informal gesture. "You may proceed, Captain Scott."

"Captain Schrock, I've heard some reports that you and your crew failed to render assistance to the fire engine from the shore. Had your men been drinking? Is this why no help was given—because you allowed your men to get drunk?"

Schrock stared back at Scott, anger coursing through his body. His words came out fast and in English, lest Scott or any of the other British there think him just another dumb German—as, in his experience, some were inclined to do.

"My officers and crew had not been drinking, Captain Scott, and I don't like that you imply that. They had no time to drink in three sleepless days on our approach to Port Stanley. They worked tirelessly to keep the fire at bay. And there was no drink to be had when they reached land. Had you been there, you would have seen exhausted men—men wet, cold, and nearly suffocated from ten full days of breathing smoke. They weren't able to do more than they had already done, and, I would say, done with courage given what they faced." Schrock continued to glare at Scott.

After a short silence, Scott spoke, keeping his focus on Schrock. "No more questions, Your Honor."

There were several questions from other assessors, but none as provocative as Scott's. Schrock was able to answer each of them without difficulty. After being on the stand for nearly two hours, he was finally dismissed. He returned to a seat in the front row, not sure if he'd said anything the assessors could interpret as negligence on his part. Relieved to be finished testifying, he felt weariness deep inside. His shoulders scrunched involuntarily, his body's attempt at easing the tension. Then he heard the court clerk's call for 'First Mate Ludwig Deetjen' to the witness box. Oh Jesus, he'd forgotten about Deetjen. He'd hardly seen him in the last two weeks—the mate had been reclusive. What state of mind was he in?

Deetjen looked nervous as he settled into the witness box, took the oath, and was asked to give his story of what happened. Schrock gripped the oak arms of his chair until his knuckles showed white. Deetjen struggled through a similar, although much shorter account of Schrock's testimony, but said nothing bizarre, nothing about the statue. Enormously grateful, Schrock's fingers loosed their grip. Then his eyes quickly shifted to Captain Scott as he heard the arrogant shipmaster clear his voice, preparing to say something.

"Mister Deetjen," Scott asked, "in your report I didn't hear you speak to the actions of your captain. Tell me, throughout the voyage, did Captain Schrock conduct himself properly in all aspects of his duty?"

Sweat started to form on Schrock's forehead. In querying Deetjen, of all his crew, Scott didn't have any idea the depth of the container he was attempting to pry open.

Deetjen paused as if something clearly troubled him. Schrock looked questioningly at his first mate. Deetjen met his eyes for an instant. Then the mate turned his head in the direction of the magistrate.

"Yes, the captain took every possible step to save the ship, the crew and all the passengers. His conduct was excellent in all ways."

Schrock quietly exhaled. Captain Scott wiped his hand across his nose, his face squinted in irritation.

"Seeing no other questions, you are dismissed, Officer Deetjen," said the magistrate. Schrock did his best not to show his relief. He wanted to kiss Deetjen for suppressing his religious ravings, superstitions, hallucinations or whatever it was that colored his version of what was behind the ship's disaster.

The first mate's testimony was followed by statements of several other members of the crew, the harbor pilot, the marine surveyor and then locals who had come out to the ship to give assistance. Scott continued his adversarial examination of witnesses. After nearly a full day of Enquiry, the hearing was adjourned for the assessors to begin their deliberation.

Schrock felt uncertain of the outcome and slept little during the night. Over and over in his mind he replayed the day's events: the testimony, the tangle of people. He grieved the loss of his ship and most of all, wondered why a statue should perplex him, the imagined picture of it lying out deep in the water sifting his thoughts.

He was at the court early next day, along with the rest of his crew, for the reading of the verdict. He sat down again in the cold courtroom, a place, after today, he never again wanted to come near. Still unable to trust the magistrate, and now Captain Scott, Schrock felt like the room grew chillier when the magistrate walked in and took his bench. The justice straightened his wig, then his papers, and finally began to read.

"The Assessors of this Court of Enquiry have provided the following opinion:"

Schrock's breathing became shallow, his vision narrowing to the man speaking.

"The *G.F. Haendel* was destroyed by fire which originated through the spontaneous ignition of the coals laden on board. There was a great body of fire in the ship before she was brought into port, so great in fact that saving her was an impossibility. From the time the fire was discovered until the ship arrived in the Bay of Port William, every reasonable precaution was taken to keep the flames under control. On turning the ship back to the Falklands promptly upon discovery of the fire, Captain Schrock took the only course that was open to him under the circumstances, having in view the lives of the crew and passengers. Taking the above into consideration, the court has unanimously decided that no blame can be attached to Captain Schrock and his officers as regards the loss of the vessel, and he and they are acquitted of all blame accordingly." The magistrate closed his file. "The court wishes to express thanks to the assessors for their time in this matter. "This court is dismissed," he declared. The gavel bang made Schrock's mouth open involuntarily. "Mother of God" he mumbled. He slowly rose and went out front to the porch of the building. He looked up at the sky. He could remain a shipmaster.

His senses were numb as he talked briefly with both Maus and Brandt and several of his crew. Then Deetjen approached him.

"Sir, I know I was out of line when I had the statue pushed off the ship without your order. That was wrong. And… and I'm grateful you didn't set out to suspend my papers. Thank you, sir."

"I—you're welcome, Mister Deetjen." He wanted to ask Deetjen what had been going on with him all that time, but knew it would need to be in private, some other time. After brief farewells he left the courthouse alone, heading out along the waterfront road, his eyes on the ruts below him.

He wasn't sure why, but he didn't feel as comforted by his exoneration as he should have. Focused on not being found negligent, he hadn't allowed himself to consider more why it had all happened. Was there any way to account for 'bad luck'?

He continued at a stroll down the gravel road. There was part of him that wanted to connect the statue to the disaster. Not like Deetjen, because it was cursed, but something larger and more complex that he could never expect to unravel. However, there was his talk with Johann about superstition. He had tried explaining to his friend that centuries of mariner superstitions had come about in order to assign cause or blame to the randomness of sea disasters—or to give some protection from disasters ever happening. Maybe what happened with the *Haendel* and the statue of Kamehameha the Great would be the start of a mariner superstition that begins here: *A ship with coal cargo will be sure to burn and sink if it carries a bronze statue on board.* Old sailors would repeat the credo on docks and in brew houses of ports around the world. Johann Kessler would surely find some humor in that.

Schrock stopped to gaze out at two ships anchored close ashore, his thoughts tumbling. If Deetjen had brought up his version of the disaster's cause during the enquiry, the statue business would likely have been disregarded. In such enquiries, topics like superstition aren't taken into serious consideration. They can't be—the legal process won't tolerate it. But some of the mariner assessors who'd participated in these enquiries were often the same men who at sea acknowledged, practiced and even swore by superstitions. And given the Falklands are British, the irony was that British mariners are the ones who'd been the biggest source of sailing superstitions. Apparently when they stepped into assessor shoes, they put on blinders so as not to look foolish.

Distancing himself from the town, Schrock dismissed the deteriorating weather, his mind moving at the pace of his feet. He'd ignored persistent thoughts about some livelihood other than sailing. Now here it was. It all stemmed from Johann Kessler's invitation to come to Honolulu—that he could help find work for him. When Johann got passage on the ship to Honolulu, Schrock hadn't really acknowledged the disconcerting idea that his own future could be something other than that of a mariner. If he had been convicted of negligence and lost his shipmaster's license, his choices would be limited. What could he do, really? Sell books, play rugby again? The difficulty was that being a sailor and then a shipmaster left a person fit for little else. It was an acquired life mold. How could the herder's sheep dog be suddenly expected to perform as the master's bird dog? Johann had planted the seed. He could voluntarily change direction. The idea was unnerving... or was that excitement he was sensing? Change was tricky, if not dangerous. But there was luster to the idea of becoming a man whose life and profession would plant both feet on the ground—even if it was on an island situated in the very middle of the Pacific Ocean. Then again, if he didn't like it, he could return to sea.

The wind pressed a cold rain into Schrock's face. He turned and headed back toward the Globe Tavern. He needed a drink, and likely two or more. Out of the mist, the man on the road walking toward him appeared upright and purposeful. As the space between them narrowed, the familiar face of Deetjen under his cap came into focus.

It was puzzling to find his first mate a good half mile from the town center. Twice in one day after two weeks of no sightings. "What brings you out here, Mister Deetjen?"

"I was actually hoping to find you, sir. Mister Ronitz said he saw you head out in this direction. I thought I should talk with you a bit more."

"I need a drink, Mister Deetjen, so I was just heading back to the tavern. Join me out of this weather. I'll treat you—we can talk on the way."

"I'll join you, sir, but you know I don't imbibe of spirits."

They walked in silence for a while. They were used to standing next to each other for hours at sea without exchanging a word. It wasn't something that made either of them uncomfortable. "It's like this, sir. I'll just say it—my faith has been shaken. I don't know why it is the ship burned and sank. I prayed hard that it wouldn't, and it still did. It made me wonder how God lets these things happen to faithful servants, and I include you as one, even if maybe you don't see yourself that way."

"You're right, Mister Deetjen, I don't. I'm surely a sinner through and through."

"But, sir, this is the second time for me—being on a ship that goes down." His voice was choked, sounding as if he was on the verge of tears.

"Kullrich told me about the vessel you both served on and something about what happened. Why hadn't you ever told me about it?"

"Because I didn't want you to ever think I couldn't perform my duties—that I might buckle in the worst storm or emergency."

"Why don't you tell me more about what happened with that other ship? I'd like to hear about it."

"I do my best not to think about it—it was so bad, so many lives." He paused, shaking his head. "That captain wouldn't hear me. He was a callous man, concerned most with bonus money. It was my first voyage with Captain Rechter, and we didn't get along that well. And then he told me I was foolish for saying we shouldn't leave Valparaiso on a Friday, Crucifixion Day. So we put out and it was night on the day we reached the coast near San Francisco Bay. We had ten foot swells and high fog so thick that we only caught glimpses of the lighthouse that sat up high in the fog. I told him we should hold off trying to get through the bay gate until morning—head out to open water for some sea room and put our anchor in drag. He was having none of it, still talking about the bonus money if we lost a day. 'Follow the fog horn until we see the lights of the city,' he said. It was when the fog cleared a bit I could see the rocks in the bay channel, so close we could have thrown a rope out to them. Captain Rechter, well, he froze. I screamed at him to give the order but he did nothing but stare. I shouted to the helmsman to come about to port, but in the next minute the hull hit the first rock underwater. It threw us all onto the deck. The rock grabbed the bow and pulled the ship to starboard and further to shore and the rocks. After that there was no hope of freeing the ship. The swells rolled the ship over and over against the submerged rocks. It only took minutes for the hull to open up and take on water so fast there wasn't time to get but one deck-boat freed up. Men were yelling, falling into the water as she foundered. I was spilled into the water and was able to grab onto a hatch cover. Then I saw the lone boat, with one man in it. I shouted and he was able to get over to me—pull me in. The ship was on its side and we had to stay back from being tangled in the rigging from the masts and yardarms sticking out of the water, or being pushed into the rocks while we rowed around and looked for others. We found one man and pulled him in. There was no one else. Captain Rechter and fourteen good men drowned that night. It was horrible, sir."

"I believe you, Mister Deetjen."

"Ever since then, I don't have to tell you—I haven't been all that steady. I'm sorry, sir. I sleep badly, have dreams about drowning. And I've had a hard time talking with people—you know, ordinary talk."

"What happened to you has put you in an extended purgatory, hasn't it?"

"We Lutherans don't believe in that. But that's about what it's been, except it was you who took me on again as your mate. Without this berth, working with you, I would have drowned in despair. I'm not sure why you did. Most captains are wary of disaster survivors."

Because I didn't know, thought Schrock. Would I have taken you on had I known? I can't tell you that this voyage has been the best case for letting you on any ship of mine.

The mist turned into a slight rain that swept across the low, scrub-covered hills, making the two men involuntarily pick up their pace in the direction of the tavern. "Even if I'd known all this before, I'm sure I wouldn't have changed my view of you," said Schrock, "as a capable sailor and officer. But you must know, Mister Deetjen, your insistent Christian beliefs, especially about that statue, did become a problem on this voyage."

"I know sir. I can't... my Christian belief is part of who I am. Besides being an officer, it's what holds me together."

"I see." The buildings of Stanley were coming in and out of view now, the mist behaving like gauzy clouds with occasional valleys, ridges and gaps that revealed a surprising ship's mast or a white-painted house that appeared and then would disappear. As they strode along in the direction of the tavern, Schrock blurted, "Mister Deetjen, if I might ask, just what were you thinking when you pushed that statue overboard out there in the bay? It should not be bothering me now but it does."

"I'm not really sure. It was something like a force compelling me to do it."

"You told me it was to save it for salvage purposes later, to prevent it from being burnt."

"I had to tell you something. I knew you would be displeased, sir. But in truth, it wasn't God telling me to do it. It was something else rather leading me to do it... I'm still not sure what. I can't explain it."

"Can you try?" Schrock tried not to show he was overly curious. "It, uh, interests me."

"Well, sir, I believe I was more like possessed. My motions, I mean—not demonic or anything like that—just a feeling like I was out on the water being thrust about on the top of the waves." He scrunched up his face. "I know that sounds strange."

"Yes, it does." He realized what Deetjen was describing was not unlike the sensations he had felt when the statue was being loaded on board and then when it went overboard. It had been like a force coursing through his body.

"I apologize, sir."

"Don't, Mister Deetjen. Whatever occurred, it was probably for the best."

As they stepped inside the tavern, Schrock watched Deetjen scan the room, searching for the devil's harbingers or whatever it was troubled him about places like this.

They sat at a table for two on the side. "I'm ordering us some fine red wine, Mister Deetjen."

"Like I said, I—."

"Didn't Jesus drink wine? It's in the Gospels—he served it at the last supper. We'll have our own little communion, and I don't want you to tell me it's blasphemous. You, my friend, are in need of a drink as badly as I am."

When they had been served, Deetjen grinned slightly after he'd taken the first few drinks of wine. "It's been quite a while."

Schrock held up his glass for examination in the light. "America's Franklin was supposed to have said something like, "Wine is sure proof that God loves us and wants us to be happy. What do you think about that, Ludwig?"

Ludwig Deetjen was flustered at hearing his given name rather than a title. "I... well I admit, I haven't spent much time thinking about God's wish for my happiness. Mostly redemption of my soul. Maybe I should reconsider that some."

"Yes! I said you needed a drink. *Prost!"*

Schrock put down his glass. "There's something I need to let you know, Ludwig. I'm not returning to Bremerhaven. I've decided to give up sailing, give it a go for work on land, in Honolulu." He anticipated this would be jarring for his first mate, but not that the man would look like he'd been hit in the head with a belaying pin. Schrock couldn't remember ever seeing Deetjen's squinty eyes so wide open with so much white revealed.

"Why... but why there, sir?" asked Deetjen, glancing around the inside of the tavern, looking disoriented. "That's a far run from the homeland."

"I need a change, and an opportunity has presented itself," said Schrock. "Besides, I'm ready to be warm for a while." He hoped he could soften what he was telling him. "Johann Kessler—from the ship—you remember him of course, told me he'd assist me in finding work there. He's apparently been successful in business in Honolulu for a number of years. I'm not sure what it is I would do. Compared to what we've been through in the last month it should look like a holiday."

"I can't imagine you not at sea, sir."

"Mister Deetjen, drink up. This might come as a surprise to you, but I can imagine you employed on land. What do you think about that? With your head for calculations, you would prosper at whatever trade you were involved with. I'm sure Mister Kessler would help you to find employment as well. You should come."

"No sir, I'd be clumsy at anything other than sailing. Two left shoes and all that."

"Well, whatever it is you do, I shall miss being able to depend on you as my mate. We've certainly turned over a lot of water together."

"Yes sir, and almost got ourselves turned under," he said, not smiling, although he'd allowed his wit to emerge. Instead, he appeared momentarily miserable. "I will miss you, sir. You have been there for me all along."

"You know what this means, don't you?" asked Schrock, trying to lighten the mood. "From now on you won't be required to call me captain or sir anymore. Mister Schrock or even Gerhard will do just fine." He was second guessing if he should go this far, since the man was habituated to formality. Just the same, it was unlikely he would ever see Deetjen again. If he left him without the burden of their official relationship, it might lessen whatever guilt his first mate would clutch on to about their ordeal on the *Haendel* or his role with the statue.

It was early the next afternoon when Schrock peered around inside the Ross and saw only a few patrons at the tables. He'd languished in bed, missing breakfast at the Globe, and went looking to eat where he remembered the kidney pie and boiled eggs as edible. A well-dressed man he recognized waved him over to sit down. It was Captain Berglof, the German shipmaster appointed as one of the inquiry assessors. Berglof insisted he sit with him and ordered ale with his food for Schrock. Berglof, trim-bearded and portly, seemed eager to give Schrock more information about the enquiry.

"You know, that stuffy magistrate was a better sort than I thought. He was clear-headed about the facts when we met to review the testimony. He set Captain Scott straight. That conniving Brit wanted to find some way to make you at fault for the loss."

"That was obvious," said Schrock, shaking his head.

"I'm not sure what got under his skin, but our shipmaster brotherhood seemed to have turned into a wrestlers club for him. I think he must have been done in by a German at one time, and he just wanted to pay it back. Hell, it could have been any German. But he just chanced to look out over the waves, and lo and behold, it was your face that appeared in front of his spyglass."

Schrock had been unsure about talking too much with Berglof, but after an hour of drinking and conversation, he felt comfortable enough, and just inebriated enough, to tell him about his consideration of giving up sailing. After he'd ordered his food from a portly South American waiter, he gave Berglof a serious look. "I can't quit the sea, can I? It doesn't make any sense. Why would I give up my years of training and experience? You know how difficult it was for us to get our certificate."

Berglof looked concerned and equally tipsy. "I do, and altogether it was a rat's nest of years to sort through, wasn't it."

"I've been comfortable with the sea until now," Schrock went on. "I've had my face to the wind since I was a young man." He took a drink of his ale and looked out toward the ships at anchor in the bay. "And I've mostly inhabited tall ships, not houses. I've more time in boats than on land—a good life, careening over the oceans all these years."

"That–is–it–exactly!" growled Berglof, ale foam shaking from his beard. "And what's a usual day for us is strange and fearful for the dirt-kickers. They'd shit their britches were they to do the kinds of things we do. It's true—we mariners are God's real men. Why, the both of us have surely been born to be at sea." Berglof held up his mug to Schrock in a toast.

Schrock could tell Captain Berglof was more than pleased to be able to brag with someone of his own kind. But this wasn't helping him decide what he should do next. This kind of talking was only helping him to grasp the ropes that kept him tethered to the mariner's life. And in the tangle of all those ropes was the one rope that was his reputation, frayed as it now was. If he did leave the sea, what would relations or old acquaintances back in Germany say? They would think he had succumbed to a storied truth—that men on sinking ships suddenly decide they'd like to spend more time on land.

Schrock took another long drink from his mug as he felt resentment poke at the back of his brain. *To hell with them all and to hell with Pfleuger and his shipping company.*

He looked up at Captain Berglof. Berglof could help. His ship was leaving for Honolulu in two days. He was beginning to like this man. He would request passage on his ship and go to Honolulu. Maybe he could become someone new. Being a landsman might be more satisfying. Maybe this would be a way to get over Susan McGinnis and find someone to be with him. It had been a long time since he'd had the singular feeling of having a woman put her arms around him when it meant something. With all the idle time in wait here, he stewed way too much about what it would be like to be loved again.

CHAPTER 13

Schrock sat in the bow of the small ketch that ferried him out to the *K.B. Wolff,* at rest in the bay. He surveyed the large, three-mast schooner, pleased that he would be sailing on such a new ship. As his boat came alongside the vessel, he quickly pulled himself up the side ladder, impatient to be on board and away from the island he'd come to despise. When his feet touched down on the deck, his body sensed the familiar sway of a ship at anchor. But the experience felt muted or maybe just different, like climbing into a strange bed. It wasn't his ship.

Captain Berglof came down from the quarterdeck to greet Schrock. "Captain Schrock. Welcome aboard the *Wolff.*"

"Glad to be anywhere but in Stanley, Captain."

Berglof offered a slight smile. "I couldn't agree more. Seaman Kleinholdt will show you to your cabin. I've set you up in quarters close to mine, and you're welcome to take your meals with me if you'd like. We'll weigh anchor and part within an hour. Make yourself comfortable."

The day after they'd met in the tavern, making sure he'd heard Schrock correctly, Captain Berglof had questioned why Schrock wasn't planning on seeking another command of a ship. Schrock had tried again to explain to Berglof, but in truth wasn't himself sure. He just knew he felt compelled to make stark changes in his life. He was grateful Berglof didn't belabor the issue. The captain had even sounded sympathetic, telling Schrock that other shipmasters compared losing a ship to losing a wife you dearly loved.

"Recovery from such a devastating blow seems to resolve differently with each man, depending on how much they cared about the ship," Berglof had said, "—or the wife, for that matter." It wasn't surprising he'd kept a straight face when he said this having already shared his losses of both a ship and a wife.

Captain Berglof looked genuinely pleased to have Schrock along on this arduous leg of the voyage around the Horn. For his own part, Schrock was glad that he could travel with a captain he wouldn't have to retell the story of his ship to or be bothered by more questions. He thanked Berglof for his hospitality and was shown to his room. He stored his few possessions in a small sea chest on the floor and lay back on his bed, feeling fatigued, as if the successes and failures of his life had reached this very bunk.

His mind floated back to Berglof's comparison of loss of a ship to losing a wife. The irony was that the *Haendel* had been his wife, his mistress and really his whole reason for being. He was thirty-five and had never married. What a misguided fool he'd been. He could have accepted Susan McGinnis' love for him when they were together in Sydney.

He sat up on his cabin bunk, staring at the knots in the oak floor. For more than a year he'd both embraced and been cursed with the memory of her nearly every day until he had heard the news. His insides seared remembering again how he'd told her he would come back. How could he have been so unsure about what he'd wanted or needed? He'd been successful at deluding himself for years—that he was a man wedded to ship and sea. What prosaic drivel that was! Even though he had a hard-won post as a shipmaster, in truth, the lure of the oceans had been diluted by the crush of responsibility, buried fear, and worst, the solitude. But it was the great irony that it had been the sea that he thought he loved that took Susan.

He rolled down on his face in the narrow bunk and pounded his fist into the mattress. He lay there, his face burning with fury at himself. After a while he took in a deep breath and exhaled. He closed his eyes so his mind could escape to the place where his dreams were.

He awoke a half hour later to the sound of the ship's bell and bosun's whistle. He had no interest in seeing Port Stanley as the ship was setting sail out through the bay channel. Nevertheless, as a cordial gesture to Captain Berglof, he left the cabin and made his way back to the quarterdeck. Berglof was occupied at the helm with the port pilot, but acknowledged Schrock with a wide smile. After a quarter hour, the captain walked over to Schrock and gestured to the mizzen mast with his outstretched arm.

"That's it. You can see the bracing and steel bands on the mast we cracked trying to get around the Horn the last time." He turned to his first mate and shouted an order to luff the sails in preparation for the pilot's departure. He looked back at Schrock. "I'm going to do everything I can to make sure we get around the Horn in one piece this time. Like you, I'd hate like hell to have to come back to this dreary asylum." Despite the cold and damp, Schrock stood on the deck for the next several hours, watching with indifference as the Falkland Islands turned into dots on the horizon and then disappeared. Although he was going back to the sea again, he recognized the paradox of this being a voyage to break the sea's hold on him. It was bracing and fear-provoking at the same time—this thought of leaving the sea life behind, learning to walk all over again. He wondered if living in a new place could fill the void of the life he would be leaving behind.

That evening, Schrock had dinner with Captain Berglof in his quarters, larger than his had been on the *Haendel*. The room had the odor of a man who'd lived in it for years, smoking the same pipe tobacco, and eating the same fish soups. Berglof had made the space comfortable with small paintings, Chinese wall ornaments, and a long, carved pipe holder. Schrock used the opportunity to thank him for his company and for giving him a decent berth on his ship. Berglof acknowledged his gratitude with a nod.

"Schrock, there's something you need to know about the enquiry I didn't tell you before. That English bastard, Scott, was probably raging inside from having his wife *shtuped* by a wily German ship's officer," Berglof said, smiling. "At least that's the rumor I heard. And you must have reminded him of whoever that officer was. Whatever it was he didn't like about you, I had the impression he wanted to get you down to his ship's rope locker and thrash you just for being German. But more to my point, if he could have persuaded the court into revoking your shipmaster papers, then all us scoundrel German mariners would be indebted to you in your sacrifice for each of our sins."

As he laughed with Berglof, Schrock realized he was only able to because he was a survivor of the enquiry ordeal. But he hadn't been left unscathed; the process had been humiliating. He knew it could have been worse. If he'd been convicted of negligence, there would have been nothing to joke about.

"You know, Schrock, I've got twenty-two years of sailing behind me," Berglof declared. "I've met other men like Scott who had a bone to carve on. I suspect your time in the Sandwich Islands will be a lot easier than being at sea. But as sure as I am sitting here, you will run up against other disagreeable peckerheads like Scott. My advice to you is what my father taught me when I was learning Latin at school. 'Son,' he said, '*non carborundum illigitimae.*' Don't let the bastards wear you down. And especially the British ones!" he bellowed.

"I'd have drunk ales with your father," said Schrock with a smile.

After a week's time, sailing without any new weather damage or setbacks, the *Wolff* prepared to round Cape Horn into the Pacific. Despite the massive swells and high winds that perpetually surrounded the Horn, Schrock felt oddly tranquil. He reckoned that for once it wasn't any of his responsibility to get the ship through this perilous stretch of sailing. It would be a new experience seeing this magnificent and deadly piece of ocean only as an observer. Maybe he could enjoy it, particularly if they made it past the Pacific side without being pushed back numerous times by the notorious winds and currents. He was hoping for no delays to keep him from the nameless engagement with his future.

———————————

Two months with nothing but ocean to look at or smell, the scent crept into Schrock's awareness, waking him from a restless sleep. Berglof had told him the previous day they should be getting close to the Sandwich Islands. Rubbing his eyes and taking a drink of water, he left his cabin and felt a warm breeze in his face; they were in tropical waters. In the quiet of the night he acknowledged the solitary helmsman as he made his way to the corner of the aft deck rail and leaned on it with both forearms. He marveled at the glow of phosphorescence trailing the ship's wake in the darkness. He'd watched it for decades at sea and yet he couldn't rinse away the child-like explanation that Heinrich, his first sailmaker had given him, that the sparkling water was nothing less than a mirror of all those stars in the night sky.

Spelled by the glittering shine of the water, his head jerked back as a massive black form broke through the surface just feet from the stern of the ship. Simultaneously there was a loud whoosh as vapor shot high above the deck from the creature's one-foot diameter blowhole. The pungent fish-smell of the spray carried into Schrock's nose. A piercing eye, glistening inside the black skin, looked directly at him, holding its gaze as it slid along the surface. Schrock shivered to his core as he watched it slip under the surface with the same powerful grace as it had risen, while the ship continued to cut through gentle two foot seas. He scanned the water, his heart pounding as if he'd been running, hoping to see it surface again, to lock eyes again. Was it too much to believe the warm-blooded colossus had come to greet him, to welcome him to the Hawaiian Kingdom? He blinked several times, hoping to see clearer but there was nothing but ocean.

It occurred to him that given the recent disaster he'd been through, perhaps this whale could just as well have come to warn him about looming trouble. But as a university professor had liked to say, that sort of thinking was anthropocentric nonsense.

He remembered his conversation with Johann Kessler about his evolving like a dolphin or whale if he stayed at sea. What occurred to him now was that unlike his life, sea creatures always had a clear sense of purpose as they moved about. All the same, he knew he had held onto just enough of an imprecise bearing to have gotten this far.

In early daylight, the ship began its passage through Kaiwi Channel between Molokai and Oahu islands. While the day passed, they traversed the mountainous rollers of the treacherous strait, and then rounded Oahu's southeastern peninsula into gentler seas of Mamala Bay as the ship headed in toward Honolulu's natural harbor.

Gerhard Schrock peered through his telescope, holding it until his arm ached. From the bow of the *K.B. Wolff*, he could just make out what was known as Diamond Head on the southwest coast of Oahu. The soft morning light and warm tradewinds brought the scent of ginger flowers and the sound of waves on the shores. Schrock's nose could sometimes detect land when he had been at sea for long periods, especially when he couldn't depend on his sense of sight. If the wind was right, the terrain of tropical climates sent out a mix of both floral growth and decay. Along with the warmth, it made the air—how could he describe it—soft. Germany, as he remembered it, was rarely like that.

His mind was playing tricks on him. The ship wasn't near enough to land for these sensations to be genuine. He was reaching out over the waves, testing, because he wasn't coming here for commerce. This time he was coming to stay for a while… or perhaps for the rest of his life. An instant of clarity passed like a single gull whisking overhead.

He wasn't used to becoming aware of anything akin to grace. He would be grasping at a second chance for life with intention.

Seaman Percy, a short, dark-complexioned crewman was near his side on deck. "A good sight, wouldn't you say, Captain Schrock?"

"Yes it is," Schrock agreed. "I'm very pleased to see this small piece of earth. Three months, a long wait."

Schrock realized it was odd to speak so fondly about land. During all his years as a sailor, then as a mate and a ship's captain, he'd always assumed that being at sea was the best life there could possibly be. As a boy, he was taken by stories of a friend's father about the great life at sea. On a ship he could break away from the restrictions of mere mortals. He had lived this myth until the years of harsh loneliness had finally bent him to recognize how he'd denied his deepest needs. It would be awkward to admit any of this to Seaman Percy.

Percy's voice broke his reverie. "I hear tell you're quitting the sea, Captain."

"Yes, I'll leave it to you and the hearty ones to carry on." He couldn't say more, and then have to stumble through his litany of reasons for a changed heart: the strange circumstances of losing his ship; coming to Honolulu and testing life on shore; meeting Johann who had encouraged him to come; and, most palpable, needing a woman to share his life with.

Seaman Percy gripped the rail with both hands and looked down at the ship's frothy wake. "Truth be, Captain, I ain't sure how I can go on with this kind of life. Every day I wonder if I can make it through another." He stared down at his feet. "It's just that it's the only thing I know how to do."

Percy's confession surprised Schrock. But he didn't need to hear more about what life on a merchant ship was doing to this man. He himself had covered up the scarcity of that existence, narrowing his choices and challenges year after year, convinced that seafaring was to be the sum of his life. But he couldn't share these thoughts with this sailor if he didn't want to be somehow complicit, should the man decide to jump ship while in port. Schrock thought about what to say and compromised, gesturing toward Oahu. "If you ever consider staying on land again, consider a place like these islands. I expect it's the climate you'll be grateful for." He took another look at Oahu through his telescope. "It's been a pleasure, Percy."

In the next hours as the ship moved into the harbor's placid waters, Schrock was heartened to again see the tall green peaks setting uneven but graceful lines against an azure blue and cloud-mottled sky. As he remembered from before and was able to see, rainbows highlighted some of the valleys of these mountains that ranged the length of the island. He stood at the rail as the ship moved into a harbor full with sailing vessels and steamers at anchor, while local Hawaiians in outrigger canoes plied the waters in all directions. On the shoreline, he could only make out tall trees that towered over where the town was, along with several white church steeples that poked higher than the ragged green belt above the ship-strewn waterfront.

Eventually the *K.B. Wolff* was towed and pushed through the harbor by two of Honolulu Harbor's new steam-powered tenders. After the mooring lines were secured at the dock, the crew maneuvered the ship's gangplank into place. His farewell and thanks given to Captain Berglof, Gerhard Schrock stood first in line at the top of the walkway. Ahead the seven other passengers on the freighter, it wasn't the customary position he found himself in when he was a schoolboy. 'Confidence without apology'—it was Captain Sanders who'd told him that. But it'd taken these hard sea years for it to sink in.

CHAPTER 14

Honolulu, Kingdom Of Hawaii
February 1881

Stepping down the *Wolff's* gangplank, a newly self-exiled Schrock was more awake than he'd been in days. Not being an officer or even a crewmember on the ship, the voyage had seemed interminable at times. Carrying a small tote filled with all his possessions, he headed toward the wharf on the worn, thick-planked docks of the harbor. The warm air sent on tradewinds had been permeating his whole being for the last day. Now on land, it was a sensation unlike any other, a subtle form of being deeply intoxicated, not unlike the time he'd smoked opium in Shanghai, except that now he could still move his body. He took deep inhalations through his nose. Hanging his jacket over his shoulder, he stopped and scanned the buildings in the distance, where he could make out palms and other greenery. He held them in a kind of reverence he'd not done in the past two layovers he had been in this port. During those visits, he'd only conducted business, eaten, drunk excessively, slept it off and left.

"Can you tell me where I can find the office of a Johann Kessler?" he asked the first dockman he encountered.

"I could, and you're in luck, 'cause it won't be far," the dockman replied. "Down at the end of the dock, go right on the wharf to Kilauea Street. His office is in the building on the south corner, facin' the water."

Schrock decided to first walk beyond the buildings fronting the docks toward the center, where he could get up close to the vegetation. He'd discovered that as the years went by, the ocean's absence of woody, sweet-green growth and flowers was something that took a measured levy of his soul. Oaken ships of age were inevitably musty and saturated with the odor of dirty cargos. At sea, he sometimes lived for months in close quarters, usually unbathed, along with the smells the crew and any passengers brought on board. Coupled with periodic bouts of seasickness and other digestive ailments anyone had, the ship sometimes took on an aroma served up like badly spoiled soup. Seeking a cure for the sailing invalid he felt he must have become, Schrock was drawn to touch greenery near many of the buildings. In addition to the hedges and shrubbery that surrounded the wood and iron-fenced houses, he was astounded by trees so tall that their foliage cast deep shadows far across the lawns and streets. Some were peppered with flowers of flame-red that after months of the nearly monochromatic seas all but assailed his vision. Everywhere were flowers in hues of yellow, orange, white, and lavender, with varied and unusual scents assaulting his nose, unlike the singular, familiar smells that had come with his ship and the sea. He had a momentary feeling of having truly arrived. It was odd—not like at a destination, as any port, but a place of consequence. Schrock stopped, not moving, a feeling coursing through him almost like he was supposed to be here at this very moment. It was another one of those unexplainable sensations, like on his ship. It seemed to course through him like moving water. He looked all around him, saw no one, and turned back, following the dockman's directions to Johann Kessler's.

When he entered his office, right away he saw Johann behind a desk in a glassed inner office. Johann looked up and came quickly to his door to greet him. "Well, I'll be damned! Welcome! Let me shake the hand of the relentless survivor. I had a strong feeling I'd see you again, and hoped I would. How are you? What ship did you come with? Tell me about the outcome of the enquiry."

"That's a lot to tell. I am in good health and as to the outcome of the enquiry, I was acquitted of any negligence. I will keep my shipmaster rating and am allowed to go back and captain another ship in Germany—if I want to."

"That is good! But your appearance here is intriguing, especially since I'm positive Germany is in the other direction. But sit down, Gerhard, please," Johann gestured. "Have some water and tell me more. Yes, I am very delighted to see you."

"And I you." Schrock picked up a glass from the side table and took a drink of the sweet-tasting water. Not months old keg water, he thought, and crystal, not crockery. "Well, I'm here because I think something's changed for me… or maybe I've changed. I had a lot of time to find out I want something else for my life—or perhaps better said, *need* something more." Based on their previous conversations, Schrock felt safe talking like this with Johann. "And this place you live in; I must have dreamed about living in a setting like this," Schrock went on. "It's intoxicating, these tropic breezes—just how the air make me feel. You must have it good here, Johann."

"I do, and so does my family. Except for some of the cultural challenges, we've done well."

Schrock didn't falter. "I'm leaving the sea behind—at least for a while, and I want to try something new. I—you know, what you said— I was hopeful your offer still stands to help me find work."

"Of course it does," said Johann with a smile. "I was hoping you'd accept my invitation. This makes me very pleased. Don't worry about anything. You'll get rested at my home, and Stina, my wife, will fill you up with good Hessian cooking. Then we'll get to finding you work and a suitable place to live. I'd like for you to become as contented here as I have."

In the next week, Schrock stayed with Johann and Stina and their two children, while he looked at newspaper work advertisements and had several interviews for positions recommended by Johann. He used his free time to explore Honolulu, occasionally taking horse carriages to the furthest ends of the city.

On one excursion, he passed by a racetrack at a place called Kapiolani Park on his way out to the small beach community of Waikiki, a fishing village that had been turned into a tourist retreat. Although there were few places to stay, there were beach huts for changing into swimming attire. Schrock didn't consider swimming as he saw some people doing, but he felt like pulling up his pant legs and wading in just to cool off. He stood there watching locals riding long wooden boards on the surf, something he'd observed in Samoa as well. He let himself imagine what that would be like. He doubted he needed hazardous thrills at this point in his life.

In downtown Honolulu, he walked for blocks in a city teeming with life, where grog shops, saloons, brothels, and gambling halls flourished. But he also saw the signs of western refinement, including department stores with fine wares, first class hotels, a good-sized opera house, and a building with a marquee that read *Royal Hawaiian*

Theater. He hoped they had a concert hall orchestra somewhere that played European compositions.

As he traveled around, he couldn't help but notice there were cats everywhere, to keep down the rat population, he supposed. He'd seen similar hordes of cats in other seaport cities. It was an unfortunate certainty that rats were a measure of ships and ports of call. The balance to this thought was that wherever he went he was still able to catch the fragrance of tropical flowers and see their colors cascading off building walls and fences of the streets where few businesses were located.

It was a month later Schrock caught himself repeatedly rubbing the back of his neck as he walked down the dock toward a three-masted freighter, ready to review the ship's cargo manifest prior to her being off-loaded. It was his third week on the job, and he felt uneasy, well aware of what was causing his anxiety. After staying a week with Johann and Stina, Johann had returned from work one evening to give him news about a job, telling him, "The cargo supervisor for the Pacific Mail Freight Company was unlucky enough to have his skull collide with a crate swinging from a ship's hoist. He was knocked about badly and will likely be out for quite a while… or he may never work again. It's a sad affair. But listen, I've spoken with Pacific's manager about you. He says the job is yours for now if you want it."

Even though Schrock had taken full advantage of being free to explore the streets and sights of Honolulu, he'd been eager to launch into a new livelihood. After dining alone on Saturday night, he paid a visit to Johann's house. In the library, Johann leaned back in his chair and leafed through a book, glancing at Schrock as he paced.

"I'm not sure I'm cut out for this work," mumbled Schrock. "In the end, what am I supposed to be able to learn here?"

"Well what was it you thought you would?"

"When I was a master mariner, I'd about learned everything one needed to know for that employment. And best of all, at sea I eventually answered to no one. But here, instead of being able to tell people what needs to be carried out, all the captains and pursers I deal with seem to think it's their right—hell—their duty to give me grief or back-talk, tell me the way things should be done. And those are just the people I can understand. There's the native people working the docks who are nearly impossible to understand speaking their Pidgin English. If they at least spoke a little German. I don't know what to say. I'm not sure who I am anymore."

Johann gave Schrock a familiar grin before he spoke. "My friend, this is exactly what you need to be learning. Certain humility, if not guile, is required of the land-bound who wish to get by. Honolulu and the docks can't be another fiefdom of yours. With open arms, Gerhard, I welcome you to *terra firma.*"

Johann's demeanor irritated Schrock. "That's easy for you to say. But what if I'm too set in my ways and don't want to waste my time with this back and forth wordplay business?"

"You're still getting your land legs, Captain Schrock," said Johann. "In time you'll find your way and you'll start to feel more at home here. It took me a while to slow down when I did business here. For the most part, locals are not interested in making their first million gold marks like Germans are."

It took three more months before Schrock started to believe that he'd both adapted and changed. He now did his job without frequently regretting he wasn't a shipmaster. During another evening visit to Johann, he was boasting about how far he'd come in fitting into his new routine when Johann caught him by surprise.

"I hate to disabuse you of the notion that you've changed," Johann said. "I fear I can still see the old Schrock in there—the captain who lets the years slip by as he stands at the helm of his ship, self-absorbed, soulless and alone. I know when you first arrived here I heard you say you wanted change. But in my experience, real transformation occurs at about the same speed that moss grows. So I advise you to allow yourself closer reflection before you proclaim your admission into the gates of Valhalla."

"What in the hell are you talking about, Kessler?"

"I'm referring, among other things," replied Johann, "to the fact that you don't seem to have any intention of ever getting married."

Schrock wagged his head. "Good God, you're aggravating, Kessler. I haven't been here that long. Give me some time. From now on I'm referring to your house as a church, and I'll only come here prepared to ask forgiveness and do penance."

"Sorry, Schrock. That must have been my mother talking."

———————————

Two weeks passed and Johann sent word to Schrock to come by his office.

"Listen to this," Johann said, his voice animated. "Kaole, one of my workers, told me that his uncle, a man named Nakea, related a story about your statue."

"Not my statue."

"You know what I mean. So this Nakea is a *kahuna kilokilo*—a priest, but not like what we think of—more like a seer. Kaole says that his uncle became involved with a ship carrying the soul of their beloved Kamehameha the Great. He had something to do with it as it caught fire and sank. Gerhard, that couldn't be any ship other than the *Haendel*."

"I'm not sure I understand what you're suggesting. What could a priest on land have had to do with a ship catching fire out at sea? Even if there were a shred of truth to it, how, why would this priest do such a thing?"

"Kaole said it's because when the statue was to arrive on a ship— in my mind clearly your ship—the King and the legislature had intended to erect it in Honolulu. But the island of Oahu wasn't Kamehameha's birthplace. He was born on the island of Hawaii, on the north coast, in a district called Kohala. Apparently, the people from Kohala were so troubled by the dishonor of taking the image of their sacred king to Honolulu, they sent their main *kahuna* priest here for Nakea's help."

"What kind of help?" asked Schrock.

"You need to understand that practices of the native priests have been kept up, even after all the repression by the church and the government. Kaole says Nakea is a *kahuna* who has been given special training and powers. Supposedly he can do something like fly, go wherever he wants and cause things to happen through his dream trances. Hard for us to comprehend." Johann opened the shutters and looked up into the sky. "In the realm of the supernatural, I'd say."

"So what did he supposedly do to my ship?"

"Kaole said another *kahuna* came to Oahu and got his uncle Nakea to agree to help the people of Kohala by making sure the statue never reached Honolulu, but instead went to Hawaii Island and Kohala."

"You don't believe any of that, do you?" asked Schrock. "I mean, it all took place a half world away from here."

"I agree," said Johann, "but maybe there was something—."

"Don't. You're not beginning to suggest that some pagan mystics were behind the loss of my ship, the complete upheaval of my life and of my crew."

"I don't know what to think," said Johann. "What baffles me is that Kaole said his uncle told him about this well before anyone here heard about the *Haendel's* sinking or saw the account of it in the papers. That's why he decided to tell me about it. He knew I was friends with you and I'd told him about your ship and the ordeal we had. Ordinarily, he would never speak about what his uncle does."

Johann's serious tone made Schrock increasingly uneasy. He sat down hard in his chair, looking at Johann as if he were a stranger.

"It seems like something unusual may have happened," said Johann. "It certainly has got my curiosity up. I think you and I need to find out more about this."

"I doubt there's any truth to any of it, Johann. It's probably pointless, but if you insist, I won't deter the man of science."

PART III

DECEMBER 1881
THE WAY HOME

CHAPTER 15

Falkland Islands
December 1881

With the sails slapping in a mild wind, the *Earl of Dalhousie* slipped through the fog into Port Stanley, quietly setting anchor in the harbor. John Jarvis's aging, bark-rigged ship was carrying more than three hundred men, women and children from the Portuguese Azores, recruited to be plantation workers in the islands of Hawaii Kingdom. The twenty-three-year-old Captain Jarvis went ashore in a skiff, along with the ship's purser, Alban McLeod, while the rest of the crew and the passengers remained aboard. In addition to arranging purchases of food and water, Jarvis planned to have McLeod set up shop to enlist more plantation workers. Those convinced to sign on would receive 'free passage' to Hawaii in exchange for their agreement to be indentured laborers in the Islands' rapidly expanding cane sugar industry.

Captain Jarvis was motivated by the planters' exceptional price for every live head he delivered to Hawaii. Any additional body procured would make the extra time in Stanley worth the delay. McLeod, nearly twice Jarvis's age, was unusually persuasive. Jarvis was confident his thin and bespectacled cohort would make him more money.

As soon as he had passed the shipmaster's exam in Scotland, Jarvis had become captain of the four-masted *Dalhousie,* a thousand-tonnage freighter and former troop ship turned emigrant carrier. An exceptional and brash sailor at such a young age, Jarvis had created cause for his recognition in British maritime circles. It was said of him that his innate ability to navigate and command a ship was surpassed only by his ambition.

After several hours securing supplies, Jarvis left McLeod with a borrowed hotel table and chair to recruit laborers just outside the

Globe Inn, one of the few gathering places for locals in the seaport community. Because dense fog had made it risky to sail for another day or more, Jarvis set out walking toward the water through the enveloping mist. Ashore, most men his age would usually be looking for alcohol and women, but his impulse was to see some of the island. Curious as a small child, for Jarvis, exploring new surroundings trumped sins of the flesh.

He headed out on the road that followed the waterfront, walking past the homes and business establishments. Farther from the town center, the road narrowed and the buildings became sparse. He walked briskly, enjoying the abnormal sensation of his feet being on ground. The flat, treeless landscape gave him the familiar sense of emptiness he'd grown accustomed to at sea. In the distance, through the swirling fog, an anomalous sight caught his eye, floating in and out of his vision like an apparition. He stopped and stared, momentarily confused. The shape he saw standing on a slight knoll above the beach didn't belong in the outskirts of this small town, or for that matter, resting at a desolate stretch of coast on this remote island.

Jarvis moved nearer, the curiosity of his childhood overtaking him. It appeared to be a statue of some imperial warrior. As he neared it, he saw the likeness of a man nearly ten feet tall and cast in bronze. The figure's gilded cape and loin cloth, as well as a sash tied around the waist and draped over the shoulder, were all badly tarnished. A Roman-like helmet was set on its head. One arm of the warrior was held out toward the sea in a noble gesture, while a long and formidable spear was held upright by the other.

Because the shape was shrouded in fog, Jarvis was all the more transfixed by his strange discovery. This wasn't like the castings he'd seen of British or European war heroes. The face seemed to be of an indigenous warrior, although he'd never heard of any such tribe in the Falklands. The dark patina of the bronze only obscured the answer. It was hard to imagine how or why it would be here in Stanley. He needed to learn the story behind this effigy.

Jarvis scanned the rise behind the beach. The mist opened enough for him to see a small warehouse on the other side of the road, surrounded by rusted machinery, assorted ship fittings and piles of scrap metal. Heading for the building, he went in to find a weather-grizzled man with thin wisps of gray hair clinging to his forehead.

"G'day," the old man greeted. "Bill Wainwright, sole proprietor of Stanley's only salvage yard. What can I do for you?"

"John Jarvis," the captain replied, tipping his hat. "I saw that statue over near the water," he gestured. "What can you tell me about it?"

"That's the conqueror of the Sandwich Islands. I was told he was the first king over there. It was salvaged from the bottom of the bay near a wreck. Port pilot named Radcliff knew all about it. I did him the favor of taking it off his hands."

"Anybody offer to buy it yet?"

"Nope, but I expect to get a good price for the bronze when the scrap-broker's ship passes through here... if it ain't sold by then." Wainwright looked over the well-dressed captain, and smiled. "Say now. You look like a man who appreciates art. Maybe you'd like to buy it?"

Jarvis intuited that there was probably some significance to this "conqueror" statue. Doubtless there could be important people in the Hawaiian Kingdom interested in having the monument, perhaps whomever had it commissioned in the first place. If he could buy the statue for a low price, there was a good chance he could double or triple the price in Honolulu.

"Well, then," said Jarvis, "I don't know if it has any value as art, but I could probably relieve you of it and ship it back myself for scrap." He paused and looked idly around the warehouse at other items lying around. "Tell you what," he said casually. "I'll give you 1,400 pounds sterling, or three hundred U.S. dollars if you prefer, and you can be done with it."

Wainwright feigned a look of astonishment. "You'll have to do a lot better'n that. I could get double that from the scrap dealer when he shows up."

"If one shows up," Jarvis said. His attention wandered to a small winch lying on the floor. He squatted down to examine the workings of it, pulling the handle to test if it functioned. He stood and, while still looking at the winch, made a gesture of reaching for his wallet. "But let's say I give you three hundred fifty dollars right now and make you a happy man."

Wainwright turned his back to Jarvis and walked to the stove. "It's a bit chilly in here, don't ya think? Why don't I put on some tea and we'll warm up a bit. Maybe I can school you some on the value of metals."

Wainwright brewed tea from an iron pot on his coal stove and talked about Falkland Islands weather. When it was ready, they sat down at the desk.

The scrap dealer slurped his tea. "Last I heard they're buying bronze scrap in London for two'n twenty pence a pound, and it's goin' up every day 'cause of demand. If the weight of that nice statue be somethin' like 1500 pounds, then it'll fetch a price of more than six hundred dollars." Wainwright rattled on about the scrap metal business longer than Jarvis was ready to listen. Suddenly he gave Jarvis his counter offer.

"Five hundred fifty dollars and not a penny less," the grizzled man said, "and you'll be gettin' a good deal, my friend."

"You're not taking into account the cost of shipping this junk," Jarvis countered. "I'll give you four fifty." The two men continued haggling, with the old man's bargaining skills becoming apparent to Jarvis. They dickered some more and finally settled on five hundred dollars.

Jarvis figured that was about two hundred more than its scrap metal value in Honolulu, but it was much less than the amount he planned to ask from whoever might want it in Hawaii. He suppressed a smile, thinking about the profit he'd make on this transaction. He could tell Wainwright was pleased, even though the man pretended to pout like he'd given away the store. Jarvis shook hands with him and let him know that people would come by to move the statue to his ship next morning.

Captain Jarvis left the salvage office and started walking back toward the town center, feeling pleased and whistling a tune he recalled from childhood. He never whistled on his ship. He thought about the superstition of whistling on board ship—it being a sign of wind and potentially inviting dangerous gales or worse. How odd that was. It was understandable that the mates used whistles for crew commands, but no one else on board was allowed to whistle, so as not to interfere with the mate's orders. But he was sure that long ago some ship's mate had concocted this myth to ensure any whistling was the closely guarded purview of the mates.

As he continued back, it occurred to him there was something unusual about the statue he couldn't place. He hoped it wasn't some superstition he'd yet to learn about shipping statues.

By the next day, Captain Jarvis had hired a lighter-barge owner named Penbock, an extremely thickset man, to move the statue off the beach and load it onto his ship. Penbock and the barge crew proved as inept as their equipment was inadequate. The barge rigging was too small for the job and the process slow and clumsy from the start. They hooked the statue around the torso and the base with heavy ropes, intending to winch it out into the shallows and then lift it up onto the barge. As it was being dragged from the shore and Penbock shouted commands, the top-heavy bronze tipped frontwards.

"What the devil!, you ham-fisted bootlickers," Penbock jabbered. "How'd you let that happen?" But they all watched helplessly as the incoming tide slid over the back of the bronze effigy lying face down in the shallows.

It took them a couple of hours to locate a team of horses who were able to pull the monument upright. The fall had broken off the upper part of the statue's spear as well as the extended forearm. They all argued over who should go back into the turbulent and near-freezing water to look for the broken statue parts, the outcome being that none of them went to the trouble and the pieces went unrecovered.

They still needed to get the statue on board the ship before dark. Working against the diminishing daylight, the barge's boom was suspended over the water as they pulled the statue up above the surface. The dangling statue veered out of control as it swung back over to the barge. The casting thumped into the corner of the ironclad boat, punching a sizeable hole in the bronze cape of the famous conqueror's likeness.

Captain Jarvis was working in his cabin when his second mate informed him the statue was finally being loaded on board. The *Dalhousie*'s lift boom wasn't large enough to easily load a piece of cargo as ungainly as the uncrated statue. Jarvis came out to inspect his purchase just as the boom slammed the statue down onto the deck.

His eyes widened as his jaw dropped. "What in God's name have you done?" he raged to Penbock. "You've ruined it. Even the salvagers pulled it out of the water in one piece!"

Penbock averted his eyes toward the bay.

"And where are the broken-off pieces?" Jarvis asked.

Penbock mumbled as he looked at his feet. "We lost 'em in the quick tide. We figured they was only a few pounds of scrap."

Jarvis exploded. "I'm not selling it as scrap, you horse's ass, and now I can't sell it in this condition. Botching this will mean your fee."

Jarvis glared at Penbock, then turned to McLeod. "Give this son-of-a-bitch half the money and get him off my ship before I bloody him."

McLeod counted the money and held it out. Penbock gingerly took his payment and slowly backed away, furtively glancing at the agitated Jarvis, standing a full foot taller than him. When Penbock reached the rail, he turned and quickly pushed his sizable bulk down the ladder, most likely moving faster than he had in years.

Jarvis spit over the side onto Penbock's barge before looking again at the statue. He turned toward his first mate. "There's nowhere else to put it. Lever it up front the main mast and secure it there, then prepare to get us underway at first light."

As the daylight faded, the ship rocked easily at anchor, waiting out the fog and a morning departure. The *Dalhousie* had seen more than twenty years at sea, and was forever moist from leaks in the bulkheads. As frequently as they were allowed, the emigrant passengers came up on deck to get out of their damp and stifling quarters in the lower decks. Depending on the weather, they were allowed up on main deck for a short respite after the supper meal. This evening, when the first of them emerged up through the hatchway, they were stunned to see the spectacle of the enormous effigy on the deck. The poor and largely unschooled sharecroppers had never seen statuary of this size, or any large statue, for that matter. Only small wood crucifixes and figurines of the Virgin Mary adorned the chapels in their villages, if there was a church at all. Seen through the murkiness of the fog and halo-lit by small deck lanterns, the sight of this colossus appeared especially eerie to these unwitting souls. They were at once awed and frightened by the statue's presence, on a ship to which they had reluctantly entrusted their lives.

Middle-aged and religiously devout Franco Marcella was terrified but not struck dumb by the vision. "Holy Mother of God, save us from this devil," he mumbled to his friend Silvo next to him. "What sins have we done to be visited by this evil? It is surely a sign we are going to die on this ship."

The two of them and others skulked back down the hatch to the lower-deck barracks. They talked hurriedly among themselves, arguing about what the apparition was doing there and what it meant for their fate. When they spread the word through the crowded quarters that there was a demon on the ship, the story created near hysteria. Most of them had lived their entire lives in the Azores, an island culture of outsized myths and superstition that was tied to both ancient and Catholic beliefs.

Several of the younger men and women were as curious as they were afraid. They cautiously moved topside. Seeing the statue lashed to the deck, the lantern light playing shadows on its face, three terrified young women in the group cowered back toward the hatch and disappeared down the stairs. Prompted by the power of suggestion from Marcella and the others, they had no difficulty verifying they indeed had seen a demon.

Within an hour a number of the emigrant men approached the only two Portuguese crew members, seamen Correja and Morillo, and said that a large group wanted to be let off the ship and taken ashore in Stanley. "We won't go out to sea again on a ship that has a demon. It will be a voyage that will end in our death."

Correja and Morillo went to the first mate, urging him to tell the captain about the new development.

"Captain," the mate said as he carried the message to the captain's cabin, "we got a problem with our sheep down in the barracks."

"And what might that be?"

"A bunch of 'em are scared pantless by the statue. They want off the ship."

"What? You mean they want to be put ashore here in Stanley? Where the hell would they go? Are they crazy?"

"It appears they're all dumber than a keg of salted mackerel."

"They've signed contracts," Jarvis said, shaking his head. "They have to honor them."

"They said it only applies if they're taken to the Sandwich Islands, and they want off here in Stanley."

Jarvis pursed his lips. He wasn't used to being patient with people not his equal. But he didn't want to lose out on the money for each 'mackerel' he could deliver to the Sandwich Islands.

"Get Correja and Morillo," he said to his mate. "Let them know I'll need their help. We'll go below and explain the statue—change their minds about leaving the ship."

Jarvis decided to give the émigrés a hero example—remind them of Vasco de Gama: the only Portuguese hero-figure he could remember. Then he would tell them the statue was the likeness of the first king of the land where they were going to live, that he'd been a brave and heroic conqueror. Something like de Gama. Maybe they would understand that.

Most nodded when they heard their own famous sea explorer's name mentioned. But they still wondered how this forbidding effigy had come to be on the ship, especially if this supposed king was from the far-away Hawaiian Kingdom. Telling them the story of how it happened became a tiresome process. With Correja and Morillo's limited English, the two of them struggled to do justice to a Portuguese translation of Jarvis's narrative. After several hours working their way through the crowded barrack rooms, Jarvis decided his sailors could finish the explaining. He'd had enough of the noise, the smell and the squalor.

Going topside, Jarvis told his first mate to get to the harbor pilot and let him know that the *Dalhousie* would be ready to set sail at first light. It was just a matter of keeping the emigrants on board until they were out at sea. Then the only way they were getting off the ship was jumping overboard, something he didn't expect even the most superstitious of them would do. However painful a human loss it might be to some, if any decided to try and swim and then drowned, God forbid, it would be the financial sting he would suffer from the most.

The weather was clear enough to leave at dawn the next morning. They had a fair wind as the harbor pilot gave his leave of the *Dalhousie* at the harbor's outer edge. The crew set full sail, and not wanting to awaken the passengers, they headed out to sea as quietly as Jarvis could get the sailors to work. Through Yorke Bay and into a trackless ocean, the captain pushed the *Dalhousie* down the coast of South America and westward in less than a week's time. Getting his ship around the treacherous Cape Horn in difficult conditions was touch and go, but he finally rounded the Cape and reached the waters of the Pacific. He still hoped to make Honolulu by late March of '82. It would be nearly four months from when he'd left the Azores. He knew it would be none too soon for the emigrants, crowded below, anxious and fearful of the statue. But from his perspective, none of the mackerels had jumped ship or died. And the bronze statue was still lashed to the main mast, despite the battering from heavy seas encountered off the Cape. He didn't see any further damage to his "fine piece of art," as he had become fond of saying to McLeod when he talked about it.

CHAPTER 16

Honolulu 1882

Near sunset, Schrock and Johann met at Schrock's rooming house a block from the harbor, where his room overlooked the forest of masts that grew from the ships docked at the piers and anchored in the harbor. The small quarters were just able to accommodate the two of them as they sat in front of the jalousie shutters that framed the open window.

Schrock tugged at his collar, too warm to notice the cooling air from a tradewind breeze drifting into the room. "Even though I'm doubtful about it all, the tale of your clerk has gnawed on me some. I'm not sure why. Just the same, can we find out more about his uncle's claim?"

"I think it's a bad idea," said Johann, "but maybe you'd like this *kahuna* questioned. You know sorcery is against the law in Hawaii."

"I've thought about that," Schrock replied. "Even if I wanted the police involved, I wouldn't imagine they're likely to take the story seriously, except if they're native Hawaiians. And even then, they'd probably follow the law." He waved his hand as if to dismiss the suggestion. "Look, what you've told me is all just idle talk. It can't be credible, can it?"

Johann's face squinted in concern for his friend. "It raises questions, though, doesn't it?"

Schrock studied his hands as he clasped them. "We should talk to this *kahuna* directly. Could you arrange a visit through your man, Kaole?" asked Schrock.

Johann shrugged. "Possibly; come by my office when you're off work tomorrow and we can both see what Kaole says about it."

After Johann had gone, Schrock was left to think more what it was about this bizarre story that puzzled him. It was like the anomalies he'd sometimes witness at sea when strange weather conditions happened, like when he saw a complete rainbow cast a generous arc over a massive black cloud, a cloud that sent down a torrential waterspout, as if it was Poseidon's own design. Or while sailing near the African coast, a solar eclipse occurred and sea birds, assuming night had fallen, landed by the scores on the ship's spars and rails. But if something was made to happen to his ship that was caused by a mystic, this would be something of a different sort, except thinking about it was ludicrous and a waste of time.

When Schrock showed up at Johann's office after work, Johann introduced him to Kaole, a large, dark-skinned young man who carried himself easily. "Kaole, this is my friend, Captain Gerhard Schrock. You've surely seen him here before. Gerhard, this is Lincoln Kaole."

"I'm pleased to meet you, Captain Schrock," the young man said with a broad smile. "Just call me Kaole. Everybody does."

Johann had told him Kaole was very intelligent and amiable, both reasons he'd hired him as a front office clerk. Also, because of his years in a missionary school, Kaole's English was good, but, Johann had noted, often infused with Pidgin.

"Kaole, the captain and I would like to talk with your uncle about the sinking of that ship you told me about."

Kaole's infectious smile crumbled.

"It's important, Kaole," Johann continued. "The captain wants to know if that was his ship. Perhaps you could take us to speak with your uncle sometime soon?"

Looking nervous, the young Hawaiian hurriedly replied, "My Uncle Nakea live way over in Waiale," he said, loosely motioning a direction with his hand, "and he only speak Hawaiian."

Johann wasn't dissuaded. "We could go in my wagon… and you could translate for us, couldn't you?"

There was an awkward moment before Kaole answered this time.

"Mister Kessler, all the *kahuna* learn the special things they do from *kahunas* who come before them. They expert of those things like healing, growing the food, canoe building. They earned the right to practice among our people—but they don't talk about what they do. They keep it close," he said, crossing his arms in front of his chest.

"Are you saying what your uncle does is secret?" asked Schrock.

"What they do they hide from people who don't understand. Those the people who report them to the police. And how they do their work always been kept secret, protected like a treasure. The only person that learns about the practices is their apprentice." Kaole's face took on a pained expression. "I'm sorry I said anything about that ship. I should not done that."

"I know this could be uncomfortable for you," Johann insisted, "but we need to talk with your uncle. We are curious about this and we'd be very grateful if you could help us. We would not go to the police. I promise we'll do nothing to get you or your uncle in trouble."

Kaole exhaled deeply. "I think I'm the one gonna be in trouble with my uncle." He paused, looking at the corners of the ceiling as if a solution was waiting there. "I'm not sure what you learn from him," he finally said. "But maybe I take you both for a short visit on Sunday, Mister Kessler."

After saying goodbye, the young Hawaiian left the office, his head hung low.

"I know what you're thinking," Johann said. "But if we want to get to the bottom of this, it's likely the only way."

———————————

Two days later, Johann, Schrock and Kaole rode in Johann's horse-drawn wagon south of Honolulu around the back of Diamond Head caldera, bouncing heavily on the rutted dirt road. It took more than two hours to reach the fishing village of Waialae, a collection of two dozen pole and thatch houses, *hales,* that sat near the ocean. Johann reined back the horse in front of a *hale* Kaole pointed out.

"*Aloha makua,* Nakea!" Kaole shouted. An older native Hawaiian man came out, stooping over to pass through the small doorway of the palm thatch structure. He was dressed only in a loin cloth, which to Schrock, dressed in a suit, seemed like a good idea. The man seemed like an older Kaole but much thinner, his ribs visible. His long gray hair was braided and held back with a twisted scarf. He smiled when he saw Kaole, and the two embraced and touched noses in greeting. "This is my uncle, Nakea," Kaole introduced. "He is my mother's oldest brother."

The man nodded and smiled at Johann and Schrock, as if he knew them. Schrock was sure he had never seen this man before. Nakea gestured for them to sit on the wooden stools outside the *hale,* then stood surveying his visitors like he might his own children who'd just returned from a day of play. Kaole looked down at his feet as he shuffled them in the dirt. Schrock glanced around at the nearby *hales* to see how much attention they were drawing, but his attention came back to the silent, diffident old man. Finally, Johann broke the silence by asking Kaole how long Nakea had lived there.

Kaole responded without asking his uncle. "He live in this place maybe thirty years. He came from Molokai because his wife's family was here."

Schrock decided to get right to the point. "Kaole, please tell your uncle that I'm the captain of the ship that burned and sank. Ask him what he can tell us about it."

Kaole shifted uncomfortably on his stool. Schrock knew he was still uneasy asking his uncle about a matter he should never have spoken about, and now doing so on behalf of two *haoles.* But as Kaole began translating Schrock's question, Nakea's face lit up. When Kaole finished, the old man started speaking Hawaiian in a slow and measured way.

"He knows who you are," Kaole translated. "He saw you on the ship."

Schrock's head jerked around toward Johann, as if to confirm the statement he'd just heard.

Kaole rubbed the back of his neck, appearing embarrassed to be the one to try and explain this to them. "You were part of his crossover dream," he said, his face in a frown that questioned whether they understood. "In the dreams he can go most anywhere and make things happen."

Schrock and Johann were at a loss for words. Their eyes flicked back and forth between Kaole and Nakea. Schrock was mostly dubious.

"But Nakea says he's very glad to talk with you. He thought maybe you didn't want to find him, or maybe you died," Kaole continued. "He is pleased you were able to come here." *Yes,* thought Schrock, *I'm damned relieved I didn't die, nor did anyone else on the ship. If this old man actually had anything to do with the Haendel's demise, he sure wasn't displaying any remorse that more than a score of us had almost been killed.*

"Ask him what he knows about the ship burning or sinking," Schrock said, making an effort to keep his voice even.

It sounded to Schrock like Kaole asked his question warily, trying not to transgress the unseen boundaries. While Kaole listened to his uncle respond, Schrock whispered to Johann, "I wonder if we'll get a straight answer."

Then Kaole turned to translate. "My uncle says his cousin from Hawaii Island is a *kahuna kaula*, like a prophet. He came to see my uncle with news some *haoles* made a statue of Kamehameha. He says what those *haoles* who made it didn't understand was that it put Kamehameha's *mana*, his divine power, in that statue."

"Do you believe that, Kaole?" Schrock asked. He had never considered that more than just the memories of the person could reside in the minds of the people who viewed a statue.

"Yeah, I believe this can happen."

Kaole listened as his uncle spoke again, and then pursed his lips as he turned back to Schrock. "My uncle says this where the big problem started. A strong but very bad *kahuna ana' ana* name Naholehua tried to destroy Kamehameha's *aumakua,* his spirit body. *Kahuna 'ana'ana*... they do what *haole's* gonna say is black magic. Naholehua did his own kind of crossover dream and made your ship catch on fire, to burn away Kamehameha's spirit body. My uncle says this is a terrible thing, to harm Kamehameha's *mana*. It's bad for all us in *Hawaii nei*," Kaole stressed, spreading his arms wide over his head to show he meant all the islands. "So my uncle did battle with Naholehua."

Kaole remained quiet and Nakea sat there, placidly looking at Schrock as if to say there was nothing more to tell about the matter. Schrock wasn't about to let it stop there.

"How did he do this battle?" he asked, insistent.

"This kind of knowledge need to stay in a sacred place," Kaole translated. "So he's not gonna say how he does battle. But he tell you what he did. He pushed the killing wind back inside that stink-eye *kahuna*, Naholehua."

"What does he mean by that? What did he do?" asked Schrock.

"He needed to save Kamehameha's *mana*. He says something like... like he didn't let your ship roll over or the fires burn it until you reached the land."

"That's what happened to us, to the ship," Johann cut in, his eyes wide. "Astonishing."

"What else does he say about the statue?" asked Schrock.

Kaole asked Nakea and then said, "My uncle had Kamehameha's statue pushed into the water by some *haole* crew on your ship," Kaole added. "That way Kamehameha's spirit body is protected from burning. He is safe in the water until he can find his way home to Kohala."

Schrock and Johann looked at each other with hollow expressions. *My God,* thought Schrock, *this is frightening. He's saying he somehow acted through Deetjen to make this happen.*

Nakea was silent, his head turned to stare out at the ocean. Kaole addressed them again, picking his words carefully. "All *kahuna* like my uncle get, how you say, ordained, the master of their work. Nakea come from a line of *kahuna* who are *'uhane hele*—that like a dream priest—and they come from the god Kane. All his life Nakea learning how to travel in his dream body to help our people. It isn't like the dream you know. It's… it come as a gift, and then must be learned. It is so very hard to do. But one more thing he practice is how to stop that *'ana'ana* killing. We call it *ho'opi'opi'o*. Nakea turn back the trouble of this one bad *kahuna 'ana'ana*. That's what he did for your ship." Kaole's brow creased. "You understand what I'm telling you?"

"More or less," Schrock responded. "You'll have to tell us more." At times he struggled with Kaole's sing-song speech and then had to filter it through his native German. Worse, he felt like he was sailing in a storm of strangeness. Johann only nodded, looking like the sleeper just awakened by the watchman.

While Nakea remained nearly motionless, Kaole fidgeted, preparing to say something. "This is what my uncle doesn't say. I know about Naholehua, that *kahuna 'ana'ana*. He come from the family of Kalanikupule, a long time back he the *moi*—the paramount chief of all Oahu, Maui, Molokai, Lanai. He was the last big enemy that Kamehameha the Great conquered in battle. So the family of Kalanikupule always hate Kamehameha. In those times, for many years, Kamehameha and Kalanikupule… you know, they were at war. But then Kamehameha brought a huge army in canoes to attack Oahu where Kalanikupule was with his soldiers. He won a big battle at Nuuanu and conquered Oahu—over there in the *mauka*," Kaole said, pointing back at the mountains above Honolulu.

"I read about that battle. Thousands died," said Johann.

"Yeah, maybe ten thousand," Kaole said. "Kamehameha's warriors captured Kalanikupule and sacrificed him at the *heaiu,* a temple.

Listen now. With that sacrifice, Kamehameha took Kalanikupule's *mana*." Kaole made a gesture like he was pulling something from his chest. "*Mana* is strength we get from the gods—it's very important to Hawaiian people." The squint of Kaole's eyes let Schrock know the young man was determined that he and Johann appreciate this essential concept. "The children of Kalanikupule's children always want revenge for his death and for taking all his *mana*. That's why that *kahuna 'ana'ana,* Naholehua, did this wicked thing to your ship— because Kamehameha's *mana* was in that statue."

Schrock sat motionless. His mind was still trying to sort out the improbability of what Kaole was saying.

"These things don't... they just can't happen," Johann whispered.

Schrock nodded almost imperceptibly.

"Kaole," Johann said, "I know there are strict laws meant to stamp out *kahuna* sorcery. What your uncle says tells us that it is still practiced anyway."

"The laws are because the missionaries and most *haoles* don't understand our long time practices," Kaole responded, sounding agitated. "But the laws just make *kahuna* do these things in the shadow."

"Then why is he all right with telling us about this?" Johann asked.

The two watched as Kaole conferred with Nakea again. The old man said something softly and smiled. Kaole's mouth pursed as if he was having a hard time believing what Nakea told him.

Kaole turned to Schrock. "He thinks that if you're not good men he wouldn't see both you so clear in the dream when he pass through to your ship. And now... you came to find him."

Nakea said something else to Kaole.

"My uncle says Kamehameha would probably not let you live if you were weak. He saw you both got hard shell." Kaole looked down at his feet as they outlined little circles in the dirt. "You know, Mister Kessler, I don't know him to ever say that about any *haoles* before."

Nakea slowly stood up and started to leave. In deference to him, they all stood. He stopped to face Johann and Schrock and said a few words in Hawaiian, ending with an "*Aloha*." Kaole moved close to his uncle. The two spoke for a minute, embraced, and the enigmatic holy man turned and walked toward the beach without looking back.

"Thank you for bringing us here, Kaole," Johann said.

Kaole nodded.

The three men got back into the wagon without talking. On their return to Honolulu, Kaole looked subdued. Schrock allowed that he might still be perplexed by his uncle's disclosures to them.

A bumpy mile later, Kaole spoke without preamble. "For a long time *haoles* have taken away *kahuna* ways from *lahui*—the people. Nakea thinks that if you learn more, it will help us."

"I'm not sure what it is we can do," Johann shrugged.

"He expect a lot from people close to him," replied Kaole. "He ask a lot from me. And you two... he say you more important than you know. He gonna ask you to come to his *hale* another time... to tell you more."

Schrock wondered what the more might be. The three said little for the remainder of the jarring ride back to Honolulu, taking Kaole to his home on the return to Johann's house.

"Extraordinary," said Johann, as they walked through the front door of his home, "to take a look through the door of old Hawaiian practices is something I'd guess not many *malahinis* are allowed to do."

"Or, by choice, most of us never venture to look at," added Schrock. "But now I still question all this. There's just no basis in fact for anyone to have supernatural powers like those."

"Again," said Johann, "what about Nakea's account of the ship sinking—well before the news had traveled here from the Falklands? How could he have possibly known about it, and the details about our near sinking, and Deetjen and the men pushing the statue into the sea?"

They were silent while Johann began mixing them each a drink.

Schrock realized the visit had put a crack in his armor against an unseen world. Other than their discussion about mariner superstitions, it was something he'd had little reason to dwell on before. "This has made me more curious about the lives of native Hawaiians. Imagine what else I don't know and will probably never learn."

Johann handed Schrock his drink. "Like the time we talked about European intolerance when we were at sea," recalled Johann. "I've only experienced a small part of the Hawaiians' culture when I see them on the streets or if they work for me."

"I've gotten the impression most whites see Hawaiians as hopelessly backward," Schrock said, "and have little concern about their welfare or rights." He looked at the floor and shook his head. "It's as if they're impeding progress and commerce. Am I wrong?"

"Unfortunately, you're right. The attitude that they are mentally and morally inferior is pervasive. The Hawaiians' way of life is far removed from what we've been taught to believe is important." Johann slumped down in his chair and sipped his drink. "Do you realize that most places in Germany it would be unthinkable just for us to be talking like this? Any thought of rights for remote island savages? You can see that the missionaries and we businessmen have done our very best to stifle native beliefs and customs." He stared into his glass. "We can't... we shouldn't colonize these islands. And there's always talk of it behind closed doors. What's happening here... it's spinning out of control. The future for the natives, those who are left, seems bleak. And I've been too accepting of it all."

Schrock saw Johann's mood darkening. "Then you need to be part of some solution." He held out his glass to Johann, having downed the last quickly. "Starting smaller, we need to consider what to say to Nakea if he invites us to meet with him again. Maybe you can find out what he thinks we should do to make up for your ways. And for me, though it seems something like conjuring, maybe he can tell us how it is that Kamehameha's spirit got inside the statue."

"Hopefully he will, since Kaole says we're important and Nakea's going to enlighten us more."

Johann made two more drinks of rum with fresh lime.

"So here's a toast to us—and discovering Hawaii," Schrock said, lifting his glass.

"And uncovering her mysteries," Johann added, touching his glass against Schrock's. "It's curious, you know, that if not for what happened to your ship and the development about this sorcery, I might have never considered there were mysteries to discover here."

Schrock thought Johann's tone was of someone who felt humiliated about unread books that had been sitting on his shelves for years. Even through the haze of the alcohol, he felt oddly cautious about what they might uncover if they started probing. Intriguing as it was to each of them, the supernatural was all uncharted water. Maybe they would be better off stifling their curiosity. Then again that's the approach his father would take. His father... still lurking around in there.

CHAPTER 17

Molokai Island
January 1882

Naholehua's apprentices, Makia and Palmele, finished their requisite cup of *awa* and waited for their master's pronouncements. They always know it's something that troubles the *kahuna* when he performs this same ceremony. Makia has learned that it's not unlike a murder pact that he carries out; a ritual that ensures they are to be complicit in his next questionable undertaking.

"There is a new problem," said Naholehua, his eyes appearing to Makia deeper and more ominous than usual. "I have brought about the sinking of the ship and watched the Kamehameha image buried in the waters of the sea." He stared vacantly out at the ocean. "It did not turn out so well—there were some difficulties, because that statue was not destroyed." He hesitated again, looking around as if he'd misplaced something, then seemed to collect himself, while the tremor in his hands was obvious. "Now, as some turtle shit floats, the master of that ship appears to have come to *Hawaii nei*. Though he is a *haole* I have seen that some of Kamehameha's *mana* seems to have rubbed off on this bastard. I don't know how but it has. The gods of Kamehameha must have made this *haole* some kind of protector of the pretender king and brought him over here on another ship to Honolulu."

"What will you do?" asked Palmele.

"We, Palmele, we shall have to find him and see what he does. And I think there are others who were on that ship who he is close with in *Hawaii nei*. We may need to watch them too. It could be that they might come to an unfortunate end. For our family, this means we must move to Oahu and stay at the home of my cousin, Kaiena."

For Makia, this was something to make him start to believe... for the wrong reasons. He had only been to Oahu one time for a school visit. This was a chance to see Honolulu. Palmele wouldn't question going—Palmele rarely seemed to question Naholehua. But going to Oahu might be shortchanged, because when Naholehua states someone might come to an unfortunate end, he means that he intends to pray them to death or maybe even figure out some other way to kill them.

Naholehua started throwing his hands up as he talked. "Kamehameha's *kepolo,* his devil *mana,* should have been sealed under the water but I have begun to see that it is not over." Makia could tell his stepfather was becoming resolute now, almost fervent. "They all say he was a god but that was never true. And now his likeness is an evil spirit on an errand of destruction. If somehow he rises up out of the water, we must cut off the arms, legs and then the head, destroy the *mana* and stop the ruin of our family's gods, our *aumakua.*"

Makia was conflicted. This was only family by marriage, but after twelve years with this man and all his relations, including Palmele, he discovered why the family was so set on reclaiming its honor and heritage. They had all been taught the story in the schools. In Kamehameha's merciless ambition to control all the islands, he had invaded Oahu with a massive army of 12,000 warriors carrying Western cannons, and then had killed upward of 8,000 Oahu combatants during the battles. But not much was said about what also happened. Kamehameha didn't just kill Naholehua's family forefather, King Kalanikupule. Kamehameha's priests had extracted Kalanikupule's *mana* and erased all evidence of his life in ritual and sacrificial fire. No wonder Naholehua was on a mission to set right those wrongs, those unforgivable insults. Makia couldn't help but sympathize some. He just cursed the fate that had enlisted him to help carry out this undertaking.

CHAPTER 18

Honolulu

Schrock got out of the carriage and made his way along the path and up the steps of Queen's Hospital, holding his bandage tightly around his forearm with his right hand. He was feeling the sting of the cut now. He hadn't noticed the sharp broken metal cargo strap as he was checking the large crate. The slice through his jacket sleeve had gone fairly deep into his arm and then bled like a sieve before he could wrap it tight to stem the flow. It made him embarrassed that he'd let it happen and angry that it had ruined his jacket, now torn and bloody.

After he was checked in, he was taken to an exam room and seated. A man in a white coat followed by a woman in white dress and cap appeared after about ten minutes.

"Hello, Captain Schrock, I'm Doctor Ferguson and this is my assistant. Let me see what we have here." After a cursory examination he said, "This laceration is quite deep. I'm afraid it will require some stitches after it is cleaned up properly. My nurse, Miss Braden, is going to assist me. It seems I've developed a slight tremor from arthritis in my hand, so she's taken to conducting these kinds of tasks for me. She is very skilled at sewing; she's a woman, after all." When Schrock saw the wry smile that accompanied the doctor's remark, he also detected the slightest grimace on his assistant's face. "I'm backed up with a number of patients," he went on. "I'll return in a bit to see that it's all done right."

The tension in the examination room eased considerably as the door closed. She began her work with confidence and efficiency, the movements of a practicing physician. "Captain… may I call you that? As I do this, it will pain you considerably. I plan to make you as comfortable as possible, but I will have to strap down your arms and legs on this table to keep you from moving around so I can put in the sutures correctly. Is that okay? Good."

Schrock hadn't finished nodding his approval when she proceeded readying. She had clearly become the person in charge in the room.

"I want to give you the opportunity to have a portion of alcohol with a small concentrate of opium," she said. "It is used often in our surgeries here." She was holding out a glass with the liquid, giving him little choice to refuse. "I would if I were you. Men much larger than you ask for it to avoid pain."

Schrock downed the drink, confused about whether he'd complied like a schoolboy with his stern teacher or succumbed to the wishes of an exciting woman.

"It will take a few minutes for the anesthetic to take effect. In the meantime, please lie down and I will place the straps on you. So, Captain, you will need to return later to have the sutures taken out and the wound examined. When will you be sailing next?"

"Well, Miss Braden, you see, I'm no longer sailing. Recently I've taken a position as a cargo superintendent here in Honolulu. People still call me Captain, just a title that people like to use."

She said nothing to this, just glanced into his eyes occasionally as she went about fixing the straps, preparing his arm. She was directly over him, moving about him, touching all his limbs, brushing his sides. He watched her face, the skin on her neck and arms. All came into sharp focus. The alcohol, opium, her; he was feeling warm all over. He didn't want whatever she was doing to stop. He watched her intently, taking in her olive skin, blue eyes, and dark hair pulled up into a knot behind her head, held back with her nurse's cap. What would her hair look like without that cap? At first he thought she might be native Hawaiian, a *kanaka maoli*, the term he had just learned from Kaole. But there was something about her beyond her light skin, blue eyes and somewhat Caucasian features that reminded him of one of Johann's girls. It was how she turned up the corners of her mouth as she smiled at him. My god, she was smiling at him.

"How are you doing, Captain Schrock? Are you feeling okay for me to proceed?"

"I think so, Miss Braden. Miss Braden?" his head was plummeting slowly over a cliff. "Could you tell me your first name so I might call you by that… only if it's, you understand… okay with you?"

She gave him a sidelong glance, then her smile appeared again. "It's Uilani."

"That's a beautiful name, Uilani. Uilani, start sewing. I'm sleepy. Uilani, my name is Gerhard. *Gute nacht.*"

Even though his arm throbbed for the next two days and was sore to the touch for three more, after that the days couldn't pass quickly enough for his return to Queen's Hospital to have his sutures removed. It was the persistent picture of Nurse Uilani Braden's face he kept trying to visualize, and her touch... and just her presence. Jesus, Johann would laugh at how easily taken he was.

CHAPTER 19

Niu Stream, Maunalua Bay, Oahu

Makia watched Naholehua's cousin, Kaiena, come up the path from the bay to his *hale*. They had just arrived and were settling in at the cousin's place outside of Honolulu, a collection of four thatch hales and some animal pens. Kaiena walked just like his name implied, his feet wide apart. Born that way, with a burly torso on top of thick legs, it reminded Makia of how bulls sauntered. From what his neighbor had said, it had given Kaiena an edge in becoming Oahu's best-known *Haka Moa* wrestler when he was younger. Makia had tried it, the standing chicken fight, but he was too tall to be any good. The two contestants hold their left leg with their left arm, grasp their opponent's right arm, and try to wrestle the other to the ground. Because of Kaiena's low-centered body, Makia figured Kaiena was probably impossible to throw.

"All you boys get ready to eat, 'cause we gonna do that now," Kaiena told the three of them. He was jovial, not at all like Naholehua. He was okay with the idea that his *kahuna* cousin was trying to right the ancient wrong done to their family, but since they had been staying at his place, he'd made it clear he wasn't ever going to miss a meal over what happened a long time ago. Furthermore, he didn't have time to be fooling around with such things. He had a farm to tend.

After they had eaten, Naholehua took Makia and Palmele down to a secluded area on a lava ledge, where the sea swells pounded below. They sat on the white coral sand collected in the lava pockets, the older Makia thinking that they would hear the *kahuna* tell them what their next move would be. But Naholehua only seemed to be talking to himself, repeating how the ship should have burned at sea.

Makia decided to take a risk. "Just so I can learn, *Kahuna*, so I know, what were the, uh, difficulties you had burning and sinking that ship with that Kamehameha idol out at sea?"

Naholehua eyed Makia hard, evidently considering the insolence of being questioned at all by his stepson apprentice, a young man he didn't much trust in the first place. After a long pause, he said, "You should know about a *kahuna kilokilo uhane* who lives here on Oahu. I knew this one when I was young—we were both apprentices to different *kahuna* on Molokai. He has a reputation here. His name is Nakea. It was him—he was there too, getting in the way and saving that ship from burning and sinking out at sea." Just saying those words made him shake.

"How—," Makia's mouth shut quickly when Naholehua glared at him as if he were about to tear his tongue out.

"You ask too many questions. I'll tell you what you need to know," Naholehua mumbled and looked around. "He can do some things. I guess he learned *uhane hele* or he couldn't have traveled there like me. That ship should have sunk and then when it didn't it should have burned. But somehow he did things so it could sail to an island where it did finally sink. Like I told you, the idol was not destroyed and is in the water close to land, and that captain lived. That damned Nakea— he got stronger than I would ever have thought."

Makia tried not to show his surprise at what he had just heard. Naholehua had led him and Palmele to believe that he was the most powerful sorcerer in all *Hawaii nei*. Now the *kahuna* himself had sown doubt about that. And Makia could sense that his stepfather wasn't telling the part of the story of most consequence. There was more that happened; this other sorcerer had badly outwitted him, or even done something that had left him somehow damaged, wounded.

CHAPTER 20

The day finally arrived when Schrock was ready to return to the hospital to have his wound checked and the sutures removed. He had followed all the orders in keeping it dry and changing the dressing. He knew about infection, had seen it on sailors while at sea and early on ascertained that having an amputated arm would be impractical.

When he arrived, Dr. Ferguson greeted him and bent his ear for ten minutes about problems in administering his department of the hospital, which the doctor was sure a ship's captain would understand. The doctor did, however, pique Schrock's interest when he mentioned his working knowledge of *kahuna* healing techniques as they had been utilized in the hospital sometimes in the past. Without telling him too much, Schrock said he was interested in *kahuna* sorcery and would be interested in finding out more from the doctor at a convenient time. Dr. Ferguson sounded enthusiastic about wanting to share what he knew and agreed to have a meeting. He un-wrapped the bandages, looked at the wound and declared it healed enough to have the sutures removed, bid Schrock a good-day and said that nurse Braden would be in shortly to see to it.

He followed her entrance as closely as he could while trying not to be conspicuous about his boyish interest. She came in with self-assurance, greeting him with a subdued smile. "Hello, Captain Gerhard Schrock. I myself want to see that wound and how it has healed before I do anything."

"Hello, Miss Uilani Braden," he said, trying to find her eyes as she picked up his arm to examine it. Her touch was professional, but it was her touch. He realized he'd been waiting for days to feel her skin against his. "I—I'm pleased to see you again. You did such a nice job suturing me, I am very grateful. I know I will have normal use of my arm again. I felt almost nothing while you did it. The next morning I had a sizable headache from the anesthetics but I'm fairly sure it was worth it." He heard himself babbling.

"Yes, Mister Schrock, otherwise you would not have liked being pierced with a needle that many times. And now it looks like you will be able to hold on to the wheel of your ship."

"No, no; it's like I said, I'm no longer a ship's captain. I work at the dock warehouses now."

"Oh yes, I forgot," she said, snipping at the first suture.

He didn't think she'd really forgotten. Could she have?

He felt the tug of the threads coming through the skin and watched small droplets of blood appear. As she wiped clean the arm and began applying a new dressing, she occasionally glanced at his face. He stared at her, trying again to connect with her eyes.

"What was it that brought you to the Hawaiian Kingdom, Mister Schrock?"

"Why, besides the fine weather, it's a long story. You—uh—probably don't have time to hear it now."

"I suppose not. I have more patients to see as soon as I'm finished here."

Schrock's mind raced. He couldn't let this moment slip. "Well, maybe if I'm not being too forward, we could have lunch on a day you are off work, and I would be able tell you the longer story. Of course I would very much like to hear about you, your life here. Would that be possible?"

There was silence as she seemed to be taking measure of the boldness of this man. "If we were to do such a thing, at what kind of a place would we be having this lunch?"

"I'm not sure, since I'm new to Honolulu. I would leave that to you to suggest a place… and a time. However, I'm most free on Sundays."

From where he stood on the wharf, Schrock looked up from his cargo ledger and saw Kaole walking past. "Ah, Kaole! *Aloha*. How are you doing?"

"I good, Captain Schrock. I'm taking papers to the ship over there," Kaole said, gesturing vaguely toward the half dozen ships secured down the dock where the multitude of masts were silhouetted against a backdrop of empty blue sky.

"Do a favor for me, will you? When you return, tell Johann that I will be coming by right after work. Tell him to stay until I get there."

"Glad to, Captain. *A hui hou aku.*"

Schrock felt bad about holding out on Johann. He wasn't even sure what would become of this new friendship... or whatever it was. He didn't know if he should tell Johann about her—he'd maybe give it a try this evening. He just knew he hadn't been so taken by a woman since Susan McGinnis. It was so unexpected.

He stepped into the office marked: *President - Kessler Shipping and Accounting Services, Ltd.* As soon as he sat down he said, "I met a person of interest."

"Interest to whom and about what?" Johann asked, smiling.

"Our mutual interest," Schrock replied, ignoring Johann's sarcasm. "At Queen's Hospital I spoke to a doctor who treated me for this cut a week ago." He pulled up his sleeve and held out his bandaged arm, a trace of dry blood showing through the bandage.

"That looks like it was bad. Is it?" Johann asked, a note of concern in his voice.

"I suppose. I wasn't paying attention—got cut by a broken lift strap on a cargo crate. I needed sutures. But that's not important; it's healed nicely. This doctor is a Scot, named Donnel Ferguson, been here about four years. He worked at some big New York hospital called Bellevue. From our short conversation, I took him to be a competent historian of early Hawaiian people and culture. He's especially interested in aboriginal medical practices. When I told him I'd been exploring some troubling stories about *kahuna* sorcery, he said he had learned quite a lot from Hawaiian patients he has treated. When he's had more success with them than what they've gotten from a *kahuna* healer, they're more willing to open up to him." Schrock hesitated, unsure. "I'm going to see him again in two days to have this wound dressed again. I think he will be able to help us. When I'm there, I'd like to invite him to meet with us for dinner... at your home if that would be possible. It's because—you know—my place is just not that large."

Johann was quick to respond. "Of course we can have him at my place. I'm sure neither of us would want to put up with your cooking anyway. If he accepts, just tell me what evening it will be and I will let Stina know."

"There's something else about the visit—," Schrock began, his voice trailing off. "Never mind. I can tell you later."

"Tell me now. I'm not going anywhere." Johann already seemed to intuit when Schrock had something of import he wanted to spin.

"These stitches; they were done by an assistant, not the doctor."

"Is that so unusual?" asked Johann.

"I'm not used to women surgeons, that's all."

"Aha, a woman! I see." Johann was like a cat playing with its prey. "Say more."

"It was nothing. Well, she was very skilled—not really a surgeon, a nurse—the doctor's assistant. I told you that already. The doctor said he has developed some arthritis in his hands and depends on her to conduct his minor surgical procedures."

"What else?" asked Johann.

"What do you mean? Never mind, I know what you mean. Yes, she got to me. Actually, she was stunning, something very special about her. Our eyes met a couple of times while she was working on me, and she said a few words—not too much, since Doctor Ferguson was right there. A sweet voice. But I talked to her alone in the office when I returned to have the sutures removed. Somehow I convinced her to have lunch with me in a week."

"My god, Schrock, you're smitten. I'm seeing a side of you I thought was drowned at sea."

"I might be slow, Kessler, but I'm not dead."

"I'm shocked—actually delighted for you."

Stina and the two children were at the table the following Saturday when Johann, Schrock and Donnel Ferguson had a cordial exchange about what each of them did in their professions. Doctor Ferguson's story about emigrating from Scotland to New York seemed interesting to everybody except Schrock. Ever since his return visit to the hospital nearly a week earlier, he hadn't stopped thinking about Uilani Braden. But he was also anxious to discuss sorcery with the doctor. The whole idea of it gnawed at him; the stories he'd heard, told as facts, were so confounding.

Johann picked up on Schrock's impatience when more than once he saw Schrock shift uncomfortably in his chair. "Children, you may clear the dishes from the table," he announced to his two girls.

"Friends, let's adjourn to the salon for an aperitif." They thanked Stina for the dinner and moved from the dining room into the salon. Johann closed the room's double doors.

Schrock changed the tenor of their conversation immediately. "Dr. Ferguson, I've been anxious to hear what you've learned about sorcery among the Hawaiians. I told you some about these two *kahuna*. Because of their interest in a statue of the first Kamehameha carried on my ship, it was said they were somehow involved in the fire that caused my vessel to sink far away in the Atlantic. As far as I know, they hadn't been near it, so logically that would be impossible. One of them, an *'ana'ana* sorcerer, supposedly caused the fire on the ship. As we heard it explained by a nephew of the other sorcerer, they each came to my ship while in some dream state. The other sorcerer, a *kilokilo 'uhane*, told us he countered the malicious actions of the first, and protected the ship until it made port in the Falklands and sank in the harbor. Here is what remains a mystery to us: they told others about their actions long before word of the sinking ever reached the Hawaiian Kingdom. By all rights, there's no logic to that either. We would be grateful if you could shed any light on what might be the truth of these accounts."

Doctor Ferguson swirled the brandy in his snifter. "Soon after I arrived in America, I wanted to understand medicine of the North American Indians. It led me to wider study about shamanic healing practices around the world. Let me put what I've learned about *kahuna* healing in some context. In many aboriginal societies, there are similarities in the practices to which these specialists have been called or chosen. We know them as shamans, medicine men, witches, sorcerers. You probably know that Hawaiians have many kinds of *kahunas,* all revered as the experts in whatever they practice. Sorcerers are just one of many occupations in this class of people. Even if it is something as commonplace as a *kahuna* navigator or canoe maker or seer, each *kahuna* has learned how to integrate visions and the dream world within their own reality. Because of my personal interest, I've been focused on learning about the *kahuna lapa'au*. These are the healers. What I've learned is that after performing healing sacrifices and rituals, the *lapa'au* go to sleep, or sometimes into a trance, and they dream or vision the cause and the remedy of their patient's illness." Ferguson paused to take a sip of his brandy. "This is quite good. You'll have to tell me where I can purchase some of this.

"Anyway, where was I? Oh yes. There are also those in the priestly occupation, the *kilokilo 'uhane,* like the man you spoke with, whose skill seems to be tracking the activities of the spirit or soul through the same mediums—in dreams or visions. From what I can understand from my patients, these *kahuna* can penetrate diverse realms. They are said to journey at will in these domains, travelers between worlds who do their bidding on behalf of their family or the community. They are in the belief that unlike most of us, they have developed the skill to observe the patterns that lie beneath day-to-day existence."

Maybe that's what it is we're trying to understand, thought Schrock, *happenings in another realm.*

"There's one thing that might speak to your inquiry," said the doctor. "When the *kahuna 'ana'ana* prayed your ship to sink, it is much like a Christian prayer of intercession for a sick person one wishes God to heal. These *kahuna*s perceive they are in the business of healing something out of harmony in their family or social structure, even if they need to kill it. Their methods are more akin to the black arts. And we have a difficult time understanding it all because it is a practice cultivated and refined here for a thousand years. But an aspect I find most interesting is that through their trance or dream states, space, time and location seem to be irrelevant to these journeys they supposedly take." Ferguson glanced at his watch. "But I am guessing there was something that the *'ana'ana* sorcerer or his family thought was out of harmony."

"In this instance, I think it was more like his family clan wanted to settle a very old score," explained Schrock.

"Well, these two *kahuna* are the kind of sorcerers who can have malignant tendencies," Ferguson said, frown lines on his forehead. "As to them supposedly having foreknowledge of the ship sinking and so on, I'm sure that can be consigned simply to hearsay." He settled back in his chair and looked at Johann and Schrock. "Does that help?"

Schrock pressed the point. "From what you have told us, Doctor Ferguson, I've not heard whether you believe that these two *kahuna* were actually capable of destroying my ship."

Doctor Ferguson's eyes opened noticeably wider in response to Schrock's statement.

"Well," he hesitated, "in a cultural context, I certainly find such accounts very interesting. However, I have never deemed to consider any of them scientifically credible. I would think adoption of such beliefs will remain with those without the benefit of formal education. Don't you agree, Captain?"

Schrock tilted his head in frustration. "Yes, Doctor Ferguson. That must be the case."

After additional small talk about the Honolulu liquor mercantilism, and formal leave taking, Ferguson was ushered to the door. When the door closed, Johann smiled at Schrock.

"One step forward, one step back, eh, Schrock?"

Despite the useful background information Donnel Ferguson had given them, Schrock couldn't help but remain frustrated, and decided that the consolation gift was the reality that tomorrow he would be meeting the good doctor's nurse for lunch.

———————

He met her at a restaurant and tea room owned by a British couple. A pink-cheeked girl Schrock assumed to be their daughter seated them at one of several service tables in a small courtyard in the back. The sight of Uilani out of her nurse uniform and her hair down made him shiver and left him unable to talk.

"My father used to bring me here for lunch or tea when I was young," she shared. "It reminded him of Ireland a bit. Being here makes me think about him."

"I'm probably not as fond of tea or the British, but I like the European feel of this place," he said, glancing around. "I am glad you agreed to have lunch with me." He fumbled with his napkin. "I—I did want to find out more about you and your life here and if you'd still like me to tell you how it is I arrived here."

"I hope your feelings about the British don't include the Irish. My father always told me his people were only British by geography. But let's order some food and then, yes, I would like to hear how this sailor washed up on our island and decided not to get back on a ship."

The food had just enough taste to remind Schrock of Stanley and his miserable time there. He tried to block that out as they ate and talked superficially about her work at the hospital.

"So it seems like you're lucky to be alive," she said, after he told her an abbreviated version of the sinking of the *Haendel* in the Falklands, the enquiry, and his decision to give up the sea and come to Honolulu at the urging of Johann Kessler. "Do you like this work as much as being a sea captain?"

"No, not really. But I do like that I'm not under constant threat of dying from forces beyond my control. I respected the power of the sea, but now that I'm on land for a time and able to put it into perspective, I realize that being a mariner meant giving up on life in a certain way. I was taking risks year in and year out that far outweigh most dangers on land."

"What risks are you referring to, Captain Schrock?"

Odd question, he thought. *Wasn't it obvious what the perils of the sea were?* "Hurricanes, typhoons, storms bringing waves the size of mountains, winds so ferocious that the ship is thrown hundreds of miles off course, and then fog so thick there is no way to take a nautical reading to find out where you are; icebergs; fire; disease on board; crew drownings; being stuck in the windless doldrums and running out of water. Is that enough?"

"Yes, Captain, that is quite enough."

Schrock could feel his heart racing. "I'm sorry, Miss Braden. I didn't mean—."

"That's all right. I just wanted to confirm something I already knew. You see, someone I cared about died at sea. He was a sailor."

"I'm sorry." Schrock saw the hurt in her eyes, even though she didn't say anything else about it. They finished their meal in uncomfortable silence. He had to assume he'd overstepped somehow.

When he'd paid for the meal, she looked at him long and carefully. "I am not sure we are very compatible, Captain Schrock. And this is the reason. Deep within me, I am and will always be a Hawaiian by my blood and by culture. Even though I am more than just that, that's what is rooted so deep that I have found it hard to accept those who are not. It has been complicated for me, but it is who I am. However, I am here with you today because I do like you in some peculiar way. What's more, there is something curious about you I don't understand, something I need to find out about. That doesn't make much sense, does it? To want to spend time with someone for whom I believe I am not well-suited? Anyway, I am rather tired and I think we should go."

CHAPTER 21

Honolulu
January 1882

Summoned to Johann's office after work, Schrock slumped down in a chair. "So?"

"So I want to hear about your lunch with your new paramour."

"She's hardly my paramour. She says she doesn't think we are even very compatible. I'm not sure where it will go. I plan to ask her to lunch again, though. I'll let you know what happens."

"Well then, if it makes you feel any better, I've been invited to a meeting and I want you to come with me," said Johann. "It's a luncheon at the home of the prime minister; you know, Walter Gibson."

"Of course I know who Gibson is," said Schrock, shaking his head in mock disbelief. "It would be hard not to with all the appalling things said about him."

"What else do you know about him?" Johann asked.

"I knew he had something to do with commissioning the statue. Beyond that, all I know is that he's considered an odd duck by his American brethren and that he's loathed for whatever he does by most of the old-guard *haoles*."

"All true." Johann got up and paced behind his desk. "He's ambitious and very eccentric, I'll grant them all that. But there's more to him. I do know he's been a defender of the monarchy and Hawaiian culture."

"I see little wrong with that," said Schrock.

"Politically, you know he's unpopular with most of the *haole* businessmen for being behind the king's excesses and against annexation of Hawaii by the United States."

"I can see why he's unloved," said Schrock, "but I also would guess he's right about the annexation business."

"Well then, he should like you," Johann said. "He also does a remarkable job of understanding Hawaiian culture. He's one of the few white politicians fluent in speaking and writing the Hawaiian language. He even edits and publishes a Hawaiian language newspaper. The 'Hawaii for Hawaiians' slogan on his paper's banner and in his editorials really works for him. It's helped him get the native Hawaiians' vote in elections and in the parliament."

"A clever man," admitted Schrock.

"Ahh, but he's also considered an opportunist and a schemer. After getting the king to name him prime minister, he appointed himself minister of all the kingdom's big departments except finance. And for that piece, he seems to control much of the government's money, money through supposed loans that come from a non-conformist sugar baron. Now his detractors have taken to calling him the 'Minister of Everything'."

"It sounds appropriate. I wonder how he juggles it all," said Schrock. "Anyway, I get what you're saying. If I can come with you, I'll be watching the weather while we're inside his house." *If my mind isn't wandering back to Uilani Braden*, he thought.

"The meeting is for merchants, but I'm sure I can have the invitation extended to include 'The Captain' Gerhard Schrock. It's for Saturday afternoon. I know that's a short day for you. It would be a good opportunity for us to hear our own Minister of Everything up close. And if it's useless, at least there will be food."

"So what's the meeting about?"

———————————

It was only two days later that Schrock and Johann sank deep into the red brocaded armchairs at the home of Hawaii's controversial if not reviled head of parliamentary government. Johann had told him he suspected that Walter Murray Gibson would be talking about his grandiose vision for establishing a Hawaii-centered empire of Oceania throughout the South Pacific.

In the salon of the Prime Minister's two story clapboard house, the tall and sartorial Gibson greeted the seven invited guests with formal handshakes and slight bows. Located not far from the monarchy's Iolani Palace, his new home was ornate by Honolulu standards, fronted with turned-wood columns that supported the large porch and entryway. It was a house grand enough to fit the current occupant's opinion of his deserved status in Hawaii's government.

Currently, King Kalakaua and Prime Minister Gibson had control of the votes in the legislature, the plurality of those seats being held by native Hawaiians. It was their unofficial political "palace" party. However, during Gibson's rise to power, he'd accumulated a myriad of bitter political enemies, mostly sugar industry growers.

But Johann was one of a small group of *haole* businessmen with sizable shipping and manufacturing enterprises in Honolulu who weren't entirely antagonistic toward Gibson or the king. Notably for Gibson, these few men, like Johann, held Hawaiian citizenship. Because they all had money and were eligible to vote, Gibson needed their support for the audacious dream he'd held onto for years. How Gibson looked and carried himself was his statement of self-importance. Impeccably dressed in a black, long-tailed suit coat and white bow tie, they paired perfectly with his coifed silver hair, mustache and beard. It took Schrock back to some of his university days lecture halls, mostly an atmosphere he found tedious and long-winded.

"My friends," Gibson opined, his arm stretched out, "keeping our monarchy strong and your business interests in harmony with the king's intentions will lead Hawaii to its rightful primacy in all the islands of the southern Pacific Ocean. Because of influential men like you, our great Hawaiian archipelago has an unrivaled command of Western commerce."

The Prime Minister cast his deep-set eyes around to the faces of his guests, making sure to make eye contact with each. "With your wherewithal and this nation's ability to rule, we have the opportunity to administer governance in all of Oceania. And this is the best part, gentlemen: the recognition of the Hawaiian monarchy as the center of a Polynesian confederation will, without doubt, result in a considerable increase in business and trade for each of you as well as our other houses of commerce." Now he reminded Schrock of a seller of snake oil. By this time, Schrock knew Gibson's mention of other houses was an indirect nod to the sugar plantation interests, the force behind Hawaii's economy. Johann told him later it was also a coded acknowledgement of Claus Spreckels, the 'sugar king', a man un-allied with the other sugar barons, the one who was said to shamelessly give the king large loans and to have his hand in many of the manipulations of the king and of Gibson himself.

Johann nudged Schrock with his elbow as they watched Gibson's face take on a kind of radiance while he warmed to what was reputed to be his favorite topic.

"And imagine this if you will: sovereignty presided over by the Hawaiian monarchy. If this vision is to become a reality, our king needs a pledge of your assistance in promoting this magnificent and beneficial great Pacific islands kingdom."

Ah, the pinch, thought Schrock. He pondered just what kind of assistance would be required in the creation of this South Pacific realm. As the prime minister droned on, Schrock concluded Gibson had already positioned himself as chief administrator for his king in this Oceania Empire.

Johann said that Gibson had been outspoken in siding with native Hawaiians' welfare as well as having spoken out in favor of their cultural traditions. An American himself, he opposed what he called the "Americanization" of the kingdom and preached his slogan, "Hawaii for Hawaiians." On the other hand, the missionary-plantation business community largely saw the native population as unsaved, unwashed and morally degenerate. They despised Gibson for being a standard-bearer for native Hawaiians and the King.

Despite Gibson's undisguised appeal to the group, Schrock felt sure that none of the men there was being taken in by the prime minister's bigger agenda, his grandiose Oceania pipe dream. Even though Gibson needed all the *haole* support he could get, it seemed that he was preaching to a diminutive choir in a church of the uncommitted.

As Gibson paused for a drink of water, his guests looked at each other with creased brows and pursed lips of doubt. Schrock assumed that, like he and Johann, they were wondering what Gibson would propose next.

"Gentlemen," he resumed, "in another matter of importance, as chairman of the Privy Council's coronation committee, I am pleased to let you know that we are making great progress in plans for the coronation of King Kalakaua and Queen Kapiolani. I assure you that this event will not go unnoticed by other world governments. At the finish of the two weeks of magisterial ceremony, our monarchy and parliament will assume a rightful place in the pantheon of world governments."

Schrock could see why the prime minister had acquired his reputation as grandiloquent, along with other undesirable attributes his critics had ascribed to him.

"We will erect a formal, sheltered pavilion in front of the royal palace where the coronation ceremonies will take place. In addition, a grandstand will be constructed to provide seating for several thousand guests. We have invited royalty and persons of position from other kingdoms and republics throughout the world. And for your continued loyalty and support of the king, you and your families are to be granted preferential seating for prime viewing of the ceremony. You will also have seating near the king at each of the performances by the Royal Hawaiian Band, and at the luaus, the balls, the dinners, the horse races, and the fireworks—all of which are now being arranged. Grand, wouldn't you say? Of course, any contribution you make to defray expenses for the coronation will be gratefully appreciated by the king."

Schrock and Johann both stifled grins.

"As of recent, there are vacancies in several councils and boards of great import to the high function of our nation." The prime minister lifted and opened a large ledger book, looking up and down the page. "This afternoon I wish to ask you to make yourselves available for possible appointment by the king to positions in our government." He studied the men. "I have the greatest confidence that you could each make a valuable contribution to our nation, should the king ask you to serve."

Two of the other businessmen put their shoulders back and raised their chins, puffed up by the sudden importance they perceived having just been granted to them.

Gibson continued. "I will be talking to you individually about these appointments in the near future."

Neither Schrock or Johann was about to take him up on the offer, but Schrock recognized Gibson's political shrewdness in suggesting he could grant a piece of the political power in exchange for a contribution. He decided to pay closer attention to the prime minister, not sure what to conclude about this man.

"A very important element of our ceremonies will be the long-awaited unveiling of a statue of Kamehameha the Great, a magnificently rendered bronze, beautified with gold leaf. It will be presented on the second day following the coronation. Gentlemen, you will not want to miss it."

Shocked, Schrock sat up straight, unprepared for what the prime minister had just said. But Gibson made only a few more references to the statue and then moved on to other topics during an agenda that stretched out like a sailing leg between distant ports of call, finally ending the meeting so they could eat.

He and Johann didn't feel like after lunch was the right time to question Gibson about the statue. The two men thanked their host and Johann added that he would like to have another meeting regarding the coronation activities, to which the prime minister said he would gladly be amenable.

CHAPTER 22

Niu Stream, Maunalua Bay, Oahu

Back at Kaiena's, after they had eaten, Naholehua took Makia and Palmele down to the secluded spot on the ledge near the water. The two apprentices sat on the ground while their *kahuna* asked them what they had found out about the *haole* captain and his companions while they were in Honolulu the last four days. When they had nothing to report, the old man struggled to his feet and paced several unsteady circles around his apprentices, who remained seated on the ground. "I know what you want to ask," he said, stopping and looking down at Makia. "How do we know how to find this captain?"

That isn't what Makia wanted to ask. It was more like when this futile quest would come to an end.

"I saw him there on that ship in my dream," the *kahuna* went on. "And I saw him come on another ship from that island where his ship sank. I might know him again if I see him. That ship he came on, I have a picture of that ship's name in my head. We need to know the names of the people on that ship, and if that captain was one of them. Palmele, get me something to write on. Maybe I can draw the letters."

Palmele ran back to Kaiena's place to retrieve a pencil and paper and then set it in front of his master. Naholehua closed his eyes for a long time, and then slowly drew out letters:

KB WOL FF.

The next day Makia went to the ship's registry office near the harbor in Honolulu to see what he could find out about a ship with that name that might have come to Honolulu, and who the captain was, or the passengers. With the help from a clerk he found what he was looking for, and when the *Wolff* had arrived and left. It was 13 months ago. The captain, a man named Berglof, was the same both coming and going in a week's time. And yes, there was also a captain as a passenger. This had to be the man he was looking for, thought Makia. Now he had to find out if he was still here. The clerk, thinking he'd already done quite enough for this *kanaka* boy, was perturbed to have to pull out all the sailing passenger manifests for the same number of months in order for Makia to check if a Captain Gerhard Schrock was one of those passengers who had then sailed out of Honolulu. Eyeing Makia, he asked sarcastically if he had ever heard of searching for a needle in a haystack.

After five hours of pouring through the books and with very tired eyes, Makia had to conclude that this Captain Schrock had never left and was still somewhere around. Hopefully he had at least stayed in Honolulu. Heading back to Kaiena's, he couldn't help but think how his training had become so contrary to what he was used to. Instead of the quiet hours memorizing prayers and doing his best to gain knowledge of the obscure world of soul sleep, now he was forced to be a criminal, an errand boy and a detective for this errant, one-time spiritual leader of their people.

That evening, Naholehua gave Makia a hint of praise at his success: "Good thing your mother sent you to missionary school to learn to read," but then mumbled how Makia should have found out where the captain went when he got off the ship. Makia wondered just how he was supposed to have done this. So when Makia suggested to Naholehua that the only way they would find this captain was to have the sorcerer find him through soul sleep or go into Honolulu and look, the usual curses and accusations began. And nobody was going to tell him what to do, especially an apprentice. When Naholehua finally said he would go into town, both Palmele and Makia convinced him they would need to wash and braid his oily, disheveled hair and dress him properly so that he would appear presentable in the city. But when it came to the process of getting him ready, he acted like a child, complaining the whole time. Makia felt pain for his mother with the thought of all the years she'd had to give to this demanding and petulant man.

CHAPTER 23

When Naholehua finally agreed to go into town, Makia and Palmele loosely followed Naholehua around the center of Honolulu to look for Captain Schrock. Naholehua had made the correct assumption that the best place would be either in the taverns or around the docks. But because the *kahuna* didn't like alcohol or the kinds of people who were in places that sold it, his first wanderings were around the docks. On his second day scouring hundreds of *haole* faces, Naholehua was sure he recognized Schrock at his cargo workstation at the head of the pier. He made a gesture to Makia, who was about twenty feet behind him. As Makia neared Naholehua, he could sense that the sight of the man his stepfather was staring at across the pier had welled up instant feelings of hatred for that man. Makia knew that if at that moment his supposed master could murder this *haole* intruder it would give him immense satisfaction. Makia put his hand on Naholehua's shoulder in an attempt to squelch his fury. The old man turned his head and stared at Makia's hand, malice oozing out of his dark-lidded eyes. Makia withdrew his hand.

Naholehua looked out over the water. "You make sure of his name and this is the right man. Then we will need to find out who else this captain is connected to. His death will have to wait."

When Palmele caught up with them, Naholehua pointed out Schrock. "Now you must both follow him and find out who are the people he is close to—see what they are up to. They may be in the way, protecting the statue. We will need to deal with them as well."

In the following days, diligent and careful sleuthing allowed Makia and Palmele to discover that Schrock spent his off hours either with a businessman named Kessler, the *hapa*-looking woman who worked at the hospital who he seemed to be courting, and the *kanaka maoli* who worked for the businessman. The process was so tiresome, Makia had begun to have thoughts about signing on as a sailor just so he could escape on a ship. But he knew he would never abandon his mother to the wretch of a man he was bound to as an apprentice.

One evening when they had gone back to Kaiena's and met with Naholehua out at the ledge, Naholehua asked the two of them, "You got plenty more time there in Honolulu, Makia. What you find out about this captain and who his people are?"

"Yeah, the captain, he talk a lot with that *kanaka* out on the docks, like they were good friends. When I remember, I think I know this one, like maybe I met him once. It was when the missionary school in Honolulu sent some of their students to Molokai and we had a competition with them in spelling and catechism. Maybe this captain and the *kanaka* could know something about your kind of *kahuna* or somehow figure out that you over here on Oahu now."

"Why you think that? That's foolish talk. You show me again what a scared boy you are."

Makia wanted to strangle his stepfather at that moment, but didn't show it.

"What about you, Palmele. You find something out?" asked Naholehua.

"Yeah, maybe. I been seeing him meet up with that woman… she sure look like a *hapa* to me, and they walk to a park and talk there and then they both leave. I see where they each live. I follow her one morning and find out where she work at the big hospital. She a nurse I think. That's all."

"Palmele, you need to find out more about this *hapa* woman. What more could she have to do with him." Naholehua's dark eyes then speared into Makia's. "And you, you so worried about this *kanaka* boy, go back and find out what he does, where he goes, why he is a friend with the captain."

When they went back to eat with Kaiena, Makia thought how disappointing it was when Naholehua told Palmele to follow the woman, instead of him. He liked how she looked and would have preferred watching her. At least it would make it more interesting, maybe even exciting. Then there was the *kanaka*. There was something about him. Maybe he did really know him from the past. He and Palmele would trade off watching him and the captain, since the woman worked all day inside the hospital. The vagueness of their task was such that he had no idea just what they were supposed to find out. Oh, how he missed Molokai.

CHAPTER 24

Honolulu

The tradewinds blew through the salon as the sun was setting. Schrock looked through the glass at his second drink: rum mixed with ripe passion fruit picked from a tree in Johann's yard, a yard resplendent with tropical fruit trees and multi-colored flowers. The drink blend had become the standard of their frequent evening get-togethers. Schrock's cheeks puckered as he swirled the mixture in his mouth. "I'm still not sure what's so good about this slime and seed concoction."

"Why, the rum, of course," said Johann. "Anyway, here's to our most recent revelations about the ship." He held up his glass, but Schrock's dour face revealed that he had little conviction anything Prime Minister Gibson had told them would somehow improve their health.

"So, your statue of Kamehameha will make it here after all," said Johann, his eyes showing a wicked gleam.

Schrock glowered. "It's not my statue. And it's not the one that was lost."

"It might as well be, considering how much this king's likeness seems to have played a part in your life. If the statue's not yours, then instead maybe it's taken possession of you. What about that?"

"Foolishness," scowled Schrock, taking the bottle of rum from the sideboard and holding it close to his chest, pretending to keep it from Johann. "You need to drink less—or more," he said, pushing the bottle toward his friend. He didn't want to divulge that there may be truth in what Johann was saying.

"Admit it, Schrock," Johann countered. "One way or the other you are linked to this image of Kamehameha as if it was family. And since you've been so slow to marry and start a family, apparently it has become your, well, your surrogate kin!" he said, laughing so hard he had to grab the back of a chair to steady himself.

"I'm not amused, Kessler," Schrock said, shaking his head and putting the bottle back on the sideboard. "You're having a lot of fun at my expense."

Johann held his hand up in feigned apology. "But after all that's happened to you, you're an easy mark. Stina doesn't appreciate my jokes, so you'll have to do."

"And may God turn you into a statue of salt, well to muffle you," said Schrock. He lifted his drink and finished it with one gulp.

"I'm sorry," Johann said, still chuckling. "I just want to see you get some humor back in your life. Something is bothering you these days... besides the ship and that statue."

"This is all absurd, you know," Schrock said.

"What's absurd?"

"That this Naholehua or Nakea could have somehow projected themselves out into the Atlantic and muddled about with the *Haendel*."

"Then why, Captain Schrock, have we both given it a moment's consideration?"

"Because we are like little kids listening to a good story," replied Schrock, "and we've been mesmerized by the fantasy of it. We need to know what happens in the end. I admit I wanted to see this through, but I didn't know I would take part in a fairy tale. I thought it would be—how should I say, more orderly," he said, his index finger flicking an imaginary line, "like a detective solving a murder case."

Johann examined the fish-roe-like fruit seeds in his glass with the same interest Schrock had shown earlier. He raised his tumbler and downed the rest of the mixture. "Hell, we've both had to pick our way along a path on this very different kind of story. Don't forget, I was on that ship. It's turned out to be intriguing for me as well. And it's coincidental that you should bring up a fairy tale. Yesterday when we left the prime minister's, I thought what this mystery reminds me of." He paused to see if Schrock would bite.

"Yes, reminds you of?"

Johann's eyes sparkled. "Why, a story by a couple of our most famous German scholars, the Grimm brothers."

Schrock looked incredulous. "You're calling them scholars?"

"I realize I'm embellishing, Schrock, but they are awfully bright boys, wouldn't you say?"

"Of course," Schrock responded in a voice that mocked Johann. "So, which of their tales is it?"

"*Hansel and Gretel,* of course. Remember, the two children are led by their wicked stepmother to the woods to be left to starve to death, but Hansel leaves a trail of bread crumbs so they can find their way back home. However, after the children are abandoned, they find that birds have eaten the crumbs. Now they are lost in the woods."

Schrock rocked on his heels. "For God's sake, Johann, I know the story!" He was doubtful that Johann's narrative was taking them anywhere he was interested in going.

Johann was undeterred. "Try to imagine this. We are the lost Hansel and Gretel who tried following crumbs. Are you following me?"

"Don't patronize me, Kessler."

Johann ignored Schrock again, his tone a pretense of gravity. "After days of wandering, the two children follow a striking white bird to a clearing in the woods. That would be Prime Minister Gibson taking us on a wild goose chase. Then the children discover a cottage built of gingerbread and immediately start to gnaw on it. That would be Naholehua's house of '*ana'ana,* yes?"

"No. I'm supposed to imagine I've been eating a sorcerer's house?"

"You're getting it, Schrock! But let's say you've just been biting around the edges. Then the door opens and a very old woman comes out and lures the children inside with the promise of soft beds and delicious food." With one eyebrow cocked, Johann gave his friend a feeble parody of the evil eye. "They are starving and tired, so they go in, unaware that their hostess is a wicked witch who accosts children to cook and eat them. Now, in our story, who do you think is the wicked witch, hiding in that house?"

"I suppose it is Naholehua."

"Yes, but it's more than that," Johann said. "You see, the witch is the sum of the great unknowns, the mysteries of life, like the ocean, or death, or what lurks in the dark side of our souls—."

"Or like why my ship burned," Schrock interjected.

"Hopefully that, too. But all of these larger things lay in wait for us. They'll devour us if we don't try to understand them."

"That's all cock and bull—far too complex for a simple fairy tale. Any child knows the witch stands for the wicked side of the struggle between good and evil. That's all it is."

"Well if that's the case," Johann said, "maybe you haven't thought about how we end up in this fairy tale."

"I'll bet this is going to be good." Schrock's words were edged with sarcasm.

"We know the witch locks Hansel in an iron cage to fatten him up and forces Gretel to become her slave. But later on Gretel tricks the witch, shoving her into the oven and slamming the door shut." Johann hunched his shoulders and clasped his hands together. "The witch gets burned to ashes, screaming until she dies. I always liked that part."

"Could you get on with this?" asked Schrock.

"So Gretel frees Hansel from the cage. They discover a vase full of precious stones in the house that they take with them as they set off to find their way home. A swan ferries them over an expanse of water they can't get across. I know that is the channel between Naholehua's Molokai and here, but I'll admit that I don't know how this bird fits into our quest. Maybe you can figure that out."

"I don't plan to," said Schrock, irritated.

And now," Johann let out an exaggerated exhale, "they make it home with the witch's wealth and live happily ever after." He looked at Schrock expectantly. "I can tell you're waiting for the rest of my parable explanation."

"No, but I'm ready for another drink."

Johann took Schrock's glass and moved over to the sideboard. "I'll be Gretel, so you don't have to be a little girl," he continued.

"Generous of you. How do you think all this stuff up?"

"Hmm, I don't know, it's just there. Anyway, because you have to be Hansel, you've been put in a cage to be fattened up. I'm sure that means you were being prepared for some interesting revelations."

"I'm to be eaten by the truth, then," Schrock said with a derisive tone.

"To the contrary. Tricking the witch is us getting wiser the more we discover. The witch's jewels are the truths that we'll uncover on our journey, along with the authentic story of your ship and the statue."

"That's too obvious," said Schrock, lowering himself into a stuffed leather armchair. "What about the witch-ed stepmother?" He was having trouble forming his words as he worked on his fourth drink.

Johann chortled when he heard Schrock's question. "You almost had it right, Captain. The wick–ed stepmother and the witch are, metaphorically speaking, one in the same. For us, they have to represent 'ana'ana sorcerers."

Johann was starting to sound weary to Schrock. It was confirmed when Johann turned and slumped into his favorite armchair. "What I find in all this is that my doubts about mysticism and sorcery are being eroded," Johann said.

Schrock said nothing while Johann's confession settled in.

"And what I see for you, Gerhard, is that the more you look at it, this path is guiding you to what it is you really need to find." Johann paused. "I think you need a woman in your life."

Schrock's eyes opened wide as he reacted to Johann's statement. Schrock thought of something else to say. "I wonder—," but he found his mouth unable to form the words. His eyelids drooped and then they slid shut. His mind saw a woman reach out toward him. He fell asleep with an indistinct image of Uilani Braden.

Schrock woke up later than usual at home the next morning. He sat at his table sipping coffee, trying to clear his head and summon the answers to solve the quandary of this wildly ambivalent woman—to understand what she wanted from him. It frustrated him when he realized that he wasn't going to be able to apply navigation or maritime engineering skills to the problem, their interactions not something he could touch or draw schematics to reflect on. It should be matter of fact, yet what they had was so… nebulous. It seemed like there was something that was directing him toward her and only her. Couldn't she tell? He was trying to show her how much he wanted her, in every way he could think of. She should be receptive to him or else clearly tell him to go away. Every time they were together she was elusive or unpredictable, signaling him one moment to come aboard and the next to stand off. She admitted being conflicted about him but that wasn't doing him any good. How long was he supposed to wait in her purgatory while she sorted through her feelings? He hadn't heard of this kind of torment from any of his friends or acquaintances. But then he'd never given much time to listen to that kind of talk before— talk he'd considered trivial.

It was midweek in Johann's library when Johann eyed Schrock accusingly. "It cost me, you know."

"What?" asked Schrock, still miserable because he had asked Uilani to a lunch later in the day and was confused why he had done it.

"This second meeting with Gibson," said Johann. "The information we wanted; it cost me. You remember I met the prime minister on the premise of assisting with the coronation, so it would have been completely faithless if I left without making a donation. But at least he was forthcoming about the statue. He was surprised that I was so interested until I told him the connection I had."

"So get to it."

"Well it turns out that this replacement statue was secured with an insurance policy the government took out on the original. The unveiling is to be a showpiece of the coronation. It will be erected in front of the Hall of Justice, across from the Palace." Schrock watched Johann pace around and talk faster than usual. "Even though the hundred-year anniversary of Cook's death is coming up, to Gibson's credit, it was his idea that a tribute should instead go to Kamehameha the Great. And it was Gibson who got the legislature to commission and fund the statue."

"I don't think I've seen you so excited," Schrock observed.

"It's because I assumed the statue was all King Kalakaua's doing," said Johann. "But Gibson put himself in charge of the statue committee in order to make it all happen. The King had plenty of input, but Gibson picked the sculptor and then oversaw the design and casting, from start to finish. Before it was shipped to Honolulu, he personally made sure they took out an extra insurance policy to cover the cost of a replacement, if anything were to happen to it in transit. Fascinating, wouldn't you say?"

"If you say so, but how does that relate to what we know?" asked Schrock.

"First of all, I didn't know Gibson was so involved with the statue," said Johann. "Secondly, he mentioned there were unusual circumstances surrounding the sinking of the ship that carried the original statue. But he didn't say what the circumstances were. I think he wanted to imply that antagonists in his political opposition had something to do with the sinking. So after the meeting, I asked him what he meant by 'unusual circumstances'. He was hesitant to tell me anything at first. But when I told him about you, and that I had been on the *G.F. Haendel* through the whole disaster in the Falklands, that got his interest."

Schrock's brow furrowed. "I'm sure it did. But what has you so worked up?"

Johann stopped pacing and looked directly at Schrock. "He told me he had been warned by a native Hawaiian legislator that there were rumors a *kahuna* sorcerer would make sure the metal image of Kamehameha would never make it to Hawaii."

"What?" blurted Schrock.

"Understand this, my friend," Johann went on, "Gibson said the legislator heard this well before the *Haendel* left Bremerhaven or sank in the Falklands."

The worry lines in Schrock's face deepened. "This sounds more than coincidental with what Kaole told us, wouldn't you say?" He got up and stared out a window facing the bay.

"Here's the most intriguing part," Johann said, his voice rising. "I told him about our conversations with Kaole and Nakea, although I didn't tell him their names. But I also told him about Naholehua, the *kahuna 'ana'ana* who Kaole said carried out the sorcery to sink your ship. As soon as I said his name to Gibson, his gray face lit up like a torch. That name really astounded him."

"Why?" Schrock asked, now rapt.

"Because Gibson said he spent his first years in here as a Mormon Elder on the island of Lanai. While he was there he met this very same Naholehua, knew his reputation and said he even naively tried to convert the man to Mormonism. He later heard Naholehua moved to Molokai. He told me Molokai is where this practice of *'ana'ana* sorcery has always flourished."

Schrock rumpled his hair. "Well, that fits with what we learned about Molokai from Nakea."

"Unfortunately Gibson had another meeting, so we had to cut our conversation short," said Johann. "But he told me he would like to meet with you again, realizing you are the captain of the ship that went down with his statue. He didn't say his statue, but it's what he meant. He wants to discuss all this with us. If you're agreeable, I've arranged for us to meet with him. He'll let me know when he has time."

"He's made a good case for me wanting to talk with him. But now I have to leave."

CHAPTER 25

Uilani had agreed to meet Schrock for lunch at a small eatery near the docks that was open on Sundays and always served fresh fish.

"I do like this fish, Captain Schrock. Dorado, Mahi Mahi, it's always good if it is prepared right. They know how to do it here, with ginger."

"I come here often because it is so close to work and my apartment. Whatever the fish of the day, it has always been excellent." To Schrock's dismay, that burst of conversation was followed with silence as they ate.

Schrock decided to take a risk. "When we are done eating, Miss Braden, if you don't mind, I would like to walk over to the docks and show you where I work, explain a little about what happens. How would you like that?"

Uilani's face showed indifference as she looked up from her plate. "I suppose we could do that."

"I assume you have been out on the docks before?"

"Yes, at times, to see someone off."

When they left the restaurant, they walked the block to the quay and out onto the main dock. The smell of fish remains and detritus in the water mixed with sweet ocean breezes. "This is where I spend a good part of my day," he said, nodding his head to an open-front office shed at the head of the dock. "I manage cargo shipments of four different shipping companies and others on occasion. There is a lot that comes and goes through here—more companies and ships than just the ones I work with. Honolulu has become one of the busiest ports in the Pacific. Sugar and rare woods out, everything else in."

"I'm impressed. Is this more work than being captain of a ship?"

"Yes and no. It is more constant when I am working, but then I get the whole night off, and Sundays. On board a ship, I was on call day and night the entire voyage, which could be as long as six months. Of course there was some relief from the first and second mates—four hour periods of sleep when they each had the watch, except in heavy weather, emergencies or coming into port."

"I'm not sure I would like sleeping in those conditions."

"I got used to it. I think all sailors do—you have to. And one more thing: at sea I had the final say about everything that happened on board. Here, those same ships' captains and pursers feel free to argue with me when they please. That has been a big adjustment—harder work."

Uilani just nodded her head, appearing to know what he was getting at.

They walked further out onto the docks, past a number of ships at berth. Schrock stopped. "This ship, this is a bark, like the one I sailed that burned and sank. It is about the same size and deck plan. I watched it come in yesterday. It makes me feel strange to look at her."

"Yes, Captain Schrock, you seem more uneasy than I've seen you before." She glanced up and down the dock at the other ships. "Now I think I have seen as much as necessary. We should go." She turned and headed back down the dock, not waiting for his response.

He stood there still staring at the ship. He finally realized what she had said and looked over his shoulder to see her at a brisk pace twenty yards down the dock.

CHAPTER 26

March 1882

It was a few days later when Schrock heard the news. He was headed back from checking on a sugar cargo bound for California when Kaole approached him with a mischievous grin.

"Kamehameha find his way. His statue on a ship over there," the young *kahuna* in waiting said without introduction, pointing out past a tangle of ships' masts.

The words jolted Schrock. "You're joking, Kaole."

"No, Captain. I'm not making a joke. We told you."

"Which statue?" Schrock demanded, puzzled by what his Hawaiian friend was saying. What ship?"

"That one was on your ship, Captain. It's on a ship named Earl... Earl Duh... something hard to say." The side of his mouth twisted as he tried to recollect the name.

"How do you know it's the same statue?" asked Schrock.

"I know—I saw it on the deck. He look Hawaiian, like *ali'i* warrior. I went on board and asked. A sailor told me that ship came from the Falkland Islands. He told me the statue was pulled out of the sea over there."

Schrock shook his head, skeptical.

"Nakea told us," Kaole said with conviction, "Kamehameha would find his way back home."

Schrock exhaled deeply. "I'll be damned on judgment day, Lincoln Kaole. This is some news you are giving me. Nakea did say that all right, except, if it's really the original statue, and it's here on Oahu, I guess it still needs to make it to Kohala, doesn't it?"

"That what I thinking already, how that's gonna happen." Kaole's face said it all for Schrock—a reminder that he and Johann could have a role in seeing the statue made it to Kamehameha's birthplace.

"I still can't believe how this could have occurred," said Schrock, mystified. "Sorry, I shouldn't be saying that. I'll go see it today. Thank you, thank you for telling me. And please tell Johann when you go back to the office."

"Yeah, you know I will, Captain. And I gonna tell Nakea when I can. But he probably already know. *Aloha*."

Schrock was both stunned and curious to distraction about Kaole's information. This was about the only thing that could compete with his single-minded thoughts about Uilani. He hurried to finish his work, having a hard time focusing on his tasks. He checked to find out about where a ship named "*Earl* something" was moored. He discovered it was the *Earl of Dalhousie*, with British papers. He left early and made his way along the wharf to find the ship while trying to sort out how the statue could have been salvaged, and then wind up here. What were the chances this would happen? After the *Haendel's* destruction, he had wanted nothing more to do with the wreck—to be through with it all and move on. Any salvage to be done was someone else's business. But after arriving in Hawaii, he'd had a few regrets about not making an attempt to salvage the statue when he was still in the Falklands. And then he would remember he wasn't in a state of mind to do much more than finish the enquiry and get out of there. He suddenly realized it had been just over a year since his arrival in Honolulu.

He tried to finish up his work but couldn't keep his mind off Kaole's revelation. As Johann kept telling him, his life seemed to have become entangled with this bronze figure. The more he learned about Kamehameha, the more his appreciation grew for what the king had done. After nearly a thousand years of tribal warring, the unification of this island nation had profoundly changed its fabric. There was a reason for this monarch's consecrated memory for Hawaiians. He symbolized their land and way of life... now being taken over by the Europeans and Americans. In exchange they had brought killing diseases like cholera, influenza, syphilis and tuberculosis, and were taking their land and culture. Uilani had reason to feel as strongly as she did, including the feeling she might have about him.

With the appearance of the statue here, he had to think there might be some truth to Johann's words about what had taken place. Whether there was anything to First Mate Deetjen's religious dread of carrying a pagan god, or that a sorcerer had tried to pray down his ship because it carried Kamehameha's *mana*, his life was on a different course.

Unable to do anything else, he locked up his books and headed out to the dock. He spotted the *Earl of Dalhousie* gold lettering on the stern of the aging four-masted bark he was looking for and walked up the gangplank. As he stepped onto the deck, he leaned back on the rail, immobilized, unprepared to see the exposed statue lashed to the mast of this other ship. It was disorienting to see it here, despite what Kaole had told him. The bronze sculpture was tarnished and broken, and from his vantage point, the lifelike eyes of Kamehameha's image seemed to be gazing at him. The disquiet emanating from the face through those eyes was unsettling. He had the same feeling he'd had as a child when he saw Jesus looking down on him from a cross at St. Johns Church in Bremen. He clearly remembered what his first reaction had been when his mother walked him up the long aisle of the vast parish, trying to avoid looking up: 'I didn't do it' he'd repeated to himself. That was the unlikely purpose of what his mother had in mind when she took him in there on that visit. But in this case, it could well be said that he 'did' do it.

Eventually a lone ship's watch inquired what his business was. After saying he wished to speak with the shipmaster, Schrock was ushered into the young Captain Jarvis's cabin.

"Captain Schrock, is it?" asked Jarvis, repeating the name told him by the ship's watch. "Welcome. What can I do for you?"

"Thank you for seeing me, Captain. I'm here about the statue on deck."

"It's for sale if you're interested. But you may have to bid against the government. I've sent word through my purser to the king's offices."

"I'm not interested in buying the statue so much as I am in finding out how you knew to bring it here. You see, the statue was part of the cargo of my ship that went down in the Falklands. I was the captain of the *G.F. Haendel*."

"Aha, it was your ship that carried it," said Jarvis.

"Yes," said Schrock, "and since it had been shoved overboard before the ship burned and sank, I'm also very curious as to how it was found and came into your possession."

"I'm sorry for your loss, and, well, it's a bit of a story," replied Jarvis. "But I'd be glad to tell it to you, and if you're comfortable in doing so, I'd like to hear more about how it was your ship went down and how it is you're here now."

"Fair enough, Captain," replied Schrock.

Jarvis poured brandies and a half hour later, as they exchanged their stories in Jarvis's cabin, Schrock was able to laugh as Jarvis told him how the Azorean immigrants had been scared by the statue.

"I only laugh," said Schrock, "because it was the superstitious fears of my first mate that made him push the statue into the sea. If he hadn't, it would have burned in the fire, probably turned it into scrap metal. And you would never have found it for sale on the beach that day."

"I guess you're fortunate that it was even salvaged," said Jarvis. "An old man who ran the salvage yard told me that a port pilot named Radcliffe who does salvage part time was the one who pulled it up. He somehow knew where to look for it, since it wasn't with the shipwreck."

"Hell, not that weasel, Radcliffe!" exclaimed Schrock. "I remember him. I never thought he'd have the skill or equipment to do it. Bumped into him in a tavern in Stanley, the same day he pulled that piece of information from one of my crew." Schrock suddenly remembered 'crow-face's' look when the pilot had heard the inebriated Kullrich mention where the statue had been shoved overboard further offshore.

"Well, according to the old man, this Radcliffe must be more of a salvager than you thought. He has the latest Deane's diving helmet and suit, and he rented a big enough barge to pull up the statue once he dived down and tied it off with lines. The problem is, they buggered it up more trying to get it onto my ship."

"I'll be damned," said Schrock, shaking his head.

"It's all quite a story, isn't it?" said Jarvis with a smile. "It had better be worth the trouble for me to bring it here."

"It's been both a curse and a strange sort of blessing for me," said Schrock. "I hope you get a good price for it. You know, there is a replacement replica that's been commissioned for Honolulu. So that will affect the price you'll get for this one. But whatever happens, I'd like to see this sculpture end up where a lot of Hawaii natives would like it, near this king's birthplace on Hawaii Island."

"I wouldn't know about that. What worries me is who will have enough money to meet my price," shrugged Jarvis.

Schrock stood up and moved toward the cabin door. "I can get word to the chair of the legislature's statue committee. He's the prime minister, a man named Gibson. He will likely be the person still interested in the statue. Maybe I'll get to him sooner than your purser."

"Thank you, Captain. I would appreciate your help in the matter. It's been a pleasure." As Schrock left Jarvis's cabin, he paused for another look at the statue before heading down the gangplank. A shiver coursed through his body as he took in the object that had woven its way into his life. It didn't escape him that the king's eyes still followed him.

At the prime minister's office, Walter Murray Gibson asked for clarification from Schrock about what Schrock had just said. "But that's not due to arrive from Europe for at least another four or five months." Gibson was distracted, as they stood in his office foyer, acting is if he had other pressing business.

"This is not the replacement statue," Schrock explained again in his shipboard captain's voice. "It is the original statue, the one that was on my ship."

"How could that be?" Gibson sounded confused. "You yourself told me that the original was at the bottom of the sea somewhere off the Falkland Islands."

"I just told you. It was salvaged."

Schrock finally convinced Gibson to accompany him to the dock. Ten minutes later, while on the walk toward the wharf, Schrock filled Gibson in on the story he had heard from Captain Jarvis. As they reached the end of the dock, the statue-committee chairman's jaw dropped as he caught sight of the towering statue. He appeared as awestruck as Schrock had been at his first sight of it. "This is quite remarkable," Gibson mumbled. They boarded the *Dalhousie* and, alerted by the ship's watchman again, Captain Jarvis appeared and was introduced to Gibson by Schrock. Jarvis steered the men over to the statue.

"It's in good condition, given what it has been through," said Jarvis, quickly assuming a salesman's role.

The wily Gibson, dressed immaculately and somewhat out of place for the setting, slowly walked around the statue several times, carefully surveying its condition. "The right hand is broken off, the spear is broken, and the cape has a hole in it," Gibson stated matter-of-factly. More than twice Jarvis's age, the articulate minister's words flowed confidently. "Moreover, the finish has suffered dreadful damage." He walked around it several more times. "The gold leaf is worn away—a very expensive repair I might add. It looks nothing like it should. You understand, we have a beautiful new replacement coming soon, so this has little value to us now."

Schrock could tell by Jarvis's face that Gibson's tactics were working. Jarvis tried his best to counter Gibson's objections by listing all the time and costs he had incurred in getting the statue back to "those in the government who commissioned this fine work of art." Captain Jarvis was no match for the elder statesman's negotiating skills. And Gibson was his only likely buyer, other than perhaps a scrap dealer. In the end, the young captain agreed to eight hundred and seventy-five dollars in payment, offered by Gibson on behalf of the Hawaiian Government.

The two men shook hands and Gibson promised to bring the money and a crew the next day to unload the statue. After Gibson left to return to his office, Schrock stayed on to talk more with Jarvis.

While Jarvis made arrangements about the statue with his purser, Schrock couldn't keep from staring at the statue. It had been such a curse. But now, clearly looking at the image of Kamehameha, he was finding it enigmatic and promising at the same time. He wondered if the warrior king was saying something to him. For a moment, his mind tussled with these absurd notions. Jarvis's grumbling jolted him out of the reverie.

"I expected to get a lot more for my trouble," Jarvis complained. Then Jarvis's tone changed as he made an attempt to salvage his pride. "But it's a nice bonus over what I got from the plantation bosses for delivering the immigrants." He gave Schrock a roguish look. "Captain Schrock, I do believe it's time to celebrate. If you would be so kind as to lead us to the nearest establishment that provides quality spirits, I will be pleased to buy you a drink."

CHAPTER 27

Captains Schrock and Jarvis stepped down the *Dalhousie's* gangplank onto the worn, splintered dock. "We'll go to my favorite tavern," said Schrock. "It's only a short way uptown. We can get something to eat there as well."

The two men had downed two ales apiece in a dark corner of the decades-old Posner's Inn on Alakea Street and now sipped brandies after finishing their dinner. Jarvis put his empty glass back on the table.

"Schrock, you've given me a better opinion of that damned statue. I've more knowledge about it than I ever wanted to find out." He looked down at his folded hands on the table. "But what you've told me about the history of this king makes me concur with your sentiments—this statue needs to set near this warrior's birthplace. We can only hope Mister Gibson or the current King Kala-something will decide to make it happen."

"King Kalakaua." Schrock twirled the remainder of his brandy. "Since I've come here, I've found out how complex things are between Europeans and the natives. And from one day to the next, it's hard to tell what will happen with the government or the monarchy. But it's clear to me that foreigners have the upper hand in nearly everything."

"Are we not bringing them progress?" Jarvis asked.

"Maybe, but along with commerce we've probably brought a lot more misery." When Jarvis had no response, Schrock wondered what the captain was thinking. "I can only hope we will at least let people here honor their heroes the way they want to."

Jarvis's smile spread on his face again. "Well, between the both of us sailors, I think we've given the ancient king a hell of a ride to get him this far, wouldn't you say?"

Schrock, somewhat appreciative of seeing a measure of humor in the whole affair, gave him a tip of his glass.

Jarvis held his glass out toward Schrock. "I know it's not kind of me to say, what with you losing your ship and more, but at least on my voyage I made some profit off their famous king."

Schrock touched his glass to Jarvis's. "Here's to your success. And don't feel sorry for me, Captain. I've somehow landed on my feet and learned a few things along the way. As it is, I just might have discovered that I'm done with life on the sea."

Jarvis's eyebrows rose. "I find that hard to believe, Captain."

"Yes, I'm probably through with it. I've had a few more years at sea than you to get to this point. Losing a ship can change you. And you must know by now that being alone is wearing. Me, I'm at the point I can't be without a wife anymore. And if I find one, I surely won't want to be away from her for years at a time." The image of Uilani and how much he ached for her flashed through his mind.

"I understand all that," responded Jarvis, "but I'm a few more years out before getting caught up in marriage. I need to have a decent purse before I even start looking for a wife. And right now, I can't imagine leaving the sea life, married or not."

"You'll do well, I'm sure," said Schrock. "You seem well suited for it."

"It has been a pleasure to eat and drink with you," Jarvis said, pushing his chair back from the table. "I'll be getting back to my ship to start readying her for the next leg."

Schrock pressed himself up from the table. "Godspeed," he said, as Jarvis turned to leave. "Look for me next time you're here."

Schrock felt a pang of envy. Jarvis held one of the elements missing in his life now: the unquestioned authority that comes with being master of a ship.

Schrock didn't want to return to his apartment yet. He knocked on Johann's front door and was let in by Johann's daughter.

Johann came out of his library. "What brings you here this fine evening?" he asked, ushering Schrock into the parlor. "I would guess it's about the bronze king. Kaole told me your statue turned up on a ship down at the docks. I went down to look at it before I came home. Quite a sight to see, after we've spent so much time talking about it."

"It's astonishing," said Schrock, "especially after everything that's happened. It's still mystifying to me what Nakea said—that Kamehameha would find his way back home. I'm becoming humbled by this old man and his seeming clairvoyance."

"So what will happen with this statue?" Johann asked.

"I went to Gibson's office to tell him it was there. He wasted no time getting to the ship and bought it from the ship's captain, on behalf of the government, he said. I was with him when he saw that it was damaged. So I think the government or the king will wait to see if the replacement arrives before they decide what to do with this one."

"If they can't figure out what to do with it, I definitely think you should buy it," Johann said, his face not giving away his intent. "You could place it right outside your front door, if you ever settle down enough to have a house of your own. It would be like family."

Schrock threw Johann a forced smile. "While you are occupied mixing me my drink, I'm going to grant you the ability to be serious for a minute." He paused to consider what he was going to say. "I have been spending more time seeing Doctor Ferguson's assistant."

Johann stopped in the middle of his task, his eyes fixed on the glass. "I'm listening."

"It's like this," began Schrock. "First of all, my social life is drinks and conversation with you and occasionally some of the dockmen. And then I read. I've been through half of your library and now been forced into reading books in English, for God's sake."

Johann smirked. "Well, even the British and a few Americans have several smart things to say."

"Not enough for me. Listen, you do remember my telling you about meeting her at Queen's Hospital?"

"Of course, but knowing how sensitive you are to these matters, I've held my tongue and didn't ask you about her, even though I wanted to. I knew you were really taken by her."

"Her name is Uilani, Uilani Braden, and I've been trying to see her as often as I can manage."

Johann's face didn't hide his smile. He handed the drink to Schrock. "You didn't tell me much more than you were going to have lunch with her."

"Well, I did, and it's more than that. She's nearly all I think about now. But I've probably made a total mess of it."

"And how have you done that?"

"She's let me see her a number of times, but it's been slow going. She feels like she is drawn to me for some reason she doesn't understand, that there's some connection. She's mixed race: her father Irish and her mother Hawaiian. But at the same time, she regards herself as more Hawaiian and doesn't think she could ever have a lasting relationship with someone who's not at least part Hawaiian. It's put me on my heels."

"So how have you handled it?" asked Johann.

"I just wasn't prepared. It's something I've never had to think about before. I just thought... I don't know what I thought. I guess I assumed because she was well educated and her father Irish that she'd be interested in a European like me. Schrock looked around the room and shook his head. The two men were both quiet for a moment. "The last time I saw her I think I got desperate, told her that maybe if she spent more time with me she could accept her Irish side as much as her Hawaiian side."

"Hmmm."

"I know, it was the wrong thing to say. Not only didn't she like my suggestion but she gave me a swift lesson about the Hawaiian people being dismembered by *haoles* since the time of Cook's arrival here."

"All true. Are you still treating those bruises?" said Johann.

"Not amusing."

"Listen, we all make mistakes," Johann said, as he finished mixing his own drink, "although that may have been... well, a rather critical one if you were trying to change her mind."

"Yes, you're right. I got on the horse backwards."

"This is what I think. I've not met her and hate to second guess your heart, but perhaps it's best," said Johann. "It makes one wonder if you came down the wrong chute when you were born. So given what you are, you might have an easier time of it all around if you found a European or an American woman and didn't have to confront these... what shall we call them... cultural impediments."

"Damn, Johann, don't be an ass. That's not the issue. She is extraordinary, maybe the whole reason I was supposed to come to Hawaii. I expected to tell you more about her someday, and what it is about her—." He laid his head down on the table between his forearms. "I still would like to... I really do want to change her mind."

Johann pulled himself out of his chair and moved over to the sideboard to mix another drink. "I'm sorry, Schrock. She's obviously important to you. This has to be difficult. What can I say? Those things I just said: that was my mother talking again."

CHAPTER 28

Naholehua again questioned Makia as the three of them sat on the ledge near the water. "You been watching that captain for days; you must have found out something useful by now."

"Yeah, we did. Besides that *hapa* woman he goes to the park with, Palmele sometimes was following that *kanaka* boy," replied Makia, "the one who the captain talks to a lot. Today that *kanaka* walks way out to a ship moored at the end of the pier that has something big on the deck, and when he goes on board and talks with the watchman, Palmele thinks that thing might be the statue, that somehow it got here. So he tells me about it." Palmele affirms this information with eager nods of his head.

"Yeah, I go out and look at it and I'm sure it was the Kamehameha statue on that ship. It looked like it been in the water a long time and maybe got broke a little. It's very big," continued Makia, not wanting to admit to his stepfather that he is excited about the discovery but that it also affected him in a way that left him worried and with strange sensations in his body when he was near it. Right away he watched Naholehua nearly explode in anger. The old man shook his head back and forth, looking as if wanted to kill the messengers, and then lumbered away from their fire, cursing and spitting. After he was gone a while, he returned, seeming to be reinvigorated, motioning for Makia and Palmele to watch while he drew a ship in the sand and what he wanted them to do.

"This Kamehameha image did not burn out there at sea and I have seen it coming up out of the sea and being brought here by this other ship. Now we have another opportunity to destroy it by fire it as sits on that ship. We must act quickly before it is moved. You two must go tonight and put that ship in flames and see that the statue burns with it. This is our chance to right what is wrong."

Like a flash of sunrise inside his head, the recognition of what Naholehua had just said woke up Makia. Why else had the old man been so infuriated when they told him about this ship? His stepfather had a chance to destroy the statue but he had somehow been foiled by this other sorcerer and could not admit it. Or worse, he fell out of his soul sleep because he'd had too much *awa*—which had been happening more in the last year. He'd failed to take care of it when it was out at sea, was covering up his mistakes, and now he wanted them to do his dirty work. Maybe it was during the time he got so sick, it looked like he was near death. He was also lying; he had never really seen the statue being taken out of the water and making its way to *Hawaii nei*. He was losing his gift to see, throwing it away piece by piece every day. It was depressing to think what this meant for him and Palmele, to be apprenticed to such a moldering and dangerous *kahuna*.

Makia's thoughts were shaken at Naholehua's haggard voice. "We'll find some burning wax for you to take. You need to leave before the sun sets." Makia heard an unmistakable order rather than a request, one that if resisted implied dark consequence.

About two in the morning, Makia and Palmele reached Honolulu harbor and made their way out toward the quay. Palmele stayed behind as a lookout at the head of the dock where the *Dalhousie* was moored. There was no one on the dock as Makia moved toward the ship. It was quiet except for some sailors reveling on another ship anchored further out in the bay. Nearing the *Dalhousie* he quickly saw a problem. The ship's large mooring fenders would keep it too far a reach from the dock for him to press the flammable wax onto the side of the ship. He would have to go on board. He'd never done anything so risky. Bile began to flow in his stomach and sweat ran down his temples. At this moment, he would rather try to kill Naholehua than go through with this, but a dead *kahuna* master wouldn't help him reach his goal. He had to do this. He crept low along the dock, sweating profusely. He stood up briefly and saw no one on the deck of the ship. His heart pounding, he lowered his head and slinked up the gangplank to the top. Keeping an eye out for any crew, he hurried to midships where the statue stood and glanced up at its piercing eyes lit by a deck lantern.

He was sure he felt its presence course through his body. Could it be true? *Yes,* he thought. *The king's mana was in this image. Don't look up at those eyes again, those eyes that were seeing inside of him.*

He pressed wax into a wooden crate near the base of the statue and lit it with a match. It flared up. He walked as lightly as he could to the stern and pressed wax around the base of the wheel helm. After that he headed to the gangplank and lit a fire next to it for good measure. Then he heard the noise behind him and quickly looked over his shoulder to see a watchman coming back out on deck. When the sailor spotted the flames he ran straight at Makia and the gangplank, belaying pin in one hand and Enfield pistol in the other.

"You savage bastard!" he yelled, "What the hell are you doing?"

Makia bolted and turned at the same time, tripping and tumbling backwards down the gangplank. He heard a blast of the pistol and felt the shot as it passed by his ear. The fall likely saved his life. On the dock he jumped up running, the darkness obscuring the watchmen's aim as more shots flew by Makia, pinging the dock boards and bollards. The yelling and shots continued, and he ran as fast as he'd ever run, down the dock and past Palmele, who didn't need to be told that he should run too. They ran, heard the ship's bell clanging, and Makia knew that meant the watchman had probably returned to the ship to roust whatever crew was aboard to put out the fires. Even though his legs and arms were pumping and he gasped for breath, the awareness of failure set over him as if he were in quicksand that was sucking his body uncontrollably down, and all he could do was flail his arms and scream.

An hour later, making their way back to Kaiena's, Makia pictured Naholehua's dark and accusing eyes as he would hear what happened. He feared his *kahuna* stepfather now more than he ever had. At the same time a rival feeling was a loathing for Naholehua so intense he found it hard to express. That his mother continued to be married to this man made it confusing. What was it about him that she kept on with him? Did she fear him and not show it? She would never tell Makia when he would hint at that notion, or when he said that Naholehua wasn't good enough for her. She would just laugh at him and tell him it wasn't his trouble.

After they had eaten and gone down by the water again, Makia and Palmele were surprised when they told Naholehua and he didn't fly into a rage. His eyes burned with fury but he didn't berate them like he usually did. It was as if he had predicted this might happen.

"You know you are not done with this," he said, searching their eyes in the torchlight, "and it will be more difficult now. The police will be watchful for a native fire starter. But you will have to find out where the statue will go next. You need to watch the dock and wait for it to be unloaded and then follow it to wherever it is taken. You cannot fail again. How can this be so difficult? Be there early tomorrow. It is a matter for eternity."

Makia couldn't help thinking that if Naholehua were such a great *kahuna 'ana'ana*, why couldn't he get into a sailor's head on that ship and make him cause a fire? Or just pray to death these people who get in our way? It was a stupid thought, one that he already knew the answer to.

As dawn broke and the harbor came to life, Makia and Palmele stationed themselves at opposite ends of the quay where they could observe any cargo movement on the *Dalhousie*. They both tried not to look suspicious, a tricky undertaking since nearly everyone else seemed to have a purpose for being at the harbor, doing one task or another. Makia cursed his *kahuna* stepfather again. It was hard not to think that the man was leading him to die or to jail chasing this statue. How will he ever gain this man's power if this discouraging quest goes on?

Not more than an hour later, Makia and Palmele saw a crew of men with a large horse-drawn platform dolly being pulled along the dock to the *Dalhousie*. They watched another two hours of unloading until the statue, now shrouded in canvas and sitting on the dolly, was pulled by the horses back down the dock. The two of them followed at a distance, aware that the statue was now accompanied by two policemen. It was a slow, seven block journey for the statue, with plenty of onlookers trying to discern what might be under the tall shroud. Some called out to ask policemen and the crew but their calls were ignored. When the statue arrived at a foundry, it took another hour to unload it into the building. Makia and Palmele waited until everyone was gone before they dared to venture past the foundry on the other side of the street, taking sidelong glances to see what it would take to set the building on fire so it would burn down.

CHAPTER 29

Schrock stood in his covered stall, shaded from the mid-afternoon sun, signing a bill of lading and handing it to a ship purser. As his client walked away, men descended down a gangway from a ship that had docked down the quay minutes earlier. He continued working through the papers in front of him, occasionally glancing up at the men passing by him. But the irony of seeing someone you don't expect, someone who looks a lot like Ludwig Deetjen, was jarring, especially when he realized that it was him, in the flesh. "Mister Deetjen!" he called out. "Over here!"

The first mate came to attention at the sound of his perpetual captain and quickly walked over, appearing just as amazed to see Schrock. Schrock could hardly believe his eyes, not really imagining he'd ever see his first mate again, even though working where he was it would be plausible, since mariners came and went all the time.

"Mister Deetjen! Hello, it is good to see you."

"Hello, sir. I didn't know if I'd really find you here. So soon—this is something. I'm pleased to see you again, and praise the Lord I'm off that barge they told me was a ship. You wouldn't believe how slow we were."

"Did you get an officer berth coming here? You're here on layover?"

"No, sir, Captain," said Deetjen, lowering his eyes to the planks under his feet. "I came on passage. It's... well, I thought more about what you said about working as a landsman. And I've come looking for work, like you seem to have done."

"I'll be damned to hell!" Shrock caught himself. "Sorry, Mister Deetjen. What I meant is it's very good you came. I told you you needed to see what it's like to be off the decks and out of the brine.

And now here you are. Don't worry, Mister Kessler and I can help you out. You'll do well here." Schrock considered what a man as rigid as Deetjen must have gone through to make such a change—and then actually pay passage to come. "We'll have to talk more about how you arrived at your decision. But what's most important now is that we get you an adequate room and good food. You'll be glad to know Honolulu has enough of both."

Schrock could see former First Mate Ludwig Deetjen had yet to give up his personal dress code. He still wore the mate's cap and military style jacket. The tropical heat caused sweat to trickle down his cheeks. Schrock realized that his own dress code had loosened since his arrival in the Hawaiian Kingdom. For daily wear he'd abandoned most of his wool clothes for cottons, except for a silk jacket tailored in a Chinese shop, worn at work.

Schrock scribbled on a piece of paper. "Look, here's a good boarding house. It's only about four blocks from here. Head down that street and ask anyone for directions. Go get yourself cleaned up and when I get off work at six bells, I'll come by and fetch you so we can go for dinner."

"Thank you, sir. I could use cleaning up and some fresh food. And sir, I have to say, you look to be of very good health, sir." An inexact smile creased Deetjen's face as he nodded and began to walk away, tote in hand. "Mister Deetjen. I forgot to mention. I have some surprising new about that statue you cared so much about. I'll tell you when we dine."

The next day, Schrock was in Johann's office before he went to his own job. "I had to let you know who showed up yesterday: First Mate Deetjen."

"He's here, in Honolulu?" Johann seemed amazed.

"As sure as I bow to you, and he's also looking for work that won't make him fish food on the sea floor. When we were still languishing back in Stanley, I put a worm in his ear about coming here. Apparently it grew to serpent size. I really didn't think he'd do it. I thought of him as a religious sailor for life, you know, the kind that comes out of a mold whose casting is permanent."

"How about your mold, Schrock—let me see, lost seeker and sailor?" Johann snickered. "Why in hell's name are you standing here now?"

"Okay, I can't predict everything. Occasionally some things elude me."

"Anyway, will you help me find work for him? He's a master of calculations and tables. I'm sure he could handle most office jobs—that is, if he can tolerate staying inside for long periods of time."

"Sure, I'll start asking around," said Johann. "Bring him by when you can so I can talk with him. I'll also ask Stina when might be a good time for him to join us for dinner."

"Thanks, my friend. I know he looked to be a broken man, but from my conversation with him, I think he may be on the mend."

"Wait here a moment. I think I have the card of a business associate I just thought of who might be a contact for work."

Schrock fingered through a book on Johann's study desk as he waited for Johann to return, then sat down hard in his favorite chair.

"So, Schrock, how is it going with Miss Braden?" Johann asked with a flourish as he returned and handed him the card. "You haven't said much about her lately."

"Not that I could tell you much. I don't know what's going on. I'm going crazy and not making any real headway. I think it's my fate, or comeuppance: something I hate to admit even to you." He studied his feet. "But I probably deserve it for how I treated Susan McGinnis." Johann stared at Schrock before saying anything.

"I am appalled at what you're saying, Captain Schrock. You of all people should have gotten beyond ideas like that. You have got to see your way through this without stumbling over misplaced guilt. Until she out and out rejects you, you have a chance with her. That is the natural order of things. Do you understand?"

"About as much as I understand multiple dimensions." Schrock gave him a mock salute. "I will give it a go, sir, and soldier on. But only because I'm under your orders."

"Thank you. And I expect you to keep me posted. Is that clear?"

"Rather. I'm having lunch with her today." He stood and opened the door to leave. "Maybe something will happen I can report, although I am more than doubtful."

"By the way, Schrock," Johann said just before the door closed, "you are going to introduce Uilani to me sometime, aren't you?"

"We'll see. When the time is right."

CHAPTER 30

Schrock met up with Uilani after work on a weekday evening, unusual for them since their times together had almost always been on Sundays. It took Schrock some time to convince her but she had finally agreed. After she had returned home and changed, he picked her up in a carriage that took them to a restaurant near the Royal Palace, one that Johann had recommended because he too would be there, hosting the two of them for dinner.

"If this is the only way I'm going to meet the lovely Miss Braden, then I'm pleased to have you as my guests this evening," Johann teased as he greeted them at a private table in the upscale restaurant, one of the few in Honolulu. "I'm very pleased to meet you, Miss Braden. Gerhard has spoken so highly of you."

"I'm pleased to meet you, too. Thank you for inviting us for dinner. It is very generous of you. And yes, I would guess that he has had some interesting things to say about me," she said, glancing at Schrock.

Schrock turned red but said nothing. After they were seated and had ordered their food, Johann asked Uilani about her work and then filled her in about his. They had all ordered different fish dishes and were working on their second bottle of white wine when Johann was bold enough to ask about Uilani's parents.

"Gerhard tells me your father was Irish. It happens that I've read a few Irish writers whom I liked, especially Jonathan Swift, because I learned satire in a way most Germans will never understand… and Thomas Moore as well."

Uilani's face showed interest. "My father was an avid reader and regularly brought home books for me. I've read some of both Swift and Moore. Moore's *Fudge Family in Paris* was nearly impossible for me to follow, but like you, I began to understand satire by getting interested in Biddy, the daughter who wanted to marry a commoner who she thought was royalty in disguise. All *kanaka* girls here think they want to be married to royalty but they rarely see the downside of that life."

"What could possibly be the downside, Miss Braden?"

"Why, always having to dress formally in uncomfortable clothing, to stay silent unless asked to speak, to be required to attend functions with stuffy people—not that I would ever have to worry about even being put in that situation."

Schrock was hearing more things and opinions from Uilani than in as many outings he'd had with her. What was it about Johann? "I've just met you," said Johann, "but I would say you have the makings of a royal should that be your desire. I know Mister Schrock believes as much." Schrock had never thought that for a second. Although he had wanted Johann to meet Uilani, he now wondered why he had allowed himself to go along with this formal occasion. His friend knew how shaky the relationship with her had been. Why was he leaving more rocks in the road?

"I wouldn't want her anywhere near royalty," corrected Schrock, aiming his words at Johann. "I like the person I see, without any of those trappings."

"I'm sorry, Schrock, I meant it more as a metaphor. But I shouldn't have assumed anything. As an aside, we German immigrants to the Kingdom are small in number here, but we stand in our support of the monarchy and against colonialism."

"You know, Mister Kessler, you remind me some of my father. He had a gift of talk and certain charm that made him very likable." The waiter served a dessert of pound cake with lillikoi compote topping, interrupting the conversation while they tasted their sweet course. "I was thinking about what you said," said Uilani. "You need to know that I am glad that Mister Schrock is satisfied with how I am. Don't get me wrong, though, I am a strong supporter of our king and all his efforts to restore the ways of the Hawaiian people. As much as I learned to love books, in many ways I prefer the oral traditions here. It is how all the history and culture of *Hawaii nei* has been carried down through the centuries. And my mother and her family were all wonderful storytellers. As Mister Schrock has already heard me say, my Hawaiian side calls out to me most."

"You have made that clear," Schrock said, doing little to disguise his irritation.

After that exchange, conversation for the remainder of the meal languished in the doldrums, small talk filling in the slow periods. When they had left the restaurant and Uilani was delivered to her home by carriage, it was Schrock who spoke first, over the sounds of the street traffic around them. "Well, Kessler, are you satisfied with your grand banquet introduction to Miss Braden? I appreciated the dinner but I'm not sure you did me any favors tonight."

"Thank you and yes, I am somewhat satisfied. I do like her. First of all, I would say that she is one of the most stunning women I've encountered in a long time. You have impeccable taste, my friend. Secondly, now I am at least more privy to what you've been up against. You have a challenge that is formidable... but not impossible. You are just as intelligent and capable as she is and she likely knows that. The fact that she continues to see you tells me she is still interested. You will need to determine what set of keys remain to unlock her heart. Although she is a force to be reckoned with, I am sure she has a warm heart, despite her ability to put on a cold front. What do you think?"

"You, Kessler, are an unremitting optimist."

CHAPTER 31

A week after Deetjen's arrival, Schrock met up with Johann for lunch to see how finding work was going for the first mate.

"You may well understand this, Schrock," said Johann, "Stina has taken a liking to Ludwig Deetjen, taking him under her protective wing as any good mother would a lost orphan."

"Likening him to an orphan is a bit demeaning. I know the man," replied Schrock.

"Well then, in this case, he's a stray who carries with him a fervent Lutheran bent that speaks to Stina's conventional values. And she has felt it was her place to introduce him to Honolulu while he waits to find employment and more permanent rooming. I'd have to say they are like birds of a feather. I don't remember seeing the man ever speaking that much on our entire voyage. Their finding affinity in the fear of God and adherence to the Lutheran way must be pleasing bishops somewhere."

Schrock rolled his eyes. "You know that may or may not serve him well in whatever employment he finds, depending on his employer."

When the occasion for a dinner arrived at the Kesslers with Deetjen and Schrock as guests, the smug look of a university lecturer came over Johann. "Actually, Captain Schrock, I think the timing of Mister Deetjen's arrival here was in Nakea's purview. I'm sure he's still looking out for your well-being and he means Mister Deetjen to be here, most likely to help you in some way."

Stina looked puzzled, but Schrock smiled and nodded, being on familiar terrain with Johann. "Johann seems to think that since we sailed from Bremerhaven, I've been under the protection of the man he's talking about, the *kahuna* wizard the two of us… how shall I say, have since encountered."

At the word 'wizard', Stina's head jerked back noticeably, although she said nothing.

"I think it's more that he planned our rendezvous," revised Johann.

"Hard as it is to for me to understand what all might have happened with Nakea, I admit I've built some respect for him," said Schrock. "Those things he supposedly did with my ship… if you think about it, he's had a lifetime of practice after having all this knowledge passed on to him from many generations of *kahuna* seers, healers and wizards who came before him. More and more, I wonder if he might actually be able to do some of these extraordinary things, moving about in his dreams."

"I, too, have begun to respect what he can do," said Johann. "That's why I think he's protecting you."

"Wait! Stop this talk!" cried Stina. "What did he do to your ship? And to you, Johann? Is this man a sorcerer?"

Johann looked at Schrock, biting his lip. "No, Stina, I don't think he should be called that, even though he may know how to do what they do. He's a *kahuna* seer, a dream interpreter, a kind of social healer for his people—and likely more things that we don't know about or understand."

"And like I said, it appears he is a dream traveler—or even interceder," explained Schrock.

"That's crazy talk," said Stina. "Don't you agree, Mister Deetjen?"

Ludwig Deetjen nodded.

"For the record, Schrock," said Johann, "I still have trouble envisioning the man moving through the ether in his dream-state undertakings, especially if he's making contact with us when he's doing that."

While Stina just shook her head, Schrock and Deetjen were quiet, apparently contemplating Johann's notion.

Then Deetjen spoke up, his demeanor brightening. "Haven't you had dreams you were flying, like a bird? What if they weren't just dreams? Wouldn't that be something? I would find it interesting to meet this man, this *kahuna*."

Everyone's attention was turned to Deetjen, who'd said so little up to that point. Not only that, Schrock thought it was out of character for him to say something so secular. Stina was now wide-eyed, looking at the three of them as if they might have all turned feral. Johann had told Schrock that as tolerant as Stina was, she wasn't one to give credence to such un-Christian practices as *kahuna* divining, healing, or anything that leaned in a direction the church considered sorcery. It was Deetjen's surprising statement which also caught Stina off guard. Meanwhile, Johann and Stina's two young daughters were taking in everything that was happening, their eyes darting back and forth between the speakers, apparently delighted to be allowed in the room for such unusual talk.

Schrock did his best to avoid Stina's look. "I would like Nakea to meet Ludwig," he said. "And if somehow we were able to pay him a visit again, it would give me a chance to ask him more about how or why I've become some kind of collaborator in his world."

"God have mercy on the lot of you," Stina said quietly, shaking her head and raising her face toward the ceiling. Johann held up his hands in surrender, long accustomed to hearing Stina's church-acquired condemnations.

"Remember when Kaole told us Nakea would ask us to come to his *hale* another time—to tell us more?" asked Schrock. "Maybe you could ask Kaole if that time has come."

Stina couldn't disguise how perturbed she was as the conversation between Johann and Schrock evolved more into speculation about whether *kahuna* mystics have any of the powers that may have affected them. She cut in, "The good Mister Deetjen had expressed an interest in taking an evening walk sometime while the air is fresher. I think this is just the time, and so if you don't have any objections, Johann, I'll go with him right now before it is too late. I'd like to point out a few of the evening sights just along the streets with gas lamps. I imagine we'll only go as far as the park and return. We shouldn't be long. Come, Mister Deetjen," she said, rising, as all the men stood in response.

Embarrassed by Stina's gesture, Deetjen looked over at Schrock and then Johann. Because it was more a declaration than an invitation, he didn't appear to have a choice unless Johann nixed the idea. Smiling, Johann said, "Have a nice walk, my dear. Don't be gone too long."

As an afterthought, Stina looked at her two daughters, who wore anxious expressions about what was transpiring in this evening of novelty. "Don't worry girls. Mister Deetjen will take good care of me. Johann, they should be off to bed soon."

Stina led an uncomfortable Deetjen out and onto the street. However, Schrock knew that by now his former first mate was feeling at ease with this woman who had been more than kind to him, and from what he'd shared in a conversation they'd had, she was certainly more understanding, if not forgiving, than his own mother had ever been. He had told Stina about the shipwreck that killed everyone but him and two others. She had listened with unusual sympathy and was genuine in her belief that God must have forgiven him for whatever responsibility he thought he might have had for that tragedy.

———————————

It was nearly two hours later when Stina burst through the door to the library with Deetjen in tow, excited and breathless. "You won't believe what happened to us!"

"What is it, my darling?" said Johann, alarmed. "You've been gone too long. You both look disheveled. We were becoming worried and were about to come looking for you. Here, have some water."

"Listen to this," Stina said as she caught her breath, both arms gesturing. "By the time we had walked several blocks down Ward Avenue, Mister Deetjen suggested that we divert off a side street to the foundry workshop where you had taken him to see your Kamehameha statue that's being repaired. He thought there might be enough light for me to see it through the windows." I thought it odd, but he said it was because, you, Captain Schrock, suggested that maybe he could better understand the statue as a venerated symbol to native people here in these islands."

"Yes, sir, I've been trying to let go of my conviction that the statue is a pagan god. I am really trying," interjected Deetjen.

"Hush now! We were very close when we saw the shadow of a figure down on his knees in front of the shop. When we got closer, we saw this man setting a fire. Mister Deetjen yelled and took off running toward him. The young man—he was a good-sized native man—stood up and came charging at Mister Deetjen. They crashed into each other and wrestled to the ground. As he was wrestling with this fool, he called to me to put out the fire. There was wax or something on some rags and sticks, so it flamed up quickly in the door portico. I took off my hat and filled it with dirt from a nearby street garden and threw it on the flames. I kept it up, doing it over and over, running back and forth as the two men struggled with each other. I needed Mister

Deetjen's help but he was having a tough go, still fighting with this man who looked very strong."

Deetjen nodded vigorously at everything Stina was reporting. "I was, for sure. He was a young brute, he was. I been sitting around too long with no work and I was feeling bested. But I just wanted to be able to make a citizen's arrest of this villain. All of a sudden, he did this move I'd never come across before in fights, where he flipped up onto his feet from his back. Then he came down hard on my head with his fists. I had to let go his legs, and he was off running like the devil he was."

"It was probably best," said Stina, "because Mister Deetjen was then able to help me put out the fire. Mister Deetjen had the good sense to yank a picket board off a nearby fence and use it to dig up soil from a garden that we loaded in our hats to put on that fire. I don't think we could have stopped it otherwise. When we finally extinguished it, we hurried down to the King Street Police Station and notified them of what had happened."

"Yes sir, I told them they ought to put a guard on that place, else that guy might try and burn it down again. Do you think it has something to do with the statue? I kind of have a notion it does."

"I'm certain your suspicion is correct, Mister Deetjen," said Johann. "If I were to guess, I'd say it was connected to a sorcerer named Naholehua, who did his best to burn the *Haendel* and sink it in the first place."

"And as I had just told Johann," said Schrock, "I recently heard a report that someone—probably this same fellow—tried to burn the ship that carried the statue as it was moored at docks."

"It all goes back to a wrong done to his family by Kamehameha. A never-ending need to settle scores," said Johann.

"I think that about sums it up," nodded Schrock, thinking it hardly summed it up at all.

Stina looked vexed. "What on earth have you men gotten yourselves mixed up in? You, Johann, you should know better."

CHAPTER 32

When Makia returned to Kaiena's place to report that he wasn't able to start the fire at the foundry, he quickly realized he'd put a match to the flames of malice at Naholehua's core, a sorcerer who unless he was shown another option, would now do his best to kill him as punishment, even though he was his stepson. Makia knew he was a long way from having the advanced skills to counter the *'ana'ana* that Naholehua would use to pray him to death, an infliction that would induce madness and pain into his dreams and waking hours, until he died a horrible, mind-raging death, a death that didn't have any visible signs of trauma or disease.

On his way back, he had steeled himself to the kind of abuse he would be facing on his arrival. He'd predicted correctly. Trembling with fury enhanced by his excessive *awa* drinking, Naholehua told him he was worth less than a dung fly and too childish to ever grow into a real man. As Naholehua continued to seethe, Makia knew that if he was to live through this he would need to convince his *kahuna* master that there was yet another way to destroy the statue. He hoped he had arrived at an idea that would appease this devil man.

Without looking over at Palmele, he pictured his cousin by marriage as his brother in blood. They had been first brought into a bond of *kahuna* apprentice secrecy. Now they had been thrown into unholy crimes that could put them both in jail for a long time. However, his little cousin might hold the key that would get him through this deep shadow of death that Naholehua threatened. Back when he was in school, his dodgy friend had an uncle who had worked on Maui where they blasted water tunnels. The uncle had learned to use dynamite and explained it all one day to his friend and Makia. The uncle had even stolen some blasting caps that they took out to a remote beach and exploded with stones. At the time, it had never occurred to him he would be using dynamite for anything—or could even have access to any. They needed dynamite, and Palmele's skill of getting into and through small spaces would be necessary for them to steal some.

Here in Honolulu, it seemed like everything was to be had. In their trips back and forth between Kaiena's at Niu Stream and Honolulu, they had passed over a place where a road crew had been blasting some lava rock with dynamite to build a bridge for the road, which up to now dipped down through the running water. Once they had been held back for an hour while the dynamiting took place, impressing them with the sound and shock wave they felt. As they passed by the work site, they had seen an enclosed wagon with *Danger/Explosives* painted red on the side. Makia also didn't fail to notice the one small window on the back, even though it had bars over it, which he knew shouldn't deter them. The other thought he had was they would need some light to search inside the wagon, but knew he couldn't use a lantern or torch. Yes, dynamite would be the best solution. Then finally he could get back to where he had intended to go with his life.

Naholehua had no reservations about their plan. To Makia, he seemed almost excited about the use of explosives, walking around mumbling with his face showing what could only be interpreted as a grin under the hollows of his dark eyes.

It was two in the morning with a three quarter moon when Makia and Palmele tied up the horse well off the road and walked by foot for the last quarter mile to the explosive storage wagon. Makia carried two critical items in a bag, a heavy metal pry bar and wrapping cloth. Palmele carried the small mirror. They sat and watched the area around the wagon for a long time to see if there was any movement or guarding of the site. When they approached slowly, the area looked abandoned. Makia checked the wagon door and could see that it would be impossible to break through. They quickly went to the wagon's window and surveyed how difficult it would be to break through. The bars over the small window were thick but rusty, as were the bolts that held them to the wagon. Makia pushed his pry bar between two of the crossbars and the wagon wall and began to pry. At first there was no movement. He took a breath and tried again, giving it all the muscle he could muster, feeling some give in one of the bolts. He repositioned the pry bar and tried again, then again. Pulling for ten minutes, until he thought he had strained all the muscles in his back and arms, the crossbars suddenly came loose with a near explosion as all the bolts on one end released at the same time. Between him and Palmele they were able to pry back the bars enough to create an opening, just wide enough for the wiry Palmele to slither through head first after Makia lifted him up. The young man thumped to the floor, hands-first to break his fall, knocking something off a shelf that held boxes, a clatter of noise. They both panicked and didn't move for minutes, but heard no reaction or shouts, so Palmele started his search, feeling around on the shelves. Makia had drawn pictures of dynamite sticks and blasting caps so Palmele would have a clear image in his mind of what he needed to find. Makia stood back from the window with the mirror, doing his best to catch the moon's reflection and aim it through the window to create some spears of light for Palmele.

After a while, Makia whispered through the opening, "You find the dynamite?" Just then he heard a rattling noise and something dropping to the floor of the wagon. Makia dropped to the ground in panic. His heart was pounding so hard it was the only thing he heard. Realizing there had been no explosion and that he might live, he got up slowly and put his mouth to the window. "You good? What happened?"

"No, I not good. I been crying. I'm scared, Makia. I knocked over something." There was a pause and Makia heard sniffling. "Yeah, I'm gonna feel to see what it is." Makia heard some soft shuffling noises. "I think it's those blasting caps. Here, I got some in my hands. Put your hand up to the window."

"Be careful, little brother."

CHAPTER 33

As they were walking, Schrock wondered to himself how the man with so many enemies still managed to hold the reins of political power. It was a weekday evening that Prime Minister Gibson had invited Johann and Schrock back for a meeting at his residence, several blocks away from the palace. By the time they arrived just before sunset, he felt the sweat that had built up under his shirt collar from the remains of the evening heat. Johann had said formal attire was expected in the home of the prime minister. He cursed his English suit, which he found little occasion to wear anymore, as did Johann.

The butler showed them to a dim room lit with chimney lamps. Moments later, Walter Gibson entered to greet them. Only a few pleasantries were exchanged before Gibson seated them and started asking questions, his intense, heavy-lidded gray eyes looking like a hawk in search of prey. "Captain Schrock, can I ask you what you think was responsible for the sinking of your ship and the subsequent loss of our Kamehameha statue?"

Schrock tried to speak in the same level voice he had used at the Falklands maritime inquiry, reciting for Gibson a short account of what had occurred. "Eventually the fire sank her and we lost all the cargo."

"I am sorry for the loss of your ship, Captain," Gibson said, his expression earnest. "After my conversation with Mister Kessler, I have a feeling there's more to learn about what happened."

Schrock frowned and glanced at Johann, trying to decide whether to say more. Johann nodded, giving him encouragement to go ahead. Schrock chose his words carefully. "What I don't know for sure, Mister Prime Minister, and I know this sounds crazy, is whether there was something extraordinary, some greater force responsible for the ship's demise, something that controlled the weather or the fire."

Johann spoke up. "We've been led to believe there may have been supernatural causes, that there were two *kahunas* who were possibly involved in this. It's beyond anything the captain and I are able to comprehend. But some of the facts we've heard give it some credibility."

"What facts, Captain?" queried the prime minister, staring at Schrock. "And you're both telling me there was more than one sorcerer in this?"

"We are. But we only speak in the greatest confidence about the *kahuna* we met with, because we gave our word not to speak of him. We don't want to expose him to any harm. However, we also know that you've been an advocate for native rights."

"You needn't worry, Captain," replied Gibson. "Your confidences will be kept. Native culture, in all its forms, has been suppressed too long. King Kalakaua and I are working hard to end that repression."

"This *kahuna*... let's call him 'Kahu'," began Schrock, "told his nephew about the ship's sinking long before word of the disaster could ever have reached these islands. It would have been impossible for him to have that information beforehand."

"It sounds like the foreshadowing I heard," said the prime minister.

"The difference was that the other sorcerer, Naholehua, was practicing *'ana'ana*," said Johann. "Kahu is a *kahuna kilokilo uhane*, a spirit diviner. His nephew told us Kahu is also able to counter *'ana'ana* sorcery. The native people from Kohala asked him to intervene against Naholehua's witchcraft. He claims to have done it by allowing the ship to reach safety before it burned and the statue was destroyed."

"So what happened?" asked Gibson.

"If we accept Kahu had that ability, somehow he made it work," said Schrock. "My crew and passengers were all able to safely disembark in the Falklands before the ship burned. As for the statue, in truth, some of my crew pushed it overboard into the bay before the ship burned and sank close to shore. Kahu claims to have had something to do with that as well. We thought the statue was somewhere out there in the deep. But then, of course, it was salvaged and brought here by Captain Jarvis on the Dalhousie."

Gibson looked uncomfortable as his eyes darted around the room. "Your story is remarkable, and a bit hard to take in." He sat down and studied his hands. "But for me, it confirms the warning I heard: that something would happen to the statue to keep it from ever getting to Honolulu. As I told Mister Kessler, even though your ship's owner presumably had insurance on all their cargo, that's why I still arranged to have the government take out an extra policy on the statue… as a precaution against the possibility of a loss that would not be covered."

Johann gave the prime minister an inquisitive look. "I find it interesting that at that time, before you knew any of this, you took out the policy because of a vague warning about an improbable event."

Gibson stood up and glared at Johann with an intensity that made Johann shrink back into his chair. "No, I didn't know of a specific threat then. But after you've lived many years among these people, as I have, you begin to believe. Despite my Christian faith, I make allowances for Hawaiian cultural practices. Just because we can't understand their beliefs, it doesn't mean that they aren't real or credible. If this Kahu of yours says this is what Naholehua was able to do to your ship, then I believe it could very well have happened. And do you know why? Like I told you, I knew about Naholehua. His sorcery was legend on Lanai. I personally knew of two cases of people who died at a very young age, of no apparent cause. And it was Naholehua who was reported to have killed them both by exercising 'ana'ana on them."

Gibson sat back into his chair as if exhausted. "What I don't understand is why this wretched little sorcerer did this?"

"Mister Prime Minister," Schrock said carefully, "there's something else we learned about Naholehua you might not have known. He's a descendent of King Kalanikupule, killed by Kamehameha's forces after the battle of Nuuanu. His family apparently has held a deep hostility these many years. They saw burning and sinking the ship as a way they could both avenge Kalanikupule's death and kill Kamehameha's spirit—by taking away the Conqueror's *mana*."

Gibson sat forward in his chair and cocked his head toward Schrock. "Well, that explains a lot, and I'm fairly certain it wasn't my political enemies who sunk the ship after all. Strange as it all is, in a way, that's a relief." He looked pensively at Schrock. "I'm sorry you were caught up in the middle of this, Captain."

"Believe me, I am too," said Schrock. It makes me wonder how different my fortunes might have been if you had instead commissioned a statue of Captain Cook and I'd loaded that onto my ship." He and Johann shared a grin that seemed to pass by the prime minister's awareness.

"I've wondered at times the same thing... about why we didn't choose to do a Captain Cook monument. We all know that someone, and it is probably Naholehua, is still doing his best to destroy the statue, now that it has finally arrived here. The fire on the ship, then at the foundry—we have had to provide police protection for it ever since. I'm just glad the insurance policy is still in effect."

"We wish you the best on that account. As for the sorcery and my ship, Mister Kessler and I both still have questions about all of it. But because the door has opened, we plan to take a look inside while we can. If it affords us an opportunity to learn more about Hawaiians and a dimension of the mystical, I guess we should welcome it."

"A valuable pursuit, Captain Schrock. And for you too, Mister Kessler." Gibson looked tired. "Hmmm, gentlemen, if there's anything I can do for you in the future—." Uncharacteristically, Gibson's words trailed off as he ushered them to the door.

CHAPTER 34

A mist of rain from passing clouds interrupted the otherwise predictable late afternoon skies while Schrock walked with Uilani Braden as they headed toward Thomas Square Park. They were coming from Uilani's apartment several blocks from the park, close enough and a place they had both agreed on. Up to this point, her agreement on anything was rare. The sun showing through the raindrops made them glisten like millions of daytime fireflies. Without saying anything, she pointed at a rainbow that had formed up over the mountains, glimpsed through the branches of the trees. They continued another block in a kind of awkward silence before Uilani spoke. "Why is it that you continue calling on me, Mister Schrock? I've told you my misgivings about our compatibility. What do you think?"

He had to conclude that this annoying line of inquiry was her way of keeping him off balance while still allowing him to see her. It had been this way since the first time he'd called on her, and for the succeeding weeks. At least she wasn't addressing him as Captain now. He watched her speak as she walked, still unable to get over how striking she was. Despite her confusing messages and how miserable she made him he was drawn to this woman like a dog begging for scraps under the table. But when he was thinking straight, he had actually wondered whether the aggravation was worth it.

"If you'd like me to return you to your apartment, I will. But you see, you did agree to see me and I do enjoy spending time with someone who doesn't work on the docks or is from Germany," he said, trying to sound humorous. He wasn't telling the whole truth, like knowing Kaole or about his involvement with Nakea or Prime Minister Gibson. Or that he was lusting for her. How else could he describe it? Right now he wanted her more than he wanted food. He wanted his arms around her. It was a breathtaking and painful dance that had steps with which he was totally unfamiliar. The truth was he hardly knew how to dance at all. And he was fairly certain there wasn't music playing to accompany their movements. The silent walking dance was wearing and Schrock was relieved to sit when they found a park bench under a Banyan tree that spread its branches as wide as half the length of a ship.

"Tell me more about your family, Miss Braden. You haven't said much about them."

Uilani looked at him as if to assess again whether he was to be trusted with information so personal. He knew from experience that despite his size, the features of his face were not intimidating, particularly to women.

"You can probably tell by looking at me and by my name that I'm not a *kanaka maoli*," she said, "full Hawaiian, you know. Because my mother is Hawaiian and my father Irish, I'm considered a *hapa haole*. But the way I see it, I'm not *hapa*. I'm a *kanaka haole*. I was born here, so Hawaiian first, as I've informed you and your friend, the good Mister Kessler. I loved both my parents, of course, so I've had to settle into the idea that I'm a mix that has both the good and the bad for me." She fiddled with her hair.

"What's been the bad part?"

"It hasn't been easy here. Many people don't like it if you're not one thing or the other. *Hapa haole* is a sort of indeterminate state. On the one hand, you're seen as matter of fact, because there are a lot of us in *Hawaii nei*, but on the other hand you're seen as just half a human because you don't belong to either race. It was a little easier when I was at nursing school in Boston, but not much. People there didn't know how to identify me, so they usually called me a native. That was better than a lot of other things I've been called."

"It sounds like that was a hard way to grow up. I—I'd never considered what someone in your situation might have to face."

"I suppose you want to hear what the good side of my *hapa* life has been," Uilani said with some sarcasm.

"I would. Truly."

Her feet pushed leaves around for a minute before she said anything. "My father was a very good doctor, born in Ireland but educated in London. He came on a mission to work at the public health department but became disillusioned with the corruption and went into private practice and surgery at Queen's Hospital. He was a good man, who always treated me with the respect of a whole person, not a half of anything. And he didn't differentiate that I was a girl. He expected the most from me. The best thing he gave me was a love of reading. He read to me a lot and as I told Mister Kessler, he brought me books all the time."

"You speak about him in the past. Is he still living?"

"No. He died of a cancer when I was fifteen."

"I'm very sorry to hear that."

"My mother helped me accept his death. She understood... she could see." Schrock wondered what Uilani meant by that but didn't ask. She got up and walked around a few steps and then sat down again. "He did give me an appreciation for medical practice, which finally led me to attend nursing school, and he left enough money for me to get my education."

"And your mother; what can you tell me about her?"

Uilani searched his face again, a gatekeeper deciding whether to lift the latch and let him in. "You know, Mister Schrock, I don't usually talk about my parents with anyone I don't know well. Even Doctor Ferguson really knows very little about my mother."

"Then you don't have to say anything else if you don't want to."

"I want to tell you, though. I'm not sure why... it confounds me. I somehow feel like it's important." She stood and began pacing again. "You see, my mother has passed too. She was a traditional healer, a *ho'olomilomi,* as was her mother. She grew up on the other side of the island in a place called Waimea, where she apprenticed under her own mother. Later, when she was a young woman, some people working in public health convinced her to move to Honolulu, where they would help her become licensed as a physician of traditional medicine. There is such a need to work with the local population. As you must know, terrible diseases kill off so many native people. That's when she and my father met."

"Your father, how did he... well... come to know your mother?"

"That is something I'd rather not talk about right now."

"I'm sorry, I simply wondered if there was a meeting of the minds between the two of them—coming from such different backgrounds."

"Actually, Mister Schrock, it was not a meeting of the minds between them. And what I think you're referring to is the problem you and I have. And it is a larger dilemma the Hawaiian people are faced with. The Europeans and Americans have brought religion and science to *Hawaii nei,* but repression and diseases at the same time. And all along they've thought they can provide the best religion and the best of everything else while the people here continue being killed off and their traditions buried. As I see it, there aren't any good reasons for Hawaiians to be so accepting of foreigners." She stood. "As you might understand, talking about this perturbs me. I'm sorry, it's probably better I go home now."

Despite her harsh words, Shrock was disappointed with their short time together. When he and Uilani got up to leave, in the shadow of a nearby tree, Naholehua's apprentice, Palmele, moved his head just enough to continue watching them as they headed out of the park.

CHAPTER 35

It was three days later when Schrock and Uilani again walked to the park's familiar bench under the Banyan tree. Uilani sat down almost abruptly. "You said you wanted to know more about my parents. I've thought about it and decided I should tell you more about my mother. I don't know why and I don't know why I trust telling you, because honestly, Mister Schrock, I still don't see much of a future in this relationship. And I don't know why I have to keep telling you this."

Schrock wondered if that meant he should just quit trying or try harder. He remembered he was bound by Johann to at least try. But what was she actually telling him to do? It didn't sound like she knew herself.

"There's another thing," she said, as if the conversation of a few days past had just paused seconds ago. "My mother also gave healing to people through dreaming or visioning. She helped people with their physical problems and their relationships. When I turned eleven, she allowed me to be with her a number of times when she did this at home. She would offer prayers and then make a sacrifice of some plants and sometimes a chicken, then for a long time she would go to sleep or into a trance. She would sit like that for hours—so I would go and do something else and come back to check on her. I was never able to develop this ability before I went away to nursing school. It's a gift from our family gods that I'm not sure I could ever receive anyway, even though she told me I could."

Schrock was considering if he should tell her about Nakea and the things he'd already learned from Kaole about *kahuna* soul sleep and dream travel.

"I think I've told you more than I intended to. We should go. I've enjoyed the walk but I do need to work tomorrow. One more thing,

Captain Schrock—Uilani is an *inoha po* name, a dream name. It came to my mother in her sleep. It means spirited, restless and likely to chafe under control. So maybe you should roll that thought down the dock."

That felt as painful as some of the blows he'd received as a rugby player in his youth. Even worse, there wasn't a hint of a smile when she said it. The walk back to her place was almost wordless. All he could think was what was he doing? More baffling; what was she doing?

CHAPTER 36

As soon as he'd sat down in Johann's library, Schrock made an unmistakable gesture that his friend needed to make him a drink. "We need to have the conversation."

"You're awfully demanding this evening. And which conversation were you referring to? You're finally asking for advice about Uilani, is that it?"

"No! She bothers me constantly, but I don't want your advice and I don't want to talk about her right now. It's pointless, maybe hopeless. But maybe later." He took a deep breath. "Look, there's something else I can't believe isn't bothering you, Kessler. There are moments when I try to sort it out and it makes me think I'm living a dream."

"Say more, Schrock," said Johann, feigning indifference as he began mixing drinks.

"We have been educated to experience our world and our universe in three dimensions. I'm trying to understand how that balances with what we understand are Nakea's celestial movements, his supposed traveling into and through other dimensions. I don't know about you but despite some of the evidence we have, I can't believe it really happens."

"Aha. I see why this is 'the' conversation. Of course, I'm as perplexed about it as you."

"Good," said Schrock, feeling agitated just from having to pull Johann into the matter. "Through dreams, trance—this is a concept that has never been—would never be acknowledged in our own world of science, where one can move about willingly with instant speed and... I try to imagine this, into another place in time—the past—or for all we know, the future. The addition of time as a dimension to all of this is monumentally harder to grasp, isn't it? Do you see the problem?"

"Maybe it shows how self-limiting we've been in science," suggested Johann. "Is it that we've been closing the doors with what we call reason? More and more I've been thinking the same thing about established science. Just remember the words typical of your learned friend, Doctor Ferguson. Although he generously found all such accounts of dream travel very interesting, he never considered any of them scientifically credible. I believe he said that adoption of such beliefs were for those without the benefit of formal education."

"God's teeth, Johann!" barked Schrock after slurping the last of his drink. "How are we or anyone going to wrap minds around this? What scientist in which discipline would go out on a limb to use the scientific method to observe, measure, formulate and then test something like dream travel? How could they even start? Here in the Hawaiian Kingdom what the *kahunas* do is privileged and shrouded knowledge, only passed on orally; Kaole made that clear. We are likely among the few outsiders to have had even the tiniest glimpse of what takes place with someone like Nakea."

"You are talking about a thousand years of being outside, culturally speaking." There was sort of a dazed silence before Johann spoke up again, setting down his drink. "I'm not sure where we can go with your ponderings, Schrock, but I have thought how amazing it is that Nakea has described his supernatural journeys in such detail. It has made me think at times that if it is real, I should like to have such a skill. The power and influence of it would be remarkable in scale." He looked into Schrock's face, searching for confirmation of such a bold idea. Schrock stared back at him, incredulous, and shook his head.

"On the other hand, I think not. I'm sure I wouldn't be up to the years of training and preparation it must take. Then there is the small matter of my not being born into a family of generations of such holy men."

Schrock shook his head again and held out his empty glass. "You have been no help and had one too many drinks. And I told you I won't be asking for advice about Uilani or reporting anything to you, at least not today, sir."

CHAPTER 37

It was Sunday afternoon when Schrock met Uilani a block away from the harbor at the Belfast Tea and Cake Shop, a place she had suggested. After their last time together, he was surprised that she would accept an invitation to do anything. He was equally surprised at himself for even asking again.

The establishment seemed out of place in the row of maritime supply businesses, tucked in between a soap-and-lye products store and a rope-and-cable supplier. There was a green canvas awning that extended out over the entry with paned and leaded glass windows on either side of the door. The salt-corroded door hinges squealed in protest as they entered. Uilani went to a small table next to the wall without hesitation, causing Schrock to assume she'd sat there before. After they were seated, Schrock looked up at the ceiling where two cut glass candelabra provided the light. A filigree iron gable separator gave the impression of dividing the space into two rooms.

Uilani sipped her tea and took the initiative to ask Schrock to tell her more about what his life had been like as a sea captain. He tried to summarize his years and travels for her but thought he might be telling her things he'd already told her or she had heard before: unpredictable weather and seas, dirty and dangerous cargo, unruly crew, the tedium of time at sea... the loneliness. He surprised himself by revealing this last thing to her, allowing her to see that he was vulnerable. He wanted to pinch himself for letting that out. But what did it matter, he wasn't winning, doing whatever it was he'd been doing. "It's one of the reasons I've given up the sea. It's a hard life out there."

"You know, Mister Schrock, I had a companion who was a sailor, except he wasn't an officer like you. He was Hawaiian—beautiful to look at. But the man didn't have a lick of good sense. He told me a lot about life at sea and how lonely it was. But then he'd go and ship out again. So I'd see him for a few weeks and he'd be gone for months and months. He didn't have any large ambitions and would never have been anything more than a sailor. He was big like you, and always making jokes. I liked being with him since my work is always so serious." She took a sip of her tea and didn't say anything more, but simply stared into her cup.

"So what happened, if I may ask... I mean, between the two of you?"

"He died—at sea—in a storm near South America. He gone to *papa lani*—that other world of *Hawaii nei*. He got a presence with us now." Schrock noticed that just bringing up the memory of her former love seemed to have added a pidgin edge to her speech.

"I'm sorry about what happened. I know too many good men who died at sea. And I know about the pain of losing someone." He paused and watched her face, seeing if she had more to say about the matter. He tried to frame what he would say next.

"You know, I'm never going to be a handsome Hawaiian and I'm not much of a joker, so you're probably right... what you've been saying about us not being compatible."

Uilani looked up from her tea, almost alarmed. "I didn't tell you that you had to be like him—like Niku—that was his name. I maybe wish you were Hawaiian, but I actually think you are a fine-looking man, Mister Schrock. I like your eyes. I also like that you seem to know where you are going. By now you may have figured out that's important to me. What I don't understand is why I was drawn to you in the first place. I never expected to become at all interested in you. There is something about you that is unusual. I just can't figure out what it is... or even why I decided to go to lunch with you that first time. And now there are moments... mind you, *moments*, when I am getting used to being with you."

Schrock had a hard time keeping himself from falling off his chair. How and where had this come from? "Really, Miss Braden, I am shocked, particularly after our last meeting."

"I'm sorry if I was a little terse," she said, seeming regretful.

He blinked, thinking her being prone to understatement must have come from her father.

"It's something else I never thought would happen with a chance German who just got off the boat, so to speak."

"So to speak, I should be grateful you didn't tell me everything you were thinking from the beginning."

"I'm sorry, I don't mean to push a suture needle into that thick skin of yours again, but I find you people from Europe carry yourselves stiffly. When I went to nursing school in America, it was as if everyone there was suffering from severe constipation, but I find the English and you Germans even worse."

"Now I'm confused. Does this mean you're getting used to how I am or has your diagnosis of Germans changed?"

She eyed him. "I'm not sure. I'll let you know."

In the park again three days later, Schrock and Uilani sat under what was becoming their usual Banyan Tree, a foot closer to each other on the bench. She didn't seem uncomfortable with the closeness or the silence.

"I know I promised to talk even more about my mother."

"Yes, you did."

She shrugged. "Do you know why I'm a nurse? It's not just because my father was a doctor. It's because of her, my mother. I told you she taught me things about *mauli ola,* the power of healing, different than European or American medicine. It works to heal the whole person." He felt her quiet gaze, imagining she was looking back in time.

"I've learned a little about *kahuna* healing," said Schrock. "It appears to get lumped in with sorcery and all the other traditional practices the missionaries didn't approve of."

"To me it is one of the greatest wrongdoings that have beset the people of *Hawaii nei.*"

She didn't say more, like that was all that was to be said today or forever about that subject.

"I know you didn't want to talk about your mother and father coming from such different backgrounds. Maybe it's like your insistence that we aren't compatible, you and I."

"Which could be one of our problems, Mister Schrock, and is why I don't want to talk about it."

Schrock felt his skin prickle. "You are close to convincing me."

I'm sorry, it's probably better that we go," she said, starting to get up.

"Wait, we just got here. There's something I wanted to tell you."

She sat down on the edge of the bench, irritation written across her face. "What, what is it?"

"When we last talked and you told me about your friend Niku who died… you told me I didn't have to be like him. Well, I didn't know if it was the right time to tell you about a former love I had, a woman named Susan. I wanted to tell you, to let you know about her, that you didn't need to be like her either. But the thing is, she also died by drowning."

"I'm sorry. How, what happened?" She sat full on the bench, attentive.

"I'm not sure of the details. It was in Australia, where I met her, and I only heard about it in a short letter from her father. She was in a small boat in the harbor when it was hit by a barge. The boat was crushed and she and the other person in the boat went into the water and drowned. She was an assistant harbormaster, doing some kind of inspection, I think."

"I'm so sorry for you."

"I have grieved for her for more than a year. It has been hard. I only hope that like your belief for Niku that she is in a heaven." Schrock was quiet, debating how much more he should say. "I—I was intending to return to Australia. I'm sure she was waiting for me. I said I would return. I put it off… unsure, for all the wrong reasons. And then she died. I was miserable because of it. Her widower father must have been devastated. She was his only child. It didn't help that I never returned to her. I should be thankful that he even chose to write to tell me."

Uilani watched Schrock's face carefully for a full minute. Finally she said, "You have to see that given how interested you are in seeing me, I question what you learned from all that. I guess this is complicated for you, but you must see that I will be left to wonder what your intentions are with me." She looked up into the Banyan branches and then pulled some strands of hair off her face. "The other side of this, Mister Schrock, is that I am glad you have been honest with me." She stood and walked around in a circle and sat down again. "Because you have been honest with me, I'm going to tell you about when my mother and father met, so you might know me better."

She put her hands on her lap and looked at him. "It was when they were both working for public health and he was fascinated with traditional healing and how it seemed to work in so many difficult cases. He thought my mother was a savant. He actually told me that once, before I knew what it meant. But he also said she was the most beautiful woman he had ever known. It took her a couple of years to accept the idea she could be with a *haole*. My father, he was persistent. She finally agreed to marry him and they were happy together—they made it work somehow. I am their only child."

Schrock thought the story of their long courtship sounded too familiar. He cringed at the prospect of a two-year expedition to win this woman's heart. "I like what it was that brought them together. I'm sorry to hear they are both gone. It sounds like you are the product of two remarkable people," he said with sincerity, reaching out and lightly touching her hand. She stared at him as if he'd broken an unspoken trust, then let her expression melt into a faint smile. "What of traditional healing did you learn from your mother?" he asked, trying to salvage the moment.

She was silent for a moment, staring off into the low-hanging Banyan branches. "It will have to be some other time. I would just say that I was lucky enough to have my mother pass on as much as she could before she died and I went away to school. My father had insisted I attend private boarding school and nursing school. I understand why, it just left me unable to learn enough from her to be useful as it could have been."

As they headed back toward Uilani's home, again they didn't see Palmele, watching them through a thicket of trees.

CHAPTER 38

Schrock surveyed the familiar shelves of Johann's library as Johann handed him a brandy. He envied the stability and escape his friend could find in this room. At the moment, the thought of sitting there and reading until he died took on a certain sheen.

"I understand your frustration," said Johann. "You must understand that she is probably still trying to find out if you're a worthy suitor. Besides, you shouldn't feel like you're so damn unique. Courting is a process that crosses all the species. Hell, Stina made me jump over all kinds of obstacles just to let me kiss her the first time."

"It surprises me that you ever got that far."

"I'll make note of that, Captain Schrock. What's more, at the time, I wasn't the only dog in Stina's circus. What I'm trying to tell you is that you don't have to be funny or dashing or to help Miss Braden resolve her feelings about her father. You're a man of honor, strength, intelligence and one of the more tenacious people I've known. Those, my friend, are the kinds of things that women are wanting in a man. If you're patient, maybe she will recognize that about you at some point."

Schrock stood up and paced the room. "I've grown comfortable here, and I'd miss your friendship were I to leave and go back to sea. Believe me, I've thought about it. But I can't get by being alone anymore. I'm not at sea, so I don't have any excuses to avoid marriage. I think it's you who's driven me to the brink of this cliff. I want to try to make something happen with Uilani. I wonder if the statue has anything to do with any of this."

"If you weren't talking so fast, Schrock, I would think you're almost making sense. Love is blind but apparently it can also induce insanity as well."

Schrock banged his glass down on the table. "What help are you? Can we go out to your garden?"

Johann gestured with his head to follow and they headed out, down the porch stairs and into a warm night. The spicy scent of ginger blossoms saturated the air as their feet crunched lightly on the crushed lava stone of the winding garden path.

"There's something else I wanted to tell you," said Schrock. "Uilani may be able to understand Nakea better than we do."

"What makes you say that?"

"She learned traditional medicine from her mother before she passed. Her mother was a *kahuna* hands healer, and Uilani was just beginning to be apprenticed to her before she went away to school, and then her mother died. I think Uilani is probably acquainted with *kahuna* sorcery. I'd like her insights about how any of this witchcraft may have played out in the events around the ship and the statue. I don't know how or when to broach the subject with her, though."

Johann stopped and stared up at a star-laden sky. "That's putting a lot of faith in what she might know. But if she is of help, then you should take the opportunity. Although from how it's going, it doesn't sound like you can rely on much from her."

"On occasion she says she is curiously drawn to me, but I'm sure she's more interested in things Hawaiian than in me."

"Anyway, Schrock, what about your ship and the statue still bothers you? Didn't we have that conversation and sort of arrive at a conclusion that some things have to remain unknowable? And really, won't we always be at a disadvantage, being empiricists and born German? Of course if you lived in Hawaii long enough, it might somehow allow you to break out of the limitations of your stilted upbringing and allow you to perceive other dimensions."

"Damn, Johann, I know you're joking, but for once I hope you're right."

"For once?"

"Thanks for listening, you bastard. I feel like a lovesick boy. It seems like your life never has these stupid dilemmas."

Johann turned away from Schrock and they walked back into the library. The only sounds in the room were the tree branches being pushed against the house wall by the breeze. "Don't fool yourself. I have my burdens... and a monstrous one I've held from you." He turned back to face Schrock. "I should have told you by now." He sat down heavily in his chair. "Remember the time we were drinking and you said you never saw the dark side of my soul? Well, it's there." Johann looked as if he was searching crevasses in the basement of his mind, his haunted eyes meeting Schrock's with a stare. "I killed a man in Germany and then ran away from it. That's the reason I came to live in Hawaii."

Schrock sat down hard in his chair, shaken, attentive, waiting for more. He could hear the distant street noises make their way into the silence as Johann's words lay there like hot embers.

"I had only been working in sales for a couple of years," said Johann. "I traveled to towns near Bremen. I'd gone overnight to Holzminden—you must know where that is."

"Yes," Schrock murmured.

"It was summer, warm out. I was having a late dinner outside in front of a small hotel. I was the only customer and there was hardly anyone on the street. I was tired, focused on my food and I didn't see anyone approach. The next thing I noticed was someone running, and I turned to see this man going around the corner with my valise. I got up and chased him. I don't think he figured I would be so quick because he slowed down in the middle of the alleyway and it was just enough for me to catch him. I grabbed the back of his coat and he went down. I remember being incredibly angry. I pulled him up and he still tried to run with my valise. I hit him in the face. In school I was a boxer and could hit hard. I'm sure my fist broke his nose because he went down with blood all over his face. And then he didn't move. I shook him and he didn't come around and when I checked his pulse, there was nothing." Johann paused and looked up at the ceiling. "I kept shaking him to bring him back. I didn't really want to kill him." He held out his hand and looked at it. "Either he hit his head on the wall or I hit him too hard. I don't know. But he was dead. I killed him." Johann exhaled deeply, and reached for his drink, his hand shaking.

Schrock's jaw went slack. "So—so what happened?" he asked quietly.

"I collected myself at first. I wiped the blood off my hands, straightened up my clothes and went back to my table. When the waiter came back out, he was very cordial, so I assumed he hadn't seen anything. I decided not to report it and just went back to my room. That's when I began to panic. I thought the police might somehow figure out it was me who killed the man and could possibly charge me with murder. You never know what will happen in the courts. I couldn't imagine spending years in jail. Before dawn I took the first carriage back to Bremen. When I got home, I told Stina what had happened and why I was afraid of taking the chance of confessing. She was very scared and she agreed we needed to get out of the country."

"That must have been hard for her," said Schrock. "How did you know where you were going?"

After heaving a sigh, Johann continued. "We knew a man who had immigrated here—he's since died. He'd sent us letters that mentioned what good business opportunities there were. So we made a plan to leave Germany at once—to come to Honolulu and start over. We had only been married a short time and had no children. It was a simple solution. I guess it's worked out—as far as I know they haven't come looking for me yet. But I've never gotten over it. I still have nightmares about it, and I still worry. I had to make some quiet inquiries to see if I was on Germany's immigration arrest list before my trip back."

"Why are you telling me this? And why now?"

"Because, Gerhard, believe it or not, you've become my closest friend. I have other acquaintances, men in business I spend time with, but that's different. I've come to think of you as the brother I never had... someone who I can always talk to, someone I can trust."

"I think of you in the same way, Johann," Schrock said, realizing that being brothers was an apt description of what they'd become.

CHAPTER 39

Johann's story played out multiple times in Schrock's mind as the week passed. He felt bad that he hadn't made time to see Johann. What more could he say to him? The account made him depressed when he turned it over again and again. He figured he probably wouldn't have done it any differently had he been in his friend's shoes, but what an albatross for Johann. He thought he'd come to know the man, and yet he realized how long it takes to really know one another or even understand ourselves. He was only beginning to have a dim idea of what he himself was made of. And Uilani—he was still feeling his way around in a dark room trying to find her.

At the end of the week, he dropped by Johann's office near closing time. Kaole walked in holding a packet of papers he said he'd retrieved from one of Johann's customers. After Kaole handed the papers to Johann, Schrock smiled and shook his hand warmly, thinking how much he liked seeing the young Hawaiian. From the start, Kaole had accepted him, a *haole* newcomer. He had come to depend on Kaole for help in learning the basics of native-born Hawaiian ways, everything from proper *kama'aina* greetings to respect for the spiritual nature of the ocean. He always showed the customary warmth extended by his people, given freely even though they had little reason to like the European and American foreigners. It made him wonder about the graceless time he was having with Uilani.

"So you saw the first Kamehameha on that ship?" Kaole asked Schrock.

"I did. I was amazed. It's a miracle that statue made it here. Something good finally came out of my ship's ashes."

"It's not a miracle," Kaole acknowledged in a matter-of-fact tone. "Nakea made sure that happen."

Schrock felt puzzled. "You said Nakea kept the statue from being destroyed on my ship. But surely it was just luck the captain of that ship, a man named Jarvis, found it and brought it to Honolulu."

Kaole's face wrinkled in charitable frustration, a look Schrock recognized. "What don't we understand?" Schrock asked, glancing over at Johann.

"Nakea made Naholehua sick to death. Then he wasn't able to find out about that *Earl* ship and try to sink it."

Schrock's draw dropped. "Did he—you mean he tried to kill Naholehua?"

"No, he just made him wish he was dead."

"How—how did he do that?" Johann stuttered.

"The way they do all *ho'opi'opi'o*, you call sorcery. He did that through *moe uhane*, his dream time. Naholehua never saw this sickness coming. If he had, Naholehua could make that sickness go sideways."

"You mean he could have kept what Nakea did to him from happening?" asked Johann.

"Maybe. But my uncle say Naholehua was full of himself, and he drank too much *awa*. He's got slow and stupid and was gonna die bad some way. He smart and stupid all his life. Then he got stupid sick. He is *kahuna 'ana'ana* that get what he earned."

Schrock noticed Johann's worried face after hearing his clerk's pronouncements.

Kaole must have seen that he looked skeptical, which Schrock knew he was. "Naholehua is a very bad man," he said. "He did more than make your ship burn and try to destroy Kamehameha's *mana*. For a lot of years, Nakea says he broke many things with *'ana'ana*."

"What do you mean 'broke things'?" asked Schrock.

"He was trained as a healer, but he just messed about with those families in the village. He hurt people—even made some die. It brought shame to all the *kahuna* priests."

The other men let Kaole's revelations set in for a moment.

Finally, Schrock said, "I'm surprised you're telling us these things. Would Nakea approve?"

Kaole's face was serious. "You're the only *haoles* we get to know who don't want to take *mana* away from *Hawaii nei*. I know you won't do anything bad with what I'm telling you."

"We wouldn't betray your trust, Kaole," Johann said. "That will never change."

"And you're going to take care of Kamehameha's statue that came on the *Earl* ship," Kaole said, nodding toward Schrock.

"What do you mean by that?" asked Schrock. "Nakea says you are protecting Kamehameha's *mana* in that statue," he answered, looking straight at Schrock. "He doesn't know why a *haole* has anything to do with this, but he says it is you."

Schrock was confused and moved. "I'm honored by this confidence in me, Kaole. But I don't think either of us can do much about the statue now; it's the property of the government."

Kaole smiled. "It's good you told Gibson to buy the statue. Now you can make sure Kamehameha gets back to Kohala on Hawaii Island, where he was born. Nakea says you can do that, too. And I'm gonna help you."

Hell have mercy, the seas are rising again, thought Schrock. Like Stina had asked, what had he gotten himself into? Kaole hesitated. "One other thing I'm gonna tell you." His head turned toward Nakea's home on the other side of Diamond Head. "I am Nakea's apprentice now."

Schrock was uncertain of what to say. "That must be an honor for you."

"Yes," agreed Johann, although Schrock could see the surprise in his face.

"Yeah, I get very honored," said Kaole. "My life's gonna be different. I was worried about telling you both before, especially you, Mister Kessler. I'm not sure how much I can work for you now. I have to see how much time Nakea wants me. I've been his student for long time, but only when I wasn't at missionary school or working here. He's getting old and wants to take me to next levels of knowledge. It takes lot of time."

Schrock and Johann stared at Kaole with new respect. Schrock considered that the young man they were talking to might someday assume skills they would never comprehend.

"Kaole, would you have dinner with me at Fish House?" asked Schrock. "I want to hear more about why the statue needs to be over on Hawaii Island, and how we can make that happen—all of us."

"Make sure he pays," said Johann with a wink.

"Good plan," Kaole said, patting his stomach. "We'll go eat and I'll tell you the whole thing."

It was a peak cane harvest season and more ships were squeezing into the harbor to unload their cargos before their turnaround to have holds filled with raw sugar for the United States. It meant the longer work days for Schrock kept him from paying a visit to Prime Minister Gibson. He still needed to inquire about the disposition of the recovered bronze, "Schrock's statue," as Johann kept referring to it, now that there was another copy to be erected across from the palace. In any case, he doubted he could influence the eccentric Gibson, the man who was the *de facto* legislative statue committee. But Nakea and Kaole's belief that he, Schrock, had an important role in seeing that it ended up in Kohala continued to weigh heavily on him.

Johann waited at the entrance to Posner's Inn, on time for their meal together before Schrock went to meet up with Uilani. "Hello, my friend," Johann said in greeting, studying Schrock's face with concern. "You look put out. Having a new love must be taking its toll."

Schrock waved off Johann's comment as they went in. As soon as they were seated, he said, "I'm getting by. I don't have any assurance that there's love coming from her direction. The irony is that I wonder if she'll ever come to see me as a whole person—the woman even makes me question if I am."

"What does she say that reduces a big guy like you to squirrel proportions?"

"Thank you. It's things like what I intend to do to fend off this movement toward colonialism, which she fears with some basis is about to happen. And she wonders if I've ever made a political stand about anything I believed in, as if I've ever had the time on land to do such a thing."

They ordered their meal and as they ate, Schrock carped on about Uilani. He realized he was talking faster than usual and sure Johann could see his agitation, he signaled the waiter to bring a bottle of wine. As the waiter served them, several men sat down at a table next to theirs.

Johann leaned in closer to Schrock, speaking in a lowered voice. "I don't want to change the subject that's driving you to distraction, but have you thought more about Kaole's account of what Nakea did to Naholehua and the other things he told us?"

Schrock took a deep breath and exhaled through pursed lips. "It's hard to believe but I like to trust Kaole. After the things we've learned about their kind of sorcery, I can't completely discount it. And I'm still baffled that Kaole assumes I have responsibility for the statue. What do you think?"

Johann sipped his wine before he spoke. "I have no reason not to believe any of it, other than it doesn't fit our agreed understanding of how things are supposed to work in the universe." He grinned. "And the more I hear, the bigger the ditch I need to leap over to get to that other side. I guess I'm rather an agnostic on this, like you seem to be."

"We need to grow longer legs," Schrock said, holding up his glass for a toast.

Johann touched his glass to Schrock's, then took a bite of dark bread and chewed on it for a minute. "What's most intriguing is Nakea's interest in you, Gerhard. It's almost like he's been looking out for you all this time."

"What do you mean by that?"

"In his world, and probably Kaole's, they say you've had a vital role in protecting Kamehameha's *mana*—the spirit or maybe its divine power they believe exists through the statue. At the same time, he's been protecting you and your ship from the moment we sailed from Bremerhaven."

"If that's the case, I wish his protection could have been more thorough. We all nearly died on that voyage. Remember when we first met him and he seemed to recognize us, when he told us he thought maybe we had died? That didn't sound like he cared."

"Ah, but we didn't, did we?" Johann replied, a glint in his eye. "I think he was just making sure he got your attention. And if we accept what Kaole told us, Nakea is doing his best to protect us from this Naholehua."

"Even though it's hard for me to get over the loss of the *Haendel*, if there's any remote truth to all this, I suppose we owe Nakea some gratitude for saving our lives. Either way, I've wanted both of us to visit Gibson and talk to him again about putting the statue on Hawaii Island. We know what Nakea, Kaole and apparently a lot of other Hawaiians want. And remember what Gibson last told us, that if there was anything he could do for us in the future... I know it was a little vague, but I'd be grateful if you and Kaole would go with me to visit the Prime Minister and try to convince him that the government needs to erect the statue in Kohala."

Johann reached for the wine to refill his glass and shook his head. "He's a slippery one, that Gibson. Besides, that's supposed to be your duty."

"I know, but you're an upstanding businessman, with money," Schrock declared with a smirk. "You're likely to have more influence with him than I would, and because Gibson understands and speaks Hawaiian, Kaole can convey the native perspective of why it needs to be placed there."

"Of course, I'll go. And if Kaole will go, you know we'll give it our best."

"Thank you, friend," said Schrock, feeling some weight come off his shoulders. "There's one more thing I've been thinking about," he added. "Kaole has an exceptional mind. I haven't heard you mention giving Kaole more responsibility in what he does for you. I know I'm overstepping my relationship with you by saying this, but maybe he should have the option of advancing in your business, in case he decides he doesn't want a life as a *kahuna*."

Johann's brow furrowed. "Don't worry, I agree with you. And believe me, I've thought about it. But my guess is that becoming more immersed in Western ways won't be what he wants."

"You're probably right," agreed Schrock.

"I'm not sure he even has a choice." Johann was quiet, swirling the wine in his glass. "I will talk to him. He deserves a chance to prosper, whatever he chooses to do. I do want to keep him as long as I can. Yes, I was thinking I'd give him more challenging assignments to warrant a pay raise."

Schrock filled both their glasses. They grinned at each other and regarded the nearly empty bottle of wine. "We might need another," said Schrock.

"Indeed," Johann nodded. "Is the wine doing anything to ease the burden of your lonesome heart?"

"Not much. I'm sure I'm in love with Uilani, at least with what I know of her. I'll probably be a shipwreck if she won't have me."

"You don't know what will happen. This woman may be thinking more about you than you suspect. And don't worry so much—it's unbecoming of a swarthy ship's captain."

"And you should go for a swim," Schrock said into his glass. "You know, Johann, the seas have made fools of the smartest sailors. But I'm beginning to learn that women are a force more likely to baffle solid men."

"You could be right, friend. However, I think the problem could be you. It could be that you waited too long to embark on this exercise of finding a woman to be with and while you dithered, your naïve advantage was lost."

"Why are you always talking in cipher, Kessler?"

"It's like this. Had you ventured more into this match-making as a young man, you could have absorbed the give and take of it all… with tears or maybe even rage instead of this lengthy and painful rumination you're in now. It's possible you are intimidated by all this."

Schrock's expression wasn't generous. After a silence, he said, "I'm going to take into account what you just said. Do you remember Bürgerpark in Bremen, where they kept all those poor animals? I used to be fascinated watching the reindeer during Octoberfest—it seemed like it was always about the time the mating happened. A big male would make a lot of those strange noises and try to gather as many females around him as a sort of harem. The bull with the biggest antlers always had the most success. Well, in this park I'm left to wonder whether I have any antlers at all."

"So it seems."

"But there's something going on that I can't explain. I'm being drawn to her like the pull of tidewater. I think by now you know me well enough to know that I probably wouldn't tolerate this standoff with another woman. Even though at times it makes little sense, all I can say is that something is telling me I need this woman—almost like I need to take my next breath."

CHAPTER 40

A drone of voices echoed off the high walls in the main corridor of Queen's Hospital. Along a counter, several clerks conducted intake with patients, as others made conversation while waiting to be seen. Today, Nurse Uilani Braden felt distracted by the hallway noise she could hear in the examination room where she was applying a plaster cast to a man's leg. The merciless afternoon sun beat through the large windows, compounding her irritation. Sweat dripped under her high collar. She pulled back the hair that strayed over her damp forehead and did her best to focus on the problem at hand, the foul-smelling patient who hadn't stopped talking since she'd entered the room.

"I'm sorry, Captain Beenhower, if I have that right—," she said, keeping her voice level.

"But you must see my position," the man said, his waxed mustache bobbing up and down, his voice rising. "This is no way to accommodate the needs of an important trading partner to your little country." From the moment she'd heard him come through the doors on crutches, his booming voice filling the ward with his presence, it had been obvious this Dutch sea captain was full of himself. "I'm no doubt losing a great deal of money by your having made me to wait," he sputtered, his face taking on a darker shade of red with each word. "Those natives didn't look so sick that they couldn't have waited."

Uilani subdued the urge to roll her eyes. It was clear he felt entitled to impose on others by virtue of his European heritage and captain's status. She spoke as evenly as she could while she continued applying the layers of plaster to the cast. "We see our patients according to when they are admitted and the urgency of their need. Some of those 'natives' who were seen before you were a woman going into labor to give birth and a man with appendicitis requiring immediate preparation for surgery. They just don't make a lot of noise about their discomfort."

"But my time is valuable," the captain shot back. "If it weren't for our ships, you people would have little dishware to eat from or pipes to smoke or—or guns to shoot."

"I'm sure Hawaiians fully appreciate the importance of the Dutch trade," said Uilani, eyeing the captain. She felt nearly overwhelmed by his smell, a months-at-sea body odor he had attempted to cover with equally offensive cologne. She looked him straight in the face. "You don't think that there should be a difference in how we serve people at the hospital, do you, Captain?" In his eyes she thought she caught his recognition that he could see her Hawaiian facial features beyond her light skin.

"Whaa, well—," the captain growled, "I've never seen such shoddy management of a hospital."

"Then you might consider another hospital the next time you are in need of one in Honolulu, Captain."

"You know there isn't another one!"

"Is that so?" Uilani completed her task of laying the plaster layers in silence. "I'm finished with my work here, Captain. You will need to sit still for half an hour for this to dry. A clerk will notify you and request your payment. Good day."

"The hospital administrator shall be hearing from the Dutch consulate," he snapped.

As she moved to the nursing desk to find out her next charge, Uilani thought that the malodorous captain was doubly perturbed that he hadn't received his treatment from a doctor, and worse yet, a *hapa haole* nurse. Later, when she caught sight of him walking out the door, his purser in tow, she wondered why she wanted anything more to do with self-entitled patients. His vulgar presence lingered like a jellyfish sting.

That evening, as she caught the horse tram heading toward her home near Thomas Park, she thought about the other captain who had troubled her since the moment she'd treated him at the hospital. It was vexing why she continued to be attracted to a German *malihini*... or to any foreigner for that matter. This Captain Schrock was handsome enough, polite, educated and actually interesting, and he had been successful. But he wasn't Hawaiian and knew little of *Hawaii nei*. So why was it that when she expected herself to have a blanket of indifference about this man, instead she felt the pull of a mother cat wanting to carry her kitten off to safety? It was maddening, what her mind was telling her about shunning him while the rest of her ached to act on. Was this what love was? If it was, then it was a strange proposition she'd never imagined. She couldn't go on seeing him. He would just have to stew in his juices until she understood.

CHAPTER 41

The note arrived by post in Schrock's mail on Tuesday morning.

Dear Mister Schrock:

I want to thank you for all of our walks, meals and the company you have afforded me in our time together. You have interested and challenged me in ways I have never experienced before. However after considerable deliberation, I still am unable to see a future where we could become compatible in a permanent manner. As such, for the time being, I think we should suspend our meetings. As always, I wish you the best.

Yours Sincerely,
Uilani Braden

By Wednesday evening Schrock was in Johann's parlor and sitting upright in his chair. Johann hadn't finished making a drink for him when Schrock came out with: "I've done a lot of thinking about this and it is time for me to move on—get back to the sea where I belong."

Johann's face dropped as nearly did the glass in his hand. He put it on the side table, sat down and laid his hands firm on the arm rests, focused on Schrock.

"And don't start lecturing me, Kessler. I've made up my mind. I'm looking for passage to Bremen where hopefully I can get another shipmaster berth."

"You had best say more," said Johann looking alarmed. "What's happened?"

"Uilani happened. Or didn't happen." Schrock had been sure he could make this all clear when he came by to explain. However, Johann's expression made him feel like a child again. "After everything, she has decided not to see me. I don't know. I guess I didn't have it. I didn't have what it takes to win her." He turned his face away from Johann. "I don't want to stay here any longer."

"How do you know? What did she say?" asked Johann, sounding incredulous.

"She sent me a letter—repeated what she's been saying all along, that we aren't compatible enough to be a couple."

"I find this hard to believe. Do you want to show me the letter?"

"No. It's personal."

"Show me anyway."

"Who do you think you are? Here, you bastard."

Johann unfolded the letter and read through it. He looked up at Schrock and shook his head. "Can't you see! She is not ending this at all. She's saying that she is putting it on hold until she can understand what is going on between the two of you. She used the word 'suspend', not 'end', and 'for the time being', not 'forever'! So it is completely rash of you to do what you sailors do and jump ship, or in your case, jump land or whatever."

"You are reading too much into this, Kessler. You don't know this woman—she is hard willed. That is it. I will not be dragged around any longer. You need to consider me gone. I thought you should be the first to know, given our friendship and all that you have done for me. I will keep you informed about my departure." Schrock rose from his chair and gave Johann a long hand shake before he turned to leave, suppressing tears. "Good evening, friend."

CHAPTER 42

The next morning, Johann decided it was fortuitous that Kaole would be reporting to work on that day, one of the two in the week that he still worked for him now that he was Nakea's apprentice. He had slept little, turning over in his mind what he might do to change Schrock's mind. He could see that appeals of logic or reason coming from him would be pointless. Having nothing else, he had arrived at an idea that seemed like an outside chance.

"Good morning," he said as Kaole walked into his office.

"*Aloha makua,* Mister Kessler. It is a fine day, don't you think?"

"I would, Kaole, but I want you to sit down while I tell you about a problem we have."

Johann explained the situation with Uilani, whom Kaole had yet to meet but he knew a little about and had seen with Schrock on two occasions.

"This is serious, Kaole. He is my friend and yours. We can't just let him leave over this setback. I think there is still hope."

"You bet this serious, Mister Kessler. This is bad and for more than he is our friend. He come to *Hawaii nei* for a reason. You know he gotta help get Kamehameha back home to Kohala. Nakea see that. He expect that."

"I don't know if that is enough to make him stay. He has been turned upside down by Uilani."

Kaole was silent, looking at Johann for a while before saying anything. "There is something else you don't know about, maybe only Nakea should be talking about. But I gonna do it, before it's too late. This woman, Uilani—Nakea has seen her. She is meant to be with Mister Schrock."

Johann was wide-eyed. "What do you mean, seen her? To say that you must mean, like in his soul sleep, yes?"

"Yeah, Mister Kessler, you got that right. She is a special woman and we have to make sure Mister Schrock know and she know that too."

"Kaole, you are a blessing today. If what you are saying is true..." Johann rolled his eyes and shook his head. "Sorry, I shouldn't question Nakea... then this could be the way to get that pig-headed Schrock to see the light. Would you be willing to meet Uilani and talk with her?"

"Mister Kessler, I have to do it. Nakea gonna want me to. This so important it further than big."

Schrock followed the shipping ledgers closely, looking for any ships passing through the Port of Honolulu on a return to Bremerhaven. After a few days, he saw a ship with German registry coming out of Shanghai to Honolulu but without the next destination cited. It could be bound for San Francisco or Europe, depending on the changeable nature of cargo shipping. Furthermore, it might not arrive here for two weeks or more. He banged down the paper holder on his desk, then went over and slammed shut the metal folding doors of his work site, with a single mind of going straight to the saloon.

Kaole returned to work two days later, even though it wasn't his regular day to work.

"So how we gonna do this, Mister Kessler?"

"We'll take my carriage after work and go to her place so I can introduce you. I'll invite her to have a small dinner, somewhere she'd like. I'll let you two get to know each other. Then I'll say I have to go attend to picking up my children at their friend's and return them home, with a promise to return and pick you up afterward. That will give you time to talk... in Hawaiian if maybe that would be best."

"You got a plan, Mister Kessler. I think we can do this."

Johann knew enough from Schrock's accounts about the time Uilani usually arrived home from work. He allowed a short time for her to collect herself; then he and Kaole knocked on her door.

"Mister Kessler!" she exclaimed when she opened the door. "What a surprise to see you. How are you? What can I do for you?"

"I'm fine, thank you, Miss Braden. I came by hoping I could take you out for a short dinner this evening at a place of your choosing. This is an associate and friend of mine, Lincoln Kaole. I've long wanted you to meet him and to have him tell you some about his uncle Nakea, who is a *kahuna uhane hele* who lives over in Waialae."

Uilani's demeanor was one of polite questioning. "This is nice of you, although I'm not sure… just why it is you would like your associate and me to talk? Mister Schrock has, of course, spoken of Kaole and likes him very much," she paused and tilted her head slightly, "so does this have something to do with Mister Schrock?"

It was Johann's turn to be uncomfortable. "In all honesty, it does. Kaole and I are both very fond of Gerhard and, well, he seems to think that the relationship with you is over and therefore he has little need to remain in the Hawaiian Kingdom."

Shock registered on Uilani's face. "Oh, oh."

"But you see, Kaole is privy to some information about Gerhard's connection to the spirit of the statue of Kamehameha, the one that was on his ship when it burned. He believes it is extremely important that Gerhard remain here so that the statue's destiny can be fulfilled." Johann paused. "I know that is a lot to accept, but that's why I think it would be good for you to have this conversation. You see, we think you may have an integral role in this. Will you do this, Miss Braden, as a favor to us?"

Uilani agreed, regardless of her skepticism about their motivations, and fifteen minutes later, the trio boarded Johann's carriage and made their way through busy Honolulu streets to a small Chinese restaurant that Uilani knew about. Settled into a private booth with two red lanterns on the wall and candles on the table, they ordered their food.

Uilani wasn't shy about making an attempt to get to the bottom of the questions that this raised for her. "Kaole, Mister Kessler, how is it that Mister Shrock never told me about your uncle… that he knew about him? Did he know, does he think he has some special connection with this statue? This is all very strange."

As Johann listened to Kaole's responses, he thought the young man was masterful in how he provided her small pieces of information at a time, allowing her to digest them before asking more questions.

"You gotta know, Miss Braden, what all *kahuna* do are private. We been trusting Mister Schrock and Mister Kessler, 'cause they were on that ship that carried Kamehameha. It was for a reason."

As the conversation went on, he could tell that Kaole wasn't ready yet to tell her that her relationship with Schrock may be a key to everything. Johann wasn't even sure how that worked or if that was even true. But he wanted to believe it was.

When the waiter began clearing the plates from the table, Johann said, "Something I didn't mention, but I need to leave for a few minutes. I'm afraid I must pick up my girls at their friend's and return them home. I will return as quickly as I can."

Uilani looked perturbed at this.

"Don't worry. I will be back shortly with the carriage to deliver you safely home, Miss Braden. I want you both to order a sweet dessert and continue your conversation. I promise you will be in the best of care with Lincoln and I'm guessing you have more to talk about. I'll be as quick as I can."

Before Uilani could register a protest, Johann was out of his chair and moving toward the front entrance of the restaurant.

CHAPTER 43

Schrock wondered how many more weeks it would be until he quit the same daily routine. Without the interest or anticipation he had experienced when first settling into his land existence nearly two years ago, he unlocked the closure to his dock work site, folding the two accordion sides back to side walls. It was now taking him two cups of coffee each morning to get himself out of bed, down the stairs and to the waterfront. Seeing ships come and go that he managed cargos for, it seemed ironic that he couldn't also direct their oceanic course to get him out of here. A strange fate, or again, something he probably deserved.

In the early sunlight, he watched down the dock, which was coming to life with native Hawaiians pushing wheelbarrows and carts, filled with loads of ship provisions for sale or delivery, sailors making their way back to ship after being out all night in saloons, brothels and Chinatown's opium dens. Already the harbor water was in motion, the first daily interisland coasting schooner leaving with a load of passengers and freight, being passed and crossed by countless *kanakas* in canoes and men in small Chinese boats. In the distance, crew on the deck of a British war vessel at anchor appeared to be readying to weigh anchor and put out to sea. He had been somewhat aware that was happening, there having been some sort of a departure festival or *luau* at the palace—was it last night or the night before—he couldn't remember.

He reluctantly brought out his ledgers, and began scanning through what would be on his plate today, the nearly non-stop review of manifests, cargo inspections and ship holds. Seeing the long list, he remembered he liked that he was kept busy at his work—just not here these days. At sea, he could put distance between himself and Honolulu. He would be unreachable.

His thoughts were interrupted when out of the corner of his eye he noticed the approach to the desk front of his first client for an order or manifest inspection signoff.

"Supervisor Schrock, I presume?" the voice said.

Schrock looked up from the ledger, mouth open and wordless at seeing Uilani's face. "Good morning. I wanted to come by before I went to work, to make sure and see you, to talk to you. Is it acceptable that I am here? Can we speak for a minute?"

Her mere presence instantly bored into his protective armor. "Yes, I guess, of course."

"I am here to apologize to you and to ask you to forgive me. Mister Schrock, you have been nothing but a dear and devoted companion these past months." She looked at him, suppressing tears. "I now realize that I have made life miserable for you. I have been inconsiderate in my inability to decide about our relationship. That note to you; that was not intended to bring any finality to our relations. It was meant to give me more time—to try and understand why it is that the two of us, so different in our backgrounds, have been brought together."

"I read it as being final," he said, "although I admit that some of your words were less so."

"It was not, and I am sorry now that I sent it. Will you forgive me, and allow me to see you again? I now know that what we have is unfinished, if that is the best way to say it."

Schrock began to feel a slow erosion of his plan to be away from her. Her words flowed through him like music—sweet, coming from that beautiful mouth. For an instant he was scared, wondering if he was like a Greek sailor being lured by a Siren. She extended her hand to him across the counter. He considered it and then held it gently. "Since tomorrow is Sunday and our day off, if you are willing, and I do hope you are, I want to take you for a picnic," she said, her eyes sincere. "Would you do that with me?"

"I am at loose ends to know what to make of you, Miss Braden. This is all quite sudden." He hadn't let go of her hand and felt the warm pulse in her wrist, muddling his judgment. "But yes, of course I will try to forgive you and I will be pleased to join you."

"Good! And I know you won't like this, but I took the liberty of asking your friend Mister Kessler if we could borrow his surrey for the day and he agreed. He will have it ready for you to pick up at nine a.m., and then you can come by to call on me. I will have some food and drink prepared to take with us. Are we agreed?"

"I'm not sure what to say, other than I am glad to see you again. I didn't expect——."

"I understand. I am very glad to see you too and will be equally so tomorrow."

As she smiled and turned away, Schrock's immediate thought was that it had to have been Kessler. He'd had something to do with this. He had showed him the note. It had to have been him.

CHAPTER 44

Honolulu - South Coast
July 1882

With Uilani seated beside him, Schrock held the reins, scarcely noticing the rough bounces of the surrey as they traveled south along the coast. They had a clear sky and cool breeze, but it could have been raining and he would have been content. It had only taken him the night to rekindle the fire that he had done his best to extinguish. How odd, he thought, the way the heart works. He also wouldn't deny that he wasn't the first man with sexual cravings.

It was south of the city and past Waikiki where she directed him to stop at the base of some low sand hills held together by scrub trees and grasses. After hobbling the horse to graze, they walked a distance over a rise and down a path to a secluded white sand cove, where she told him she used to come as a child. It was a very short stretch of beach, secreted by the trees and rocks. They laid out a blanket in the sand under a cluster of Hala trees that shaded a group of rocks, settling in with their backs against a large boulder, eating a fresh fruit and listening to the ocean. Each of them pointed out different shore birds. Schrock was silently confident that his time at sea and in ports had afforded him a fair bit of knowledge about birds.

"I wanted to tell you more about my mother, the kind of healing she did," said Uilani, as if she'd just noticed an unusual bird. "The reason is because it may help you to see why it took me so long to understand what it was about you that brought us together, unusual as it may seem. It was my mother who taught me things about *mauli ola,* the ways of healing the whole person—different than European or American medicine. It's what made me want to become a nurse. As I've told you, it wasn't just because my father was a doctor. Remember

I told you my mother came from Waimea, where my grandmother was her teacher?"

"Yes. I would like to go over there someday," Schrock replied. *With you*, he thought.

"Because my mother was a *ho'olomilomi*," she said, laying her head back on the blanket, "she often healed me with her hands when I had an illness or injury. My father never interfered—he always preferred that she work on me first and then use Western medicine as a last resort. I learned from how she took care of me the ways she could cure people. When I grew older, she often had me sit with her while she worked with the people who came to see her. She would tell me that it was a way to create harmony and balance in those people, in their circumstances. She often started by using special heated stones to increase blood flow to certain parts of the body. Then she used her hands, elbows, her forearms to massage affected areas of the body. So I know some of the practice of *ho'olomilomi*. Occasionally there are times it helps me in my work to this day."

"Why didn't you tell me more about this before?"

"I didn't think you would appreciate it, or like most *malahinis,* would reject it out of hand as some sort of sorcery. But I think you have been the one who has been holding out. Mister Kessler introduced me to your friend, Lincoln Kaole."

"What? When?"

"A few nights ago, the three of us went to dinner. That's not important. What is important is that I learned about Nakea and your involvement with him through the statue of Kamehameha on your ship."

Schrock pulled his hands down from rumpling his hair. "I know I should have told you about the both of them sooner but it didn't seem right… given how it was going between us."

"It would have gone better if you had. I've learned some but would like you to tell me more, Captain Schrock," she said, seeming to imply by using his title that he start at the beginning.

He wasn't used to taking orders but her tone was unambiguous. "I guess it is my turn to apologize. This will take a while."

After he told her about hearing Kaole's revelations about the sorcery of Nakea and Naholehua, she shook her head and gave him a hard look. "If you'd told me all this sooner, I might have been able to help you sort out what is happening through the Kamehameha statue, to help you be more trusting of what they were telling you. I was aware of Nakea and that he is respected by many native Hawaiians on Oahu. I'm fairly sure my mother knew him. Maybe you could allow me to meet Nakea… sometime soon."

"It isn't up to me. He invites us when he wants to. Not often."

"I think if you get word to him through Kaole that I would like to, it might be different now. I am not sure, but Kaole said that Nakea has seen there is something important about the two of us. I think we both know that—we have both felt it, but I would like to hear it from him."

Astonished to hear and try and take in this new piece of information, he could only say, "I will do my best."

"Mister Schrock, you are impossible. How could you have held out when you wanted to get to know me? Don't answer. I think it is time that you swim," she said, her voice feigning seriousness.

"Swim? Why swim? Is this my punishment?"

"No. Because the closer you are joined with water the closer you are to becoming Hawaiian."

"That's nonsense. We're surrounded by water," he said, sweeping his arm around, "there's no need to get in it."

"Take off your clothes. We are going in."

"What? No. I don't want to go in. I—I don't swim that well. Actually, I can't swim at all. I can sort of float around. At the maritime academy we had survival training—learning to float by kicking off our shoes and coat and leaning back with our arms out to keep our head above water. All the cadets called it the turd float."

"You are in *Hawaii nei* now Mister Schrock. You need to learn how to swim in this water, not just sail around on top of it. You are no longer a captain and you are not a missionary who finds swimming sinful. You cannot be here and not swim. Look, there is warm water everywhere," she said, gesturing around, dangling her dress that she'd just pulled off over her head. "My parents brought me here as a child many times to swim, and we never wore swimming attire. It was a Hawaiian's beach, and there was never anyone else here anyway."

"I don't take off my clothes in public," he said, trying not to see what he was seeing.

"That is absurd," she said with a smirk. "There is no public here. It is just you and me here, and I am a nurse. I've seen all kinds of naked men, alive and dead, so don't worry about me."

By this time, she had pulled off all her underclothes and lay them on a rock. Seeing her standing there naked and smiling made him shudder. He knew this would never happen where he'd grown up. In all his days, he had never been graced with a sight so breathtaking and exciting. Her breasts were perfectly shaped; in fact her whole body was as faultless as he could imagine, highlighted in the sunlight by her light olive skin and long dark hair. Carefully, he began taking his shirt off, feeling very self-conscious about the sheer whiteness of his own skin.

She smiled and walked toward him. "Hurry up, take it all off. You might not be any part *kamamaina* but I gonna do my best to make you think you are." She gave him an impish grin, turned and took off at a trot down the beach and up to the water's edge. He was following the view of her nude backside as she ran, trying not to fall down while he quickly tore off his pants, socks and underwear. He ran down to catch her, feeling at once very newly exposed and exotic, suddenly having to let go the lifetime of shame covering. When he came up beside her, she took his hand and with a sidelong glance at him, smiled and led him into the small waves. As they waded in, he began to feel alive again, an entombed man now freed to the warmth of this clear blue water, the sun able to reach all of his skin, and the acute awareness of her hand in his, a miracle in itself after all this time longing to touch her.

Panic came as he watched a swell roll toward them and quickly form into a large wave. He jerked to turn back but she let go his hand and in a split second saw her dive under it while it knocked him over, slamming him back into boiling surf and sand. The water washed back over him as he struggled awkwardly to get back on his feet, wiping saltwater and sand out of his eyes. She came up on the outer side of the waves and easily swam outward from the shore. Fifty feet out, she turned, waved at him and started heading back, reaching a point where her feet could touch the bottom. She floated up and down in water that came up to her neck and down below her breasts, her hair flowing out over her front and back. She laughed and called to him to dive under the next wave. She was so enticing to look at, he did what she said. He used all his courage to close his eyes and plummet under the next roller, trying to erase the reality that he was naked. When he emerged, sputtering, in the flat water out beyond the surf, she grabbed his hand and began patiently teaching him the basics of arm-stroke swimming and how to float lazily on his back. When she put her arms under him for support, it was all he could do to keep himself from pulling her body into his.

After a half hour, she said, "You look like you are on your way to truly living in *Hawaii nei*. I think we should go in now." He had been holding out, aching for her to finally embrace him in the water, but he complied, ready to take a break, feeling fatigue in muscles that weren't used to this.

They made their way back up the slope of the beach. A big breaker pounded the shoreline and they both turned to see it about to spill them over. He grabbed her to keep her from falling as the wave rushed over their thighs, shaking them both. With the wave subsiding, they turned and held each other close as the water slid back down over their legs. He leaned down and kissed her. She kissed him back, leaning hard into him. His heart hammered in his chest as if they had both come alive. It had been so long, he had almost forgotten how sweet the taste of a woman's lips and mouth were. He hadn't been sure of her desire for him, but she took his hand to her breast and held it there. She kissed him deeply again, then led him back up the beach to the blanket. He held her back from him a brief moment, to look at her, to ensure this was real. The earnestness in her eyes was something he hadn't seen before now and it told him what he needed to know as he pulled her to him, feeling her body soften and let go. He picked her up and she wrapped her arms around his neck and folded her body firmly around his. He laid her down on the blanket with her still holding on. They kissed each other feverishly, searching. The discovery, the newness, pounded his body and soul. And then he was in her. As they moved, he felt he'd never been joined so closely to anyone like this, bound in an unbreakable seal. *It is the two of us—it's not just me anymore. My god, there is no other place or sound, just us, here, now.* They moved like they already knew each other and it felt as if all his years of isolation at sea were torn away by the storm of her breathing and the waves that pounded inside him.

———————————

They lay there catching their breath. Schrock felt a sense of peace that seemed to have been locked away for a long, long time.

"You know, I was worried," she whispered in his ear, "the moment you first looked at me in the hospital room, that way you do."

"Umm... what way?"

"It's your uncomplicated yearning and your wanting to give—and your curiosity—all of it at once. There's a lot in your eyes, Mister Schrock. But there was that other thing that I couldn't explain... that I sensed I would need from you. It drew me in and made me very anxious."

"I did want you, oh so much, but there was something like that for me too that I could never understand," he said. "What do you think that was?"

"I still don't know. Something happened… a kind of sensation would go through my body. Not what I might normally feel when I'm attracted to a man. I tried to brush it off—brush you off—I really tried, as you know, but I couldn't. That sense of being drawn to you hasn't gone away. Trite as it may sound, it is like we were intended to find each other." She held him tighter. "I didn't like the feeling at first. I fought it, I really did. I wanted to make some kind of decision about us, based on… well, that was the problem. I didn't know what."

"I've felt the same thing about you from the moment you walked in that room," he said, "that feeling about being drawn to you—just you—that somehow we were ordained. It made me keep coming to call on you even though you seemed intent on pushing me away. You've made it so hard. Maybe someday we'll learn what it is."

"I am still so sorry for how I treated you. I am. It pains me. You know, Kaole told me how important you were to the spirit of the statue, and that you needed to follow through on helping to see that Kamehameha finds his way home. That you couldn't leave *Hawaii nei*. He hinted at—sort of implied that I had a role to play because of my relationship to you." She searched his eyes. "That is when it came to me, really made it clearer for me—there was a reason we were meant to be together."

Schrock leaned back and looked at her face. "You know, if my parents were alive, they wouldn't even begin to understand my journey and how I came to find you. I'm not sure I do. But they would be happy that I finally found someone. I could never explain any of this and it would probably have been a big adjustment for them. If they got to know you, they would love you as I do. Did I say that? I did. I love you, Uilani." He was saying it with more meaning than anything he'd said in years.

Uilani touched his cheek with her hand. "I'm finally certain that I love you, Captain Gerhard Schrock."

"Uilani. I like saying your name. It rolls off my tongue better than most Hawaiian words. Besides making me the happiest man anywhere, you have also made me very hungry. Could we eat some of the food you brought?"

"Gerhard. I think I can call you that, yes? I like it. My father would have liked you. Maybe even my mother after a year or two." She grinned and wrapped her arm around his waist. "I think we should only eat if afterward you would consider another swim and then do what we just did again."

"You are a tireless woman who must know I will do whatever you say."

"I didn't tell you the full meaning of Uilani—more than spirited and restless."

"And what would that be?"

"Always seeking pleasure," she said, nibbling his ear. "I didn't want to encourage you back when I first told you its meaning."

Along with their dried fish, bread, cheese and pieces of lillikoi and mango fruit, they finished off a bottle of red wine. They talked about their parents as they ate. Schrock told her about his childhood in Germany and more about his parents.

"And when they both died of the cholera seven years ago," he said, "I admit that even as an adult, I felt like I had been orphaned."

"When my mother died," she said, "it was worse than when my father went. The thought of it makes me sad because I was so close to her. Since I didn't have brothers or sisters to lean on, I, too, felt I was an orphan. You, me, orphans—we do have that in common, don't we?" She positioned herself so her head was on his lap. "You know, Gerhard, I miss my mother so much even though she's still with me in many ways."

Schrock lay back and pulled her into him so they could lie in each other's arms. He lay there in this new world of pleasure, feeling as if his body was shimmering, aware of being naked in the open, feeling her warm skin, hearing the waves. Of all the misery he had been through to get to this moment, he would subject himself to it again if it turned out like this. The sounds of the surf continued in soothing repetition. He sensed Uilani was asleep. Looking at her face, he wanted to nestle under those soft eyelids in the same way he'd been inside her. Instead, he felt his own eyes grow heavy.

A while later, he didn't say anything when she nudged him from his sleep, pulled him up and led him out toward the water.

Schrock could hear the clanging bell on the nearby dock warehouse, telling him he could officially close his station on the quay. He had a good Swiss watch but he continued to let the bell be the timekeeper for the end of his business day. Old ship habits aren't buried without ceremony. He liked holding on to the remnants of who he was, or at least had been. Thoughts of Uilani lying with him on the blanket had floated to him throughout the day, giving him spasmodic shivers that made him close his eyes tight while catching his breath.

He couldn't wait to break the news to Johann. He hadn't resolved how much he should tell him. A gentleman never telling was something he'd had little reason to worry about with his friend. Since his relationship with Johann was now like that of a brother, he could trust him to not disapprove and also provide... what, advice? In uncharted waters again, he would need some. And then he would interrogate him about what had happened between him, Kaole and Uilani in that dinner that had turned her head.

———————————

Johann's library felt too warm, despite all the jalousie windows being opened. "Could we go sit out in your garden?" asked Schrock.

"Take our drinks and I'll get some water. It looks like you have a lot on your mind and I wouldn't want you to get a dry mouth in the telling of whatever it is."

When they had settled into the rattan chairs next to a small wrought-iron table, Schrock held up his glass to Johann's for a toast.

"Here is to a fine day, with a good friend, in a wonderful kingdom."

"Hear, hear," said Johann. "I don't know that I have ever, and I mean ever, heard you sound so positive. So spill it, Schrock. What brought this on?"

"If you don't know, then you've been asleep while the thief emptied your store. It's simple... Uilani's accepted me. I think we're in love. I know I am."

Johann's eyes widened. "How? I knew if you were patient it could work out. What's happened to bring this about?"

"You tell me, you pretender. You know, don't you? You got Kaole to help change her mind about me, didn't you? And don't lie about it. She told me you had a dinner talk."

Johann held up his hands in defense. "It was a last ditch effort to keep you from leaving. I'm not sure what all was said. I left the two of them to talk while I ran an errand. They did all their talking in Hawaiian, so I'm not sure what Kaole told her. But what I did hear him say was that Nakea believes you are integral to the statue and how needed you are here."

"I am angry that you messed with my love problem, Kessler. And I will be forever grateful to you for doing just that, my friend. You may have saved my life."

"You are welcome. Now tell me what has happened."

"She came by my work to apologize—for the note, and for how she had been treating me. I was shocked, to have her show up there in the morning. But she got to me. I melted and forgave her. It was her idea to go for the outing when we used your surrey. We went to a beach she had been to as a child and we made a day of it. It was down the coast—secluded. Things went well."

Johann pulled at his ear. "Things went well. That's it. That's all you're going to say. It went well?"

Schrock felt himself reddening. "She convinced me to go in the water, but we had no bathing clothes! Johann, it was amazing, so outrageous and liberating all at the same time. And she is so beautiful, I mean, in the flesh. Like a goddess. I felt like I had died and gone to your Valhalla, particularly after, you know, we made love right there on the beach. She is everything I've ever wanted: headstrong, fearless, and she wants me. I am so lucky, so happy that I don't know what to do with myself."

"Amazing is right! After what you've been through with her. I'm scandalized! A nice German boy like you." Johann's straight face finally split with a grin and something like a giggle. "So what do you plan to do… next, I mean? Will you finally marry?"

"Yes, I hope, if she will have me as her husband. I plan to ask her tomorrow, when we are going out to dinner. Of course I will first buy a proposal ring. What do you think?"

"It sounds right to me. If she says yes, I would be glad to help you with whatever you need for a marriage, including having your wedding reception right here at my home, if you would like."

"Kessler, you are going to make a grown man cry."

"And if she refuses?"

"Damn you. You can kiss my ass hanging from the stern of the ship I'll sail with."

CHAPTER 45

South East Honolulu, Niu Stream

Makia and Palmele uncovered the box with the dynamite and blasting caps they had hidden to be sure it was still well protected and dry. Satisfied, they reported back to Naholehua, frustrated that nothing was happening that would allow them to get at the hateful statue, the bronze still sitting somewhere in a well-guarded warehouse.

"Why can't you boys find out where it is?" Naholehua asked them.

"We told you," replied Palmele, "they moved it at night from that foundry we tried to burn to some other place. Nobody is talking about where it is. All we have heard is it's still being repaired."

"You're worth nothing anymore if you can't find it. We have a way to wipe away this stain on the family and you tell me it has gone into a dark hole. Good dynamite is being wasted."

Makia wondered again why such a powerful *moe uhane* soul-sleep traveler couldn't find this annoying effigy, that he expected the two of them to be his detectives because of his shortcoming, his wasted talent. Suddenly the old *kahuna* raised his arms and started shouting, pointing at the two of them, "Go find it so we can see it exploded to pieces, into tiny grains of sand!"

CHAPTER 46

Stina was all business when it came to something like planning a wedding. "You stand over here, Mister Schrock, and you here, Miss Braden," she said, directing the rehearsal in the chancel of the Lutheran Church the Kessler's attended. She had assumed this role for the bishop before, and he was just as glad not to be bothered. Stina also had shepherded Uilani through all the things her own mother was not there to do for her: choosing a dress, selecting flowers, bridesmaid's dresses and the like. Uilani actually had mixed feelings about it all. She'd once imagined that if she ever married, it would be a traditional Irish wedding that her father had told her about, with her father standing proud beside her; or maybe it would be a Hawaiian wedding, several of which she had attended with her mother, completely different but probably closer to who she was. In the end, it felt best to do something that she and Schrock would both be comfortable with.

The wedding ceremony was on a Saturday morning, when the air was still cool and fresh. It was an intimate wedding party, made up of a few of Uilani's close friends from childhood, her aunt, uncle and two cousins who had traveled over from Waimea, and several hospital co-workers. Schrock's invited included Johann, Stina and their girls, Kaole, Deetjen and three of his co-workers.

Schrock, hair cut and pomaded, wore a black silk suit and white tie tailored especially for the day. He'd refined his normally rugged features to the point of such a severe changeover that he was startled when he'd first looked in a mirror. He stood uncomfortably at the front of the chancel, along with the bishop, Johann, as his best man and the bridesmaids. When the music began, he turned to see Uilani brought up the aisle by her uncle. The sight of her made him feel like the bones in his legs were dissolving. He'd never seen her dressed so stunning. Her hair was done up high on her head and she wore a pearl-adorned unconventional white dress that highlighted the olive glow of her skin, from her face, down her neck to her bare shoulders. As she neared the altar, he found himself reaching deep for a breath, much like in the torrential gales at sea, when the sheer power and spectacle were nearly overwhelming as he struggled for mouthfuls of air.

When they all arrived at Johann's house for a lunch reception afterward, the mood was lightened mostly by Kaole, who was a natural at bridging gaps between *kanaka maoli*, *kama'aina* and *haole*. Schrock appreciated his skill as he watched him ensure that Uilani's family and friends were at ease, making introductions and opening up conversations around the room.

As the afternoon wore on, Schrock had mixed emotions about what was taking place: to be finally married to a woman of his dreams and at the same time be uncomfortable with the formal trappings to make it happen. He didn't take the news well when Johann said it was considered bad form to serve alcohol at a Lutheran reception. He could do with a few drinks about now, as it would likely make him a more amiable and conversant groom.

He felt Uilani's arm slip through his. "Hello, Mister Schrock. It's so good that you could come today. I hope to see more of you later." She gave him a coquettish smile and moved on to talk with more of the guests. How did she know what he was thinking, this mischievous angel who had just rescued him? He'd make it through the day's events without a drink. He turned and headed toward Uilani's uncle.

"Well, what do you think of the view?" asked Schrock, pointing toward the bay through the upstairs window. He and Uilani were in an upstairs flat of a house, a place they had rented, large enough for the two of them. This was the solution, since neither of their own places felt adequate. It was the first morning after their one week trip to the Island of Maui, where they had explored parts of the island.

"I know you wouldn't have had it any other way—being able to see the water," she said. "But yes, I like it, especially being up higher and picking up the ocean breezes." Schrock watched Uilani move about in a thin dress. She made the morning as bright as the sunlight coming through the window. Each of them going off to work would be a new adventure, as would having each other to return to in the evening. What a change it was going to be. The thought of it gave him that now-familiar shiver.

It was dusk as Uilani held Schrock's arm as they walked back to their apartment after eating out with Johann at a small nearby restaurant. "You know, to hear you two talk, it seems like the king, the prime minister and their supporters in the palace party are the last political force against the unraveling of what's left of the people who are *kanaka maoli*."

"You would know better than me, but that's probably true. It seems that the king and Gibson's only other allies here are trusted *kama'aina* friends and the American they call the 'Sugar King', the big grower and exporter named Spreckels."

"We all know about him."

"Then you know the king is rumored to be heavily in debt to Spreckels," said Schrock. "Unfortunately, that gives the opposition more cause to fight whatever he and Gibson want. Most native people don't know how to maneuver the new laws of land ownership or business regulations that heavily favor the *haoles*. The white population ever more controls the land and the economy. And as you can guess, when the whites talk among themselves, most still consider natives who don't conform to our ways as being savage." Saying 'our ways' made him instantly feel self-conscious, a stranger in a foreign land.

"I guess that would make me a *hapa* savage, at least some of the time."

Schrock looked at her face and could tell she wasn't attempting any humor, that slights like this ran deep for her.

They did their best to avoid the mud through another intersection. "So is there anything you and Johann can do to make a difference?"

Schrock didn't look over at her as they walked, not surprised that she would get to the heart of things.

"The problem is that neither of us has any experience in politics. And Johann—well, he wants to keep his name out of the papers—a matter perhaps he will tell you about sometime. I should get more involved now that I'm here to stay. And there must be a few other Europeans with influence who care something about the injustice. I just haven't run into any yet, especially Germans."

Uilani gave him a look that seemed to expect a clearer commitment, turning her head toward his until he caught her eye. Of course she would. His response had been feeble. He knew he'd wanted her for more than companionship. This was a reminder she could be counted on to untie the rest of the package he'd bargained for.

CHAPTER 47

Kaole had made an arrangement with his uncle and with Johann to continue working for Johann a couple of days a week. Schrock was pleased to see his friend again, both on the docks and in Johann's office. There was much he wanted to talk with him about, especially the arrival of the statue.

Over the next two weeks, he ate with Kaole several times, including one afternoon with Uilani, when the three of them sat at a small waterfront café, enjoying fish soup and black bread. Uilani seemed comfortable asking him questions about his new undertaking as an apprentice to Nakea. Kaole eased into more pidgin as they spoke. He didn't give away much about his training, but described for her Waialae, Nakea's village, and how much he loved it there. He was talking about how the Waialae village fish pond functioned when he mentioned the invitation, as if it were part of the same conversation.

"Nakea want you, Miss Uilani, Mister Kessler and Mister Deetjen to come over there for *ho'o pili haipule*."

"Come over for what?" Schrock asked, not sure what he'd heard.

"*Ho'o pili haipule*. It like a ceremony."

"I was with my mother at one of those when I was young, up the *mauka*," said Uilani. "I think it was to honor a new chief of our district *ahupua'a*. So what is this ceremony for?"

"He didn't tell me. I only his apprentice," replied Kaole, his face giving nothing away.

Schrock had wanted to hear more from Nakea, and to introduce him to Deetjen, but instantly he started thinking what they might be in for if they accepted. There was ample reason to be wary of the *kahuna's* abilities. If any of his claims were true, how many other times might Nakea have crossed Schrock's path without his knowing about it? Had this man altered his life's trajectory beyond what he'd already been told? Losing his ship and all the other difficulties that had come behind was monumental enough. But then, there was this connection to Uilani through him—.

The informal manner Kaole passed on the invitation for his uncle made Schrock realize how little he knew about Hawaiian ways. The first time he and Johann had gone to see Nakea, Kaole had to be pressured to allow them to visit with his *kahuna* uncle. Now the relationships had changed, or at least it seemed that way. It was easier for Schrock when he could use his ship's telescope to see his way through mist-shrouded seas. He was glad Uilani would be along. Hopefully she could help interpret whatever they were to experience.

"What do you think this might be about?" Uilani asked after they'd left Kaole.

"Your guess is as good as mine. As a *kama'aina* I was hoping you might have a better feeling about this than me. Whatever it is, you said you wanted to meet Nakea. Now you're going to get your wish."

On Sunday afternoon, Schrock, Uilani, Johann and Deetjen traveled in Johann's surrey on the jarring road that led around the back of the Diamond Head caldera toward Waialae. As they traveled, they conjectured more about Nakea's ceremony. Was it to be a Hawaiian marriage of Schrock and Uilani that Nakea thought they were obliged to complete? Was it in recognition of Kaole's full apprenticeship? Johann joked uneasily that it might be for their induction into Nakea's world of dream journeying. The talk only left Schrock apprehensive.

When they reached the village, Kaole and his uncle came out of the thatch *hale* to greet them. After Nakea briefly acknowledged Schrock and Johann, he went directly to Deetjen, putting his hands on Deetjen's shoulders and saying words of greeting. Kaole said, "He is glad you came to see him again. He likes you very much 'cause you a man of conviction."

"I—I'm sorry," Deetjen addressed Nakea, "I don't remember having met you before." An instant passed. "He can't mean on the ship, can he, like with Captain Schrock?" he asked Kaole.

"Yeah," Kaole said. "He says he saw you tell the men what to do."

Schrock glanced sideways at his mate. He thought he was taking Nakea's revelations better than he had more than a year ago, when the *kahuna* had told him he'd seen him on the *Haendel* while far out at sea.

"I see what you've been talking about," Deetjen mumbled to Schrock and Kaole, "his moving about in the world."

"Unsettling, isn't it?" Schrock murmured back.

Then Nakea turned his attention to Uilani. He took her hands and began speaking to her. Schrock glanced at Kaole for translation. "My uncle says he knew Uilani's mother, that she was a valued healer." He listened more as Nakea spoke. "Yeah, he also say he knew her when she been in her mother's womb. He's glad to greet her again."

Schrock watched her start to well up with emotion because of the implication—that Nakea had known of her from the time she was conceived. Nakea looked straight into her eyes and smiled. She nodded while saying something to him quietly in Hawaiian, seeming grateful for this revered man who had appreciated her mother and was accepting of Uilani as a whole person.

Nakea put his hands on both her shoulders and spoke to her again. What he said appeared to stun Kaole. In a voice just above a whisper, he translated what he'd heard. She gripped Schrock's arm as Kaole translated her words to the others.

"He says she has the gift to see."

All eyes turned to Uilani. She looked relieved to have heard those words, as if someone was finally affirming something deep within her.

"I'm—I always believed there was more than one dimension," said Uilani. "Other than the visions of my mother, friends I have lost, I never expected that it would be presented to me this way." She took a few steps away and walked around in a circle, looking down. "Him saying this makes me feel like coming out of a shell. It is strange, and wonderful at the same time." Uilani moved up to Nakea and spoke to him in Hawaiian. He smiled and nodded as the words tumbled from her mouth.

Judging from the impact it had on Kaole, *Kahuna* Nakea's simple statement must have been something akin to a Catholic beatification. The difference was that Uilani was very much alive for the *kahuna's* proclamation. Schrock wasn't sure what to believe. If this was true, who would she be with him? But unlike someone being destined for sainthood, he'd prefer to think of her as the lightning in a bottle he'd first encountered at the hospital. That was enough for now.

Deetjen stood with his mouth half open, listening, watching, a newly conscripted sailor waiting to be told what to do next.

Kaole led them to an open, thatch-covered structure where they sat on a floor made of fine wave-worn stone and coral, partially covered with *tapa* mats. Joined by Nakea's wife, they were treated to a large meal of fish, poi, sweet potatoes and breadfruit, everyone eating with their hands in traditional island style. "A fine meal," said Johann. "I'm grateful to eat in the *hale* of Nakea." When Kaole translated, his uncle nodded, smiled and kept eating. Schrock was amazed at what a big appetite this priest had for being so thin a man.

Afterward, when the food was cleared away, Kaole and Nakea carried in a drinking gourd and cups. "He wants you each to drink some *awa* for this," said Kaole. "This drink used for lotta healing things and for ceremony. Some people use it too much and their head not straight. But we're not gonna do that."

Kahuna Nakea walked around the circle and poured a small amount of *awa* in a coconut shell cup for each of them. The liquid looked like muddy water to Schrock. Nakea returned to his place, then sat down and spoke.

"Nakea want you to drink, but leave some in the cup," Kaole said, "then pour on the ground behind the mat. That is thank you to the earth where it come from. I gonna tell you *awa* make your mouth feel slow for a while. And it doesn't taste so good. But don't worry, it's not bad for you. It heals lot of things." He passed around a small bowl with pieces of banana. "Eat this when the *awa* tastes too bad for you."

Nakea had seated himself cross-legged and was quietly watching them all. He closed his eyes and began a chant that went on for several minutes. When he stopped, he smiled and then gestured for them each to drink. They all followed suit, watching each other.

True to Kaole's warning, it tasted like bitter dirt. Schrock reached for the piece of banana, noticing Johann and Uilani doing the same. He felt the effects of the *awa,* with numbness in his mouth and slight nausea. They all remained silent as the solemnity of the occasion settled in. Schrock had never experienced anything quite like the sensation he was having: the surroundings in sharp focus, the awareness that he was with the people he cared most about in life, allowing himself to put his trust in this native mystic. He glanced at Uilani to see how she was faring but her face revealed little.

Finally Nakea spoke to them again and Kaole translated.

"Kamehameha's *mana* in that statue was always intended to be with *lahui*, the people of *Hawaii nei*. And it take place in a long journey that Nakea start dreaming three years ago. And even now he don't know why it happening this way, with you four. But this is what he has seen."

Kahuna Nakea paused and poured himself another small amount of *awa* and gulped it. He closed his eyes, and when he opened them he looked directly at Schrock. Schrock was jolted by the sight of the *kahuna's* black eyes appearing as tunnels leading to another world. Nakea then said a few words, and Kaole translated.

"The captain of your ship who died—he die so that ship could be your ship."

Schrock nearly fell over backwards. How could he know about Sanders' dying? "That wasn't why he died. He—it was his heart!"

"Like fish and birds and trees, we all gonna die," Kaole went on. "Nakea say that when he die, that was his time. It was the time."

Nakea continued talking, pausing for Kaole to translate. Schrock saw Uilani nodding in her understanding.

"You had to be captain of that ship, to come into the circle to protect the *mana* of Kamehameha on his journey. And then you still gonna do that after he gets where he belong—at his birthplace in Kohala… and in the hearts of all the people."

"What circle?" asked Schrock, still reeling in confusion. "All of us," Kaole said, gesturing to the group with his arm. His furrowed brow exposed how personal this was to him. "You know how the spider web is tied together." He held out the palms of his hands with his fingers spread. "Nakea is my uncle and he is my *kahuna*. I got a job with Mister Kessler and he been my teacher, too. I tied to him." He used the index finger on his other hand to point out the imaginary connection. "Mister Kessler, he comes for a long journey on your ship and then he got a tie with you," he went on, tracing an imaginary web on his one hand with a finger from the other. "He tell you to come to *Hawaii nei* so he can be your brother and your *kahuna pule*—maybe like your pastor." Schrock could see the trace of a grin on Johann's face. "And then Mister Deetjen come here too, to be with us. Kamehameha is on that ship with all of you. The Conqueror got tied to you. You all meant to be."

"But why not Captain Sanders in this circle? Why me?"

Kaole listened again to Nakea, who was looking at Uilani and then back at Schrock.

"Because of Uilani," said Kaole, "it could not be that other captain. For the reason that you tied to her… it could only be you. And Nakea say that other captain very pleased with you."

Schrock felt sweat trickle down his forehead, his mind spinning. *Jesus, can this man communicate with the dead, too? I shouldn't even be asking.* He looked at Uilani in desperation but her attention was focused on Nakea.

"You always been tied to Uilani," said Kaole, "even when you didn't think you been. Now all of us make the web that can protect Kamehameha's *mana*. Nakea says that is what he honor today." After an uncomfortable silence, Schrock said, "I find all of this hard to accept. When we were at sea I never thought about trying to protect that statue. And why us foreigners? Why would we have anything to do with the *mana* of your god-king?"

Kaole asked and then listened to Nakea's response, pondering it for a moment.

"He say you could not know any of this was happening. You have to learn to 'see' it," he said, emphasizing the word. "At first my uncle didn't trust how *haoles* have anything to do with the *mana* of the Great One. He still doesn't understand it—he just see it. When he saw that ship with the statue out there on the ocean, and see you men, he remember what he knew—all of us—*kanaka maoli* and *haole*—we all in more than one world at the same time, and there are cords that connect both."

Uilani nodded and smiled as if that statement had opened a gate.

After another period of quiet, Johann asked, "Kaole, do you believe all of this?"

"Yeah, Mister Kessler, I do. Nakea teach me to see it clear when I dream, and I know we got another soul that moves when we dream."

"I'm sure I have always felt that," Uilani said, her head down, "but never fully allowed it."

Nakea poured himself another small amount of *awa* and drank it, closed his eyes for a few moments, then began to speak again for some time.

"Mister Kessler," Kaole finally said, "Nakea says you come to *Hawaii nei* for special reason. Now you gonna do something important for *lahui,* the people. And you won't need to worry about what happened in that place where you lived. Nakea see you when you have a fight with a man and hit him. You think you killed him and then come to Honolulu, your *pu'uhonua,* your place of refuge."

Johann stared at the floor in front of him, clearly shaken by what he was hearing and embarrassed that both Kaole, Uilani and Deetjen would have learned this about him. "But he say this man not die. That man woke up. He got a very bad nose... that's all that happen. That's all. See!" Kaole's face was a picture of joy. "You meant to come to *Hawaii nei*."

"I—I can't believe it," said Johann, breathless. "All this time—all the-the agony of it. I—is he sure?" Schrock had never seen his friend so disoriented.

"Yeah, Mister Kessler, he sure. I don't want to ask him again about that. He always tell the truth what he sees."

Johann shook his head, and then started laughing. "It's absurd—amazing! It's wonderful—the whole thing." Schrock reached out and squeezed Johann's shoulder and saw that he was crying.

Nakea took more sips of *awa*, pouring some out, and then after a pause, spoke again, this time turning his attention to Deetjen.

"Mister Deetjen," translated Kaole, "Nakea says you've been taking care of Kamehameha's *mana*, like Captain Schrock."

Deetjen looked over at Schrock to see if he might know what Kaole meant. Schrock could only shrug. "How?" Deetjen asked.

Kaole queried his uncle.

"You pushed that Kamehameha statue into the water off the ship. My uncle said he helped you to do that." It was the second occasion Schrock had clearly seen the whites of Deetjen's eyes. This time it was like his mate had been struck by lightning on the top of his head. Apparently he was struck dumb, because he said nothing for a full minute and everyone else was silent.

Deetjen finally said, "I remember... I remember feeling like I'd done that for some important reason. But it wasn't God telling me to do it or the Devil. It was something else." He hesitated. "Is he saying? I'm sorry, Mister Nakea... Kaole ask him, are you telling me you were somehow there making me do that?"

It was apparent Nakea could see the deep suspicion written on Deetjen's face, since he spoke to Kaole right away.

"He says he know you believe in your god," said Kaole, "and your god does things you usually can't see with your eyes, but they still there. He is telling you he was there in his dream. He says there were some other men with poles to help you."

Deetjen shook his head. "I don't know how I would ever be able to explain any of this to my mother."

Nakea spoke again, still directing his words at Deetjen, and Kaole translated. "All those men who died on a ship you were on, they hold no blame with you. They believe you a good man and a brother at sea who should still be there, master of men at sea, where your talent lies."

Schrock watched Deetjen shake his head back and forth, then up and down, obviously trying to understand how Nakea could have known about this haunting incident in his past and what the *kahuna* was telling him. "This is very hard for me to talk about. How can he know about what happened, Kaole? Well, maybe he could know somehow, but how would he know what those men, those men who died, think of me? Did I hear you right? They want me to go back to sea. This… I don't understand."

"You heard me say, my uncle he has learned to travel in two worlds. He can have a presence with the spirits of the living and those who have passed over. It is like that for him. You must believe me, Mister Deetjen, in your life you will probably never meet another like this man."

Deetjen was quiet, appearing humbled by what he'd heard. What a shift from his zealot ways, thought Schrock.

"It is almost like Mister Nakea has read my mind. I have been dreaming about being back at sea, thinking how I missed it."

Nakea spoke again. "He say there is something you each already know," said Kaole. "Many more *haoles* will come to our islands. These people need to hear the story of Kamehameha. But most important, for the people who got heart that opens up, the strength of his *mana* must pass to them. This the only way *Hawaii nei* can endure." Kaole's eyes passed over each of theirs. "And we all gonna make that happen."

There was an uncomfortable silence as this jarring summons caused expressions of bewilderment, wondering what he was expecting.

Nakea nodded separately to Schrock, Uilani, Johann and Deetjen. He voiced a short chant, and then spoke at what appeared to be the end of their ceremony.

"You are *ohana*—family," translated Kaole. "You always welcome here."

As well as his friend Kaole, Schrock was humbled to have the acceptance of Nakea. He felt like they'd just been through a sea-storm of bewilderment and revelation with this forceful Hawaiian, a wisp of a man who seemed to straddle more than one world with agility and confidence.

"Kaole," Uilani said, "please thank Nakea again for helping bring the captain and me together… and for opening the door to who I know I am. I'm indebted to him."

"Yeah, I do that."

"And tell him," said Johann, "I'll be forever grateful for freeing me from my awful burden."

Deetjen's smile was uncommon for the strict sailor. "Mister Kaole, please tell your uncle it has been a pleasure meeting him. He has helped me in ways I never thought possible."

I'm grateful too, thought Schrock, *for whatever it is you've done, even though I can't see to understand it.* This was all making him feel regret for all his past complaints of bad luck visited on him and his ship. He now sensed that those events and what had followed had all been gifts. Today was special, even if he didn't see himself ever being able to penetrate this mystery. "Kaole, please tell him I am so very grateful to be here in *Hawaii nei*."

———————————————

The ruts in the road and the hard springs of the surrey kept Schrock awake for the journey back to Honolulu, apparently an awake of introspection for each of them, since there was little talk. Schrock tried to review what was most puzzling. In addition to Nakea's astonishing ability to travel in dream spirit, it was that he thought they had been protecting Kamehameha's *mana*. But Nakea said even he didn't understand what had pulled him, Uilani, Johann and Deetjen into its hold, four *haoles* intimately joined to this ancient cultural web. Schrock had no confidence that he would ever be able to 'see' to understand it. For Uilani, her potential appeared to be different. He didn't know if he could tell her he envied her the gift to see into something like other dimensions. He wasn't even sure that was an accurate description of what he felt.

There were traits in Uilani that snared him and reeled him in. Besides her beauty, she was unconventional, open to the extraordinary and quietly fierce. And when he was able to admit it, there were moments those qualities made him anxious about being her match. He tried to sort through who she was and who they would be, to find a place where it would fit comfortably in his mind, considering that this woman would benefit from seeing the world through different eyes than all the people he had ever known back home. Schrock glanced over at Kaole and wondered what his inner world was like.

He woke with a jolt after briefly dozing off. As the road thumped on, he began to think about how he had arrived at this very spot, on this road: his journey. It was the statue. Because of its symbolic value, the statue of the warrior king was worth protecting, as was telling the king's story. He knew the century-long clash of cultures and religion, the demise of the Hawaiian race, and the assault on the monarchy by foreign residents portended an uncertain future for this island nation. But now that they were given the charge, how were they to consciously go about shielding Kamehameha's *mana,* a shapeless, even pagan entity, to recent *haole* arrivals like him, Johann, and even Deetjen? Seeing that some essence of it had been passed on was another question. He was grateful to now have Uilani by his side, to try and manage this task with her. She might have some answers. But what was it that made him feel so responsible?

A question lingered that he had been struggling with. Nakea had asserted Kamehameha's *mana* resided in the statue. Schrock had studied theology enough to know about the concept of the holy spirit; that it is the breath, the animating power, the soul of God. From what he had heard from Kaole and Nakea, the ideas of *mana* and that of the holy spirit served the same purposes for believers. Maybe it would be helpful to use that as a starting place to grasp what they were supposed to be doing. Later they would need help on this from Kaole. As he liked to tell them, he had done his time at Christian school. He would understand their *haole* dilemma.

CHAPTER 48

Honolulu
November 1882

Deetjen was sheepish about telling Schrock his decision. His hangdog posture was almost like that of a child in trouble. It reminded Schrock of the time he had seen him on the quarterdeck, mulling over the fact that they would be loading the statue onto the *Haendel*. He always knew when there was something up with the man. "Talk to me, Mister Deetjen. What's bothering you?"

"It's like this, sir. I've taken on a berth as a first mate: a schooner sailing in three days for Bremen."

"You don't say?" Shrock exclaimed, trying to withhold a knowing grin.

"You see, sir, their mate came down sick and isn't able to travel, so they heard I was here and the captain recruited me. I actually know the man a bit… met him years ago. Good man."

"You were planning to do this anyway, weren't you?"

"Well, yessir, I sort of was. Ever since we had that time with Mister Nakea, it became very clear in my mind it's what I needed to do to be myself again. And I plan to put in for my Master papers and take the examinations when I return. Do you think I am ready?"

"Yes, you are. You will make a shipmaster who can ply the seas with confidence, confidence that comes with the knowledge and skills of abundant experience. But there is something else just as important." Schrock put his hand on Deetjen's elbow, a liberty he had never taken, and looked him straight on. "It appears to me that you've quit holding on to the harsh and judgmental God of yours and perhaps embraced one that is merciful and loves mankind, including yourself. I feel that will ensure smooth sailing. What do you think, Mister Deetjen?"

Deetjen's face wrinkled as if he were about to cry. "Ever since I arrived here, I have been treated with care and decency, by you, Mister Kessler, and especially Missus Kessler. She has been so kind to me, demonstrating true Christian charity." He paused, looked around and up at the sky. "I don't know quite how to say this, but ever since our meeting with Mister Nakea, I have not been the same. Just his telling me that those souls who died in that shipwreck did not find blame with me—whether it is true or not—has freed me in some way... lifted a great burden from me. But when he held my shoulders, looked in my eyes and spoke to me, even though I didn't understand the words, I felt something happen. Like a healing. Yessir, it must have been a healing, because all the pain in my heart seems to be going away. I know that is blasphemous for me to think that—him not being a Christian. But sir, I cannot deny that my heart feels lifted and I am now feeling generous to all living souls. It is quite remarkable."

There was a moment of silence as the two men looked at each other, eye to eye. Schrock thought that Kaole's description of them as *ohana* had really happened. He was at peace with this man. He swallowed the choke in the back of his throat.

"Well then, Captain Deetjen, we will need to have a going away event to send you off properly. I know Johann and Stina will want to host a dinner party on Sunday, before you leave. And I shall expect you to give us a farewell speech, including needed advice to the two of us about how to comport ourselves from now on with more dignity and self-respect."

For a moment, Deetjen's face screwed up in shock. Gradually, it changed to a grin as he wagged his head at Schrock.

CHAPTER 49

Honolulu, Niu Stream
December 1882

When they had all squatted down on the sandy ground, Naholehua stared at the two of them like they were thoughtless dogs. Makia felt the seething rage he saw in his stepfather's black eyes.

"We will make this captain wish he had never crossed paths with the statue of this pretender king or had even come to *Hawaii nei*," Naholehua hissed. "And we will make him pay through that *hapa* wife of his. It is very hard for me to do *ho'ounauna* or *'ana'ana* with *haoles*. But this *hapa* can have dreams that can let me in. She is going to feel the pain. You know I need to look at her first and you are going to take me to the hospital in the morning—at the time she comes to work. We will be like patients waiting to get help there."

Makia thought that Naholehua was being as coherent as he'd seen him in a long time. Wanting to hurt or kill people clearly stirred up the best in him.

Early next morning, the three of them were in a loose line of people outside the entrance to Queen's Hospital, waiting to be seen before it opened. "Palmele," Naholehua said in low murmur so he wouldn't be overheard, "you make sure and show me who she is when she come in. It would be good if you could stop her and ask her a question."

"Like what?" whispered Palmele, stupefied by the request.

"Don't be so slow," scolded Makia. "Just ask her when the doors will open and we can go in."

They waited a while and Naholehua said, "You both need to start learning about this. If you are to see to make *'ana'ana* with someone you have to get that person in your mind's eye to find them in your dream. Beside looking at this *hapa,* I want to hear her. I want to watch her face, how she walks, how she is."

Ten minutes later Palmele nudged Naholehua and gestured with his head toward Uilani, who was coming up the walkway from the carriage stop.

Uilani looked back over her shoulder at the man who had just asked her about when the hospital opened. It seemed odd; local people were usually patient, wouldn't ask something like that. The old man behind him with the long stringy hair... why had he been looking at her so fiercely? She felt something stir deep inside her and it was not good. Her body shivered with cold.

So as not to be noticed, the three men nonchalantly walked out of line one by one and left the hospital grounds. As soon as they were by themselves, Naholehua said, "We have something else important to do now. Palmele, take us to the place where she lives."

"Yeah, well she lives with that Captain now, but we know where that place is."

On their way to Schrock and Uilani's place, Naholehua explained that they were going there to get some articles of hers, maybe some clothing or hair or food leavings to do *'ana'ana.* These kinds of things were called *maunu,* to be burned along with saying *ka pule kuni* prayers. "I do this on three nights in a row. On the last of these nights, the ashes of this *hapa's maunu* I gonna throw into the sea. Then she will die in two to four days," he stated matter-of-factly. Makia's mind reeled with what he was hearing. He felt pulled by being able to have power over someone's life. Naholehua had indifferently said it just as a healing *kahuna* would pronounce that the person would be better in two to four days. Makia squeezed his eyes tight and told himself that this could not be right, that he would never be this kind of sorcerer.

Makia was good at break-ins. He had a friend at the missionary school on Molokai who was rotten to the core, always looking for ways to flout authority. Makia had been drawn to companion with him and had picked up some interesting skills. He had no trouble opening a back window of their apartment without breaking it and having the slender Palmele slip in and open the main door for them to get in. They were careful not to disturb anything and take only a select few items from the bottom of some drawers that looked as if they were seldom worn by her, some of her hair from a wastebasket, and leftover food in the sink. After he locked the front door, Palmele went out the window the way he'd come in.

Four days later, in the middle of the night, Schrock woke up to the sound of Uilani groaning. He dismissed it as her having a bad dream and went back to sleep, only to hear her again wake him with screams of pain. She was writhing on the bed but appeared to Schrock to still be asleep. He shook her. "Wake up, wake up, Uilani! What's happening?"

Her eyes opened and he saw terror as well as pain. "Oh, Gerhard, I hurt all over. I was having a horrible nightmare—stabbed by a large man-beast. Oh god, the pain, it's everywhere... my head hurts so badly! Ohhh Gerhard, it's awful! Make it stop!"

Schrock looked all over her body, quickly turning her over to examine her to see if she had any bites or bruising and saw nothing. She was sweating profusely and whimpering, making him feel frantic. "We need to get a doctor." How can he find a doctor at this time of night, he wondered? This is urgent—he could go to Johann's. He would know where to find one. But he didn't want to leave her alone. Just take her over to the hospital. Maybe there was a doctor on duty at night. Her eyes were open wide, full of terror, until he saw her squeezing them tight, as if to shut out the pain and the strange and malicious attacker come to her dream.

"No, no doctor," she gasped. "I know what's happening. It's—I'm being cursed by that *kahuna* Naholehua. He's done *ho'ounauna* on me, to make me sick. Oh dear god it's working. I feel like I am dying. It could be—maybe he's trying to kill me—maybe *'ana'ana*."

"God, are you sure?" gasped Schrock, incredulous.

"Yes. Oh Gerhard, it hurts so much. I can't stop it! I need Nakea— I need him to help me." Her face was gripped in anguish. "Go—go to Kaole, now." Schrock got her some water, hugged her, put a wet towel on her forehead and was out the door as his mind ran wild with fear. This was the first test—his trust that Uilani had the gift to see—that she knew best about a cure for whatever the horrible thing was she was experiencing.

Schrock and Kaole were driving Johann's horse as fast as they dared, the surrey they had borrowed taking every bump hard on the road to Waialae. It would be at least another half hour or more, the trip slower because of the darkness, the morning light hours away. Schrock was anxious that Nakea might not be there, that he may be reluctant to come with them back to Honolulu, that he wouldn't have whatever it was he needed to counter this sorcery that may be killing Uilani—if that's what it was.

When they arrived, Nakea was sitting out in front of his *hale* as if he hadn't slept or always got up before light. He was prepared. There were several filled *tapa* bags on the ground beside him. He rose as Kaole jumped down from the surrey to greet his uncle with *honi*. Schrock did the same, touching forehead and nose with Nakea's.

On the way back to Honolulu, Kaole told Schrock that Nakea had seen that Uilani was sick, that he would be summoned to help. That is why he was waiting for them when they arrived. Schrock thought that if he had any doubts about the powers of this man, he should let them go now. It was beyond logic, something another part of him would have to accept.

"What will he do when we get there?" he asked Kaole.

He glanced back at Nakea sitting in the seat behind them in the surrey, almost serene despite the bumpy road. "My uncle, he practice *ho'opi'opi'o* a long time. That is to stop the bad curse that *kahuna* like Naholehua do to make people sick or die. I know he has done that to help people before." There was a pause while he seemed to be considering what he would say next. "I think that we gonna have to take Uilani over to a quiet place by the water for him to do that. You understand?"

"I'll do anything," said Schrock. "We need to save her. I can't lose her." He felt himself bottling up tears.

"Nakea know that. I know that. She is *ohana*."

CHAPTER 50

Honolulu
January 1883

Schrock settled into a chair in Johann's office after work, having been summoned by Kaole. "I've been trying to guess what was it you wanted to tell me."

"First tell me how Uilani is doing. Is she feeling all right? We haven't seen either of you in days."

"She is fine. No noticeable problems since her recovery. She has been back at work for the last week. I'm sorry we don't get over here more often for a visit. Married life is different, isn't it? It's what I wanted and it's what you pressed me to have, wasn't it?"

"Yes, I suppose I did."

"Do I detect you miss my visits, bothering you with my courtship troubles and then drinking ourselves silly while we fall into existential sinkholes?"

Johann just held up his hands and didn't seem to be able to answer. "Well, anyway, before I get into the news I have for you, at least give me a description of what Nakea did for Uilani. Tell me something about what he did or that you saw him do. Kaole told me a little but I want to hear it from you."

"Kaole and I put her in your surrey. I held her; she was still in terrible pain, and we went to that remote beach she had taken me to— the one where we... you know, *swam*."

"I remember your account well, Schrock."

"When we got there, we made a small fire and laid her out on a blanket in the sand beside it. Nakea set out a number of bowls and cups, some sticks, small bags with leaves or powders, and a gourd with *awa*. Kaole and I moved back a ways and just watched. He sat there next to her and drank some *awa* and began some incantations.

Whenever she would scream in pain, he would just lean over and put his hand on her forehead... but not stop his chanting. After a long time of this, he put some of the things he'd brought into the fire, said more incantations, drank more *awa*, then settled back with his eyes closed. Uilani continued to make noises and writhe about some, but he ignored her after that. It looked like he went into a trance or sleep of some kind. Kaole told me later that was exactly what he did. It was like that for hours. Eventually, I noticed he had laid down on his side in a kind of fetal position. Kaole got up to tend the fire, even though it was getting to be daylight. I was so exhausted I couldn't stay awake; I fell asleep. I woke up after a couple of hours and Nakea was sitting up again in a trance, but I could see that Uilani was sleeping comfortably and her breathing looked normal."

"Was that it?"

"Nakea seemed to wake up when the sun was up well over the mountain. He helped Uilani sit up, and gave her something to drink. He then took her out into the water and had her sit down and immerse herself several times. He was chanting the whole time. Then he brought her back and we dried her off and got her into the surrey and brought her home. He left several things that he wanted her to mix and drink for the next few days. Kaole explained it to me. He put his hands on her head, smiled at her, gave an *aloha* to both of us, and then he and Kaole left. That was what I remember." Schrock's expression was that of a man who had inexplicably been given a large sum of money. "That man is astonishing—truly a gift to us all. Though I think I understand little of what he does, I'll always be indebted to him."

"You probably know more than you think about *kahuna* sorcery," said Johann. "I feel that as time goes on, I'm sort of absorbing what he does, rather than understanding it. What you've just told me happened confirms for me there is so much more to the unseen world." They both paused to consider that. "It's easier for me to say those words today than I could have a few months ago."

"What's happening to us, Johann? I'm pretty sure it's good."

Johann stood up and did a little dance in a circle, laughing. "I think so. And on top of that, what I wanted to tell you—Prime Minister Gibson has done something interesting... actually, just short of amazing. He's invited you, me and Kaole as honored guests to a ceremony."

"What kind of ceremony? I'm certain not the same kind that Nakea had for us," joked Schrock.

"Well, there have been more than rumors that Gibson and the king were already inclined to ship the statue over to Kohala, to place it near Kamehameha's actual birthplace."

You mean my statue, thought Schrock. But it was true: over the past several months, he'd frequently wondered what would happen with the statue over which he'd come to think he'd taken some ownership. It was an unreasonable and selfish thought, considering he wasn't even Hawaiian, but he couldn't erase his feelings.

"I told you Gibson was cagey, so I wasn't sure it was true. But I've just received an invitation from him. He said the reparation on the statue will be complete in two months, when they will ship it to Hawaii Island's Kohala for an unveiling ceremony. He went on to say that we had provided a compelling argument for them to make their decision for where it should be. He thanked us all."

"That's quite the news," Schrock replied, eyes wide. "I'm sure Kaole and Nakea are pleased with this outcome."

"They are," confirmed Johann.

"It has to be a victory for them." *And the other Hawaiians who understand the importance of this*, thought Schrock.

"As a matter of fact, Kaole told me that his uncle is planning to go to Kohala. Nakea wants to go there ahead to make prayers of preparation for the arrival of Kamehameha's *mana* at his birthplace." Hearing this news, Schrock felt a kind of relief that had been a couple years in the making. "Whatever their motive, King Kalakaua and Gibson seemed to have done the right thing."

"So the ceremony is to be the statue unveiling, and Prime Minister Gibson said the king had made a point of wanting to send an invitation to us and our wives," Johann said.

"Yes!" said Schrock. "I would be pleased with that. I couldn't go without Uilani. And I've never done more than sail past that island. But the king? How can he know about us? Gibson must have said something to him, don't you think?"

Johann nodded. "He told him about the original statue being on your ship and the interest we've had in it. Gibson wants us and Kaole there for the ceremony as part of the king's entourage."

"But what about *Kahuna* Nakea?" asked Schrock. "He probably had the most influence, or whatever it was, in getting that statue to Hawaii."

"Of course! How could I forget? We know the king has been doing his best to restore the standing of *kahuna* healers and other *kahuna* masters. According to Gibson, the king has known of Nakea for many years. Hard to believe, isn't it? He heard through his sources about Nakea's involvement in all of it and apparently it didn't surprise him. Isn't that something?"

"Holy pig's feet. I wish we'd known this a long time ago. It might have simplified things for us," said Schrock. "We might have got around a lot of our guesswork."

"Too late now. But I don't think the king expects that such a private soul as Nakea would even accept a formal invitation," said Johann. "Kaole says he'll make sure Nakea knows about the ceremony and that he gets over to Kohala."

Johann's eyes glinted with enthusiasm. "Listen to this: the king would even like us to join him for a meal afterward. So I've gone ahead and confirmed ship's passage for all of us except Stina. She won't be able to go since our girls' school will still be in session. I assume Uilani would want to join us."

"I would imagine she wouldn't want to miss anything like this," said Schrock. "It will depend on whether she can get the time off work. If I have to, I'll speak with our good Doctor Ferguson."

"I should have more details from Gibson next month. We can finalize our plans then."

"Thank you for doing all this, Johann."

Leaving Johann's office, Schrock realized he couldn't shake the feeling that Naholehua and his apprentices had not abandoned their mission to destroy the statue and its *mana*. The attempt by someone to burn the foundry where the statue was had been troubling. Kaole had said Deetjen's description sounded like it was Naholehua's nephew and apprentice, with whom he was familiar. And then with the attempt to kill Uilani, it seemed certain that the malevolent sorcerer was somewhere on Oahu.

Walking back to the house he and Uilani were renting, Schrock was eager to tell her about the king's invitation. Uilani grabbed him and kissed him the moment he walked through the door, pushing him away in the next.

"Tell me why it is that it's worked out this way, that it's *haoles* who are in charge of the hospital and deciding how everything is done? Whose kingdom is this anyway? I know it's pointless to ask, since no *kanakas* are headed over to mainland medical schools, at least not yet. Just the same, we have *kahuna* healers who could be curing many people who come into the hospital, people who are given medicines they probably don't need or shouldn't have. I'm sorry. Here, Captain Schrock. I made you a drink that you like. Sit down." She kissed him again and pushed a rum and lillikoi juice with lime into his hand.

Schrock thought that besides being set upon by some animated spirit, being near Uilani made him feel fully alive. She was the reverse of what work had wrung from him today.

"Instead I see so many patients that could benefit from *ho'oponpono*," she continued, pacing around the floor. "You know what that is? It is healing the relations that aren't settled—with their family, their friends, their neighbors—that cause mental or physical symptoms that bring these people into the hospital. But it is not allowed or practiced at the hospital. And you know why that is? It's the pressure from the missionary party. They stop it... keep a lid on almost all traditional Hawaiian ways. It is wearisome. I think there are those in the hospital, even Doctor Ferguson, who would be open to supporting more traditional practices; making referrals to *kahuna* practitioners if they could. But they would lose their jobs if they opened their mouths or stepped out of line, as would I. Gerhard, sometimes it's so hard."

Schrock got up and pulled her into a bear hug. "You make me hurt for you, love. And I have to ask myself again what good we foreign invaders brought to this wonderful land. It's clear the flood gate was opened a long time ago, and now—," he let her go and looked down at the floor, "so much good has been undone." He reached for Uilani's hand, bringing her down onto his lap as he sat. "Trying to make some small amends seems like it's been ordained upon me and Johann, and now even you. For starters, we know we have a statue we have a connection to. And we've been told we needed to see that it finds its way home. Well, guess what, my darling? The king has given us a formal invitation to attend the unveiling of the statue in Kohala in three weeks, along with Johann and Kaole. So that is a start."

"What? No! Yes!" she said, jumping up. "I knew I was marrying a remarkable man. What will it be then: Captain Schrock, his wife and party in the company of the king?" she declared with a mock flourish of her arm. "Why didn't you say so right away?"

Underneath his own anticipation of going, Schrock still wondered what quirk of fate had entwined his life with this statue... and then this remarkable woman. It was possible that wasn't even the right question.

CHAPTER 51

Makia and Palmele met up at their usual spot on the outskirts of south Honolulu before heading back to Kaiena's place.

"Palmele, why you got that keep happy smile on your face?" asked Makia. "Naholehua been vile as a moray eel since the *hapa* woman didn't die. I think we got nothing to be happy time about. What you find out today?"

"I feel like I'm one of those detective guys I read stories about."

"What you mean, little brother?"

"At the café where I went to get some food there was one of those policeman we always used to see guarding the foundry. It was crowded and we sat next to each other. I acted like I never seen him before and he didn't seem to know me. He talked a lot, this guy—and so I asked him what kind of jobs he did with police. He told me he had to guard this place that had some statue, but he said they were finished working on it and they were gonna send it out to Hawaii Island on a Russian warship in a few days. Oh dumb *kanaka*, I thought, you just dumped the *poi* bowl. He said he was really happy to get back to some regular police work. I didn't show that I was real happy about what he just told me."

"You right, Detective Palmele. We gotta tell this to Naholehua."

That evening when they went out to their private place near the beach and Palmele told Naholehua what he'd found out, the *kahuna* grunted in approval.

"You found some luck before I had to feed you both to sharks. It comes to sight we have another chance to burn this damn effigy. We will need to find out this ship they send it on—do our best to set a fire on it after the statue is loaded. But after you were caught last time, Makia, they might be watching close, especially soldiers."

Makia seethed, knowing that again his stepfather wouldn't be the one to try and set any kind of fire.

"If it is impossible," Naholehua went on, "we will need to go the Hawaii Island... kill the pretender's *mana* there."

Makia didn't say anything, waiting for it to finally settle into his stepfather's muddied brain that there would be no chance of burning a Russian warship, and that they had been saving the dynamite for an opportunity to plant it on the statue when it was out in the open and exposed. That wouldn't be on any warship.

CHAPTER 52

It was three weeks later when Schrock, Uilani and Kaole all gathered in Johann's office. "This should be no small adventure," Johann said, grinning. "Prime Minister Gibson said His Majesty will have us sail this Friday with the others of his entourage on the royal ship, *The Pride of Hawaii*. We'll head to the Port of Mahukona in Kohala, and go overland from there to a small settlement called Ainakea, where the ceremony will be on Saturday. Afterward we'll attend a *luau* arranged for the king by some of his supporters."

"*Luau!*" Kaole slapped his hand on his thigh. "Always the best food, and then *hula*."

"This should be good," said Uilani. "I've never been to the Big Island."

"Where will we be staying?" asked Schrock.

"At the home of a prominent Kohala ranch owner," Johann answered. "She was the person who headed up the Hawaii Island effort to have the statue erected near Kamehameha's birthplace."

"I'll be glad to meet this woman," said Kaole.

Johann looked around at his friends, his expression now serious. "You understand there is a lot of opposition here in Honolulu to erecting this second statue. The missionary party critics of the king and Gibson are attacking it in the press."

"I read what they are saying," said Uilani, "that it's another waste of money, especially after last month's big coronation of Kalakaua and Queen Kapiolani, and then the unveiling of the replacement statue across from the new Iolani Palace."

Schrock heaved a sigh. "You know, at this point, I'm not sure there's any government expenditure they won't condemn."

"They also think constructing the palace squandered government money in the first place," Johann said, shaking his head. "Never mind that most monarchs around the world have palaces and spend way beyond what they should. What they really want is a monarchy with no power or control of the purse strings. They want this royal to stay quiet and out of sight until they can finally see the kingdom annexed to the United States."

It was clear Johann had grown protective of his adopted home. What he was saying raised Schrock's ire as well. "This missionary party is hell-bent on taking over the government and wiping out what remains of the culture. At times like this, it brings up visions of having my old second mate here to knock heads around."

"It's good you see this, Captain Schrock," said Kaole. "These men don't like the old ways: our food, the *kahunas*, the *hula*—."

They were all quiet until Johann's expression brightened. "I was lucky enough to see Kaole do *hula* once. He's exceptional."

"I'm doing *hula* since I was a boy," said Kaole, "even though we can't do it in the open until now."

Schrock looked puzzled.

"It's been denounced by Protestant missionaries since they arrived in the islands," said Uilani.

"They call it heathen dance," added Kaole. "When our chiefs became Christians, the missionaries told the chiefs to forbid it, make it *kapu*. But King Kalakaua, he change that. We all very proud of him."

By mid-morning, the king's guests had all boarded the *Pride of Hawaii* at Honolulu Harbor's royal wharf. Soon after, a ship steward brought Schrock a message from the ship's captain to join him on the quarterdeck. When Uilani was settled in the cabin, Schrock went aft as the ship was being towed out of the inner harbor.

"Welcome aboard, Captain Schrock," said Captain Rutherford. "It is a pleasure to meet you. I hope this will be another uneventful island hop for all of us. I heard about your unfortunate adventure at sea when you carried this same statue you're off to commemorate."

"It's true—the worst thing I've ever been through," said Schrock. "But things have been working out well ever since." He realized what he'd said had not been a casual reply. He had meant it. After he filled Rutherford in on some of the events that had transpired since losing the *Haendel*, the two captains talked about the Russian warship that, two days earlier, had carried the statue to Kohala as their gesture of friendship to the monarchy. Captain Rutherford ordered the crew to host the *Pride's* sails and get underway.

"I found it curious it would be the Russians," said Rutherford, "but given how many nations have an interest in Hawaii's resources, I shouldn't be surprised."

"It surprises me, since the Russians lose so many ships to terrible seamanship," quipped Schrock. "After all that's happened to the statue, a Russian ship should have been the last choice the king or Gibson would have made to transport it there safely." He was aware of his concern for the statue. Again he was feeling like this bronze effigy had somehow settled in and become a part of him—a peculiar but not unwelcome happening, he decided. He'd make sure not to give Johann any satisfaction by telling him what was going through his mind. A Pacific Ocean upsurge rose to Schrock's eye level as Rutherford continued to talk, a string of words Schrock didn't hear as they flowed past him, mixing with the splash of tiny droplets in a sun-pierced wave crest.

On the main deck, Uilani joined Johann to explore the ship. As the swells moved the schooner up and down in a measured rhythm, the two paused at the forward railing to lean over and watch the bow slice cleanly through turquoise seas.

"It's remarkable that this is happening, Johann," said Uilani. "Seven months ago, after I had known Gerhard only a week, I was sure we weren't compatible and that he would be quickly gone out of my life. I wasn't even sure I would ever meet anyone I would want to marry."

"I don't understand how you can say that," said Johann. "I could imagine a lot of men courting you."

"I'm not looking for pity, but in *Hawaii nei*, the part about marrying a *hapa haole* holds a predictable stigma for men. Before Gerhard, much of the time I was made to feel self-conscious and out of place here in my homeland. And I never seemed to attract the kind of men that I would want to be with."

Johann's forehead creased. "If it's any consolation, when I realized what a discovery he'd made in you, I know he was beside himself to get your attention. He never once considered your parentage an issue.

He just wanted you as you are. Before I had met you, I have to admit I told him that he should look elsewhere. It looked like he was trying to figure out how to cross this cultural gap and you just seemed to be giving him a hard time. You need to know, Uilani, he all but told me to go drown myself—it was you he wanted. He said he would not give up on you."

"Really, he told you that?" she asked, embarrassed. "I caused him a lot of distress, didn't I?" She grabbed the rail with both hands as the deck lifted higher with a swell that slipped past the bow.

"Actually, you well know he was about to give up. When you sent him that letter, you might as well have hit him with a brick. He thought it was all over. I tried to point out you were just taking some time. He wouldn't believe it and that's when he decided to leave, which is why I arranged for you to talk with Kaole."

"Johann, I am so thankful you did that. But looking back, we realized we both had this feeling there was some force outside of us bringing us together, to move us beyond the differences we had. Nakea confirmed that for us, didn't he?"

"Forgive me," said Johann, "despite Nakea's role, that doesn't sound like what happens to two people who simply find themselves in love."

"I don't think you understand what I'm saying. Our coming together was like the needle on a compass, pointing to this person that we needed to go to without fail."

"I still can't abide with the logic behind all that."

"I can't explain it, because it wasn't logic. I struggled with what was happening to me. I still do. If I hadn't grown up here, and knowledge hadn't been passed down to me by my mother, I don't think I would accept it at all. Remember, I went to school in Boston. I know about logic. What made it clearer was when Gerhard told me the whole story about losing his ship and then coming to *Hawaii nei*. I realized that it was the beginning of reshaping something in him. Then I heard about his friendship with you and your family and Kaole, and then the connection with the statue and Nakea—."

Johann nodded. "Kaole and Nakea have both helped to change a lot of what I believe. Before all this, before the *Haendel* sailed from Germany, time for me was linear and space was one dimensional. If you think there was some force that helped bring the two of you together, then I probably shouldn't be the one to question it. When I allow myself to remember, I know that both of us have been saved from a cruel death by Nakea. And from the beginning, Gerhard was saying all the same things to me about something unexplainable drawing him to you. At the time I just thought it was nonsense."

"Is it such a chance thing to happen... to all of us, Johann? It feels—it has to be more deliberate than random. I am sure it is for a good reason and that Nakea must have seen it all. Kaole's description of the web that ties us all said it exactly right for me."

Johann's brow furrowed. There was a long pause while he let that settle in. "On the other side of this, I'm afraid of what Naholehua and his family can do as long as he is around. I'm not sure of what he is capable of, and now that we know what trouble he can cause, it can be no good."

The ship rolled over a large swell and Uilani grabbed the rail to keep balance. "At least having become close to Nakea has made me feel safer. When I first heard the two of you talk about him, I knew I needed to hear your accounts of what he'd done. It's not that I didn't believe in an unseen world—another dimension. Hawaiians call it *po*, the place of the gods. It's just that I had to see and hear Nakea for myself. I'm so thankful I did. There were lessons I'd learned from my mother... things I had let slip away. And now, besides saving my life, he's allowed me to start taking hold of my gifts."

Johann rolled his head back with a smile. "I envy you, Uilani." He held his hand out over the rail to catch some spray. "You know, it has been very difficult for me—to change. As you have seen, I've had to loosen my grip on things to accept what Nakea's done. I'm still bewildered how anyone can have power over natural forces. But what can I say... what he told me about my past has made me a free man. It has been extraordinary. I, too, am deeply thankful."

"That was a surprise to hear him tell you that. Do you—do you want to tell me more about what happened back there in Germany?"

Johann pulled at his chin. "It changed my life, all of that. I'm not sure I'm up to telling you the story right now. But I have a proposal for you—something I've thought about. I would like you to meet up with Stina sometime so she can tell you her version of what happened. She knows it in great detail. It would be a good opportunity for the two of you to get to know each other better. I'm sure she will grow to like you even more once that happens. And then what I would like you to do is to let her know what Nakea told me about what actually happened, about that man being alive—that I didn't kill him. I haven't told her yet. I know it sounds odd, but I knew she wouldn't be trusting of the source if I told her. She is more likely to believe you if you let her know of your confidence in Nakea and his abilities. I know it's asking a lot, but it would mean a great deal to me."

"Yes, of course I would do that for you, Johann. And I would like to get to know Stina… as family."

Schrock returned from the quarterdeck and joined Uilani, Johann, and Kaole at the mid-cabin deck to sit in the canvas chairs and enjoy the milder seas and balmy weather. A few hours later they neared Hawaii Island off Ulolu Point. As the schooner angled south toward Mahukona Harbor along the dry Kohala coastline, three humpback whales moved lazily through the water, no more than thirty yards from the ship.

"It's a male, a female and her calf," Kaole pointed out as they all stood at the rail.

"That's a rare sight in the islands," Uilani said. "Most have been taken by whalers."

The female periodically surfaced, rolled to her side, and loudly slapped her immense pectoral fin on the water. A minute later the calf surfaced and did the same, mimicking its mother.

Schrock noticed Uilani rising up on her toes with excitement. He felt fortunate that this woman brimming with such vitality had allowed him into her life.

Within another hour, they spotted the Kohala peninsula's solitary dock a few miles away at Mahukona. The water glistened from the afternoon sun, bathing the shoreline hills in warm gold. In silence, the four of them took in the sight.

Kaole broke the quiet. "You know the story why the sun stays so long in the sky this time of year?" The three of them looked at him questioningly.

Then Uilani grinned and said, "I think maybe I know. But I want you to tell the story, Kaole."

"Yeah, I do that. It's 'cause a long time ago the mother of the god Maui complained that her *kapa* cloth can't dry—the day's too short. So Maui, being one good son, he made a rope from his sister's hair, and when Sun came up in the morning he lassoed the rays of Sun. When Maui caught Sun, Sun was very scared and begged for his life. So Maui says to Sun 'I don't want you to move so fast.' Now Sun really wants to live. So Sun agrees to move slower, and make the days long in the summer. And that's why you seeing the sun over on those hills now this time of day."

They all turned to look again at the sun-warmed hills.

"Thank you for that," said Uilani, beaming. "I did know, but you make me believe again."

"So whenever I have a question about nature," said Schrock, "I need to ask you first, to get the true story?"

Kaole smiled. "Yeah, you should. I heard your creation stories at the Christian school. We got ours. I like ours better. I think maybe Uilani know better, too."

CHAPTER 53

Hawaii Island, North Kohala

Schrock took in the scenery as they traveled by carriage from Mahukona Harbor up the coast and inland. They passed through the largely agricultural and sparsely inhabited Kohala region. Sugar cane was nearly the only crop to be seen, leaving Schrock to wonder what the local diet was like. When they arrived at the estate of the sugar plantation where they were to stay, they were provided private accommodations in rooms that adjoined a courtyard. The group was treated to a dinner with their host and her extended family. The meal included roast beef that came from a large cattle ranch in the interior highlands. The four of them had had a long day, and after dinner they all retired for the evening.

Schrock and Uilani were pleased with their accommodation, and both fell quickly asleep. But Schrock had never overcome his shipboard sleeping habit of four-hour watch increments and then, even though it was much shorter now, a like period of wakefulness. He woke a couple of hours after midnight, got up, and without waking Uilani, slipped out the door to the courtyard for some fresh air. He jumped back, startled by a shadowy figure sitting on a nearby bench, illuminated by starlight.

"It's me, Kaole," the silhouette reassured him.

Relieved, Schrock went to sit next to his friend. "Couldn't sleep either, eh?" Instead of a response, he heard Kaole's rapid breathing. "What's happening? Are you all right?"

"It good you awake. I just about to get you. It's—I just talk with Nakea."

"What?" Schrock said, confused. "How did that happen?" he asked in a loud whisper.

"My uncle knocked on my room window and woke me up."

In the dim light, Schrock could just make out the tension in Kaole's face. "But how did he know you were here?"

Kaole shook his head. "I'm surprise you even ask that question."

"I'm sorry, you're right. Go on."

"My uncle, he doesn't worry much, but I think he worried tonight. He told me he want you and me to come with him. He out over there, waiting for us."

"What? What does he want us to do at this time of night?"

We gonna go near to the place in Ainakea where the statue is. Nakea, he see in his dream those men going there."

Schrock felt wide awake now. "Those men?"

"Yeah. Naholehua's two apprentices."

Schrock wondered what they would be doing out there in the darkness, these men who had already proven to be conniving as well as criminal. "What does he want us to do?"

"Nakea don't want us to kill them, if that's what you think," said Kaole.

"After what happened to Uilani it occurred to me."

"This no joke. We know Naholehua one bad man. I heard about those two apprentice—younger than me: one his stepson and the other a nephew. That *kahuna* and those boys are going there to finish what Naholehua been trying to do—get rid of Kamehameha's *mana*. Now we know they think they can do that by destroying the statue."

"They sure are determined—to come over here from Oahu. I guess we've no choice but to go out there to try and stop them."

"Not try. Nakea says we gonna stop them."

Schrock went back to his room to put on a shirt and cap and walking shoes. Looking at Uilani sleeping soundly, he decided not to wake her. He knew he'd hear about it later from her. Outside again, they headed off in the direction Kaole had indicated where Nakea was, finding him squatted down with his back against a tree.

"Aloha, Schrock," Nakea greeted, standing. He spoke directly to Schrock in Hawaiian and put his hands on Schrock's shoulders. "My uncle is very glad you coming with us. He thinks you the one to best protect Kamehameha."

Nakea turned and started leading them down the road. "Kaole, I'm still honored Nakea thinks that way but I'm just an ordinary *malahini* with no special abilities." After a short exchange between the two Hawaiians, including Schrock hearing a chuckle from Nakea, Kaole said, "He's surprised you don't see yet. But just the same, he likes that you one big guy, which might be good."

They walked nearly an hour in silence when he heard Nakea speak. "We getting close to Ainakea," said Kaole. At this point, they were off the road and on a trail through a forest of low trees, vines and thick undergrowth. His eyes had adjusted to the dark and there was just enough moonlight to see Kaole moving in front of him. "My uncle knows they out here close somewhere."

"How, how can he, it's dark, there's no sounds." Schrock couldn't contain his incredulity, even though he knew better.

"He smells them. Not like you smell something bad through your nose. That what you say when you remembered it from a dream. That what he did. He already been seeing this—you know, smelling these guys out here somewhere."

Schrock was glad Kaole couldn't see him shake his head. With nothing logical, he thought he was probably relegated to never being able to see in the way Nakea did. It would be useful to be able to view events before they took place. At the same time, he could imagine having such an ability being a crushing burden, like knowing about impending sickness or death of those closest to you. His rumination on the matter was interrupted when in the dim light he bumped into Kaole stopped behind Nakea. Listening, they heard someone walking toward them, not more than a hundred feet away. He could just make out a small clearing close ahead, and a light flickering toward it. Nakea walked into it without hesitation. Schrock followed Kaole a short distance behind.

Makia was holding a torch when he and Palmele walked into the clearing, jolted by seeing anyone at this time of night in such a remote section of the island. Nakea said something to them. They pretended to ignore him and continued as if they were going to walk past the three of them. Kaole and Schrock stood in their way behind Nakea. They were surprised by the encounter and moved up close to Nakea, saying things that sounded like they were going to hurt him. Kaole yelled at them in pidgin, which Schrock thought was 'Don't come any further,' but what he did say was, "Don't get near my uncle."

Makia knew instantly it was Kaole and the captain. The revelation was instant and awful. "Your uncle?" The pieces fell into place for him: the connection between the statue and the captain and now Nakea and Kaole. If his *awa*-weakened stepfather could only have been able to see it—dealt with them all before this. Damn him.

Makia felt desperate. "You're shark food. We gonna make you die, little brother, and you too, old man, and this *haole*."

Kaole shouted back at them, told them they didn't know who they were making threats to.

"Hey *kanaka,* I know you—that Molokai school," said Makia. "You shouldn't be out here. Get out the way. Take your uncle away from here." It was apparent he knew Nakea was the old man who was in their face, a *kahuna* force that he had been threatening.

At just that point of their uncertainty, Nakea pointed back up the path and told them something. They ignored him again and started pushing past the three. Kaole and Schrock pushed back. Schrock thought it was going to get ugly, shifting from a rugby scrum to fists any second. Then all of a sudden, Nakea yelled something loud while raising his arm over the two men. Makia and Palmele almost froze. He spoke to them in Hawaiian for a few moments. They seemed to be listening, then looking dazed, wrapping their arms around themselves. Finally they turned and left, with confused expressions. It seemed remarkable to Schrock, whatever had transpired, although by now it probably shouldn't have been.

Schrock picked up the torch on the ground, still burning, and tripped on something as they turned to walk back. He aimed the torch down to light up whatever it was below his feet and saw a cloth bag. "They must have dropped this." He picked it up and had Kaole hold the torch while he opened it and peered inside. He pulled out two bundles wrapped in cloth, laid them on the ground and carefully unwrapped four sticks of dynamite in one and blasting caps and fuses in another.

Nakea didn't appear to be as stunned as Schrock and Kaole, but it was Nakea who declared that they would take the explosives over to the ocean on their way back and sink them in deep water.

When they finally returned to the ranch compound hours later, and Nakea had gone, sitting in the courtyard, Schrock asked Kaole, "Were you worried about what those guys would do to us?"

"More I been thinking about how they could have blowed up Kamehameha. But yeah, I was worried. Makia is big guy, isn't he? I didn't know if they would try and kill us right there. But my uncle is a fearless warrior. I just look at him to remember that."

The times Schrock had seen the willowy and reserved Nakea, that notion had never occurred to him… until tonight. "So what happened out there? What did Nakea do or say that kept them from maybe killing us?"

Kaole wiped sweat off his forehead with the back of his hand. "Nakea, you could see he was calm in all this. He told them: 'You wasted your gift to become healers, only to bring misery. You learned nothing of being caretakers to our people.' Before that you could see those boys weren't listening to him. They just kept swearing at us, telling us we were all gonna be dead men."

"I could tell they were threatening us," said Schrock. "But what made them stop?" "When they start pushing and fighting us," said Kaole, "Nakea told them something I never forget. When he held up his arm, he say, 'The *kahuna* priesthood in all *Hawaii nei* gonna hear of the worthless ways of you and your master and then smother all your *mana*.' That's when they were still and listened. He said, 'Your *mana* gonna be snuffed out until you all are empty. Your names not gonna have value. You will be like nothing.'" Kaole's head turned up and he stared into the night sky, as if reflecting on the destructive authority of his mentor's words. "You know they listened to that. That's when they got very nervous and wrapped their arms around themselves, like they were cold. I would if I was them. It's like what those Catholics call ex-communication. Remember, those boys didn't say anything else. They knew clear then who Nakea was. It looked to me like they got lost when they took off up that dark path."

"This was important, wasn't it?" asked Schrock. "After all that's happened to this statue—," he didn't finish the thought.

"To Kamehameha," Kaole corrected.

Schrock nodded. "When we were walking back, Nakea said something else to you."

"Yeah. One good lesson: easy for me to say in English. You want to make somebody change their ways, shame work a lot better than pain."

CHAPTER 54

Hawaii Island, North Kohala
Naholehua's Encampment

It was late morning when Makia left Palmele at the encampment and went down the path toward the ocean, looking for Naholehua. They hadn't slept all night, he was hot and after their three hour walk back it was already warm. Makia wanted to get it over with, tell the old man what happened and let him go wild or whatever he was going to do. All he knew is that after the encounter with that *kahuna* uncle of Kaole, he wasn't about to let his stepfather send him out again to try and destroy that statue. He was done with that. That *kahuna* had scared him to death, made him more afraid than Naholehua had ever done. His stepfather could do his best to kill him first, but he'd now lost his fear of the man.

He ran out of the path near the ocean and came up on the ledges of black lava. He heard the waves crashing below just as he saw the form of a man sitting close to the edge with his legs crossed and his head down. His motionless stepfather was in a trance state, his stringy hair dangling down over his bare shoulders. He could see a gourd and a cup, a sign of the *awa* that he'd brought with him. Makia thought it was unusual for him to position himself so close to the edge, given that waves are unpredictable. Because it was so warm, he probably sat close to the water to be cooler.

Makia squatted down at a distance and watched. The old man had bragged that he would kill the interfering captain with *'ana'ana*—what he was likely trying to do. This was a *haole* he had only seen once in person, so it was a futile undertaking in the first place. After all this time, he was still mystified why the captain's *hapa* woman had never died. More often he was mixed up about what he intended to do. To Makia, it appeared as if Naholehua needed to consume more *awa* to put him into his dream state, but the result was only that it left him acting more foolish and ruthless. Makia felt like he was looking at a worthless piece of shark feces, sitting there in his state of idiocy. The thought crept into his head, persistent as an insect biting his brain, the opportunity that lay in front of him. If the old man went into the sea right now, he would drown because he was stupid with *awa*... and never much of a swimmer.

Makia tried to swat away the insect—somehow this was the husband of his own mother. But she should never have taken up with this man. He also knew his mother: she would grieve Naholehua's death for a while. Then it wouldn't take long for her to find someone else who would need taking care of. He and his mother would be happier without him.

Makia remained squatting, the sun impaling him. He still might try to squeeze some more teaching from this dirty fossil but there would be a good chance his supposed master would try his best to make him sick or kill him. And then there was that other *kahuna*. He had promised to see that his future as a priest was ruined. Makia understood the future he imagined was gone.

With a wave of forbidding failure and an insect's roar in his head, he was up and moving toward the motionless lump with stringy hair bent over the hard lava. In fierce, continuous strides he swept up Naholehua like a bag of taro corms and with a burst of fury flung him into the crashing surf deep under the jagged ledge.

CHAPTER 55

North Kohala, Hawaii Island

A day had passed since the encounter with Naholehua's apprentices, and Schrock and Kaole had tried to sort out the previous night's happening by retelling the story several times to Johann and Uilani. Schrock woke up just past midnight and again roamed around the courtyard in his usual night watch. His ritual arousal gave him a chance to think unencumbered, like the countless hours he'd spent on the ship deck, alone in his thoughts. His night awakenings were becoming shorter the more time he was distanced from the sea trade. It would only take an hour or so before he returned to bed. He thought again about Kamehameha's birthplace, said to be about ten miles from where they were at the ranch. Kaole told them it was always an aspiration of his to visit the place where The Conqueror came into this world. He said it was sacred ground, especially to *kanaka maoli* like him. Schrock felt moved to visit the place himself—a vital part of his journey. It didn't surprise him at breakfast when Uilani and Johann said they had both been having something like a yearning to go to the birthplace. When Kaole heard them all confirming their experiences, he couldn't contain his smile.

"We all gonna go, aren't we? I coulda told you this gonna happen. Nakea already been there. Now we ready for what you say... pilgrimage."

By the next day, the four of them loaded into a surrey borrowed from the ranch, along with verbal directions to find their way, and headed to the Hawaii Island's northwesterly tip and the place called Kokoiki. For the first hour, well-used roads led them to the dusty plantation mill town of Hawi. But from there they had to cut through a maze of narrow paths leading through endless sugar cane fields until they neared the coast. Because the layer of soil over the lava was too thin for cane to grow, the fields ended there. At this point in their journey, they were confronted with another series of unmarked trails that time and again left them wandering. The directions they had been given were vague about this part, other than 'head toward Upolu Point.' Try as they might, they were unable to find any signs or trail markers. Kaole and Uilani both walked ahead of the surrey at times but found none. At one point, Johann pulled up on the reins and brought the horse to a stop. Four rutted trails converged from different directions, plus the one they were on. Kaole jumped down and stood at the crossroads, looking down at the ground, and then up at the sky. He just stood there, looking up.

Uilani said nothing, but got down and walked over to stand near him. She walked around in a small circle, her head down, one hand held slightly out. Then she held an arm up, as if to test the wind, even though there was little. Kaole did the same thing. Watching them, Schrock thought they looked like two human weather vanes, measuring the ether for the right direction—which is what happened. Kaole and Uilani dropped their arms and looked at each other, conferred for a minute, then got back into the surrey and pointed out the trail that they'd need to take.

"Okay then," Johann said, flicking the reins and starting down the path.

"I had a strong feeling I could do that—that I could sense that the place was in that direction," said Uilani contentedly. "Kaole did too, didn't you?"

"Yeah. For me, it was something like looking through a lot of water."

"It was clear," said Uilani. "We're sure this is the way."

The chosen trail wound through a scrub forest, their movement slowed by the rough lava in the wagon ruts. The surrey top served its purpose as the sun in the cloudless sky bore down on them except when they were shaded beneath short trees along the way. Johann did his best to maneuver the surrey around the larger lava pieces. As they rumbled on for a half mile or so, Schrock felt himself lulled into a trance by the constant bouncing.

"Stop!" yelled Uilani.

Schrock nearly jumped out of his seat. Johann quickly jerked back on the reins just at the same moment he was guiding the horse around some large rocks. The horse and surrey shuddered to a halt, then wobbled to the right with a crunching sound as the right front wheel fell half way into a hole in the lava.

Out of the surrey, they all looked to see that the tall, wood-spoked wheel had settled into a two-foot diameter break in the lava surface. Several of the spokes had cracked with the force of the drop. Looking under and in front of the surrey, they saw smaller holes in the lava. The horse was shying leftward away from the holes. Schrock got down to examine the holes and saw that the lava crust wasn't more than an inch or two thick. He cringed as he looked down through a hole—a fifteen-foot deep chasm, a section of a hollow lava tube that ran roughly parallel to the stretch of the path they were on. Had they gone any further, the surrey could have broken completely through the layer of lava and badly injured or killed any of them.

"I shoulda seen that coming," said Kaole. I'm sorry for that, Mister Kessler."

"You couldn't have seen it," said Johann. "I had my eyes on the trail and I didn't see it."

"I shoulda seen it earlier... like Uilani saw it. The same way we knew to take this trail."

Johann and Schrock stared at Uilani. "Is that how you knew the hole was there—seeing it like that?" Schrock asked.

"It just came to me. I wasn't thinking about anything but getting to the birthplace, and then a vision of road ahead just kind of happened. I don't know... it was just there for a second. But I knew we were in danger."

"Thank god for this gift that's been let out of its container," said Johann. "Let's hope it stays with you."

"Amen," agreed Schrock.

"Maybe you should thank Kamehameha and Nakea," said Kaole, his voice flat.

Backing up the horse and pulling on the three good wheels, all of them were able to get the surrey wheel out of the hole. A repair kit in the wagon had some wire and pliers that Schrock used to fix the cracked spokes. As he kneeled next to the wheel, winding the spokes and tying them, he said, "I'd like to know why the trail was placed so dangerously close to a lava tube."

"I just walked up around the corner of that grove of trees and saw the reason," said Johann, returning from his survey of their path. "There's a high lava ridge and only one way through it for a wide stretch in either direction. Apparently this was the shortest or maybe the only way to get to that opening."

"Why wasn't there any kind of warning?" wondered Schrock aloud.

"Look over there," said Kaole. "That pile of stones mean to watch out."

"What! That little pile was supposed to warn me?" said Johann.

"Maybe it so small just to keep *malahini* away from this place," said Kaole with a chuckle. "I think it almost do the job."

"That is not amusing, Kaole," said Johann.

"Right, Kaole. You need to get down and wire up this last spoke," said Schrock.

A half hour later, they heard waves breaking on the lava strewn shores, the remains of the *Mookini Heiau* temple coming into view as they rounded a bend. Set on a flat slope to the ocean, they saw a massive, rectangular, twenty-foot-high rock-wall enclosure set back several hundred yards from the shore. They parked the surrey near the wall and got out.

"This the oldest *heiau* in *Hawaii nei*," explained Kaole. "All these stones carried over here by warriors from Pololu Valley—on the other side—a long way over there," he said motioning toward the east. "One more thing. It *kapu*, so we not going inside. But it okay to see where Kamehameha was born, wherever that gonna be."

They took their two rucksacks out of the surrey and set out on foot to search out the birthplace. A short distance beyond the *heiau* they came to a smaller rock enclosure where a large stone lay in the center.

"This is how it was described in our directions," said Johann.

They all walked around quietly, taking in the feel of the place.

"This is where it happen," said Kaole, his face tilted up. "His *mana* all around here."

All four of them gravitated to the stone and, one by one, began to lay their palms on it. Then they each began to take in their surroundings. Schrock tried to imagine why this desolate spot had been chosen for a birth. He had to guess there was a lot more going on here at the time, that people lived near the *heiau,* that there was something auspicious about this very spot.

After a while they noticed a number of the rocks along the enclosure wall at a comfortable sitting height, with fairly smooth tops. It was clear that over time, many others had sat on them, as they all chose to do without even discussing it. It was early afternoon, and

Johann and Kaole pulled the food and water out of rucksacks. With the dried meat, crackers, fruits and water passed around, contentment returned to the faces of the four travel-weary pilgrims.

They ate in silence until Schrock said what had been on his mind for weeks. "Kaole, we've wanted to know more about what *mana* is. To Hawaiians, it seems to be at the center of religious or cultural belief. But we can't do what Nakea wants us to do—be caretakers of the *mana* in Kamehameha's statue—if we don't understand it. So we were thinking it might be like the Christian concept of the holy spirit. In a theology book of Johann's, that is defined as the breath, the animating power, the soul of God that is given to man."

"That good, Mister Schrock—you getting close," said Kaole. "You been thinking about this okay, an it kinda like that. For Kamehameha and all the *ali'i*, through all time, their *mana* is divine power and say-so rule. *Mana* for everybody else is to get the power to do good in life, and to move through this world like a fish swim in the sea. That kinda righteousness we call *pono*."

"In Christianity, I believe that's known as grace," offered Johann.

"When I was in Christian school they taught us about holy spirit. It part of the trinity, things like that. I was thinking then that the holy spirit sure was something like *mana*. We had to memorize a lot of the Bible, and I can't forget this what it says in the new testament: 'I will pour out my spirit upon every sort of flesh, and your sons and your daughters will prophesy and your young men will see visions and your old men will dream dreams.' Right away when I first read that I think of my uncle. You understand… that what happens when you getting *mana* and you let it fill you up like water. I think it happening to each of you. You got lucky you here in *Hawaii nei*."

Schrock was sure that Kaole meant that.

"Another question," said Schrock. "How is it that a statue or this birth stone can have *mana*?"

"Things that are not people can have it, too," said Kaole. "It come about 'cause of what happens with that thing or that place. The top of the mountain over there on Maui call Haleakala—that got *mana,* 'cause that where the goddess Pele lives. And the whole island of Molokai—the old people always say it has *mana*. The statue, it got *mana* 'cause it created in the image of Kamehameha the Great. And it got made 'cause of his descendent, King Kalakaua."

It occurs to me, Kaole," said Johann, "that you told us about Kamehameha taking the *mana* from the king of Oahu, his enemy who he sacrificed after that big battle at Nuuanu. In Christianity, if you're filled with the holy spirit, you have it—supposedly that's it, for eternity. It sounds like *mana* can be taken away from someone, or in the case of the statue, destroyed.

"You got that about right, Mister Kessler. You been thinking about this too," said Kaole with a grin. "The *mana* can be gain or lost by actions. Yeah. It like those two boys—Naholehua's apprentices. They were on the wrong side of right. They were throwing their *mana* away already, and I think Nakea finish taking it away that night out in the forest. He didn't even need to sacrifice them." Schrock couldn't tell from Kaole's face if he was serious about the sacrifice part.

Uilani lifted her head up from what appeared to have been self-reflection. "My mother always said *mana* was the life force that she got from her mama and that had come from my grandmother and ancestors before her. She said she was passing it to me. I was never sure until Nakea."

CHAPTER 56

The early afternoon was declared "king's weather" by attendees: soft tradewinds and no rain clouds in sight. Nearly two hundred people gathered for the unveiling ceremony in the settlement of Ainakea, not far from Kamehameha's birthplace. The attendees milled around the cloth-shrouded statue. Schrock, Uilani and Johann stood next to the wood platform that held a speaker's podium, waiting for the entrance of King Kalakaua and his niece, Princess Kekaulike. Schrock looked around for Kaole, who had arrived with them but wasn't with them now.

Uilani held Schrock's arm. The movement of her hand confirmed the excitement in the air as they waited for the entrance of the king and princess. He stared at the large form covered with cloth. He hadn't seen the statue since it had been repaired and could only hope the restoration had been done well. It had become more than just a bronze figure to him. Like many of the native Hawaiians there today, he was coming to believe this effigy held the *mana* of the great conqueror and unifier of the Kingdom of Hawaii.

In the back of his mind, Schrock couldn't help wondering if Naholehua's two apprentices had ignored Nakea's shaming and gone on to damage the statue after they had intercepted them in the night, or maybe they still planned to disrupt the ceremony? Just then, Kaole moved down the line of chairs and stood by where his seat was next to Schrock. He seemed excited and agitated.

"What's going on, Kaole?"

"I been talking with a few *kanakas* over there," he said, gesturing in the general direction of where they had left their surrey. "They say he dead."

"Who? Who's dead?"

"You should feel it, Captain Schrock. Naholehua: he dead. Drowned out there in the ocean. His body wash up this morning."

Schrock and Uilani were both silent, trying to absorb the information. "What—what do you think happened?" Uilani finally asked.

"Don't know. But I heard Nakea say the *kahuna* priesthood in all *Hawaii nei* gonna hear of the worthless ways of that man and then smother all his *mana*—snuff it out until he is empty. Could be that what happen."

Shrock shook his head. "If death can destroy *mana* of mortal men, then that appears to be what happened. But how do you think he drowned?"

"Don't know. Maybe Nakea will know. Maybe not."

Kaole's attention shifted away. Schrock followed his gaze to the far end of the platform where Nakea had appeared. Kaole went to greet his revered teacher. They embraced in *honi*, touching noses as they breathed in, bound together as uncle and nephew, *kahuna nui* and apprentice. After speaking for a moment, Nakea and Kaole came to where they stood.

"He says thank you for your help in seeing that the *mana* of Kamehameha has come back to rest in Kohala. He says now the long journey gonna begin."

"What does that mean, Kaole?" asked Schrock, uncertain if he wanted an answer.

"It mean we all have a long time more to protect that *mana,* and to tell this story so it never get forgot and for *Hawaii nei* to endure. Nakea gonna tell you more in days to come. But you also gonna like this. He says he gonna have a marriage for you and Uilani when we go back to Oahu… so you get blessed the Hawaiian way, be born again, and then be justly *kama'aina.*" There was a slight grin on Nakea's mouth and Schrock saw Uilani actually wink at him.

It made Schrock uneasy to have plans being made that he wasn't a part of. He decided to change the subject by asking Kaole to query Nakea about what he knew concerning Naholehua's drowning.

After a short exchange, Kaole said, "He saw his death coming. He says that big apprentice made it happen. That's all."

"How sad for that family," said Uilani. She then said something to Nakea in Hawaiian.

Nakea nodded and then his face turned toward a short pathway that came down the hill, as if he knew what was happening before anyone else. The assembled crowd applauded as repeated sounds from a conch shell split the air and the procession of King Kalakaua and Princess Kekaulike appeared, moving slowly toward where they stood. First came two uniformed men, each bearing a *kahili,* the traditional feathered standard, followed by two more attendants dressed in traditional loincloths and feathered head pieces, carrying woven leaf fans. King Kalakaua wore a white, western military-style uniform with braided epaulets and medals pinned to the front. The radiant princess, with elaborately braided hair, wore a long black dress with high neckline and puffed sleeves adorned with lace. Each wore several flower *leis*. They made their way to the front, and with their bearers, stepped up onto the platform built for the occasion.

Able to understand very little Hawaiian language, Schrock still saw why King Kalakaua was considered an accomplished orator. He supposed the king had to be dancing with his words, since, for political reasons, the statue was never intended for Kohala. In a way, this ceremony was almost an afterthought. He knew the king had wanted to balance the moneyed interests of Honolulu with his personal interest in preserving the Hawaiian culture. Since this event served as an opportunity to erect a statue in the place sacred to native Hawaiians, he now would have it both ways: one statue in Honolulu and another one here. He'd ask Uilani what he'd said later.

Schrock's thoughts were interrupted by applause from the audience as the king finished his speech. But as the applause died and King Kalakaua remained at the podium, he began speaking in educated English.

"I wish to acknowledge the honored company seated here," he said, waving a hand toward Schrock's party, "to thank you each for your perseverance in seeing this splendid monument arrive at its rightful place. Your generous endeavors will forever be remembered by the people of Hawaii Island and the Kingdom of Hawaii."

The audience clapped politely. Schrock wondered how many in the audience had an inkling of how he or his friends were connected to the statue. It would take him a long time to tell their story if he were somehow standing in King Kalakaua's place. All he could do was turn a small grin and squeeze Uilani's hand.

At that point, Schrock was surprised when King Kalakaua looked directly at Nakea in the crowd and gave the old man an almost indiscernible nod. Schrock knew Kalakaua wouldn't publicly say anything about the *kahuna* in this largely Christianized kingdom. Foreign residents would think it preposterous if Nakea's actions were recounted. It could only be a losing proposition for the king to give any acknowledgment to what Nakea's role might have been. And Schrock was sure Nakea did not welcome any recognition, preferring to be anonymous.

Seated at the side of the platform, Schrock looked over his shoulder at King Kalakaua, who beamed with pride as he gestured toward Princess Kekaulike. The monarch announced in Hawaiian and then in English that the nation's beloved princess would have the honor of unveiling the statue on behalf of the Kingdom of Hawaii. The princess stepped down from the podium and went over to the shrouded bronze. She took the cord held for her by an assistant, standing motionless until the only sound was the crashing surf in the far distance. She pulled the cord and the veil dropped.

Cheers and applause arose from the crowd. Positioned on a six-foot high pedestal, and standing twenty feet to the top of the warrior's spear, the bronze casting seemed enormous. Schrock and his companions joined in the passionate approval.

They stared at the warrior king in his bronze splendor, at once imperial and distinctly ancient Hawaiian. One arm was held out in a gesture of welcome, the other holding a spear. To Schrock, neither the arm nor spear showed the signs of the repairs. None but a small group of them knew that late in the night he had been with Nakea and Kaole as they had likely saved the statue from further damage in a dramatic struggle of wills.

Schrock thought about how important this was to the people of Hawaii Island. Here was this likeness of the first king of Hawaii who had descended from a dynasty of twenty-eight generations of rulers before him. Now he had emerged in majesty again—on their island. And an exceptional occurrence was the presence of King Kalakaua, the sixth descendent of Kamehameha in that line of succeeding monarchs.

    Schrock reached for Uilani's hand. This remarkable moment in the journey of Kamehameha had finally come to pass. Schrock and the people he loved had been fortunate enough to be here, to be a part of it. It struck him how far he was from where he was born. His gaze turned toward the sea and the dark outline of Maui Island on the horizon. It made him think back to when he'd first seen this crated statue on the Bremerhaven dock. So much since then—being forced to accept the mysteries that had occurred, that had brought him to this place. It began to overcome him. He was seeing the fissure in his core—the constraints of having been born and raised in Germany. A wave of letting go coursed through his body along with a sensation of wanting to both laugh and cry.

Uilani reached up and touched his face. "Are you all right?"

"I think mostly I feel good. I thought I was content just having you, but there were other things—unfinished pieces."

"I tried to tell you some of that early on."

"Take that smirk off your face. Something valuable has happened to me today."

Uilani squeezed his hand, then pulled it around her waist. "I'm sorry; I can see that it has. I'm glad for you, Captain Schrock. You still might make a good island boy."

"And you, island girl, how about you?"

"I am happy that we have been brought together, that I married you. I was always worried as a *hapa* girl that I could never be happy with either a *kanaka* or a *haole* husband. What I love about you is that I know you will let me be all the parts of who I am. And what's happened to you proved that for me."

"I'm not sure I would ever have a choice but to be there for you," said Schrock, "because we were told it was ordained and, well, I love you dearly." He leaned over and gave her a kiss on her cheek. "But right now, Captain Schrock and party are about to have dinner in the company of royalty. We can't be late if you want to talk story to your friends when you get back to work." As they rose to leave, they were the last ones standing in front of the bronze king. Schrock drew Uilani closer to him, nestling his face next to hers, savoring the moment. Then they turned and hurried to catch Johann and Kaole walking to the carriage ahead of them, the carriage that would take them all to the *luau* with a king.

END

GLOSSARY OF HAWAIIAN WORDS AND PHRASES –
in the context of this narrative

---

ahupua'a—Wedge-shaped land division usually extending from the uplands to the sea.

ali'i—Chief, chiefess, officer, ruler, monarch, noble, aristocrat, king, queen, commander, royal.

aloha—Greeting, salutation; Greetings! Hello! Good-by.

aloha makua—Greeting considerate and thoughtful of parents and elders.

a hui hou aku—Good-by (literally, until we meet again).

aumakua—Spirit body.

awa—The kava shrub *(Piper Methysticum)*, the root being the source of a narcotic drink used in ceremonies. Also used medicinally.

hale—House.

haole—White person, especially American or English; of foreign origin.

Hawaii nei—The kingdom and State of Hawaii, *nei* meaning this, indicating 'this beloved'.

hapa haole—Part white person; of part-white blood; part white and part Hawaiian, as an individual or phenomenon.

hana kahuna—General sorcery.

honi—To kiss; to greet by the touch of foreheads and noses.

ho'olomilomi—A healing technique employing a form of massage with physical and spiritual rituals; used for childbirth, ailments and injuries.

ho'o pili haipule—To consecrate the bringing together a relationship; put together as parts of a puzzle.

ho'opi'opi'o—Counter-sorcery.

ho'oponpono—Mental cleansing: family conferences in which relationships are set right through prayer, discussion, confession, repentance and mutual restitution and forgiveness.

ho'ounauna—Sorcery practice of sending sickness or trouble to someone.

inoha po—Name chosen in a dream.

kahuna—Priest, sorcerer, wizard, healer, expert practitioner in certain vocations, crafts and arts. Custodians of the culture, preserving knowledge in trained memory.

kahuna 'ana'ana—Sorcerer who practices black magic by praying people to death.

kahuna kaula—Prophet, seer.

kahuna kilokilo—Observer of the skies for omens, predictor.

kahuna kilokilo uhane—Spirit diviner.

kahuna la'au lapa'au—Traditional healer; an herbalist that administers Hawaiian healing herbs.

kahuna nui—Advisor to chief or king on spiritual and other matters.

kahuna pule—Pastor, minister.

kama'aina—Native born, one born in Hawaii.

kanaka maoli—Full-blooded Hawaiian person.

ka pule kuni—The prayer uttered as part of *kuni*, black magic.

kepolo—Devil; devilish.

lahui—Nation, race, people.

malihini—Stranger, foreigner, newcomer, tourist, one unfamiliar with a place or customs, of foreign origin.

mana—Supernatural or divine power, authority, life force, spirit, soul.

mauka—Inland, toward the mountains.

mauli ola—Power of healing.

maunu—Objects used in black magic such as clothing, hair, exreta or food leavings.

moe uhane—To dream; soul sleep.

papa lani—Heaven.

poi—The Hawaiian staff of life, made from cooked taro corms, pounded and thinned with water.

pu'uhonua—Sanctuary or place of refuge for kapu breakers, defeated warriors or civilians in time of battle.

uhane hele—Dream specialist, dream-spirit traveller.

ACKNOWLEDGMENTS

I would like to thank the following for assistance in my research and to those who supported my writing in all the ways I needed:

– Professor Jim McAdam, Editor, The Falkland Islands Journal, who provided the official account of the sinking of the *G.F. Haendel*, rendered in the record of the maritime Court of Enquiry conducted following the disaster in Port Stanley, Falkland Islands.

– Staff of the Hawaiian Historical Society, Honolulu, Hawaii.

– Sharon Hayden, Former Kohala Kamehameha Celebration Committee, Kapaau, Hawaii.

– Staff of the Bernice Pauahi Bishop Museum, Library and Archives, Honolulu, Hawaii.

– Staff of the Hawaii State Public Library System: Oahu, Hawaii, Maui and Kauai Island Libraries.

– Ulrich Voskamp, Gottingen, Germany, for research on the ship *G.F. Haendel* and Captain Gerhard Schrock through the Deutsches Schiffahrtsmuseum of Bremerhaven.

– Staff of the Maritime Research Center at San Francisco Maritime National Historical Park, San Francisco, California.

– Members of the Lafayette Writers Group who were with me for much of the journey. To each of them an ocean of appreciation for critiquing, encouraging, helping to bring out the better writer in me: Laura Loomis; Stephanie Carr; Sandy Rogin; Christine Lavin; Lenka Glassner; and Gloria Lenhart, the group organizer and mother superior who more often than not was my personal writer's guide.

– Philip Elliott, the developmental editor, who gave me some good advice and then hard sailing orders that I took very reluctantly—which in the end made all the difference.

– Lisa Messinger, my copy editor who went beyond expectations in helping to craft the manuscript.

– My long-time friend Jean Swanson who did the earliest proof reads.

– My son, Jesse, conceptual artist nonpareil who drew and developed the book cover and drew the map and other illustrations.

– Jennifer Leigh Selig, publisher of Empress Publications, who provided all the right expertise and good care to bring this book to life.

– My wife Marietta, sharing a passion for Hawaii and of its culture and history, while being my fellow explorer with an eagerness to discover it all. She tolerated all the times of my being in absentia during the writing process—while she still managed to stay amazingly supportive.